GEBIRAH
GREAT LADY; QUEEN MOTHER

THOMAS A. DEARING

For Mom and Dad

"But of that day and hour knoweth no man. . ."
- Matthew 24:36

"Who run the world? Girls!"
- Beyonce

THE ISLE OF PATMOS, YEAR 96

Images washed across John's mind like the warm, steady tide crashing into the shore outside his crude island cell. Towering figures clashed in the sunset as an impossibly large city all around them was trampled, as were the people. Giant steps meant more death and more destruction. John was merely a witness to it. An interpreter, perhaps. But in the end, all he could do was watch in horror—and a twinge of fascination, if he was honest with himself—as some unknown city in his mind was torn apart by giants.

He had enough presence of mind to write down what he was seeing, to save it and help keep a shred of his sanity. Saved for posterity and for the burgeoning movement he felt a part of but not fully accepted into. John knew he would never leave his jail on the island, and was at peace with that knowledge. He believed his work—his life's work—was complete, and he served a higher calling.

Even consigned to the indignity of a jail cell on the island, he believed in and needed to complete something. Something that would not come to fruition in his lifetime, or the lifetime of his children . . . if he had any. Instead, John had taken up with a small group of desert people who shared wild stories of magic in the old cities: Jerusalem, Bethlehem, Ur, Rome, and even the far-off places of the heathens in the north. Where most people heard nonsense, John felt a stirring inside him that called as no amount of farming or raising sheep could. His parents had wept when he left the family farm. He hadn't really thought of them in years. Why were they coming to mind now?

The visions continued to dominate his thoughts. A brutal fight that toppled tall huts with walls that showed the outside and the inside? Was it madness? John did not recognize the type of adobe used to build the dream-huts. It was smooth and . . . straight? Who would take the time to smooth out the edges of their hut beyond all good measure when there

1

were crops to tend, animals to feed, and the constant threat of invasion from every direction? A smooth hut was the sign of a madman or a fool.

The fighting continued, brutal as anything John had seen in his short life around the Mediterranean, a few years in Rome, and his last two years as what the local children called, charitably, a raving lunatic. The figure in a white tunic with flowing, light hair was, to John's mind, the closest thing to an angel he could imagine. He or she—John could not be sure—fought with a flaming sword and swift, flowing movements. In a few hundred years and a thousand miles east, the art of jiu jitsu would begin to form, and were John alive to see it, he would recognize some of the graceful, strategic movements of the flowing figure in white from his vision.

The other character in this drama was a study in opposites. Brutal, muscled, and without grace, it was the definition of self-centeredness and hatred. It fought without regard for its surroundings or the people around and below. It seemed to revel in the destruction and the bodies falling around it as its clawed hand crunched into the tall hut beside it, ripping a portion of the adobe out and using it as a crude bludgeon against its opponent.

Death and destruction rained down on the peasants below. John could see groups of people fleeing the destruction, some carrying babies or small children. John thought he saw peasants, in his mind's eye, pointing tiny bricks at the rampaging giants. What would that do? What strange city had brick-pointing peasants who dressed like royalty? He tried to pray and discern the meaning but felt helpless as the images and feelings washed over him.

John was half right, and more wrong than he could imagine. In his reverie, John missed a detail that would change the course of the fight: a tiny figure, dressed mostly in gray, observing from behind a building.

"I see you, prophet," the figure said. The voice was startling. John had heard similar voices his whole life, from childhood to his enforced solitude now. It was the sound of his mother, his grandmother, his sisters, and the girls he pursued as a younger man. It was the voice of a single, solitary woman . . . but with a tone that he rarely heard from either women *or* men. Ferocious certainty. In a few years, readers of John's work would call it by a different name: conviction.

CHAPTER 1: GABBY & DANIEL

Daniel Masterson closed his eyes as "Just a Closer Walk With Thee" hit its second refrain. "Let it be, dear Lord, let it be." He found comfort and hope in the lyrics that overlapped The Beatles. He saw it as a continuation of a long, long line of spirituality that was interwoven into nearly all art—or at least the art he knew and appreciated. He loved the song and the feeling of peace it gave him. "When my feeble life is over, time for me will be no more. Guide me gently, safely over. To thy kingdom shore . . . to thy shore." In his mind, he could almost see the shore. It looked like a mundane beach from a rest stop brochure in South Carolina.

With the last "shore," the song ended . . . as did Daniel's entrancement. He loved the songs in the moment. He knew all the words and was fairly confident he knew the key changes enough to play the song despite having only middle school-level musical training and even less talent. The song's ending, though, always was Daniel's least favorite part. All of the rapturous feelings he experienced during the song vanished as quickly as they came. He carried the thoughts in his mind, but the feelings left almost immediately. It made him think of filling up a gas tank with a hole in it.

Gabby Sullivan went along with Daniel's almost-weekly church attendance. He loved the Enduring Faith Church in Falls Church, Virginia, since he discovered it shortly after moving nearby for graduate school. Gabby attended because it seemed to mean so much to Daniel. The give-and-take in their relationship had not always been easy, but it had led to stability for four years and counting. It was safe and reliable—they communicated relatively well and knew each other. Plus, Gabby could put together arguments for her thesis during the sermons. She had composed a stunning argument for women in leadership positions being more rational and forward-thinking in times of crisis than their male counterparts. Today, that had been more difficult than usual. Gabby was having a difficult time not daydreaming. She gave up working on the thesis and gave in to her wandering mind. She also was getting a headache.

"When do we get to the doxology?" Gabby asked, impatient to start their day. She never counted the time at church as "the day." She considered it the price she (mostly) happily paid for having Daniel as her partner. And her daydreams were more bleak than she cared to admit. She was eager to get outside and into the sunlight.

Gabby could tell the pastor, whose name she had forgotten—she would have to check the church bulletin later—was wrapping up the sermon by summarizing the lessons he had just shared. Soon the organ would swell with a vaguely uplifting hymn from the mid- to late 1800s, and everyone would file out afterward, with polite nods and light handshakes from the women and awkward reaches among the men and some of the older boys who tried to crush each other's hands in a strange show of church machismo. It was a ritual that Gabby disliked but Daniel seemed to revel in. Today she couldn't wait to get out, but Daniel seemed to grow happier and more assured the more people he talked to after the service ended.

Once outside, Gabby made a beeline for their car—an early 2000s Honda CR-V with 220,000 miles, several minor dents, and a fading paint job. They had loved the car since they bought it three years ago. It had been their first joint purchase. The usual Sunday ritual was lunch with church acquaintances. Gabby could make small talk when needed, but it didn't come to her naturally. She would have to think back to the news of the week she had scanned earlier in the morning to have something to talk about. Gabby thought a quick lunch followed by a quiet afternoon of research sounded wonderful. Daniel would watch football on Channel 9, while she worked in the dining room/office.

"Lunch at Applebee's?" Daniel asked.

Gabby was not enthused. "We went there last week."

"Chilé con Carnage?"

"Sounds good. Do you have change for the games?"

"There're quarters in the tray."

The lunch destination settled, Gabby and Daniel took a left out of the church parking lot and headed into the city. If they could beat the church traffic, they could get good seats to watch the pre-game and play a few rounds of vintage Donkey Kong. It was silly and something from her parents' era, but Gabby had an affinity for the simplicity of Mario's mission to reach the top of the structure, only to have to start over again—with a little more difficulty—with each success. She had mused on Donkey Kong as a metaphor for her life growing up and had even written a paper in undergrad about it. She thought it was brilliant and spot-on. Her English professor, Dr. Clayton, thought it was good and showed promise despite "the stretch for a life metaphor in such a simplistic game," and gave her a B-plus for the effort.

Gabby had argued the grade should be higher because she had tied the central human theme of growth through adversity to a video game with a King Kong rip-off and a slightly racist caricature handyman. The B-plus remained (she ended up with an A in the class), but years later Gabby still felt slighted by the grade and the inability of the professor to see the brilliance of her ten-page treatise on Life's Constant Struggle To Thrive and the game level with sentient fireballs. Story of my life, she thought.

Her thoughts drifted to her parents, and to growing up in the middle of the mountains of West Virginia, going to college and beginning to shed the habits of her insular upbringing. Although just two hours away from home, college at Davis & Elkins was a different world, where Gabby truly had felt comfortable to express herself as she never could growing up. She had experimented with long hair and short hair, taking on the air of an academic then changing to the persona of someone who was reluctantly in school at her parents' behest. It was delayed maturation at what now seemed like lightning speed. At the time, though, every semester was a chance to reinvent herself until she'd found most of the elements that she felt were her. Her hair slightly above the shoulders, T-shirts and light sweaters that were mostly monochromatic—it became her look and even had carried over into her profession as a park ranger.

In her few moments of self-reflection, Gabby had missed the exotic electric Energica motorcycle as it eased in behind them on the expressway and the piercing, focused gaze behind the driver's visor.

CHAPTER 2: CHANNEL 9 NEWS

If the talking heads and experienced anchors from Channel 9 said it, it must be true. Gabby didn't know much about the other local stations, but she was sure they would be a distant second to Channel 9. In a town known for keeping secrets, deception, and outright lies, the station's reporters were a good example of a dying breed: principled, well-sourced journalists. The station was on several televisions inside the themed restaurant as it awaited the regular Sunday afternoon crowds.

What was first reported several days earlier was on once again. In the coming week, the night sky would feature a passing meteor discovered just four years prior. Named Baomer, the car-sized rock traveled at a leisurely 37,000 miles an hour. Baomer would pass within 300,000 miles of the moon—a very close shave by astronomical standards. The anchor closed the story with the fact that five to ten asteroids whizzed past Earth every year. What made Baomer unique was an unusually high concentration of decaying iron, and it was losing mass at a small but measurable rate. Astronomers the world over were enthused about this rare happening because it gave them the opportunity to study a rarity on top of a rarity—a meteor passing close enough to the planet to be observed with conventional telescopes, and it was leaving behind a portion of itself in the form of a long, ever-expanding trail of space dust. There were discussions in the global scientific community about capturing some of this rare detritus, but no feasible mission could be mounted in time for the meteor's passing. Baomer would not pass by Earth again, at last estimate, for another 324 years.

As the meteor passed, some of its iron flakes were slowly gravitating toward a nearby celestial body with a very weak gravitational field: the moon. The television talking heads ruminated on this once-in-several-lifetimes phenomenon, and Gabby listened and watched intently. She hung on their every word but couldn't take her eyes off the screen. An old U2 song played in the background . . . something about a hill and beds of roses. On the screen, the moon appeared very red. Several astrophysicists were chattering excitedly about the extremely rare phenomenon and how fortunate mankind was to see it and record it for future generations. The iron flakes were gathering in low orbit around the moon, while the sun reflected off the flakes. It made the moon appear a deep shade of red.

Gabby began to see it very differently the longer she watched. The moon was drenched in blood. The craters slowly were filling up with thick, syrupy sanguination. Even daydreaming, Gabby enjoyed the use of archaic language. Neil Armstrong's footprints were filled in by the slowly spreading liquid. "It appears quite black," she heard in the voice of Anthony Hopkins' Dr. Lecter from *The Silence of the Lambs*. Pools of blood were rising in the smaller craters, with small rivers forming in the dust. The restaurant speakers seemed to grow louder when the song reached its crescendo, " . . . and the moon has turned red over One Tree Hill."

In her daydream, Gabby saw the singer's hairline receding every few seconds with pale skin and a slow, steady growth of horns from his forehead. The horns kept growing and began to curl in on themselves like the Fourth of July snakes Gabby's dad had brought home during her childhood. They were growing, writhing, twisting, and curling in on themselves. Blood began to break free of the moon's weaker gravity. At one-sixth the gravity of Earth, it could not hold onto the ever-growing pools. Blood began to drift, congeal, reform, and reconnect again as more of it left the lunar surface and floated into the thin atmosphere. In her mind's eye, Gabby saw a glob land on her shoe, and she let out a surprised yelp.

Her sudden exclamation did not remain in her imagination. The all-too-real daydream caused Gabby to have a minor outburst in the restaurant. It was not the sort of thing she typically did. Daniel came to her side quietly and asked if something was wrong. She was flushed and breathing slightly faster than normal—a rarity for someone who prided herself on being calm and collected. "Ugh, sorry about the mess." Gabby moved to clean her spilled drink from the table beside her and from her shirt. Even in a slightly distraught state, she was more concerned about the impression she would leave with her fellow diners and the restaurant's staff than herself.

"I'm fine," she said, running her hands down her shirt in a quick attempt to smooth out the fabric and wipe away the water spot. "I was watching the news and got a little light-headed. Waited too long to eat. Let's go sit down." The normal bustle of the restaurant resumed, but not nearly fast enough for Gabby. She was nursing a case of embarrassment as she tried to shake her daydream. Plus, she didn't know which was worse: the hot flush of knowing she had let out an abrupt shout in public—drawing attention to herself was one of her worst fears—or being unable to move past the mental image of blood flowing and filling craters on the moon. Later on, she would decide both were equally unlike her and would chalk it up to transitioning from the bright fall sunlight into the dark, windowless barcade.

***

Three booths away, a set of piercing blue eyes watched the couple enter their booth and immerse themselves in the too-large menus that hid their faces. If Gabby or Daniel had lowered their menus, they would have caught a glimpse of a man with the darkest skin ever to be seen on Earth, watching their every move. "Not yet," he murmured to himself. *It has started,* he thought. *She is on her way. After hundreds of thousands of years, my time is finally here.*

CHAPTER 3: SORTING IT OUT AT HOME

The house was extremely small but suited both Gabby and Daniel. Five rooms—the front door opened directly into the long living room that made up a third of the whole place. Off to the left was a decent-sized bedroom—as long as the occupants were happy with close quarters and didn't mind sharing one roomy closet. (They were and they didn't.) At the end of the living room was the entrance to a no-frills kitchen, complete with a small dining table that fit two and no more. This really cut into Gabby and Daniel's entertaining, which was fine by both of them because they rarely had occasion to do so and didn't particularly enjoy it. Daniel's parents had visited from South Dakota two years ago, and one of his coworkers they both liked stopped by every few weeks or so. But even those visits were becoming less frequent. With just the basics for two in the pantry and refrigerator, maybe it was a sign that maybe having regular visitors was not high on the priority list.

Gabby said she needed a nap. Her afternoon daydreaming (which was what she decided it had been) had left her sleepy and shaken. The daydream had seemed very real at the time. The edges of her vision had become fuzzy, much like the time she was smacked in the right eye with a softball in fourth grade. If someone looked closely enough, the area around her right eye was always a little darker than her left. She had been equally upset about the prodigious black eye as the fact that the runner had been safe.

Gabby thought some quality time on the couch would help her feel better. It almost always did, and she was counting on the weekly ritual of a Sunday afternoon post-church, post-lunch nap to help the odd daydream fade from her thoughts.

When she closed her eyes, however, she saw the moon again, covered in a red haze that it took nearly all her willpower not to see as blood. *What is wrong with me today?* she thought as she twisted on the couch, her head buried in a cushion in an attempt to block the Virginia afternoon sun streaming through the front window. She twisted on the couch again, spinning in an effort to get comfortable enough to doze off. It wasn't working.

A few more minutes of spinning and cushion-arranging didn't help the memory fade or help her fall asleep. Gabby was awake for the afternoon and she knew it. This was not the way to end the week.

Daniel already had dozed off in the bedroom, several hastily folded shirts that would require refolding beside him on the bed. Daniel was many things—reliable, usually slow to anger, a good housekeeper, a little slow when it came to math, and incredibly good with kids. But a folder of freshly laundered clothes he was not. To his credit, though, he never claimed to be. He was more than happy to ferry the clothes up and down the stairs to the washer and dryer combo—even hanging up what required it with no complaint—but the last crucial step eluded him. He was happy with slightly rumpled T-shirts and button-ups. Why wasn't everyone?

Gabby shambled into the bedroom, desperate for the afternoon slumber that eluded her. The week was going to be a really, really long one if she didn't catch up on her sleep on Sunday afternoons as normal. Deep down, she knew science didn't back up this outdated notion of restfulness, but she had lived this way since she was an early teenager and had convinced herself it was too late to change the habit.

"Move over, please," she grumbled, moving aside the pile of laundry. Gabby was a sprawler and a spinner, which meant the T-shirts were destined to hit the floor. Daniel would have to move over if he intended to continue napping.

Early in their relationship when they were still getting to know each other, their differing sleep habits had caused a few bruised feelings for both of them. They had adapted to it after three somewhat tense follow-up dates (with an unexpected make-out session on the third), a morning-after heart-to-heart talk and new ground rules: Daniel would give Gabby as much room as she needed, and they would invest in a king-sized bed when they moved in together—which came about seven months later.

Four years later, there still was no king-sized bed. Gabby slept, Daniel slept, and neither completely rested each night, but they made it work anyway. The trade-off of being together, they discovered, was more than worth a little sleep deprivation. Sunday afternoon naps had become key to maintaining the balance. Gabby fell onto the right side of the bed and closed her eyes. In her mind, the moon was still running red with blood. Eyes open or eyes closed, it was the same. The daydream would be with her all day, so she might as well make the most of it and take a walk. The crisp fall air would do her good, and she could turn in early for the evening.

Seventeen blocks away, the dark-skinned motorcyclist sat in his luxury apartment. Immaculately clean with a large, looming acacia tree and several strains of rare lilies, the apartment took up the entire thirteenth floor of an otherwise nondescript office building. The building's elevator didn't list a thirteenth floor (which is common), but had one (which is not). Every floor but the thirteenth was filled with small businesses, quasi-governmental agencies and on the ground floor, three nonprofits. A completely separate, hidden elevator accessed the apartment. This meant there was less chance of someone—an errant handyman or an enterprising salesperson, perhaps—stumbling into the place. It was as secure as a military bunker. The man had made sure of that when the building was built in 1957.

He sat in the middle of the large, sparse living room, listening to the sounds of the couple trying to manage a Sunday afternoon nap. He smiled as he used a new, bright highlighter to mark a passage in a very large, very old book. The yellow mark streaked the words and wore away a visible part of the brownish paper. With crumbling edges of papyrus and very crude leather for a cover, the book was older than most countries and was one of only a handful of books still in existence after 1,000 years. Its owner, though, was far older. He had memorized most of the passages in the sixteenth century and didn't hesitate to mark up the otherwise priceless tome. Good notes, he had learned the hard way, are essential to a successful plan.

CHAPTER 4: WORK CHALLENGES

A bachelor's degree in political science from a good but not particularly well-known university in Appalachia is a great thing to enhance a student's understanding of the world and see where help is needed the most. It's also a good base for pursuing a higher degree. What it is not good for is starting a career in the extremely image-conscious world of bureaucracy in and around Washington, DC. Coupled with Gabby's very low tolerance for insincerity, her career path had taken a very unexpected—and ultimately welcomed—turn into becoming a park ranger with the National Park Service. After three years of training at her first post-college job in nearby Harpers Ferry National Historical Park, she felt ready for a step up. When an opening at the Washington Monument came open, she applied and, through a field of several dozen applicants, ultimately landed a position at the landmark.

Gabby loved talking to the visitors and escorting them to near the top of the obelisk. The elevator trip was her favorite part of the tours: a two-minute trip up with a few stops to view the inscriptions on the inside of the massive stones. At the top, visitors had a stunning view and could begin to understand the genius of L'Enfant's design of the capital city. The maddening turns in the Federal District were remnants of early eighteenth-century urban warfare, designed so cannons commanded by the fledgling nation's defense could target any enemy forces marching down an avenue. This hub-and-spoke design had worked well for more than a century, but the city and the nation had grown past foreign invasions that would have laid siege to the district.

The design existed long after the need for cannon fire in the city had vanished. The cross-web of streets now served to carry public servants to their offices, carry busloads of visitors from all over the world to once-in-a-lifetime historical sites, and lastly, to consistently frustrate city residents and frequent visitors. The view from the windows near the top of the monument showed in detail what was seldom grasped from the ground. Gabby always enjoyed sharing this bit of information as the elevator neared the top. It gave the visitors something to look for from the tiny windows, and it felt as though she was sharing secret knowledge with the lucky few who visited the monument during her shifts.

Today's crowd was the same as always. Eager school kids and teachers, older visitors in small groups of four to six who wanted to see the monument for the first time or, just as often, see it again as adults after first visiting as schoolchildren decades ago. There also were the occasional family trippers and visitors from other countries. It was this last group that always surprised and impressed Gabby the most. That someone from another nation would want to visit a monument to the father of the United States always made her scratch her head. Every country had a unique history and story. Gabby thought the origins of every country were extremely interesting, and she often engaged in that topic with foreign visitors. Canadian visitors were almost unfailingly polite, and French and British ones frequently would sniff a little when the ranger talked about breaking free from colonial rule and outside influence. The guest book at the entrance of the monument often had comments from British visitors such as, "We want it back," "You've ruined the place," and Gabby's favorite, "We did it best and first." There's nothing like a sore loser, even after 250 years.

She had learned to pick up bits and pieces of French and German during her short tenure with the Park Service—"Be sure and look," "Get a photo while you can," "Americans are so loud," and the universal "Just wait until we get home." She was less adept with other Romance languages, and completely lost with Asian ones. Occasionally there were small groups from the Far East: Japan, the Philippines, Korea, and China. Most of these groups were very polite, followed directions and hand gestures, and were most likely discussing the large, emotional Americans all around them, Gabby thought. The quick, seemingly curt speech of these visitors usually left her confounded. The same was true of the even more rarely heard Baltic and Slavic languages. Then there were the melodious African languages that were too numerous to count but sounded exceedingly lovely to her.

Every so often, she would hear a language that completely baffled her. It didn't happen often—maybe three or four times in her eighteen months on this detail. But there were some languages she heard that didn't seem to have any connections she could pick up on. She had learned, over time, that the Inuit language was dying out and within two generations it may not have any native speakers. It would be preserved, but as a piece of history and not as a living, thriving language. This made her sadder than she cared to admit.

Every group since 9 a.m. had been much the same: mostly American, usually polite and sometimes reverent, with small groups of foreign visitors mixed in. As the 2:30 p.m. group advanced inside the monument's entrance, Gabby was confused by a few visitors—four of them, two men and two women, polite and nicely dressed (which seemed a little odd, Gabby thought, because hardly anyone wore dress clothes when sightseeing), but the language completely baffled her. It was melodious like Chinese with some of the guttural swirl of German—and utterly unfathomable. She focused on reciting her facts as the elevator climbed higher, but a small part of her mind was trying to decide where these visitors were from. It appeared, from their tone and stance, that one couple was having a disagreement with the other. They were barely paying attention to Gabby's talk—even the part where the elevator stops for visitors to see the markers inside the monument's walls.

"This marker was a gift from the people of Montana," Gabby said, almost by rote, as she stopped the elevator. She believed she could give the spiel in her sleep, but she always tried to make it exciting every time she gave it. She recited it nearly every day, but most visitors likely were hearing it for the first time. Gabby wanted everyone to have a memorable experience at what she had come to see as, in the months she'd been on this job, her monument. Her enthusiasm showed and it was not uncommon for visitors to remark in the guest book that the energetic ranger in the elevator was a highlight of the visit.

The unusual foursome continued their disagreement, oblivious to the rest of the passengers. Gabby still couldn't make heads or tails of it or identify the language. As an unofficial but enthusiastic student of the human experience, she was bothered by this to no end. She made a mental note to start looking for little known languages that evening.

A mild cacophony was building in the back of the elevator as the quartet's conversation became louder and more animated. The gruff, melodious banter was becoming impossible to ignore. One visitor attempted to ask the foursome to be quiet. "Would you please lower your voices?" she asked. They ignored her and kept going. Gabby restarted the elevator's ascent a minute or so earlier than usual to help get this group safely to the top and out of the close confines of the elevator, and away from the strange argument going on with the well-dressed but quarrelsome visitors.

During the abbreviated stop, had any of the elevator's occupants peered out the window past the inscriptions and down the dimly lit staircase that wrapped around the monument's interior, they might have caught a glimpse of a very dark-skinned, white-haired man sprinting up the thin metal stairs.

The elevator continued to rise, reaching its highest point several feet shy of the monument's pinnacle of 555 feet. Gabby nodded politely to everyone as they entered the tiny walk-around area that encircled the top of the spire. Four tiny windows afforded views in each direction. Upon exiting the elevator, the four visitors ended their lively discussion and walked out as if nothing had happened. Gabby was relieved and nodded to the attendants in the small visitors area as if to say, "Keep a closer watch than normal on this group." The guards were trained to watch for potential acts of violence. Family disputes among foreign nationals were not in their job descriptions. They could, and did, keep the peace in the relatively small observation area of the Washington Monument, though.

Until today.

CHAPTER 5: OBELISK DISSENSION

Visitors ambled around the small, rectangular walkway near the top of the monument. The track, with the elevator in the middle and four small windows looking out, made this observation point one of the most popular in the capital city. It could comfortably hold up to sixty people. Today's crowd was a lighter one. Forty-three visitors—including the four foreign nationals no one could understand—five guards, and Gabby.

As usual, most people ignored the well-thought-out written histories and photos and went straight for the windows. Made of reinforced steel and high-impact glass, the eight square portholes provided fantastic views of the city, with the White House and tidal basin to the east and the Blue Ridge Mountains to the west. Gabby had a little time before she had to take the elevator back to the ground level. Usually the rangers would get at least two to three groups to the top, cycle them back down as they finished their visit to the top of the monument, then bring new visitors on the return trip.

The two couples started to argue again, not paying any attention to the windows situated around the walkway or vying for a spot to look out. Gabby thought that was unusual even for these four. Their voices trailed off slightly as they went around the corner away from the elevator. Most of the other visitors gave them a wide berth, either out of respect for foreign visitors or because their group sounded as though they were almost shouting in an extremely foreign tongue.

Gabby had about ten minutes of downtime before she would take anyone ready to travel back down to the monument's base. Her relative quiet time was interrupted by the sounds of a scuffle from the other side of the walk-around. Gabby ran toward the commotion to find the four visitors had moved from quarreling with each other to accosting those around them. They were jostling other visitors, pushing and shoving them, trying to search their pockets, and, most odd of all, grasping any visitor they could—men, women, and children—by the head, gazing into their eyes, and bellowing a short, sharp shriek. Most people were too shocked by the sudden familiarity to do anything. Five guards attempted to remove the interlopers and force them to let go of the people they were accosting, but to no avail. The visitors were abnormally strong and, despite the guards' efforts— all of whom were ex-military and well-versed in crowd control— kept grabbing every visitor they could. Their chattering grew into shouting, becoming louder the more the guards tried to remove them. Children were not spared the strange interrogation, either. They and several adults were gasping to catch their breath as the guards tried in vain to stop the assaults.

Around the corner, the door to the stairs burst open—it usually was not opened from the staircase side—and slammed into the limestone of the monument, sending small flecks of century-old stone flying. The dark-skinned, white-haired motorcyclist, breathing heavily, ran through the open door, quickly scanned the area to see where the commotion was coming from, and ran toward it. "More trouble!" shouted one of the guards.

Gabby was on one side of the four, the motorcyclist on the other. He glanced at Gabby, his long white hair partially sticking to his face. She stared at him, feeling powerless to stop what was happening. They both hesitated for a moment; then the leather-clad cyclist ran toward one of the male attackers who had a middle-aged man held with his arms behind his back, waiting for his partner to perform the next shriek.

As a park ranger, Gabby was trained in self-defense and how to get an aggressive visitor to let go of something or someone. She had never had to use her training, though, and watched in disbelief as the experienced guards had no success in subduing the out-of-control visitors. Gabby's training did help in another way: escape. "This way, stay down low, crawl quickly, and make your way to the elevator," she said in a low voice to one of the visitors on the ground who had already been through the strange interrogation. "Help get people moving so we can get everyone out of here."

With the stairway suddenly inaccessible with the arrival of the white-haired man—*He has to be part of this,* Gabby thought—the elevators were the only way to get everyone out of harm's way, even if it was not part of standard protocol. A line of crawling, frightened visitors started to move past her to the elevator doors. One of the kids was shaking. "It's going to be all right. We're going to get you out of here, and the rangers are going to get those people under control," Gabby said, patting the boy on the back as he crawled past. She thought she saw a tiny smile creep onto his face as she reassured him. She hoped she was right.

Thirty-nine people in the elevator was not going to work, even crammed in tightly. They could fit maybe twenty at the most. They would have to make two trips, or try to send some people down the stairs. More security should be making their way up the stairs now, per Park Service protocol. Gabby was hopeful but not counting on it, given the limited success the security team already had experienced.

Back in the middle of the commotion, the motorcyclist had launched himself at the nearest interloper and succeeded in getting him to release his hostage. A second shoulder shove, backed up by two short running steps, sent the man careening through the air and into a section of limestone. A baseball-sized chunk of stone flew from the impact as his head and left arm bounced off the stone and the smartly dressed attacker fell to the floor with a thud. He wasn't moving. There was no blood. One of the guards quickly subdued him with handcuffs.

The other three interlopers kept up their interrogations, although they were doing them more quickly and with a noticeable sense of urgency. The guards moved in closer. "Can anyone talk to them, see what they want?" shouted one.

"Yeah, if we knew what language they were speaking," came the reply. "They sure aren't responding to English. We need to get this locked down. Plus there's the new guy . . . white hair over there." The motorcyclist had rebounded quickly from his attack. He clambered up from the floor, his shirt torn but with no visible marks on his skin. All of the visitors had been crawling toward the elevators. There was just one person left, and he had the undivided attention of three apparently extremely strong, super-skinny, and nattily dressed visitors who were bent on completing whatever they were trying to do. The remaining male interloper shouted something unintelligible as one of the women held the sole remaining hostage—a man who appeared to be in his mid-forties—tightly by the arms. The other stood slightly to the left and behind her.

The hostage was named José, Gabby learned later, and had come to the capital city from Maryland with his daughter Selah for her birthday weekend. He could see that Selah had crawled out of harm's way, out of sight of the attackers, and hopefully headed down to safety so the guards could take care of these terrorists like they deserved. It was as if they wanted to die or be caught. Why stage something crazy like this in a place with just one way in and out? Even under duress, José and the guards had been wondering the same thing. The hum of the elevator started and José hoped Selah was on it. He squirmed in the unyielding grip of the shorter, stouter of the two female attackers who had no trouble keeping José where she wanted him. The guards had the group surrounded, but José's arm bones were beginning to crack. Loudly.

Another shout from the taller woman sounded as if she gargled carburetor oil and razor blades. The result was completely incomprehensible but menacing all the same. Some things are understood on a primal level, including threats of violence. The three remaining assailants plus their prisoner were confronted by the five guards to their left, but the assailants barely registered their presence or movement. Since the motorcyclist's arrival, the three had kept their focus on him on their right and beside the stairway door. Normally these were great odds for the well-trained and regimented Park Service guards—three distracted miscreants, just one hostage, and no one else nearby to get hurt—but the last few minutes had shown this was far from a normal situation.

One of the guards ran forward, brawny arms outstretched to grab the taller female from behind. She dodged his advance, and brought her thin, bony elbow into the guard's back. It made a sickening *snap* followed by the guard's jaw bouncing off the concrete floor. The other guards saw their coworker unconscious but breathing, bloody spittle running down the side of his chin. José seized the moment and delivered a backward head butt to his would-be captor. She didn't move or react. Not one sorry muscle. "I'm dead," José said.

In the same instant the guard had moved forward, the motorcyclist produced an expandable steel rod from his left jacket sleeve, and leapt into the air. He was not tall—five feet at best—and his leap bordered on the unbelievable. Before anyone could react, his boots connected with the taller female's chin, and he wrapped one of his thick, muscled arms around her neck, bringing the rod around and delivering what should have been a fatal blow to the other female's skull. She went to her knees in obvious pain, but didn't make a sound.

The motorcyclist used his momentum to swing around, twist the neck of the taller assailant into a sickening position, and tuck and roll under the legs of José and the remaining attacker. He stopped himself with his hands mid-roll, then delivered a punishing double-footed mule kick to the crotch. (It would be recounted later as a thing of unexpected beauty by the survivors.) The kickee dropped to his bony knees and received a swift blow to the head from the business end of the staff. He collapsed with a light thud. José stood there, surprised to be suddenly free with a five-foot-tall, white-haired, dark-skinned ninja behind him. He turned around much more slowly than he ordinarily would have.

The motorcyclist was already gone, the stairwell door once again slamming against granite with the sound of rapid footsteps echoing down the stairwell. The guards looked around. No signs of the attackers other than scuff marks, cracks in the century-old stone and granite, and something everyone hoped was just funny-looking blood. They returned to where their captured assailant should have been and were greeted by a pair of bloody handcuffs, still locked, with large chunks of pale white skin stuck to the inside.

CHAPTER 6: ESCAPE

Gabby's evacuation plan worked better than she had hoped. As the melee started, she sent a very full elevator down to the ground floor. She placed an assertive-looking woman with an unexpectedly lovely name in charge. Sometimes you find beauty in the strangest of situations, Gabby thought. "You, ma'am, what's your name?" Gabby shouted over the commotion of the crowd.

"It's Coral, officer."

Gabby was impressed. "Oh, that's a great name. I'm going to remember that one. Coral, can you be in charge until the elevator gets to the bottom? Will you do that for me?" Coral nodded. "Great. See you at the bottom. The rest of us will head down the stairs." The elevator doors closed as a handful of tourists, children, and the elderly began their slow descent to safety.

With the elevator safely on its way, Gabby and the remaining eighteen visitors took the long way around the platform, ending up near the stairwell door. They were going to have to risk an encounter with anyone else who may come up the stairs. It would take more than twenty-five minutes to descend the staircase, provided they didn't encounter any armed rangers coming up to help. If so, they would have to identify themselves while the rangers ensured they were not a threat. Gabby hoped her presence would mitigate that.

She went first to begin the long trek down. Gabby appointed the calmest person she could find in the group to keep things moving in the back of the group. He seemed eager and up to the task. The group started moving down the dimly lit metal staircase. Gabby did take a moment to be thankful that no one was panicking and everyone was being helpful under duress. Ordinarily, climbing or descending these stairs was a treat. Today it was a life-saving necessity. Gabby told everyone to be sure to hold onto the handrails and not to look down. Visitors often experienced vertigo when looking down the chasm.

Less than ten minutes into their descent, they heard the sound of rangers bounding up the stairs. Gabby had the group stop and stand on the outer side of the guardrails to allow the rangers to pass by safely and quickly. She also shouted out her identity, location, and who was with her. "It's Gabby. We're coming down the stairs with a group of visitors. Most people went down the elevator. It's just the troublemakers and the guards at the top. Four bad guys. We don't know what they want." The guards all were very solemn as they passed by, eyeing every visitor warily. They knew that one determined person could slip past multiple security checks and do a lot of damage in a very short time. These nineteen all looked frightened and normal enough—but that was to be expected.

After a quiet but tense minute, the two groups moved past each other without incident. Gabby breathed the biggest sigh of relief of her life as her small group continued its descent. She considered sharing details about the many inscriptions and engraved well-wishes they passed but thought better of it.

Nearing the bottom of the staircase, Gabby and most of the group began to express relief at reaching the exit. Once Gabby heard the sounds of more guards on the ground floor and knew the last of her group had made their way through the doorway, she was able to relax slightly. That moment grew into full-blown joy when she saw the elevator riders gathered in a tight group outside the monument's entrance. Coral was tending to everyone, giving reassurance when needed and calmly talking to armed park rangers who had arrived shortly after the incident began. Gabby stopped to offer her sincerest thanks and a promise to get back in touch when all this was over.

Just a few hundred yards away, the closest gate of the White House opened and a limousine exited, surrounded by soldiers carrying heavy ordnance. The car drove over the curb and made a beeline for the monument and the survivors and guards gathered there. The monument guards spread out to make room for the car's arrival, still holding their weapons at the ready.

The car pulled up as near as it could to the monument's entrance and its ring of heavy stone benches. The passenger side door opened, and an officious-looking man in a suit got out, walked around the back of the limo, and opened the left rear door. An even more officious man exited. Most watchers of the evening news or countless cable news programs would recognize the US Secretary of State. Seeing him in person was a little disorienting for the small crowd of survivors and only slightly less so for the Park Service guards. He walked over to the survivors and one by one began to shake their hands, ask how they were doing, and thank them for their bravery.

The secretary abruptly stopped his glad-handing when he saw emerging from the monument's entrance a group of park rangers. They were clearing the way for five other rangers as they walked backward steadily, with their weapons pointing slightly down and trained on one man. A few moments later and with five guns pointed directly at him, the motorcyclist exited the stairwell. Sweat still was cooling on his brow as he gently eased the door open with his foot and walked out. He smiled at the guards and the barrels of their weapons, which all were pointed directly at him.

"You really do not want to do that," he said with a small chuckle. "It would have," he paused to consider his next words, "disastrous consequences for whoever pulled the trigger. I promise, I am not one of the bad guys. Believe it or not, I am here to help." The motorcyclist slowly advanced, and the guards moved backward at the same pace, never taking their gazes away from the curious man who walked out seemingly unharmed from a terrorist attack.

Once the group moved away from the exit, the secretary and his larger, better-armed entourage came up behind the small wall of rangers, telling them to lower their weapons slowly and stand down. "The danger has passed, officers, thanks to your dedication. And Mr. Green here." The secretary swept past the rangers before they could react to his orders, and offered an extremely courteous handshake to the motorcyclist. "This man is not a threat," the secretary said loudly. "He's one of the most patriotic men I know, and the closest thing we have to a living natural treasure. Sorry about the weapons, Gage. We owe you a debt for your assistance. Your call helped us mobilize extra security and lock down all other historic sites in the city. It looks as though you took it upon yourself to help with some of the clean-up. Words cannot do justice to the thanks the American people owe you. I've been asked by the president to give you our thanks."

Mr. Green smiled. "Thanks, Mr. Secretary. Just doing what I can. 'To whom much is given, much is required.' I was nearby when I saw the commotion. I called you, then ran inside to see if I could help. I know it was foolish. Sorry if I caused any stress up there. Or down here." He glanced at the still-stunned rangers who had lowered their weapons but had not moved an inch. "I was able to reach the top and get the door open so this young man," Mr. Green gestured toward a very surprised visitor who had been a part of Gabby's group, "could lead everyone to safety. If anyone deserves our thanks today, it is the guards and him."

The secretary smiled and nodded. "Everyone across the street agrees your request to stay out of the limelight will be honored. The focus will be on our brave rangers and this young man—the real heroes. But privately, the president would like to thank you too."

Gabby listened in shock and disbelief. *This crazy little man had flat-out lied to the secretary of state, and no one said a word. And he mentioned just about everyone but me. Maybe he doesn't like assertive women.*

To her shock, Mr. Green made his way over to her, hopped up on one of the nearby benches so he could look Gabby in the eyes, and said in a low voice, "Sorry about that. It is a long story. If you will come with me, I can make us dinner. I have a nice caprese salad I have been making for the past six thousand years. You will love it. And we can talk about the really important stuff. Like the beginning and the end of the world."

CHAPTER 7: MR. GREEN

"I'm not going anywhere with you. You sound like you're certifiable. So jump off the bench and back off." The adrenaline in Gabby's system was wearing off and she was getting antsy. Who was this strange man who spoke as if he'd escaped from an institution, apparently knew people in the upper echelons of the government including the president, and had successfully helped fight a group of terrorists? And why did she feel like she *should* go with him? She thought this and her strange dreams lately couldn't be a coincidence.

Gabby insisted on meeting Daniel first and on her own before going anywhere. Mr. Green said his people could find Gabby's boyfriend and bring him along, but Gabby wasn't having it. "I don't know you from Adam. I saw you burst through a door you shouldn't have been able to open, then get involved in a fight between some lunatics and trained security experts and live to talk about it without a scratch on you. Then the secretary of state, of all people, shows up kissing your ass and tells us to go about our business. Well, the Jedi mind trick stops here, *Mr. Green,* or whoever you really are."

Mr. Green smiled more than he had in a very long time. He liked Gabby. He stifled a small laugh as he said, "Oh, you are definitely the one—no doubt about it. The gift, as foretold. And the surprise? A temper too. Modern women can be endlessly fascinating. The other side doesn't stand a chance." His smile was equal parts charming and irritating. "Please allow me to provide an address to meet. I will be there at least through the next two days. Stop by any time." Mr. Green wrote down his address on the back of a business card, nodded toward Gabby, and walked down the grassy hill toward a waiting car.

***

Daniel had stood patiently for the temporary security checkpoint at the base of the Washington Monument's hill. He watched as several panicked families waited to hear from their loved ones. Gabby had texted him as soon as she had exited the monument to tell him she was fine, and it appeared as if almost everyone—except for the four interlopers—had emerged unharmed. When he finally made it through the checkpoint, Daniel began walking hurriedly then ran toward the group of survivors clustered on benches. He didn't see Gabby at first. He found her after a minute or so of searching. She was sitting, talking with Coral. Gabby's head was down, and her shoulders were shaking a bit. She had been crying.

"I'm so happy to see you," Daniel said a little louder than he normally would over the shoulder of one of the survivors as he tried to make his way to his girlfriend. He had to elbow through the crowd to sit beside her. Gabby raised her head, showed a small smile, and said, "Tough day at the office." Leaning into Daniel, she began to let go of the tension that had kept her going after the danger had passed. With Daniel, she could relax and rely on him for a moment. He was good that way. It was one of the things she loved about him the most.

After several long minutes, Gabby spoke. "This isn't over. There's still something I probably have to do. I'd like you to go with me but would understand if you don't want to." They got up and walked to an empty bench where no one else could hear them. Gabby recounted the day's events in as much detail as she could: the strange dress and speech of the four, the sudden outbursts and violence at the top of the monument, how the escape happened, and the arrival and departure of Mr. Green. And his curious invitation to meet.

"Well, yeah, I'll go with you. It's you and me. Always. You could do it alone and be fine, I know that. But I'd hate to miss the fun and hear about it secondhand. You know I tell stories better than you anyway." When he finished talking, Gabby looked Daniel in the eyes, and they both started to cry. Then they both began to laugh. Quietly at first, then louder and more effusively until some survivors nearby started to give them the side eye. Neither of them cared. They both loved the other a little more in that moment. She not only had survived, but she had helped every visitor—save one—get away from the observation deck unharmed. It was nothing short of a miracle.

Wrapped in an emergency blanket like most of the survivors, Gabby grabbed Daniel's hand and walked down the small incline as more police and fire vehicles showed up. News cameras were filming everything from behind hastily erected barricades. Gabby smiled slightly as she saw José the Navy veteran emerge from the base of the monument. He was the last of the people left inside—the one person she didn't help. The four terrorists somehow had escaped, but they had failed in their mission. There were no serious injuries. Every person was accounted for and in relatively good spirits. The Washington Monument had lost a few pieces of stone upstairs, but otherwise stood as it had for nearly 150 years. Gabby's smile turned into a full grin when she saw the girl who must have been Selah, José's daughter, break away from a group of paramedics and run into her father's arms. She did not let go of him for a long, long time.

CHAPTER 8: URBAN JUNGLE

Daniel insisted on going home first to find an old tape recorder. Gabby and he had used it in graduate school to record professors who talked faster than either of them could take notes. It had come in handy and had been the source of a few minor fights when they both wanted to use it at the same time. For the past several years, though, it had sat unused in a kitchen drawer. With a fresh set of batteries, it was ready to go again. Daniel said he felt like Woodward and Bernstein. Gabby said he was ridiculous but loved him anyway.

It was a twenty-minute drive to a nearby business district in Alexandria and the address Mr. Green had provided. It was like any number of office buildings in the metro Washington area: mildly modern and nondescript. Gabby always had wondered why there wasn't more diversity in the architecture around Washington. A fellow ranger had put it best: "When you're surrounded by modern masterpieces that were built to look Greco-Roman but still come across as overwhelmingly American, everything else pales in comparison." The buildings might be plain, but the contents often are not—quasi-governmental organizations, some spy agencies from the US and elsewhere, extra-posh stores and housing for some of the most rich and powerful people in the world. The longer Gabby lived in northern Virginia, the more she felt this interpretation was accurate. It also reminded her of a movie her parents loved, starring Dudley Moore and featuring patients at a mental facility who came up with advertising ideas. One of the most creative ideas from the movie was for Volvo cars: "They're boxy, but they're good." The same principle applied to many of metro Washington's buildings.

Daniel was having a little trouble finding the building's entrance. The business card gave the address—that part was easy enough—but the written instructions were very vague. "Garage, first floor, take elevator to garden level." Many buildings nearby probably had rooftop gardens, but this brutalist structure didn't appear as though it had one. It was nothing but gray, drab concrete with mirrored windows for at least twenty floors. Daniel thought it would be hard to grow a garden anywhere here.

Gabby was eager to find their destination. "Let's park on the first floor and walk around." Buildings in and around Washington frequently were built with garages underground and on the first floor, to save on valuable real estate in the ever-growing capital city. They found a parking space— possibly only because it was the early evening and most of the workers in the building had left for the day. Gabby and Daniel got out and walked toward the glassed-in lobby. The sign didn't list anyone named Mr. Green, nor did it show anything for Green Industries, which also was listed on the business card. In frustration, Gabby and Daniel walked out of the foyer and back into the garage area. "If there's an elevator, it would have to be close to these," Daniel said. "It would be too expensive to have another elevator core."

They walked around the lobby enclosure and found nothing. They widened their search in the garage, but still no luck. In the building's southeast corner, Gabby came across a plain set of double doors with a small white sign no bigger than a sheet of paper with a green outline of a tree on it. *This is either the place or where all the recycling goes,* she thought.

Gabby tried the doors. They swung open with a gentle pneumatic hiss. Inside was a completely separate lobby with one freight elevator. The sign near the elevator button had the same tree design. Daniel offered a theory. "Let's see. It's green and shows a tree. You said this guy seemed very eccentric and well-connected. He must like his privacy. This has to be the place." As they approached the elevator, the doors opened with an almost frightening silence. A pleasant voice came through a speaker somewhere in the elevator car. "Good evening, Ms. Sullivan and . . . guest. Mr. Green is pleased to have you visit his Washington residence. We look forward to seeing you in a moment."

The elevator only had up and down buttons. No numbers. *There must be more to this guy than we imagined,* Gabby thought. A private elevator. Rubbing elbows with the highest levels of the American government.

What had she gotten herself into? Her curiosity was getting the better of her. There was no turning back now. The elevator opened as quietly at its destination as it had in the garage. The view, though, was as different as could be: very high ceilings with the last bits of early evening sunlight streaming through massive windows. Huge plants of all varieties were everywhere, so much so that it was hard to believe the environment was in a nondescript office building in metropolitan northern Virginia. Walkways weaved in between the greenery, and small animals skittered about. A massive sun lamp overhead provided warmth, along with the appearance and feel of true sunlight. It was as if someone had scooped a section of a dense forest and transported it here in one piece.

Gabby and Daniel were greeted by an extremely courteous woman with a West African accent. She introduced herself as Merrison—the second of two absolutely unique names Gabby had never heard before in one day. "We've let Mr. Green know you're here," Merrison said. "He will be along . . . shortly." She tried to hold back a smile but only partially succeeded. Gabby grinned and thanked her. Daniel became more curious and ready to flip the recorder on at a moment's notice.

They could see two other people, neither of them Mr. Green, tending to the vegetation all around them and seeming very happy to be doing so. Gabby gently stopped one of the workers with a light touch on his arm, saying, "Excuse me."

The man finished with the branch he was meticulously pruning, then laid down his shears and turned around. Gabby thought he couldn't have been older than twenty-five. He had dark skin, not quite as dark as Mr. Green's, and was definitely of African or Caribbean descent. When he spoke, Gabby heard a confluence of accents—the Caribbean via Britain with a detour through the American South. It was a lovely, lilting thing to hear him speak. She asked how long he had worked here. "About two years, give or take. Best job I've ever had. The work is fun for the most part, the boss is rarely here, and the pay is good." He smiled, then returned to his pruning.

"Actually," the man added as they continued down a path with tall, large-leafed trees on both sides, "the pay is phenomenal. Most of us earn at least three times more than anyone else in our fields. We keep the place neat, the plants thriving, and the pantry stocked for whenever Mr. Green is in town. And we're asked just to . . . " He stopped short. "Excuse me." He turned back hurriedly and left Gabby and Daniel on the lush garden path in the middle of an office building in northern Virginia, waiting on a five-foot-tall ninja who was friends with the president of the United States, a relationship that was serious enough to include having his phone number.

"It seems your abilities affect even those around you. The truth reveals itself no matter what," said Mr. Green, emerging from a path beside the couple. "Or you two just have honest faces. That always encourages good people to share more than they should."

"I sure hope you start making sense soon," Gabby said, squaring herself to face Mr. Green. "I'm here because you did a brave but reckless thing, and you seem to know more about what happened at the monument than you're telling. And you seem to know more about me than you should. It's creepy. *What do you want, Mr. Green?*"

"Me? Nothing much. I just want to see the world survive for the foreseeable future. It is very much in danger of not doing that very thing, I am afraid."

Daniel was listening in ever-increasing wonder as Gabby spoke. He always loved it when she got passionate about something. After a few moments of wide-eyed disbelief, Gabby said, with irritation and very little patience, "You are out of your mind. It was a mistake to come here. Whatever you're on or whatever you're playing at, I'm done."

Mr. Green continued to smile and stand calmly, which made Gabby noticeably more irritated. "There is no game, and I am deadly serious. There are forces at work all around you that even you cannot see or dream your way through. Things and people—and I used that term very loosely—that would like nothing more than for the world to burn. We have a chance to stop it and to break a very old cycle of death and rebirth. And when I say 'we,' what I really mean is you, Gabrielle. You are the key. Those things at the monument today. They were just the first. Nothing but cannon fodder. Nearly mindless wraiths responding to . . . whatever they can sense. They knew it was close by but were too basic to not see what they sought when it stood before them. That would be you, Gabrielle. What will come next will be smarter. Much smarter and much more deadly."

"Oh yeah, since you seem to know everything, why don't you stop whatever it is you're worried about?" Gabby said with a hint of disdain in her voice. "You seem to have plenty of resources. Why don't you do it if it's that important?"

Mr. Green smiled, briefly; then quite unexpectedly, his face turned unmistakably sad, as he stared off into the greenery behind them. "I would very much like to do that. It might help a great deal with my situation, I believe. But that is not my path or my role in what is to come. I have my part to play, but you, Gabrielle Sullivan, are in this whether you like it or not. Of that I am certain, more than anything else."

Daniel, usually content to listen and watch from the sidelines, finally spoke up. "Look, sir, this is a lovely place, and we appreciate the invite. But, well, you're not making much sense. We've had a long day and maybe you have too. I mean, it's not every day you stop a terrorist attack. Maybe everyone needs some sleep, a little prayer, a little reflection, and we can get back together later. This is probably too much for one day. We really should be going."

Gabby usually disliked when Daniel tried to smooth over uncomfortable situations. She believed he often gave in too easily when he should stand his ground. But today, for more reasons than she could name at the moment, she went with it. "Yes, let's go. Don't call us, we'll call you. Or not."

Gabby and Daniel found their way back to the elevator, waited a few awkward moments until the doors opened, then hurriedly entered and pushed the down button multiple times in quick succession, eager to leave the unlikely urban forest apartment and the events of the day behind them. Just as the elevator doors were closing, Mr. Green emerged from one of the paths. He started a slow wave goodbye and to say something, but he was cut short by the doors closing and the parting image of Gabby—shocked, tired, angry, frustrated, and suddenly in desperate need of sleep.

***

"That could have gone better," Mr. Green said out loud to no one. Then he turned around, walked back onto one of the many paths through the greenery. *Maybe I should work on my delivery,* he thought. *And tell them all of the truth. That would be a novel approach. After today, it couldn't hurt.*

CHAPTER 9: OLD TELEVISION SHOWS

Gabby and Daniel pulled out of the parking garage quickly and, in their desire to get away from this latest bit of strangeness on a very strange day, a bit recklessly. Gabby spoke first. "Please tell me you got some of that crazy talk on tape."

Daniel was happy to be back in familiar territory. "Oh yeah, every bit of it. And some of the workers too. That guy is certifiable. Do you think being that short did something to him? Like, drove him a little batty? Maybe he inherited his fortune and that sent him further off the deep end. That happens. Or he's watched too many conspiracy shows. Maybe he sees himself like Charlie from *Charlie's Angels*. I definitely could see you as an angel, kind of in the Kate Jackson no-nonsense-but-still-can-kick-your-butt mold."

Gabby had to smile. Daniel had a way of looking at things that was almost unnaturally upbeat and often out of left field. He could make light of things with just enough respect for a serious situation to not be hurtful. Today, that quality single-handedly almost made Gabby glad she had gone through the day's events. Almost.

"Thanks, Daniel. I love you more than words and usually more than chocolate ice cream. Tonight, that one is a very close second. Why don't we make a stop on the way home and drown our sorrows?"

Daniel smiled. "Plotting a course for caloric intake." Once again, in spite of herself, Gabby felt the tension in her neck ease as she leaned back and tried to forget the events of the past two days. The blood moon, her visions—which she still could not bring herself to share with anyone, including Daniel—the strange assailants at work, Mr. Green and his crazy apartment and even crazier talk. *Today was positively surreal,* she thought. Wouldn't it be wild if everything was connected? That would give the conspiracy theorists something really juicy to fret about.

Gabby began to doze. Within a few minutes, she was asleep.

***

Daniel thought about ordering her a chocolate shake with extra whipped cream on top—her favorite—and having it for when she awoke, but decided against it. He didn't want to risk waking her. He drove slowly on the way home, then helped Gabby walk groggily inside, fall into bed, and close the book on what had been a genuinely frightening, eventful day.

Daniel watched the late news on as low a volume as he could manage while Gabby slept. He considered finding his wireless headphones to see if he could make them work with their eighteen-year-old cathode ray television but decided against it. Much like processing the day's events, that was a task for another day. A few minutes of the news and Daniel fell asleep as well, as the ancient TV broadcasted endlessly about the attack, the rangers who faced the attackers, José and Selah . . . and the park ranger who had led nearly all of the hostages to safety, and who had slipped away in the chaos of the attack's aftermath. The ranger's name was not given, and a Park Service spokesperson said the ranger had requested anonymity. Daniel wondered what would happen when Gabby and the other rangers returned to their jobs in a day or so. How long would they be able to keep her heroic actions from being emblazoned across screens large and small worldwide?

***

Gabby awoke suddenly, startled to see sunlight in the bedroom. The room was cooler than normal. She almost always was up and ready before daybreak, which usually was around 6:50 a.m. this time of the year. The bedside clock read 9:12 a.m.

In a panic, she threw on her crumpled uniform from yesterday, pulled back her hair, grabbed the keys to the CR-V, and ran out the door. Usually she and Daniel carpooled to the nearby Metro station, but Daniel was nowhere to be found this morning. The car was still in the drive. She could call him en route. He must have taken the day off and gone for a walk. Daniel loved to walk around their neighborhood and even downtown on the weekends when it wasn't as crowded. He occasionally would jog when he thought he had gained a little too much weight. Walking, though, was his main form of exercise and stress relief. He was attentive, and Gabby was thankful for it most days. He normally would have left a note or given her a gentle nudge if it was a workday. Today, there was nothing. Maybe he left in a hurry, trying to avoid the news crews, or even to draw them away from the house if someone had uncovered her role in the day's events. That sounds like something Daniel would do. She smiled at the thought.

As Gabby drove to the Metro station, she tried calling her boss, a genial career ranger named Stan. She wanted to let him know she was on her way and also to check on the injured ranger from the day before. Gabby noticed it was starting to snow. This was rare for mid-October but not unheard of. The weather in northern Virginia usually was mild—hot in the summer, cold in the winter, with enjoyable falls and springs to match—and she had not read about any early flurries. But here they were as she made her way into work, one day after the most harrowing experience of her life.

Stan had not answered his line, so Gabby left a message. She was sure the monument would be closed for the foreseeable future. There would be lots of work to do as part of the inevitable investigation. There also was the possibility of being reassigned to another site, but Gabby preferred to stay at the Washington Monument and do her job regardless.

She boarded the Metro as usual, and garnered some nods and stares from the other passengers. At first, Gabby worried that her name and picture had gotten out. A young girl beside her—she looked to be about nine or ten—leaned over to her to say, "Park rangers are badass," with the last word said more quietly than the rest, as if it was a sworn secret between the two. Gabby thanked her and said being a ranger is a privilege, and the key to being a good one was to be reliable and rely on your coworkers. The little girl replied, "But you saved all those people. No one helped you do that." Gabby looked at her in amazement. Maybe her photo and name had leaked despite the Park Service's best efforts. It happens.

"I had lots of help," Gabby replied. "The other rangers and the visitors. Everyone did what they could to make sure everyone made it out safe."

"What about Henry?" the girl asked in a markedly deeper voice than before. "His back is broken, and he's missing half his teeth. Why didn't you save him?"

The lights on the commuter train flickered as they passed through a tunnel. The girl's eyes seemed to glow as she stared at Gabby, questioning her actions. "I did everything I could," Gabby said. "We're visiting Henry in a few days after his surgeries when he can have visitors. His doctors say he'll make a full recovery. He was the bravest person up there."

"While you snuck out like a dirty thief," the girl retorted. It may have been the girl's form, but definitely was not her voice. It now was lower and guttural, very similar to the attackers from the day before, but in English. "Glory hound," she snorted before turning around, slinging a book bag over her shoulders, and exiting to another railcar. The lights flickered and the door hissed shut behind her. The train's wheels whined as they navigated a slippery bend in the tracks, and the train emerged from a tunnel. In the light, Gabby could see it was snowing profusely.

Gabby realized she had stood up during the confrontation with the girl, her hand gripped tight on one of the car's stabilizing poles. She took a breath then sat back down. Only about ten minutes until her station. Work would be busy and unusual, but it would be a welcome return to almost normalcy—and a good distraction from the sudden oddness in her life. The train car door opened, and Daniel walked in. Gabby had been slightly annoyed that he had left without a note or saying goodbye, but she was happy to see him. She smiled as he approached her seat. Daniel was talking with someone else. Someone Gabby didn't recognize. They passed Gabby without a second look. She didn't think Daniel even saw her sitting there. "Daniel!" she said, as he moved past her.

He didn't react or turn around, still deeply engrossed in his conversation. His companion—a tall, striking woman with dark red hair, dressed for winter—glanced back and smiled at Gabby. Or was it a smirk? It was only a moment, but it stung. The woman seemed to know Daniel and was talking close to and leaning on his shoulder. If she didn't know better, Gabby would have thought the two were a couple. Gabby thought, *Is he two-timing me?* That would be completely out of character for him, but stranger things had happened. And how did he end up on the train? Did this woman pick him up at the house then join him on the Metro?

The snow outside was intensifying. The train slowed down as more snow gathered on the tracks faster than it could melt off. The train rocked slightly. An announcement came over the loudspeaker that the train was slowing down due to the extreme weather. Gabby looked for a seat belt but found the train did not have them. Design flaw, she thought.

Snowdrifts were piling up on the sides of the tracks, and even more so down on the ground. Gabby thought it looked like two to three feet and climbing. As the train continued to slow down, it also started to rock and jump slightly as the wheels ran over rails that were increasingly coated with thick, wet snow. A slightly nervous voice came over the loudspeaker. "We are sorry to interrupt the trip, but the train can go no further. All passengers need to disembark and walk to the nearest station. We apologize for the inconvenience, but the weather is too dangerous to continue."

And walking on an elevated track is a breeze, Gabby thought. *That's dangerous all by itself, but maybe it's the lesser of the two.* She was used to thinking logically under pressure and always tried to see the positive side of things. It was one of the qualities that made her an effective ranger. There usually was an upside. *You just have to look carefully and change your perspective sometimes,* she thought.

Passengers began to disembark, carrying work satchels, backpacks, and the occasional bag of groceries. One of the attendants told them their destination was a station about a half mile to the north, where they could get shelter and warmth. The temperature was predicted to keep falling, along with the snow. All Amtrak travel was being suspended. Gabby looked around for Daniel and the mystery woman but didn't see them anywhere.

Small groups of passengers navigated the tracks slowly. Gabby thought she saw Daniel's head in the line ahead, about seven people in front of the group. It looked like him from behind. Gabby worked to pass some of the other walkers on the tracks, trying to catch up to her errant boyfriend. She got close enough to the man to see he had a beard and was carrying a briefcase—two things that definitely were not Daniel. Daniel still had a baby face, which Gabby would tease him about on rare occasions. She never would tell him, but she admired how youthful Daniel looked, even as they edged closer to their thirties. And then there was the briefcase—she could not imagine Daniel ever carrying one. A backpack or something outdoorsy slung over his shoulder would be more like him. Not that he needed to carry much to his job as a computer programmer.

She breathed a sigh of relief and stopped politely passing people on the trek to the Metro station. As the anxiety of seeing her committed other half walking with a strange woman on a Metro and not giving her the time of day passed, she lowered her head and felt a small sense of relief. It wasn't him. Just as Gabby thought she had imagined the whole thing, she saw something on the ground that made her blood run as cold as the falling snow. Daniel and the redhead walking down below, engaged in a tight embrace and what seemed to be, even from a distance, a passionate kiss. Tension like she had rarely known came into her brain like a black, overwhelming wave. She could scarcely believe what she was seeing. She started to yell at them when from behind her she heard a voice she had first heard only several hours earlier.

It was Mr. Green. She wheeled around and saw the diminutive, confident man standing uncomfortably close to her. "He's with her now," Mr. Green said with an undeniable smirk. "You're better off without him. Come with me. Short guys have game, if you didn't know." Mr. Green approached her as if to hug her. Gabby backed up and felt her feet sliding in the snow. She wavered on the edge of the elevated train tracks.

Mr. Green's expression had a sudden gleam of mischievousness as he walked forward, saying, "If you won't come with me, go to him. See where that gets you." And with that, he pushed her off the tracks to the cold, snow-covered ground more than fifty feet below.

***

For the second time this evening Gabby awoke with a start. She was sweating and breathing heavily. To her left Daniel was sleeping, the Virginia moon shining brightly through the single, large bedroom window. The projector clock showed the time on the ceiling: 12:43 a.m.

Only when she stood up groggily did she realize everything had been a dream. She tried to shake the feeling that what she just experienced had not happened, but was only partially successful. Whenever Gabby had a bad dream as a child, she would break it down in her head, reassuring herself that none of it was real. This dream, however, had been startlingly vivid. It had started off so much like her life, including the events of the extraordinary day she had just had. It still was sinking in that none of it had happened. Not the train, the snow, not Daniel being weird or the red-haired woman he had been with. Or Mr. Green.

She nudged Daniel. "Wake up, Danny. Please."

Daniel wiped his eyes, groaned a bit, then pulled himself up in the bed. He had been sound asleep, which was normal for him. It's a gift, he had told Gabby early in their relationship. The events of the day had affected him too, but he mostly had been concerned about Gabby and how she was handling one of the most traumatic days she'd ever had. He sat up, pulling his pillow up at the same time to support his back as he began to wake up. He could count on one hand, with several fingers left over, the number of times Gabby had woken him up with something urgent. "What's up, sweetheart?" he said in his usual positive tone, although a bit sluggishly.

"We have to go back. To see Mr. Green. We need to go tonight."

CHAPTER 10: THE HIDDEN FLOOR

Gabby called the number Mr. Green had left, but no one answered. On the fourth call, she left a message. "Hi, Mr. Green. It's Gabby. You know, the ranger from the Washington Monument. Listen, we really need to speak with you as soon as possible. I know we left in a hurry and not on the best of terms, but, well . . . " Gabby struggled to put into words what she was thinking. *Maybe I should just tell him the whole thing,* she thought. She wanted him to tell her what *he's* hiding. But shouldn't she do the same thing? Other than the fact that it's crazy and is very likely to earn her sent to a nice, padded cell somewhere. " . . . anyway, we need to talk," Gabby continued with the voicemail. "The sooner the better. We're on our way. It's close to one in the morning. I'll tell you my crazy story if you tell me yours." Gabby hated what she said as soon as the words had been spoken. *He's going to think I'm trying to flirt with him.* "See you soon. I hope."

Roughly twenty minutes later, they pulled into the garage and parked as close as they could to the hidden elevator. The doors opened for them. Merrison was standing inside smiling and looking as if this was a normal occurrence and it wasn't the middle of the night. "Please come in. Allow me to escort you upstairs and get you something to eat or drink. Your choice, given the hour. Mr. Green would like to thank you for your call and to let you know he is happy you have returned. He's expecting you."

Merrison led Gabby and Daniel through the greenery to a small, hidden enclave within the forest apartment. There were three chairs and a small side table. Merrison gestured for Gabby and Daniel to sit down while she slipped away to prepare refreshments. "Mr. Green will be along . . . well, you know," she said, laughing slightly at her own joke again as if it was the first time, then disappearing along one of the paths.

Daniel finally spoke up. "Gabby, what's this all about? What's going on? Why did we come back here?"

She had anticipated this conversation in the car. When that moment passed almost silently she was both thankful and fearful. Daniel took her late night request at face value and had done as she asked. Of course he was going to ask what's going on, and Gabby didn't have any good answers.

"Daniel, I'm so sorry. I understand only a very little of this, and it's getting stranger by the hour. I don't have the right to ask you this, but please trust me and stick with me. Please."

Daniel nodded and reached out for Gabby's hand. "Of course, sweetheart. It's you and me, whatever happens. You're my ride or die."

The last part was said with a grin, which made Gabby feel as if everything was going to be fine. Daniel often had that effect on her. She gripped his hand a little tighter and showed a slight smile. "Thanks, Daniel. Hey, you don't know any redheads, do you?" she asked, surprising herself with a direct question from her dream.

"He may not know her yet." Mr. Green emerged once again from the greenery, surprising Gabby and Daniel and moving toward the empty seat. "If I am interpreting what you said correctly. Lots of room for error in prophecy, especially lately."

Gabby was both relieved to see the man they came to see and annoyed that he had been listening in. "Mr. Green. How long were you spying on us? Not a great way to welcome back people you claim to want to talk to."

Mr. Green smiled. "No, probably not. But perhaps no more than a phone call in the middle of the night followed by an unexpected visit. But, here we are. So, let us talk. Why are you back so soon? What happened?"

Gabby thought about his response, decided he was probably right, and mentally let the spying thing go. "When we were here earlier, you said something about 'being the key' and 'abilities.' What did you mean by that?"

Mr. Green smiled. "So, something did happen. Something that made you rethink everything that has happened to you in the last few days. You are on your way, young lady, more than you know."

Gabby was growing irritated and mildly regretful of her decision to return. "Please stop speaking in circles and riddles and tell us what's going on," she said. "Are you causing all this? Is this some sick game rich people play? Manipulating regular folks into some twisted game? I've seen movies about this kind of stuff." Daniel once again was nodding in agreement and edged his chair closer to Gabby. It was firmly two against one.

Mr. Green smiled. Once again the temper of the righteous was on display. "Okay, okay. My apologies. I can be long-winded and forget myself, especially when I get caught up in a moment. The truth is, the three of us are connected. Not by family or coincidence, though." Mr. Green paused, contemplating his next words very carefully. He took a long breath, let it out slowly, and continued. "We are bound together by fate and by prophecy. You may not believe in such things, and I would not hold it against you if you do not. Nevertheless, it is what lies in front of us. There is no denying it, and there also is no escaping it. We must see it through."

Gabby was listening more intently this time, trying to keep her simmering frustration at bay and absorb what Mr. Green was saying. In their earlier conversations, she had discounted Green almost immediately as an unhinged rich guy who had lost touch with reality. After her train dream, though, she believed there was something to it. She wasn't convinced yet but she was getting there.

"There will be things that are hard to believe," Mr. Green said. "But I implore you, please stay with me and keep an open mind. That and steadfast dedication to a successful outcome will see us through. We have a fighting chance and no more. Of that I am sure."

Gabby spoke up. "And who exactly is 'we'? I'm the one with the weird dreams. Once again, you know more than you're saying. What's your stake in this? Why do you care so much? And more importantly, how do you even know half of this stuff? And no more of the 'thousands of years' claptrap. Tell it all right now or we walk again, and we're not coming back." She glanced at Daniel, who still was nodding in agreement.

"Telling it all," Mr. Green said, somewhat wistfully, "would take far, far too long. But the high points, I can do in about thirty minutes. Will you allow me that, so I may share why I 'care so much'? You may not like the answer."

CHAPTER 11:
THE SECRET ORIGIN OF MR. GREEN

Mr. Green walked around the couple slowly. He had shared this story many times, and the response almost always had been the same. He was not looking forward to another bad experience. "Who am I? The first thing I would like you to know is, I am on your side. Everything you have faced in the past twenty-four hours I have experienced before. I know how to fight them, and I believe I know how to defeat them. And that, my friends, is an absolute must. We may disagree at times, but we must all agree and commit to the fact that what we are facing is much, much worse than the small differences between us."

Gabby was not amused. "I'm not committing to anything until you start making sense. And that's one minute down. Twenty-nine to go, Mister Mystery. Get on with it."

For the second time in as many days, Mr. Green smiled despite himself. "Second, you need to know that I am the wealthiest man on the planet. No one else comes close. Not Bill Gates, not that Facebook kid, not any of the royal families slumming around Europe. I am worth, at last estimate, 51.2 trillion dollars. I say this not to try to impress you. I know that will not work. You two seem committed to each other and do not seem any more materialistic than anyone else. Perhaps even less than normal, which is a fine thing. It will make our time together easier. I say this because what lies before us will be difficult and costly. The difficult part will be your department. The costly part is on me."

Daniel perked up unexpectedly. "Great. Can we get premium cable?" Gabby and Mr. Green both gave him a similar, disapproving look. "Just asking," Daniel said, sliding down in his chair a bit.

Mr. Green thought, *Let's try this one more time. Maybe it will be better and help the situation. If they don't take off once they know everything.*

He took a deep breath. "Please. I am going to ask that you allow me to speak for a few minutes without interruption. It will make things easier, I assure you. When I am done, you will have many questions, and I will do my best to answer them. And most of all, keep an open mind. That is quite the overused phrase in this day and age, but if it fits . . . you will see." Another deep breath, followed by an uncomfortable minute of silence. Gabby and Daniel shifted in their chairs but didn't say a word. Mr. Green kept his head down, murmuring something to himself in a very low voice. He raised his head and took yet another deep breath.

"I am from long ago and very, very far away. I am the firstborn of all mankind and another first as well. Like so many who came after me, I am also a killer. Although I did it first . . . pioneering the concept, you might say. The first to be born and the first to kill. Small children to the aged know my name and some of my story, but they only know the beginning. They learn my story as a cautionary tale, and it very much is one. But it is also much, much more." Another pause. Mr. Green's hands were shaking slightly, his eyes welling up with tears.

"No one may lay their hands on me in anger and live. Throughout the ages that has been my curse and my very strange and unexpected blessing. Even death or disease will not come close, although I have wished for both many times. I have lived ten thousand lifetimes while those around me grow old and die.

"I cannot father children, but I have been a father to hundreds nonetheless. Perhaps thousands. I long ago lost count, but I dearly loved each and every one even though they did not spring forth from my well-worn loins." At this, Gabby rolled her eyes. Daniel stared at Mr. Green in disbelief. Mr. Green continued. "I loved them even as their names have faded in antiquity and, to my shame, my memory. I have watched those I knew as infants grow old and die while I never change, their faces on their deathbeds always the same. Silently asking, 'Why, *Avi?* Why am I leaving this world while you are the same as the day I was born? It is unnatural. It is not right. Please, share your secret with me.' This has been my fate more times than I can count. I have been a farmer, a businessman, a lover, a slave, and a killer. I have walked every inch of the Earth many times over, never once being welcomed . . . until I gained the material wealth I now have these last few years. I tried to live in peace and obscurity in the land of Nod, only to be driven from there after staying in one place too long and not aging. That was the first and last time I made that mistake. I am, you might say, the quintessential human. I have been called many things in the last eight thousand years, but you can call me the name my parents gave me.

"Cain."

A few breathless moments passed as the last words hung in the air. Daniel was the first to speak. "You've got to be kidding," he blurted out. "No one names their kid that. Who wants to be named after a murderer, especially that one?"

Mr. Green smiled thoughtfully before responding. This reaction was better than nearly all of the ones he had heard before. It gave him a slight jolt of happiness, although he tried not to show it. "When my parents chose my name, that had not happened yet."

A moment passed. Then another. The three looked at each other, and the voices of Gabby and Daniel failed them for a time. It was Daniel who finally spoke up again and, uncharacteristically, lost his temper for a moment. "What the hell does that even mean?" he asked. "How could it not have happened? Are you seriously trying to tell us you are *the* Cain? From Genesis? The one who killed his brother for having a better offering? The jealous guy?"

Mr. Green's expression changed as Daniel spoke. It had been a face of reflection, then stony silence, followed by something that appeared to be shame. Gabby was silent and wide-eyed.

Gabby spoke after several minutes. "Please go on," she said softly.

"Thank you, young lady," Mr. Green said. "That is the nicest response I have ever had to sharing that particular bit of knowledge. I am not overly fond of the name. If you would, can you please continue to call me Mr. Green, or my latest chosen first name, Gage. It is my favorite pseudonym. I will miss it when it has to be retired and I take on a new identity." The smile was slowly returning to his face and a bit of light to his eyes. "Now, let us talk about you two and how you figure into all of this. What you know from the book," Mr. Green said, "is mostly true."

Daniel interrupted suddenly. "By 'book' I presume you mean the Bible? Is that the book we're talking about? I just want to be clear in case someone else shows up. Is Paul going to come out of the bushes in a minute? Will Mary Magdalene pop out of the elevator? John the Baptist going to come strolling through your creek over there throwing holy water? Maybe your dad Adam will parachute in through a retractable roof in a loincloth?" Daniel had become so worked up over this new knowledge that he had stood up and was nearly shouting.

Gabby came up beside him, placed her hand on his shoulder, and quietly asked Daniel to sit down and keep an open mind. "Please, Daniel. I think he's telling the truth . . . or at least trying to. Let's hear what he has to say. Please."

With Gabby's urging and quiet confidence, Daniel slowly sat back in his chair, his cheeks still red with anger. "Okay, I'm sorry. Lost my cool. Won't happen again." He crossed his arms and leaned back in his chair.

The man who had just shared that he was the original Cain eyed Daniel warily. "As I was saying, most of the Bible is absolutely true. I believe there are a few embellishments in there—I was not around for all of it. I completely missed most of the New Testament because I was in what is now China and eastern Russia for about three hundred years. There are, however, some moments in there where someone must have gotten into some fine desert hallucinogens. But overall it is a pretty accurate history of the time period. The parts we need to focus on are, as fate would have it, the parts I am not as familiar with. The New Testament, particularly the Book of Revelations. Chock-full of signs and portents—a lot of them apparently completely untenable. Apparently. Old John was pretty far gone, from what I heard after the fact." Cain glanced down once again, taking a moment to compose himself.

"But he was onto something, and I am pretty sure he did have a direct line into the future. He may not have understood what he was seeing, but some of the things he wrote about have come true. It stands to reason that his other writings have a better than average chance of coming to pass. But there is a twist. The prophecies are not going to beat you over the head all of the time. Some will be subtle or not noticed at all. That is where Gabby comes in. It is John the Revelator's masterstroke and maybe the key to just about everything. It is so slight that most people do not notice it or they gloss right over it as poetry. But hidden in there is what I believe is the key to our side winning."

Gabby spoke up. "What do you mean, 'our side'? What side are we on, and what side are you on, for that matter? I didn't know I had a side."

Cain chuckled a bit. "The only side that matters. The side of life. The side of growth, of development, of kids growing up healthy and strong to become adults and start the cycle all over again. The side of the Earth continuing to spin for thousands—millions—of more years. We have it in us to win, to defeat the quote-unquote 'forces of darkness.' It is within our grasp, but we have to see it through completely and commit to accomplishing the job no matter the cost, or that is it. The world will burn and that will be the end. Evil will win, and it will overrun the planet. I do not want that, and I presume neither of you two do. Now, fate and other higher powers have placed us squarely in the middle of this. Let us do what we are intended to do and stop what is coming."

Two, perhaps three long breaths and Cain was ready to speak again. "What is coming can be stopped if we are prepared. And that, I believe, is where the lovely Ms. Sullivan comes in. She can see what is coming, and she probably will know what it means. We can work on that part. She is like an incredibly accurate radar—a spy, if you will—who can see the entire playing field and even see several moves ahead. 'No man will know' indeed." He began to smile, and the smile kept growing until it broke out into a full-fledged laugh. "Who would have thought the Almighty would hang the survival of the human race on a technicality? That is ballsy. It is . . . borderline insane. Maybe brilliant. It is all of those things. And unknowable, just as advertised."

Gabby was not buying it. "Are you saying what's happening to me is on purpose? Like it was done to me? Without even asking?"

"Yes, that seems to be true," Cain replied. "You were most likely chosen long ago for this duty. You get used to it. Being a pawn—maybe a queen in your case, *Gebirah*—in the eternal war between Heaven and Hell. It is no use trying to fight it. Believe me, I have tried. You always will find yourself right where you need to be. It is odd how it works. I have my own little theory on how this is possible."

Gabby became more interested. "Well, let's hear it. If we're going to follow some damn fool on a crusade, we should at least know why." She had done her best to paraphrase Han Solo from the first *Star Wars* film, partially because it would help put Daniel on a little firmer ground, and because she surprised herself by thinking of it in the first place. Daniel's repeated viewing of the original trilogy had left a mark on her.

Cain settled back in his chair. "Look, I do not believe any of this is preordained completely. I know that sounds odd, considering I just told you not to fight it. Please, hear me out. Then you can decide. Prophecy is, mostly, just propaganda from one side. But it is our side more or less, and the other side is not sure if they believe it or not. Not that that is going to stop them from trying. However, it is easy to foretell the future if you can actually see it, which is what I believe happened. Science today has given it the name 'quantum tunneling.' This is elaborate talk for, in essence, seeing and potentially traveling into the future. The engineering that goes into this today is incredibly complex. How a bunch of desert *schmendricks* two thousand years ago did it is way beyond me. The best I can come up with is divine intervention. Or ancient aliens. Pick whichever gives you the most comfort. But whatever and whoever went into making all this, including predicting—or knowing or orchestrating, whatever you choose to call it—that Gabby would be the key to putting the kibosh on the whole thing is, like I said, nothing short of . . . well, miraculous. Poor choice of words maybe, but it fits.

"I am the last person you should take religious tips from. But at times you have to wonder about the work that went into this and why. Why write down what is going to happen unless you know—really know—it is going to come to pass? I have found that most prophecy is propaganda in a nice suit. But the question remains: how did a few guys wandering around the desert know all this was going to happen? Probably the same way no one can hurt me and I cannot die. Which brings us back to divine intervention versus aliens.

"I was not very sophisticated during the few hundred years the actual writing was going on. I was still firmly in the schmendrick camp myself in those days. I alternated between trying to be a better man and staying drunk for decades. I did, however, know enough to question what had happened, but news did not travel fast or far then. I would usually hear about what was being written a few years after it was done. Even that was very fast. Most of the writings were preserved in casks and caves by the time I made it back from Asia. I knew from experience what we were told was not the complete truth, but I also did not know what it really was.

"Which brings us back to my latest theory. The side of the angels—that is our side, more or less—had access to something similar to what I said before: quantum tunneling. The one thing it is not, be sure to note, is time travel. That is most likely impossible. But to see—or plant the seeds for— what would come thousands of years after all of this was set in motion? That, as science is just learning today, is entirely possible. And these people did it two thousand years ago in the desert. Mind-blowing."

Gabby had begun to lean forward, her face cradled between two clenched fists against her chin. She was listening intently, and she was surprised to find she was following this strange amalgam of religion, science, and philosophy coming out of the mouth of a purportedly several-thousand-year-old man without too much trouble. Daniel had leaned back in his chair and was slouching and somewhat absentmindedly playing with Gabby's hair. It was something he did when the two of them were deep into conversation with each other at home. Gabby thought it was a good sign he was doing it as they listened to this improbable—but quite likely true— story.

Cain continued. "And how did we—humans—lose this wondrous ability and not have a trace of it left to rediscover? Nothing written down and placed in another clay pot somewhere? The ability to do this amazing thing, lost forever until it became the stuff of legend and a way of explaining the unexplainable. Humans have lost a lot of things over the years, but the absolute worst of it—and I would know—was what happened to Rome in 476. That's where we lost most of the knowledge gathered up until that point. Rome burned, and so did the knowledge left behind to help guide mankind through this mess. We were supposed to grow up and stand up to the neighborhood bully, in a manner of speaking. If you consider 'growing up' to be the steady march of progress and the 'bully' to be a gang of fallen angels who would like nothing more than to watch the Earth die a horrible death.

"Instead, to complicate things, we lost the instructions and spread out the remaining story to enough people in and around the Mediterranean throughout the years, culminating in the events of two thousand years ago, to point the way. It took a long time, but the essential story is there. Maybe those guys really did know what they were doing. But I would be surprised if they truly did. An open-minded person living in the twenty-first century would have enough trouble accepting all this. Go back a few thousand years, and . . . "

***

Gabby had been listening intently to Cain's story, but she felt her mind wandering. *Now is not the time,* she thought. *How do I get these crazy visions under control? Is that even possible?* Cain kept talking as Gabby lost focus on what he was saying. " . . . new strategy they were trying. Humans were too smart for their own good . . . messing it all up . . . engineered from two thousand years ago as a failsafe . . . other side."

Frost gathered on the windows, and the greenery in the apartment began to wilt quickly as if a stop-motion film had come to life. Gabby shivered and reached for Daniel's arm, but he wasn't there. She was suddenly alone in the massive jungle apartment.

She thought maybe she had dozed off, and Cain and Daniel had left her to rest. But that didn't sound like Daniel, Gabby thought. As she walked through the freezing greenery, the thought occurred to her that she was in the middle of a dream. The fluid movements she made when she walked, the sudden disappearance of the two men, and the sudden cold—maybe all this was part of another dream. What did Cain call them? Prophetic visions? Something about seeing into the future? She knew it was something more than a dream, but she could not pin it down any further. *Best to go with it and see what I can see. At least I know it's happening. Maybe*

I can learn something new . . .

Cain kept talking as Gabby's eyes became unfocused, and she slouched ever so slightly. Neither Daniel nor Cain noticed the change. "Anyway, humanity ended up losing or destroying what was left for them right when they could really use it, which is pretty much par for the course for humanity in general. You can thank the Caesars for screwing everything up—throwing everything into chaos and not knowing the path forward that was left for the entire species. Brilliant move, fellows. Our side was trying to reconstruct and preserve what the Holy Roman Empire—which, I would like to add, was none of those things—was busy turning to ash." Cain stopped and signaled to Merrison, who had been standing ready nearby to bring something to drink. She approached the table, set out three glasses, and filled them with water. And she did so as close to silent as humanly possible. "Regardless, that is my theory," Cain said. "No way to test it obviously, but it adds up. The bad guys certainly believe it, and maybe that is all that matters. That we stop them. The 'how' of it does not matter."

Gabby suddenly perked up. "For the sake of argument, I would think the 'how' of it would be extremely important," she said, shifting out of listening mode and moving into the conversation once more. "I mean, we could just kill them all. Couldn't we just find them, then drop you in the middle of them and watch them get zapped the moment they lay a hand on you? That would work, right? And be ethical? No foul if you're taking out someone who's trying to destroy the world?"

Cain nodded. "Unsure if it would work, but it is likely. It does not take much to activate. An unintentional jostle in the subway is one thing. Someone striking me in anger—yes, that would do it. I do believe intent on the part of the attacker factors into it. And the ethical part, sure. These are fallen angels we are talking about."

Gabby was testing what she just heard. She wanted to see how far the man before them would carry his story. She folded her arms and said, "There you go. That's how we do it. It's simple, direct, and gets the job done. I can find them, the fallen angels, demons, the bad guys, whoever. And Mister No-Touch here takes them out. Problem solved, right? Maybe that's what was intended all along."

Daniel had been watching and listening to both Gabby and Cain, thinking through the logistics. "What about 'Do not put the Lord your God to the test?' Aren't we just using this curse thing as a superpower? What if we get in the heat of the moment and it doesn't work? What if the intent factor works both ways? Has anyone thought about that?"

"It has never not worked before," Cain replied. "Every time someone lays their hands on me in anger, they die. It has been true since the day I struck my brother down until now. Hundreds of people have met their end thanks to me, whether they were standing before, crouching behind, jumping down to, or even emerging from below. The result is always the same: instant death. To my shame, I have taken out a romantic rival or two that very way.

"Not in a long time, though."

Daniel spoke up once again. "I do have one question about all this. Not about how we're going to kill the bad angels, though." Daniel stopped for a moment, then said, "There's a sentence I never thought I would say. Anyway, I do have this question. I could never figure this out. I got in trouble in Sunday School when I was thirteen for asking it. But you were, you know, 'there at the beginning.' I swear this will help me sleep better at night if you can answer just one simple question for me. I'm not saying I won't have more, but this one has been with me a long time."

Cain replied dryly, "I can hardly wait. Please. Ask your question. I will do my best, although my memory can be spotty about many things."

Daniel smiled and guffawed a few times before he was barely able to spit out the words in between laughs. "Did your parents . . . Adam and Eve . . . you know, since they were created and not born like everybody else. Did they have . . . were they created with . . . " Daniel had to stop for a moment to compose himself. He was doubled over and holding up one hand while his other arm struggled to hold his heaving stomach in place. After a moment, he blurted out the question quickly before his laughter completely overwhelmed his ability to speak.

"Did they have belly buttons?"

Daniel continued to laugh until it was uncontrollable. Gabby tried to remain stoic, but she soon was laughing despite herself. Cain smiled more than he had in a long, long time. His smile then blossomed into a full grin, and he enjoyed his first genuine laughing fit in decades. The three eventually settled down, still smiling and smirking at each other.

After everyone fell silent and were mostly finished wiping tears from their eyes, Cain spoke up. "Hell no, they did not."

The laughter didn't subside for a while.

CHAPTER 12: ONE VISION

Gabby had not wanted to let on to either of her companions that she had missed part of the most interesting story she had ever heard. She had picked up enough and was able to catch up and talk through using Cain's curse to their advantage. The jury was out on if that would work, if all of this was really true, and if she believed any of it. But she had missed some of what transpired before. She thought it had been no more than two or three minutes, but she was loathe to share that she had zoned out during Cain's story.

Her mind was full of thoughts about her waking dream/vision—her third in less than forty-eight hours. She listened to the rest of Cain's story in contemplative silence before interjecting her thoughts when the subject of how the three of them could save the world came up. She was pretty sure her suggestion about using Cain as a weapon wouldn't work, but she needed to buy some time to think and parse out what she saw. Then Daniel's awkward question had given everyone a much needed moment of levity. Laughter is always good for the soul and for seeing clearly. Now was the time to sort this out.

As everyone was laughing and bonding over Daniel and Cain's impromptu comedy routine, Gabby noticed the time. It was 3:43 in the morning. The events of the past few days, plus the visions, were taking a toll. During a lull she asked, "Can we get some rest soon? I'm starting to wear out. If you two want to stay up for male bonding, that's fine. I can drive home myself."

"Nonsense, Ms. Sullivan," Cain said. "I would ask that you and Daniel stay with us this evening. We have several spare bedrooms, and Merrison makes an excellent breakfast. Please. Allow me to provide you accommodations for the evening. It would be an honor for this old man. Plus, we can start our work early in the morning. I do not require much sleep."

Gabby smiled. "Well, we mere mortals do. Daniel, you okay with a sleepover?"

He nodded in agreement, likely already thinking of the refrigerator and the kind of food a place like this would have.

As Gabby rose from her seat, Merrison again appeared from the greenery. "This way, please."

Despite everything—the long day, the strange visions, and the revelation that the world's oldest man and its first murderer knew her name and she was staying in his jungle apartment—Gabby thought, *I will never get tired of hearing such a lovely accent.* She nodded to both men, who still were seated and apparently eager to keep talking. "See you two in the morning."

***

Upstairs in a massive, spartan bedroom, Gabby slipped off her shoes and flopped onto the king-size bed. *This is probably the nicest, most comfortable bed I've ever seen. Maybe this guy is telling the truth. Nothing else makes sense, and he seems to want to help. Maybe we should let him.* Then, still clothed, exhausted, and on top of the top-of-the-line down comforter, Gabby collapsed and within ten minutes had fallen into a deep sleep that did not bring unsettling visions.

***

The morning sun shone in between buildings and through the one-way glass that afforded a spectacular view of the Potomac River and, to the east, Washington, DC, proper. Gabby yawned, stretched, and smiled as she removed herself from the comforter. Daniel was asleep on his stomach as usual and borderline unresponsive as Gabby got up, put on the clothes from last evening (which really had ended just five hours before in the early morning), and pulled back her hair. She found a new, still packaged electric toothbrush in the immaculate bathroom, and she started an abbreviated version of her morning routine. *If the world is ending, at least I'll have clean teeth,* she thought. She was in a good mood despite the past day's events.

Gabby made her way down the spiral staircase into the main living area. The greenery made it difficult to know which way to go, so she chose what looked like the most well-worn path. She could hear the sounds of activity nearby, but the cavernous space made it difficult to find the exact source.

After a few mildly frustrating turns along walking paths, Gabby emerged near the kitchen area. Merrison was busy there cooking what looked like a very full breakfast of eggs, french toast, oranges, bacon, and coffee.

"Good morning, ma'am," Merrison said in a cheerful voice. "Breakfast will be ready in just a moment. May I pour you a cup of coffee? We have regular and decaf—your choice."

"Thank you. Lots of caffeine this morning, if you don't mind," Gabby said, still stretching and waking up. A morning copy of *The Washington Post* sat on the counter, and Gabby flipped through the first few pages.

"Excuse me, but do you know what time Daniel and . . . your boss"— Gabby wasn't sure what to call their new friend, especially to people who worked for him. She wondered if they knew his supposed secret—"went to bed? And when your boss might be up?"

"No, ma'am. They were still talking and laughing when I went to my room at four," Merrison replied. "But the boss does not seem to sleep much. I am envious."

"You mean you didn't go home? You stay here?" Gabby asked, suddenly perking up. That seemed a bit controlling.

"We all have apartments on the floor above," Merrison replied. "Each of us. There are five who manage the Washington residence. We all have accommodations here. We can stay or have homes elsewhere. It's our choice. The apartment comes with the job whether we use it or not. It's much bigger than the house I grew up in. I do stay here most of the time, whether I'm working or not. I'm saving to buy a little place out in Virginia. Just a few more years, and I'll be able to afford it."

Gabby smiled at this little bit of shared knowledge. "Oh, you're saving for a down payment? That's great," she said, trying to make conversation as her stomach rumbled.

"No, ma'am," Merrison replied. "To buy the house I want. Mr. Green says it's cheaper that way in the long run. It's in the $375,000 range. I'm almost there."

Gabby was stunned. How much did Cain pay his domestic staff? And did he have people like this at every house? It sounded unbelievable, but it wasn't the most unbelievable thing she had heard lately. Cain did say he was the richest man on the planet. Maybe he paid his employees well so they would stay quiet about his weirdness. And in case they discovered his secret.

"That's . . . great," Gabby said, a little envious of Merrison's financial situation. It sounded a good deal better than her own. "Listen, Merrison, how is Mr. Green as a boss? Nice guy? Demanding? I'm just trying to get to know him, and decide whether we should . . . work with him. I'll keep whatever you share between us. I promise."

"No, ma'am. We are asked to not share anything about Mr. Green," Merrison said, a bit of curtness creeping into her voice. "You will have to ask him directly. That's the one thing that will get us let go from our positions. You seem nice, and so does your boyfriend. But please don't ask me that again."

"I'm sorry. I don't want to cause you any trouble," Gabby said. "Please, forget I asked. I hope you can forgive me." Gabby smiled as she said this, and she meant it. She didn't want to cause any trouble, let alone for someone who seemed to love her job—even a strange job like this one.

"Yes, ma'am," Merrison said, a little cooler than before. "Breakfast is ready." Merrison set out the generous breakfast and a large carafe of coffee. She quickly cleaned up the kitchen area and departed, giving a fast backward glance at Gabby. Her expression seemed equally disapproving and deeply concerned.

Gabby ate in silence as she flipped through the newspaper. *What a strange couple of days,* she thought. Nearly all of her life has been turned upside down and she was going with it. The moon dripping blood. Not too bright demons at the Washington Monument. A strange-looking man showing up, pulling some crazy ninja moves and kibitzing with the Secretary of State. Finding out this guy is really Cain from the Book of Genesis, and he's trying to stop the world from ending?

Maybe that's a bridge too far, Gabby thought. *A little too much wish fulfillment.* They had just met this guy and he already had convinced them only they could save the world. Were they being foolish to believe Cain's story? Were there hidden cameras somewhere?

The more Gabby looked at the facts rationally, the more foolish she felt. The attack was bad, her dream afterward almost equally so, and now this. Why did she buy what Green was selling so easily?

Because it made me feel special, she thought. *Because he told me I am unique and the only one who could help.* It was becoming apparent to Gabby they were being duped. Even the dreams and visions could be chemically induced. "Cain" and his people could have been following them and spiking their food and drinks, and they wouldn't have known it. Gabby wondered why she was not thinking more clearly. What was the principle she remembered from her one philosophy class in college? Oscar's Razor or something like that? She would look it up later. First, she needed to get Daniel and get out of this place.

Gabby pushed away her half-eaten food. She found her way back to the staircase so she could rouse Daniel, and they could make a hasty retreat. Daniel was up and in the bathroom when she came in, the sounds of the shower almost completely muted by the well-insulated walls. Gabby sat on the edge of the bed. *What if these maniacs already had drugged him? I'm so stupid and gullible. Telling me I'm special, and only I can save the world.*

In the light of day, Gabby began to see that she probably was being played. Why, she wasn't sure, but she knew she wanted to get out of this place as quickly as possible. For all she knew, they were putting hallucinogens in the air. Gabby got up and talked into the bathroom door. "Daniel, please hurry up. We need to go now. This is my fault and I'm sorry for dragging you into this but we have got to go. And we have to go now."

No response. Maybe he couldn't hear her over the shower, she thought. Outside the main bedroom door, Gabby thought she heard an extremely loud bang. She walked to the bedroom door, only to be greeted by a sudden heat wave and the unmistakable whoosh and crackle of fire. She could see flames erupting on the apartment's main floor and accelerating at a rapid pace because of the abundance of greenery.

Almost immediately, emergency sprinklers overhead sprang to life and began pumping out copious amounts of water, more than Gabby had ever seen in training videos and the simulations they ran at the Washington Monument twice a year. It was barely keeping the growing flames at bay.

Gabby ran to the bathroom door, flung it open, and saw an empty shower with the water running. There was no Daniel in sight. Gabby murmured to herself, "This just gets better and better. This whole thing was a terrible idea."

She found a hand towel in the bathroom, got it wet, and walked back to the bedroom door. The fire was spreading rapidly downstairs and already had engulfed part of the stairs. Gabby placed the wet towel over her mouth and nose as she tried to break one of the bedroom windows. In the moment, she hadn't considered that they were several stories above ground. *Dammit,* she thought. *I've lost valuable time not thinking clearly. That man really is doing a number on us.* She took a moment, cleared her mind, and started looking for other ways off the floor.

Gabby stayed low and tied the towel around her head so she could breathe somewhat safely and use both of her hands. Ranger training never was this intense. *So let's see what we can do and not get roasted alive. And find Daniel and get far, far away from all of this.* The stairway was about eight feet from the door, so she went in the opposite direction. It would take her deeper into the apartment hallways, but, she reasoned, there had to be another stairway close by. The winding one was for show and everyday use. There had to be emergency stairs, even on a hidden floor.

Gabby continued to crouch-walk through the hallway. The hallway itself felt noticeably less hot. Maybe the sprinkler system was taking care of it. *Unless my optimism gets me fried,* she thought, smiling slightly under her wet towel at her gallows humor.

A right turn, then a long hallway—maybe 100 feet—with several doors on either side. At the end, though, was what she was looking for: a lit emergency exit sign. Even secret floors had design standards. Gabby made her way to the exit, opened the door, and, for the second time in as many days, began a descent down a staircase to avoid a catastrophe. Mr. Green had better not be the cause of all this, she thought, a bit darker than her usual sensible, practical self. Because if he was, ninja skills or not, she was going to kick his short ass.

CHAPTER 13: MEET THE NEW BOSS

Gabby considered going up and trying to reach the staff apartments Merrison had mentioned, but she thought better of it. Surely this place had an adequate alert system, and everyone else was evacuating. Cain might not be completely sane or telling the truth, but he didn't seem cruel either. Those were the ones you had to watch out for, she thought despairingly. The ones who were convinced they were right no matter what.

Why were there no other people coming down the stairs? Gabby thought maybe she was wrong and Cain, Mr. Green, or whoever he really was had a way to squelch the fire alarm in the building. He did seem a bit irresponsible. As she descended the stairs, she peeked through the emergency doors on the lower floors. Nothing was amiss. There were no signs of fire, no panicked people, and no fire department.

Gabby kept making her way down, passing the sixth-floor emergency exit door. She was halfway there. "If this is one of those stupid visions, I am going to be really, really mad," she said under her breath as she kept moving steadily downward. By the time she reached the bottom and was almost at the stairwell exit, she made a bet with herself that no one else would be there. Upon opening the first-floor door, she confirmed her theory. She was all alone. There were no other evacuees, no fire trucks, no emergency response teams.

What the devil was going on? Gabby immediately regretted the phrase even if it was unspoken, given the story she had heard. She still saw no sign of Daniel, Green, Merrison, or other staff from the apartment. It was just her in the early morning light, underneath the ubiquitous ground-level parking area.

This is getting weirder and weirder, Gabby thought, still not entirely convinced this wasn't an elaborate set-up for a television show. If it was, she was definitely going to hurt someone. The most likely candidate for that was the man she knew as Mr. Green, or Cain. He had been at the heart of all the strangeness in her life these past two days. And he was as smug as anyone she had ever met. Gabby walked around toward the front of the building and saw a lone person standing about a half a block away. He was staring intently in her direction, wearing a black trench coat and sunglasses in the morning. *Must be a government spy or wanting someone to think that's what he is.* Maybe he was waiting for a ride, but when she kept walking, she saw he had moved closer to the doorway as well. Gabby thought he was probably another of Green's flunkies watching her every move. *I'm going to drop kick that man when I see him.*

This new stranger came up to the doors just as Gabby arrived at the same location. "Excuse me, just coming back from a morning run to get my boyfriend," Gabby said, trying to let the man know someone was close by and expecting her.

He smiled. "We both know that's not true, Gabrielle." The man's voice was deep and scratchy, as if he gargled with rusty nails and enjoyed the experience. He also exuded confidence and had an air of authority. Gabby thought he was either a mafia hitman or the most straight-edge FBI agent she had ever seen.

"The man you have met is severely mentally unbalanced. He would have introduced himself as Gage Green, a billionaire, or as Cain. You know, like in the Bible. He claims to be thousands of years old. He may be manipulating you and your friend into thinking there's something special about you. We've seen him do this dozens of times to unsuspecting couples. He's using you and your friend in an elaborate scheme for reasons we don't understand quite yet, but we'd like to. We've had run-ins with him before. He's a very disturbed man who, unfortunately, has a large bank account that buys him more than it should. We think it's affected him mentally."

I knew it, Gabby thought. That's why all this crazy stuff had been happening. She usually had a good ability to see through deception. There were almost always clues to watch for. And she fell for it anyway, then left poor Daniel somewhere up there too. She had dragged him along and now he was missing.

"If you will come with me to make a statement at our office, we can take it from there and get this guy before he harms anyone else," the gravel-voiced man said. "He's done this before, but this is the first time we've gotten to him before he causes, you know, permanent harm. It's fortunate we were able to smoke him out. Please, right this way." The man gestured toward a large black SUV waiting across on the other side of the building's access road.

At "smoke him out," Gabby froze. She hadn't mentioned the fire, and there was no evidence of it from the ground. Was that a coincidence or did this man know more than he was letting on? What made this new stranger any different than Mr. Green?

"Who did you say you were with? And I didn't catch your name, *officer,*" Gabby said as she slowly moved back a few steps and out of arm's reach.

The man remained calm and replied, "My apologies, ma'am. Sometimes these cases become personal, especially when there are civilians involved. I'm Agent Rasch. Like 'race' but with an 'sh' at the end." He smiled at her, but there was no friendliness in the gesture.

Gabby still was skeptical and growing more so by the moment. The agent had been moving toward the SUV, expecting Gabby to follow. Gabby remained several steps behind him and asked, "And your branch of government? There's so many in DC. Are you local, state, or federal?"

Agent Rasch stopped suddenly, turned around, and said in a much lower and menacing voice, anger flaring in his eyes, "Get in the car now, girl, before I make you."

Gabby was stunned for a moment. The dreams, the impossible story of Mr. Green, the fire upstairs, and now this. How did she get into this situation? She wished she would have searched longer for Daniel upstairs despite the flames. She wanted to know he was safe. But her immediate situation took precedence, and her ranger training kicked in.

"No, sir, I will not," she replied as forcefully as she could muster. She squared her shoulders to the agent and lowered her stance just enough to be ready to move in almost any direction. The agent was four or five steps away, standing in the middle of the access road between their building and the one next door. Gabby smiled to herself as she was still on the curb. *I have the high ground,* she thought. Maybe Daniel and his endless queue of sci-fi and adventure movies were helpful after all. "Step back or I will have to subdue you."

Rasch turned completely around and very purposefully took one step toward Gabby, his right leg in front. "Oh, that's good. The hard way is so much better. Thank you, Gabrielle," Rasch said as he took another cautious step forward. His eyes had started to glow a deep red behind his sunglasses, and his fingers, already long and bony, curled into fists.

Gabby lowered herself a bit further to be prepared, hoping a swift kick to the gut would be effective. Rasch took another step toward her in what appeared to be the start of a full-on charge. On his next step, though, he completely disappeared with a sudden thump and a gust of air. Gabby thought it was a trick of the light and remained ready, her breathing calm and adrenaline fully pumping. Still no Rasch.

Approximately seventy feet down the road, a small, all-black vehicle whipped around and came to a stop. Rasch—or most of him—was plastered to the bottom part of the front grill. He was missing a chunk of his right arm, and his legs looked torn to shreds. He hissed, then yelled something unintelligible. The waiting black SUV took off quickly and drove toward him, coming to a halt about twenty feet away. No one got out.

A barely visible front hatch on the mystery vehicle visibly popped, then slid open silently. Daniel and Cain were in the front seat. Cain appeared to be driving, while Daniel stood up holding a long metal stick with electricity crackling on its end.

"Gabby! Thank God we found you," Daniel said. "Who was that guy? We have a tank and the apartment was on fire but not anymore. And I think our friend here is telling the truth." Daniel jabbed Rasch with the rod, but from a distance. He leaned in slightly toward the injured man to make contact, but kept as healthy a distance as the weapon afforded him.

"How do you like that, Razhael, old buddy, old pal?" Cain shouted, smiling at the sight of the man currently plastered across his front hood. He then hopped out of the driver's seat and down to the ground near the now-writhing agent. "Things have changed a bit since the last time you were allowed topside. What do you think of my horseless carriage, traitor?"

"Cain . . . I had planned to . . . give you a quick death," came the reply. The person who a moment ago looked like a government agent was growing ever so slightly taller and wider, his clothes popping at the seams. It was as if his entire body were unfolding into something substantially larger.

"Painful, but quick. But no longer. You will twist and burn . . . in the pits with the rest of these pitiful excuses for sentient be . . . ahhhh!"

The speech was stopped short by Daniel, who turned a small dial on his weapon as far as it would go. The man Cain called Razhael, who had survived a full-speed vehicular accident and improbably was growing just a moment ago, began shaking violently, as if he had stuck a wet fork in an electrical socket. Daniel seemed pleased with himself.

Rasch was drooling, except the liquid running down his chin was black. Cain was standing in his seat and actively taunting the man as he writhed. Daniel was grinning more that he ought to be, Gabby thought.

"How does it feel, angel?" Cain asked to the man's contorted face. "You have killed thousands with that same damned smile on your face. You have fallen very, very far, Razhael. This, after all these years, is a little payback, my feathered friend. You can thank Saint Thomas Edison for the gift."

Rasch's eyes were rolling back in his head, and his legs were shaking violently. Daniel kept the staff stuck firmly in his side with both hands holding on, his eyes watching the being before him struggle to move away. He drove the staff in further, although his hands were getting sweaty. Daniel could feel the man—or whatever he was—fighting to regain control and get away. Daniel drove the staff even harder into his rib cage.

Rasch howled in pain, twisting as 2,000 volts of electricity surged through him. It was more than enough to kill a man. Rasch, however, moved his one good arm and the other broken, bloody one suddenly, grabbing the staff and surprising Daniel with his quickness. Rasch pulled the staff further into his midsection, still growling and twitching but with an iron grip on the staff. His eyes began to glow red.

"Daniel, I think it is time to go. Make a strategic retreat," Cain said. "That souped-up cattle prod is only going to keep him busy for a minute. Hold on tight to it, and push the yellow button on the side, then sit back down as quickly as you can."

"What's the button do?" Daniel asked, shouting over the crackling electricity as he struggled to keep his grip on the rod and to hear over Rasch's ever-louder groans.

"It will send him away from the car so we can get away. Push it! Now!" Cain yelled, more than a little anxious.

Daniel gripped the staff as firmly as he could and pushed the button. The rod made a pneumatic hiss, then ejected its lower third—the one shocking the man who was struggling to get off their hood—violently, much like a harpoon spear. It drove even further into Rasch's side. Dark, foamy liquid began to ooze out. Rasch rolled to the ground with the rod stuck in him, still writhing in pain but less than before.

Then he got up.

Daniel, knocked back by the recoil, was partially inside the vehicle. "Get in, you idiot!" Cain yelled, tugging at Daniel, who was lying across part of the cockpit, frozen in horror and fascination at what he had done.

Rasch was up, the electrified rod still sticking out of his abdomen. He lunged at Daniel's feet. Cain threw the vehicle into reverse, grabbed onto Daniel's shirt, and floored it. (Daniel would learn later that the vehicle was rated for zero to sixty in 2.6 seconds.) Rasch slid down the side of the vehicle back onto the ground in a heap as Cain wheeled around and took off back toward Gabby. She had been watching the fight with fascination and more than a little fear. Cain stopped quickly, slid the canopy back fully, and said with his best Austrian accent, "Come vith us if you vant to live." He laughed out loud as Gabby shook her head and climbed in the tiny back seat.

Cain glanced in his state-of-the-art rearview camera monitor while the unlikely trio drove through suburban Arlington in a prototype tank that, when questioned about it on the evening news the following the day, the Department of Defense would deny even existed. After a few minutes, Cain spoke. "I know that guy from a long time ago. You do not want to mess with him.

"At least not yet."

CHAPTER 14: SAME AS THE OLD BOSS

"It is an electric jet tank. Pretty cool, as the kids say, right?" Cain asked as they sped down the road. "It is something one of my companies came up with. Quick acceleration and quick braking. Very maneuverable and also gives the occupants a lot of protection. Designed for urban warfare." Cain smiled. "Completely electric and completely silent. 'Silent but deadly,'" he said, still grinning. "I insisted on naming it the 'Fast Action Reconnaissance Truck' for that very reason. Although today, it has earned a new name. It is the . . . Fallen Angel Run Through!" Cain was almost doubled over with laughter at his own joke, nearly sideswiping a car in the adjacent lane.

Gabby and Daniel were slightly terrified, mostly from what they just experienced, but also from Cain's questionable driving.

"Even ancient men enjoy a good joke about breaking wind," Cain said, still chuckling and paying a bit more attention to the road. "I believe it is coded into the male DNA. It has been a consistent thing for as long as I can remember."

"And how long is that, really?" Gabby asked. The events of the past twenty minutes, along with everything from the day before, were beginning to convince her that, despite all rational thought to the contrary, this man was telling the truth.

"Defense contracting has been good to me," Cain said, ignoring Gabby's question. "It is an ugly business, but it is profitable. Some things never change. Rome was much the same way. Back then, the biggest innovations were elephants and the catapult. Innovations in this modern era, they can be very welcome indeed. The endless march of progress is truly astounding. Let us get somewhere safe."

***

Cain pulled into the Four Seasons Hotel in DC proper. The parking attendants didn't know what to do with the most exotic vehicle they had ever seen. "Do not put a scratch on it, boys," Cain said, tossing the keys to the man standing closest to him as he climbed out of the prototype tank. "I will know." He smiled, raised an eyebrow, winked at the two astonished attendants, and walked inside as if it was the most natural thing in the world. Gabby and Daniel followed close behind, both with grins on their faces despite themselves.

In the lobby, Cain walked past the service desk, smiling and nodding to the staff. Gabby and Daniel had to walk faster than normal to keep up. Cain took a turn down a long access hallway and exited the building near the opposite side they came in on. A nondescript Ford sedan with blacked-out windows was parked right outside. Cain motioned for the couple to get in, and he clambered into the driver's seat.

"Better to be safe than sorry. Someone will be along shortly to pick up the FART," Cain said, trying to suppress a smirk. "If anyone followed us, they will think we are holed up in the hotel. We will be many miles away before they discover the truth. And this car," Cain patted the dashboard, "is just as safe as our previous transportation. Plus, it looks like a police car. Our opponents will stay far away from anything that appears to belong to the authorities. I cannot imagine they want further trouble in the public eye. But I am an old man. What do I know? Maybe they have changed or, even worse, evolved."

The trio rode in silence as Cain made his way out of the city heading west. Once out of the city and on a relatively straight interstate, Gabby spoke up. "Okay, a couple of questions. First, where are we going? And second and more importantly, what happened back there? Who was that man? How do you know each other?"

Cain smiled. "We are going somewhere safe. As for that 'man,' that's a story you mostly know. I can fill in most of the missing parts. But first, and just to be sure, everyone is uninjured? Do we need to seek medical attention? If so, please say so. Do not let any injury or malady linger. We will need all of our strength and wits for the foreseeable future. We can seek treatment safely."

"I think we're fine for the most part," Daniel said. "At least physically. Mentally and emotionally, I'm not so sure. It's been a crazy few days."

Gabby nodded in agreement. "What about the people in the building? Your people working there? The other tenants? Are they okay?"

"Yes, they are," Cain replied. "I have received news that Merrison has a slight burn on her arm from helping get everyone out, but otherwise all of the staff are unharmed. The sprinklers eventually took care of the flames, along with some brave actions by the staff. The rest of the building, thankfully, was unaffected. We have shared with the other tenants that the fire was the result of a faulty heater on the maintenance level.

"When the fire broke out, I knew it had to be the work of our opponents. I am not sure how they gained access to the apartment, but that is an issue for another day. Everyone will be off work—with pay, of course—while repairs are made. Also, I appreciate your concern. Thinking of others first is a hallmark of a brave and caring soul."

Gabby and Daniel were quiet—mostly from exhaustion and mild shock, but also because compliments always made them self-conscious. Gabby was thankful for the quiet. She needed time to think and process the conflicting thoughts running through her head. The car was silent for a minute or two, until she spoke again.

"That's twice now these . . . people . . . have attacked a building with me in it. What is this? The Middle Ages? Do they think they are storming a castle? People almost died because of them. Because of me. Because I was there. I'm not saying I believe you all the way. But until there's a better explanation, we'll go with it. Plus, you helped get us out—well, you helped Daniel out. I had to do it myself. We can talk about that later. For now, how do we get these . . . whatever they are . . . to stop? How do they keep finding us?"

"That," Cain replied, "is the looming question to which I, sadly, have no answer. Those nearly brainless automatons were attracted to the monument somehow. I liken it to a bloodhound that can sniff out its target. But how they know there even is a target, I do not know."

"What about that quantum stuff you were talking about last night," Daniel said. "Can they do that too? Wouldn't that explain it?"

Cain was a little surprised that Daniel, who had been admirably stoic and faithful but did not seem to be a great thinker, brought this up. *Modern humans are always more than they seem,* he thought. "That is a possibility, and a very good thought," Cain said. "I will task some of my trusted assistants to look into it."

"How many people are on your payroll?" Gabby asked. "And how many know who you really are? If you have as many people as you seem to, it's likely that Rasch and his people got to one of them. Maybe threatened them, or made them 'an offer they can't refuse.'" Gabby did this last part in a raspy, pseudo-Italian accent.

It was Daniel who spoke next. "I doubt that. Everyone I saw stayed through the fire, trying to put it out and helping each other. They didn't strike me as disloyal, even for a price. You can't buy that kind of dedication."

Gabby looked mildly stunned at Daniel. Cain, however, was impressed. Perhaps he had judged Daniel too harshly. He made a mental note to pay more attention to the man and to begin a more thorough background check of him when he contacted his staff.

"Thank you, Daniel. The staff at my residences are extremely well-vetted. They are as loyal and discreet as they come. And they are paid well for it. I concur with you. I doubt it was an inside job."

Gabby spoke up. "Can those guys—the fallen angels, demons, whatever—can they possess people? Like in the movies?"

Gabby thought that would answer all the questions about how the fire started despite a small staff of very loyal people in a hidden location. Maybe the Devil made them do it. Gabby smiled at the thought, then grew mildly terrified that that now was a distinct possibility in her life.

"Good thinking, Gabrielle," Cain said. "A first-rate mind, through and through." He glanced quickly in the rearview mirror to see Daniel beaming and leaning forward. *He truly loves her and wants the best for her,* Cain thought. There was not an ounce of envy or self-centeredness in the man. Cain shook his head slightly at the thought, and perhaps, he considered further, he himself was envious of Daniel's worldview and attitude. Wonders never cease, Cain thought before refocusing on the tasks at hand.

"But no, that does not happen," Cain replied. "People have been using that excuse for thousands of years. Can they tempt you? Absolutely. But nothing I ever have seen makes me think that a sentient being can force another to do something against their will. Coercion, bribery, blackmail, threats? Yes, that happens quite a bit, and these people are extremely good at all of it. But mind control or some sort of hypnosis or subliminal suggestion? No."

"Okay, good to know," Gabby said. "Daniel, if we have kids and they try that excuse, we now know from a reliable source that it's no good." She looked over at Daniel and smiled. He raised his eyebrows a few times back at her and winked.

Cain rolled his eyes even while driving. "We are headed a few hours west, to the highlands of Maryland. I have a place there where we can plan and be safe."

"That sounds great . . . Cain," Gabby said.

"Oh, you believe me now?" Cain asked with a slight chuckle. "It took meeting a fallen angel who would have killed you two without a second thought to convince you?"

"Something like that," Gabby said. "I'm sure this isn't the first time you've shared your story and not had anyone believe it. I mean, you're how old? You must have confided in people over the years."

"I have," Cain said, "and I have almost always regretted it. Very few people believe it. And the ones who do tend to take off pretty fast afterward. I have been working on a spreadsheet of the times and people I have told. It is a work in progress. As I remember them, I write it down. Working on a computer is so much easier than cuneiform. It makes remembering the dates a bit easier as well."

"Wait a second," Daniel said. "In the day or so that we've known you, I've heard you say you're eight thousand years old, then four or five thousand. I know you're getting up there, but which is it? It kind of makes believing you harder when stuff changes."

Cain's face turned serious and perhaps a bit sad. "Very astute, Daniel," he said. "The truth is, I do not know. The marking of time was not invented when I was born. I grew up, had a row with my brother, and was kicked out of the house. We did not have clocks or even sundials then. It is all a huge guess. In the past few hundred years, whenever scientists discover a new fossil and announce a date the specimen probably lived, their best guess is within a hundred thousand years. I am sure science will improve and develop more accurate dating methods. I long for that day and to relearn some of what I have forgotten."

Daniel had not expected to pity Cain or feel sympathy for him. Since childhood, Daniel—like every other person who walked through a church or synagogue—was raised to believe the biblical Cain was a villain. His story was a cautionary tale about greed, envy, and anger. On the page or in Sunday School was one thing. To have the living, breathing man in front of you, driving a Ford, and telling you he wishes he could remember things— that was very, very different.

Unlike Gabby, Daniel had believed Cain's story almost from the beginning. He could accept all that he had heard. But nothing could prepare him for connecting with and having his heart ache for the pain of the world's oldest man and first murderer. What a difficult and extraordinary life he must have led.

"I'm sorry to hear that," Daniel replied. "That had to be tough over the years. We believe you, and we're going to help." Daniel squeezed Gabby's hand tightly as he said this. She squeezed back. Daniel smiled at Gabby, and she at him. Cain, watching through the rearview mirror, gave a small smile and wiped away a tear. He hadn't cried since before the Civil War, but this moment seemed like a fine one to revisit the feeling. After that, the unlikely trio rode in silence until they were deep in the mountains of western Maryland.

CHAPTER 15: AIN'T NO MOUNTAIN HIGH ENOUGH

Cain drove all day and into the early evening, taking care to stay off the interstate and well-traveled roads. It made the trip significantly longer, but it also was safer. They arrived at their destination in western Maryland around 7:30 p.m. Gabby and Daniel had dozed in the back seat for the rest of the trip.

"Welcome to Backbone Mountain," Cain announced. "The president has Camp David, and I have this—both in the great state of Maryland. Take a guess which one is nicer and better fortified against an attack. Please, take a guess."

Gabby smiled, wiping the sleep from eyes. "I'm going to guess it's no contest . . . Camp David," she said. Cain rolled his eyes, and Daniel laughed.

"You are trying to wind me up, correct?" Cain said as he stepped out of the car. Immediately, three attendants emerged from a large wooden and stone structure that was built into the side of the mountain.

"This retreat is in a perfect defensive location. Very inaccessible rock all the way around, with fortified windows and sentry posts scattered over the property. This place could withstand a nuclear attack. But let us try to avoid testing it out."

"Why do you have such a fortified place in the Maryland mountains?" Daniel asked.

"Someone has to build the bombs," Cain said. "Well, if you are a defense contractor—and I am, among other things—you know what they can do. You also learn what to do to prevent yourself from being hurt by one, just in case."

"In case of what? Global thermonuclear war? Between countries? Or between . . . you know, the 'good guys' and the 'bad guys?'" Gabby asked, only slightly distressed at the implications.

"Yes to both questions, Gabrielle," Cain said. "I have many similar facilities throughout the world. Should we need them, they are ready. They can provide food and shelter for many months without any contact from the outside world."

"Oh no," Gabby said, laughing slightly. "You're a doomsday prepper. Now I'm really scared." She and Daniel had enjoyed a television series about people who were constantly preparing for war and the desolation of the civilized world.

Cain was not amused. "I have seen that program," he said. "That you equate me and my state-of-the-art facilities placed strategically around the globe—all designed to help as many people as possible should the need arise—with people who do not even practice good dental hygiene regularly yet find it necessary to prepare for a war they would not be fit to engage in even in the most minor capacity, is ridiculous and more than a little insulting." A hint of indignation had crept into Cain's voice at the end.

Gabby had considered laughing this off as well, but she saw a gleam of seriousness in Cain's eye that she had not seen before. "Look, Cain. I'm sorry," she said, trying to smooth things over. "I didn't mean to offend you and the work you're doing. Being able to help people is a great gift. I'm sorry I made light of your intentions."

"Thank you, Gabrielle," Cain replied. "Perhaps my reaction was a little stronger than I intended. It does mean a great to me to be able to help my fellow man when I can. It is the least I have been able to do for the past two hundred years."

"Just two hundred?" Daniel said. "What did you do the rest of the time? That's a lot of time to wander the Earth. You know, like in *Kung Fu*. Hey, that guy was named Caine too! Was it based on you and part of your life? Maybe just a little?" Daniel now seemed more intrigued at the possibility of Cain being the model for David Carradine's portrayal of a wayward Chinese martial arts master than he was about the end of the Earth, fallen angels, and how they might prevent all that from happening.

Cain sighed and said, "No, Daniel. That is just a coincidence. It is not a name that gets used a lot, as I am sure you know. I believe the writers of that show used the name so audiences would not identify with the character—at least at first. They had to grow to like him despite the name. That is part of what made his character arc so compelling."

Daniel brightened up the more Cain spoke. "The original Cain watched *Kung Fu* Caine? That's probably the greatest thing I've ever heard." He continued to smile and laugh to himself.

"Yes, yes, very perceptive, Mr. Masterson," Cain said disapprovingly. "Let us get inside before you have the apocalypse solved all by yourself after bingeing on *Star Trek*."

"Hey, that might work. Don't discount the wisdom of Kirk and Spock," Daniel said.

Gabby shook her head at both of them and headed toward the front door of the fortress. "Are you two coming, or are you going to geek out in the front drive until it's dark?"

Cain and Daniel looked at each other; both started to smile and said simultaneously, "We're coming."

***

"Does this place have a library?" Gabby asked once everyone was settled inside. "I'd like to check some stuff out, see if it makes any sense."

"Have you had another vision?" Cain asked.

"Nothing lately," Gabby said. She did not like being deceptive, but she wanted to understand what she saw the other night before she could share it. The other visions had been relatively straightforward—the world was ending, the meteor was a harbinger of doom, the moon turned red. It was all fairly standard apocalypse scenarios. The last one, though, with Daniel trudging around with someone else, the snow and ice, feeling completely lost without any refuge in sight . . . that one she could not reason her way through or shake the feeling she was missing an important piece. Gabby wanted to go to the source and see what she could turn up that might mean something to her that everyone else had missed for centuries. *If I'm going to have this crazy gift whether I want it or not, I might as well lean into it,* she thought.

"I'd like to read up, especially the later books that start mentioning the kind of things we're seeing," Gabby replied. "You know, 'Forewarned is forearmed.' I'll have a better chance of understanding these things if I familiarize myself with them."

Cain was impressed. "A fine idea, Gabrielle. One of our little team here can show you the way. There's a full library—we have anticipated being here quite a while one day—along with a very reliable Internet connection that cost far more than it should have." This was the first time Gabby or Daniel had heard Cain complain about the cost of something. If he was as rich as he said he was, why would something like that bother him?

"I hate our cable bill, too," Daniel said. Cain smiled, nodded politely and went upstairs.

A man dressed for a day in the woods came around a corner after a few minutes. He was dressed head to toe in dark, muted colors with a pair of high-end Salomon boots. "Good afternoon, my name is Eric," he said, nodding courteously. "Sir, a moment of your time first, please?"

"Of course, Eric," Cain said. "What do you need?"

"There is a small issue with the pantry. Heaven knows how, but some rodents got into the stores. Everyone is working double-time to clean up the mess. You may want to consider alternative methods for meals during your visit."

"Sounds good, Eric. Anything else?" Cain said.

"Heavy traffic in the mountains lately. Although no one has been on the grounds that shouldn't be. Very close calls at times, though. Enough that we have tightened security on the north end of the property."

"I'm sorry to hear that. Please, do what you need to do to keep things locked down and safe for the retreat and the staff," Cain replied.

For such mundane tasks, he seems to be paying quite a bit of attention, Gabby thought. *Maybe he really is a good boss.*

"Much appreciated, sir," Eric replied. "You can count on the staff of the Mountain to do the right thing. First, though, there are some papers that require your signature. After dinner, would you please review them and leave them for the attorneys? Mostly, they are formalities. It's just follow-ups on property rights for some of the neighbors. Lessening their worry about our property will put them at ease. You may have questions, though."

Cain looked at Eric, stone-faced for a few moments before nodding. "All right, Eric. I will . . . take a look at all of this. Thank you for your help. I appreciate everything you do, now more than ever. If you would, please show our guests to the library. Afterward, please do what you need to do."

Eric gave a barely perceptible smile. "Yes, sir." Then he turned to Gabby and Daniel. "Right this way, please."

Daniel was intrigued with the house and the people running it. He asked Eric a question as they wound their way through the steel beam and wood house, which also doubled as a bunker apparently. "So, what's your role here at Doomsday Central?"

Eric did not smile or laugh as Daniel had hoped. Surprisingly, he stopped and turned around. He was serious but also a bit friendlier than Daniel expected after hearing the reserved exchange with Cain. "I'm the caretaker of the Backbone Mountain residence. We have a staff to keep the electronics up-to-date and functioning, and trusted people for maintenance and cleaning. Mr. Green has been visiting here more lately than in the past, so we have been quite busy. Later on, I will be making a circuit around the property to ensure our paths remain clear and the fences are in good order. If you would like to join me, I would be glad for the company.

"But first, please, let me show you to the library." With that, Eric turned around and continued down the hallway.

"Daniel, why don't you go enjoy some fresh air, and I'll spend some quality time in the library," Gabby said. "We can get back together at dinner and compare notes. And maybe, you know, try to have a relaxing moment? It can't always be doom and gloom, right?"

"Sounds good, Gabby," Daniel said. "See you in a while, bookworm."

Gabby smiled. She and Daniel usually had funny, topical nicknames for each other depending on what was going on. It was nice to hear him return to the practice after the past few days.

"See you later, mountain man," she said, smiling at the duo.

Eric stood there for a moment with a confused expression. "She means you, right?" he said to Daniel.

"Yes. Yes, she does," Daniel said proudly. "That's my girl. Some things never change. Let's go."

***

Gabby was impressed with the library's collection. The bookcases were at least ten feet high and lined a room that was bigger than the house she and Daniel shared. She couldn't hazard a guess as to how many were there, but it was as many books in one place as Gabby had seen since college. She found the biblical section and pulled off the shelf a copy of the Bible. She thought it might be helpful to look at the writings of Nostradamus too. After a few minutes, she discovered the library had a whole section on prophecy. There were close to a hundred books in the section, by her estimation, and many of them were old and tattered. She chose a relatively new one—it had a color cover, modern graphics, and an intact dust jacket—titled New Thoughts On Old Revelations.

I've had enough of old things for a moment, Gabby thought. *Let's see what the younger generation has to say about all of this.*

***

Eric climbed into the driver's seat of a white, weathered Toyota 4Runner and motioned for Daniel to take the passenger's seat. When they were both buckled, Eric said, "We'll be headed about two miles north to the edge of the property. We've had some wolf sightings. We think they've managed to get through the electric fence on the other side of the mountain. Some small rodents are turning up half-eaten. We're not sure why the wolves would eat and then leave a fresh kill without finishing it. It's unlike them. When you see one, there's usually a pack nearby. Don't worry about them, though. We have this for safety." Eric patted a bolt-action Remington rifle in a secure locking stand between the seats.

"I hope that's not necessary," Daniel said. "Aren't they just trying to survive? If they aren't bothering anyone or eating a garden or something like that, why not just leave them be?"

Eric looked straight ahead, then to the left as they took a turn up the gravel road. "If you leave them alone, they'll think this is safe territory and bring in more. One will eat a few rodents, maybe get into your garden every once in a while. A pack is a different story. If there's enough of them, and they are hungry enough, they'll go after a full-grown cow. Horses too.

I've heard they used to keep horses here about thirty-five years ago, when Mr. Green's father owned everything."

Daniel had to repress a smirk at how easily the façade Cain used worked. But who would think someone would pose as their own child because they didn't age? Most people wouldn't bat an eye. And if Cain moved around as much as he said, it would be a relatively easy deception to pull off.

Eric continued. "A single wolf might try to take down a bigger animal, especially if it's hungry enough. But in a pack, it's very different. They hunt together. They coordinate their attack. Their prey doesn't suspect anything until it's too late. They are aggressive and they work well together. It's something to see. Unless you're the prey, of course." Eric shared this knowledge with a very serious look, not glancing over at Daniel or making an effort to lighten the mood in the truck cab. Eric seemed to take his job as caretaker of the mountain retreat very seriously.

He must really dislike wolves, Daniel thought.

After another twenty minutes of driving, they finally crested a large ridge before descending into a small, very green and very dense valley. Eric stopped the 4Runner near the bottom of the north side of the ridge. "This is it," he announced.

Both men got out of the vehicle, Eric with the shotgun in hand. "It's just a little beyond that tree line," he said. "You can stay with the truck or walk behind me. Your choice. What would you like to do?"

"I'll walk behind," Daniel said. "I've been a city boy for a while now, but I grew up in the Dakotas. These aren't mountains—they're hills," he said with a slight grin. It was something his great-aunt, who lived most of her life in Washington state, would say when she visited family on the East Coast. Eric nodded, then turned around, leaving Daniel's attempt at small talk to languish and fade into uncomfortable silence. They trudged along the roadway until they came to the fence. It and the locked gate were intact, and there were no obvious signs of wolves. "Let's walk a bit," Eric said, starting off eastward along the fence line. "They don't stick to the roads like we do."

***

Gabby was immersed in her literary find. The text was easy to read, and the insights were simple but well thought out. Gabby thought the title could have been *Biblical Prophecies for Beginners* and sold quite well. The author made valiant efforts to decode complicated passages from 2,000 years ago into something a modern reader would recognize. Nearly fifty pages into the tome, Gabby froze. There on the page was one word from their first in-depth conversation with Cain. *Gebirah*. She didn't know its meaning at the time, but he had used it in reference to her. The index in the back of the book said it was Hebrew for "Queen Mother." Why did Cain call her that? As far as she knew, she was neither of those things. It must have something to do with the visions, she thought.

Even if she accepted what Cain had shared—his true nature, the fact that fallen angels are real and after her, that she could stop the Apocalypse spelled out in the Book of Revelations, and that her true nature was some sort of supernatural Hail Mary to stop it from happening—it was something else entirely to see it in black and white in a book you pulled off the shelf from one of apparently dozens of houses owned worldwide by Cain, the son of Adam and Eve and humanity's first murderer. It did lend some legitimacy to what Cain was saying. She was close to believing him already. Gabby thought Daniel, being the more religious one in their relationship, already had bought into it completely. In fact, he seemed to be reveling in it. He was proud of her, but he also seemed to relish having a part in the grand scheme of the beginning of the end of the world.

Oh wow, she thought. *Now I'm completely bought into this madness too.* She had tried—twice—to explain it away or refuse to accept the facts. Gabby tried not to dwell on the connotations of denying something two times. She laughed to herself a bit. *If a rooster crows in a moment, I'm going to lose it completely.*

And if she accepted the Bible as historical fact and what Cain was saying about her, it led to a pretty terrifying place. All these pieces seemed to add up unless it was a ruse on such a scale it would boggle the mind. For the first time, Gabby felt a degree of shame in calling Cain a lunatic during their first visit to the apartment, then coming back once she had another vision in her dreams. *Maybe I'm descended from the disciple Thomas,* she thought somewhat sarcastically. *I sure as heck doubted all of this.* Maybe this was the penance their family was paying for his—and her—doubt. That would really add up to some sort of cosmic, divinely ordained karma, wouldn't it? Gabby closed the book, half afraid she might learn something she would rather not know. Then again, she reasoned, whatever she did would lead her down this path, right? Apparently she couldn't escape it. Even if she tried, she was going to be chased down like a dog by Rasch and his goons, who definitely believed all of this.

Then I'm in for a penny, in for a pound, she decided. They would have to see this thing through completely and rely on Cain's help and direction to get there. The three of them had done okay considering two of them—although maybe it was just one of them—her, because Daniel seemed to already be bought in—didn't believe what was most likely the truth. A small part of Gabby still remained skeptical, but unless she discovered otherwise and did it fast, she was committing to the cause.

Gabby, who daydreamed through church services and had humored her beloved boyfriend with his religious notions for years, suddenly was a believer and about to become the foretold warrior prophetess in the extremely imminent and apparently already-in-progress, capital "A" Apocalypse. Her next thought was more mundane. It was her sensible side coming out to balance just about everything else in life at this moment. *I have got to stop watching Daniel's movies.* "They may be helpful and even a bit inspirational as we take on this seemingly impossible task, but they also give you an overwhelming sense of grandeur." Gabby realized she had said that last part out loud, and shook her head. When this was over, she would burn all those movies . . . She then set out to find Cain in the gargantuan stone fortress that had become their temporary refuge.

This all had better be worth it. She walked out of the library, book tucked under her arm, and started yelling, "Cain! Yoo-hoo! Where are you?" Her voice echoed through the hallways as she made her way back to the main entrance, looking around corners and knocking on doors as she went.

***

Daniel and Eric continued their walk on the north ridge, watching for wolves and trying to stay quiet. They found a few places where the fences were in disrepair—enough to allow the animals through, Eric said—but no tracks or droppings. After walking for nearly twenty minutes, Eric said it was time to stop.

"Why stop here?" Daniel asked. "Couldn't the wolves be coming in further down the fence line too?"

"It's possible, but not likely," Eric said. "This is as far as we go."

"Really?" said Daniel. "We came out all this way, only to walk for a couple minutes then turn back?"

"No," said Eric, his gaze cast downward. "That's what *I'm* doing. You're going with them."

Behind several nearby trees were Rasch and a band of people who, if Daniel had seen them with his own eyes, he would swear resembled the Washington Monument assailants. The only difference was that these beings weren't dressed in formal attire. They were dressed from head to toe in black military clothing. They emerged from their hiding places and quickly surrounded Daniel and Eric.

Rasch walked slowly up to Eric and offered a handshake. Eric stood by, then started to shake slightly. Tears welled up in the corner of his eyes. He refused Rasch's hand. "Just tell me my family is okay, and we can be done," Eric said. "This is bad enough without trying to act like we're friends."

"Oh, but we are, my dear Mr. Ballencourt," Rasch replied. "We couldn't have done this without you. We are in your debt, my dear man. And you," Rasch said, turning to Daniel. "The last time I saw you—just this morning, in fact—you were jamming a cattle prod into my side and trying to run me over. But look! No magic stick and no car. Whatever are we going to do with you? Shall we fight it out, like men?"

Daniel looked Rasch in the eye, his right leg quivering slightly. He started to recite the Lord's Prayer under his breath. "Our Father in Heaven . . ."

"Who isn't listening and doesn't care about you, Daniel," Rasch said. "He never has."

" . . . hallowed be your name . . ."

"More like hollow," Rasch said laughingly. His rail-thin companions followed suit, like a pack of animals following the leader.

"Your kingdom come . . ."

"Oh, it's coming all right," came Rasch's retort. "Coming and going down the tubes in record time."

"your will be done . . . "

"If he or anyone up there had the nerve to enforce their will, none of us would be in this mess." Rasch was talking loudly at this point, trying to cow Daniel into stopping.

"on Earth . . . "

"And everywhere in between, don't forget," Rasch said, a temper starting to show in his speech.

"as it is in Heaven," Daniel said, somewhat defiantly, his voice quivering a bit at the end.

"That's the last place anyone wants to be, Danny boy," Rasch said, cackling, which was mimicked by his accomplices. They had begun to pick at Daniel's arms and torso, testing him and trying to goad him into a fight that he would lose, badly. "And definitely the last place you—

"Wait a minute," Rasch said suddenly. He grew silent, raised his head as if he was taking in a full breath for the first time. "Wait one goddamned minute . . . " His eyes closed. *It almost seems as if he is in prayer,* Daniel thought. *But that would be the last thing he would do, right?*

Everyone was still: Rasch, Daniel, the wraiths—even Eric, who was watching the whole affair from several paces away with an odd mixture of shame and relief on his face. "Sorry, boys, we have to depart. Pack this one up and get him in the car.

"And, boys," Rasch said to the obedient but unruly wraiths, "not a scratch on him. We have new orders. Which brings us to Mr. Ballencourt." Rasch turned toward the property-manager-turned-turncoat. "You can go. Your family will be released. Unharmed . . . for the most part."

***

"Gabby! What is it? I was dozing while catching up on the news," Cain said as he came down the stairs, looking slightly disheveled while tying together the belt of his robe.

"First of all, amazing library," Gabby said. "Second, I found a great book. And, I think I'm in it."

"Really? I am glad but not entirely surprised. Do share what you have found," Cain said with genuine interest.

"You called me a name the other night. Gebirah. I didn't know what it meant. I thought maybe it was a nice way of saying 'girl' or 'young lady.' You know, like old people do," Gabby said with a wide grin. "But it's not. I know you know that, but I didn't know then. Why did you call me 'Queen Mother?'"

"It is a title given to royalty many centuries ago. I thought it fit. And of course it is similar to your own name. I thought perhaps it fit you and the circumstances you have been dropped into. I meant no offense in using the term."

"None taken, old man. But maybe give me a little heads-up as to what you mean when you drop in a word or phrase that hasn't been uttered since we've been on AD time."

Surprisingly, Cain did not laugh. "Now, my dear Gebirah, we have work to do. More than I planned on, it seems. Young Eric has been compromised, and Daniel is in danger. He may already be dead or injured. I do not know."

"What do you mean you don't know if Daniel is dead? He was just here a little while ago. Why would you say that?"

Cain hung his head a bit. "I had an ugly choice to make, and I made it. It was five lives versus one. Daniel is a full-grown man, and he has some experience dealing with these people. They had taken Eric's family hostage and were going to kill them. He was put in a no-win situation before we even arrived. He asked what he should do when we first got here. I told him to do it. Now, we will make getting Daniel back one of our top priorities."

"One?" Gabby said angrily. "It needs to be the first and only thing. Then we stop the Apocalypse."

"I think we can pursue getting Daniel back safely and our ultimate goal at the same time," Cain said. "Our paths are going to converge with the Fallen anyway. We might as well use it to our advantage.

"Speaking of advantages . . . this could have been a lot worse. Yes, they were a step ahead of us this time, and Eric's family was caught in the crossfire. That is very bad, of course, and we are taking steps worldwide to fortify every place I own and ensure the staff and their families are well protected. Lesson learned the hard way. But, as I said, it could have been worse. If Razhael and his goons were not stuck several millennia in the past, nursing old wounds and their poor decisions, they would have thought to bug the retreat. My initial thought was that they had. Think how much worse it would have been if they heard our discussion. If they knew—truly knew—how pivotal you are to ensuring the Earth and humanity in general survive. Or if they picked up something else potentially devastating they could use to their advantage. I am telling you, Gabrielle, we can beat the Fallen and get Daniel back safely. I am sure of it."

"Sure enough to bet your life?" Gabby asked. "Oh, that's right. You can't because you're immortal. Maybe you've been alive so long that human life has lost meaning to you. Maybe I was right the first time and should have stayed as far away from you as possible. Daniel would be here if I had."

Cain stood there, listening silently. A tear welled up in one eye; then he spoke. "Gabrielle, if I could have been taken in Daniel's place, I would have. They do not want me. They want the Apocalypse to proceed, and you and Daniel are on the path to stopping it. That is why he was taken. He is important, as are you. I, in the greater scheme of things, am not. I want to help, but my ability to do so is more limited than you might imagine. I have my knowledge and resources to offer, but no more. It has to be you. And I am sure Daniel has a part to play as well. I can feel it. You must believe me. And hopefully, in time, forgive me. But for now, let us set aside our discontent and focus on returning Daniel safe and sound. And roasting some of those black-winged bastards along the way."

"All right . . . for now," Gabby said. "But the next time we're going to be put in mortal peril, a little warning would be nice. Or else, as God as my witness, I will find a way to hurt you that doesn't get me flash fried. Maybe I will have a vision about that." Gabby ended her threat on an up note so that it sounded like a positive development. "And I'm driving."

CHAPTER 16: CAR TALK

Eric was gathering his things to take time off to be with his family. His wife, two daughters, and young son were scraped up, bruised, and slightly traumatized when they were found walking by themselves a few miles away on an old access road. Emergency search drones had been sent out from the mountain's information technology team, and they located heat signatures about five miles north in the woods. There were signs of a recently abandoned encampment close by. Cain said they had called the local sheriff's office and reported poachers nearby.

"No sense in alarming them about their true nature," Cain said. "They won't find them, but the police searching the area will be enough to ensure any of our adversaries remaining in the area will go into hiding or better yet, leave entirely."

"With Daniel, you mean?" Gabby asked. "Why is that good? We agreed to go after him as soon as possible. You better not be going back on your word already."

"I am not, Gabrielle," Cain replied. "If they are moving or transporting young Daniel somewhere, we have a greater chance of spotting them or getting a good tip from the local authorities. If they hole up somewhere and go into hiding, it will be much, much more difficult. Before leaving, Eric asked our technology staff to monitor all police channels. If they are spotted, we will know about it."

" . . . Thank you," Gabby said, taking a moment to think through her next words carefully. "Look, I know you made a tough decision. Maybe it was the right one, all things considered. I'm glad that man has his family back and they weren't hurt. But Daniel is missing and they *are* going to hurt him. I know it. I can feel it."

Cain's interest was piqued. "You had another vision? Please, tell me what you saw."

"No, no, nothing like that," Gabby said. "Just regular worry. The kind you get when you know a loved one is hurting and you can't help."

"I have not experienced that since the 1920s, I am afraid," Cain said. "My life the last one hundred years or so has been focused on building material wealth and creating an organization to help with our cause. But I do remember the feeling. I had someone very dear to me whom I lost back then. It was easier to focus on material things afterward than to grieve. I . . . still miss Jacqueline very much."

"I'm sorry to hear that, Cain," Gabby said, putting a hand on his shoulder. "It must be difficult. Seeing people grow and age all around you. I hadn't thought about it that much, but the toll it would take on your emotions . . . "

"Are what you are experiencing now, young Gabrielle. To get Daniel back we have to get moving. We can talk more while we are driving. Before he left, Eric ensured the garage was open and ready for us. Let us take a walk and get some new wheels. Deal?"

"Deal," Gabby said. She was more concerned about Daniel than she let on. He was kind, considerate, and sometimes fragile. He was a great boyfriend and partner, but she never thought of him as hardy. He was not going to hold up well.

***

The garage at Backbone Mountain was impressive. It housed sports cars, two-seaters, trucks, Jeeps, then more exotic sports cars, at least two of the same type of electric tanks they used the day before, and a whole section of late-sixties, early seventies GMC trucks. Gabby was choosing which vehicle would be the most helpful.

"Always go with speed, my dear," Cain said as he watched Gabby silently deliberate. "The roadsters can be fun to drive, but the McLarens are—if this makes a difference to you—my favorites. They are fast and low to the ground. Good for outrunning the authorities. But only if needed, of course."

"We are not going hunting for fallen angels and my kidnapped boyfriend in a McLaren," Gabby said. "Why I have to say such things out

88

loud is beyond me."

"Is it because you have never driven one and are afraid of the power?" Cain said. "That is a common concern."

"No, it's not, you sexist jerk. I want to get my boyfriend back from a pack of demons, and I don't necessarily want to draw attention while doing it. Is that good enough for you?"

Cain felt a pang of regret at his flippant response while Gabby was in obvious pain. "You are right, Gabby. My apologies once again. A lower profile will be helpful."

"You know, for an old man, your manners stink," Gabby said. "I don't care how rich you are. Wrong is wrong. I would hope after living so long, you would learn how to talk to people. I guess not."

Cain looked at Gabby, dumbfounded. He did not have a response, and he hung his head a bit lower.

Gabby walked toward an older, black, late-1980s Mazda RX-7. "Here. Let's take this one. It should be fast, but older and less likely to draw suspicion. Sound good . . . partner?" Gabby showed a slight smile at Cain.

"Yes, that is perfect . . . partner."

***

They both returned to their rooms to pack clothes and necessities. Gabby's had been supplied by a staff member who had asked her sizes and preferences shortly after they had arrived. She had returned a few hours later while Gabby was still in the library with a small wardrobe of comfortable, stylish pants, shirts, and light sweaters—all things she preferred. Gabby was impressed at how well the attendant had done in choosing what she liked after their cursory talk.

Cain walked back to the main entrance of the house with a small but obviously expensive suitcase. He spoke in hushed tones to the second-in-charge at the Mountain, a quiet, stern woman who wore differing shades of gray. She nodded as Cain talked and occasionally said, "Very good, Mr. Green. We will take care of it."

Gabby walked in with her new clothes and luggage in hand. She was eager to get going and to see Daniel once more. "What's going on, guys?"

she said. "Any updates? Any word about Daniel?"

"No, Gabrielle," Cain said. "Just some last-minute instructions to keep the Mountain retreat safe and secure. And I am trying to figure out where we are headed after we inspect the abandoned campsite. The car should be fully fueled and ready to go. Are you ready?"

"I was ready ten minutes ago. Let's go get my man back safe and sound."

CHAPTER 17: ALABAMA, 1852

James Richman was a sixth-generation Alabama plantation owner. His land north of Mobile had been owned by his family since before the United States was an independent country. Their 3,000-acre plantation was built for harvesting cotton. James reclined slightly on the front porch of his mansion. It was early September and time to bring the crops in. Nearly every slave able to work and not already working in the household was out in fields. The overseers kept everyone working with a combination of a pack of trained hounds and a leather whip. At last count, the Richmans had 293 slaves, making them one of the largest cotton-producing plantations in the state.

One slave, however, was not working today. James received a report that Old Smoke, their longest-living field worker, did not come out of the quarters at daylight. He pondered what to do. Old Smoke generally was avoided by the Richman family, the white overseers, and many of the slaves.

James also had a visitor. He was a relatively new owner from about six miles northwest. The visitor, Frederick, and James had been acquaintances in their teens, more than twenty years ago. Frederick had inherited his father's estate and was returning to the area after being away in New York for nearly fourteen years working as an attorney.

"Trouble with your folks, James?" asked Frederick, who was readjusting to life in the South.

"I do not know yet if it's trouble or something else. The worker has been here more'n sixty years, still works the fields just like he was twenty," James said. "My great-granddaddy brought him over, bought him right off the boat in Mobile. Said he was short but sturdy. Probably wouldn't give anyone a hard time, being so short. And he's got some muscle, so he'd be a hard worker."

"He sounds like a fine worker," Frederick said. "What is the issue with him? Can he not be tamed after all these years?"

"He works all right," James said. "When he wants to. Which is most of the time. Every once in a while, he gets a little uppity and refuses to come out."

"Well, there's a solution for that, correct?"

"You would think so. But we try to give him a wide berth, on account of his age. Also, on account of what happened to the man who brought him here, my great-granddaddy Cassius."

"Can you share the story? I'm very interested to hear about the slave that you can't discipline," Frederick said, leaning forward.

"It'd be my pleasure, although the story itself is far from pleasurable," James said, lighting his pipe and leaning back in his chair. "The story is, about four months after buyin' him, my great-granddaddy Cassius found him sitting in the fields, staring up at the clouds. Great-granddaddy Cassius, I have been told, didn't take no guff from anyone. Especially from short darkies too lazy to work. He, my great-granddaddy that is, brought out his whip and got one good lick in. Then, outta the blue he was struck by lightning. Struck him dead where he stood, whip still in his hand. On a clear day in April, no less. It was the damnedest thing anyone had ever seen.

"Ol' Smoke there, he just got up, dusted himself off, and walked back to the boardinghouse. Stepped right over Granddaddy Cassius like it wasn't nothin'. He's been here ever since. Usually works just fine. Others don't wanna mess with him, though. They leave him alone. He even sleeps in a different part of the quarters, I hear. They don't wanna mess with him, and neither do we. As long as he works, we keep him around. My daddy thought about settin' him loose a couple years ago. He tried, but the damned fool just stood there, lettin' his chains fall to the ground when Daddy unlocked 'em. He looked at Daddy, shook his head, and walked back to his quarters as if nothing had changed.

"He works mostly. Days he don't, we just leave him alone. He eventually comes back and gets back to it. He's a good worker when he's there. Don't eat too much and don't cause trouble, at least not for a long time.

"The others steer clear of him. I don't blame 'em. He looks the same today as he did when I was a boy. And my daddy and his daddy before him said the same thing. It's not natural."

Frederick was intrigued. "You think it's some kind of magic? Something he learned from a witch doctor back in Africa? I hear they have those still."

"Might be," James said. "If so, I'd like to know how to get him to leave. He doesn't seem too keen on the idea, though."

"Can I see him?" Frederick asked. "Maybe there is something unique about him that we can use. I would surely like the opportunity to meet him."

"I try not to get around him myself," James said. "Gives me the chills, the way he stares at people. But, in the interest of being neighborly, let's do it. The houses are a few hundred yards south. We can walk down if you're good with that."

"I appreciate the opportunity, James," Frederick said. "It's not every day you can see such a unique specimen. Maybe you could sell him to the traveling circus."

As the two prepared to walk to the slave quarters, one of James' other servants, a house worker named Thaddeus approached the men.

"Excuse me, sir," he said. "I've been asked to let you know Old Smoke is making his way up here. He's coming to the house and asking to see you."

"Well, that fellow is just full of surprises," James said. "Frederick, it looks like we can forgo our walk. Old Smoke is coming to us. Will wonders never cease?

"Thaddeus, please bring him to us when he arrives. And, also stay close for what should be a lively conversation."

***

Old Smoke approached the rear of the house and began looking for a way in. The doors were, uncharacteristically, secured during the daytime. He could see several sets of eyes peering out of the kitchen windows, watching his every move. *Word travels fast when people think trouble is brewing,* he thought. If they knew the truth, they would get as far away as possible. He walked around to the front and the massive front porch where James and Frederick were sitting peacefully with Thaddeus nearby. He walked up near the men, but remained on the grass.

"Good day, Mr. Richman," Old Smoke said. "I would like to speak with you, if I may?" Old Smoke was nearly five feet tall, with very long white hair, which he wore in braids. His clothes were tattered enough that the majority of his chest and a good part of his right leg were exposed as he walked. He did, however, carry himself with a great deal of dignity—a rarity for slaves.

"We're all friends here, Smoke," James said. "Whatever you have to share, you can share with Frederick and Thaddeus too. Please, tell me the reason for this visit."

"Sir, my request is a tad unusual," Old Smoke said in a hushed tone. "It would be beneficial for you and me both if we could speak privately. Please, sir."

This time, it was Frederick who answered. "Hoo boy, James, it sounds like your boy wants to negotiate. I'd never thought I'd see the day . . . " Frederick stood up and hopped down from the porch to the ground beside Old Smoke. He stood at least a head and a half taller than the slave. "Your master lets you speak that way to him? Not with me around you won't," Frederick said somewhat forcefully as well as unexpectedly. What Frederick had not shared with James was that, in addition to catching up with an old friend, his visit had another purpose. Frederick was new to being an owner and wanted to pick up some tips from more experienced hands. His boyhood friend, James, lived a very similar life, and Frederick thought a visit there would be helpful.

Frederick looked the man up and down, then delivered a swift smack across his face. "How dare you talk to your bett—"

At that moment, a lightning bolt came down from an otherwise cloudless sky, narrowly missing the porch roof, and electrocuted Frederick mid-sentence where he stood.

A man-shaped, charred husk fell over. James stood up from his spot at the table and backed away in horror. Thaddeus was wide-eyed and remained still. Old Smoke brushed his ripped shirt slightly, looking down at what remained of Frederick. Then he stepped over the smoldering heap and up onto the porch.

"Mr. Richman," Old Smoke said as he took the seat that, until a minute ago, had been occupied by Frederick. James had started to exhibit a small tremor in his left leg before wetting himself. He sat back down and asked Thaddeus for something stronger to drink. Thaddeus didn't move.

"Sir, as I was saying, I would like to talk with you," Old Smoke said as if nothing out of the ordinary had just happened.

"Leave, you demon from Hell," James said. "I thought the story about you was hyperbole and that my great-granddaddy died of natural causes. I now see that was most likely not the case. I hold you to blame for his death and for the death of Frederick Ballinger here." James gestured toward the smoldering remains on the lawn.

"Yes, I can see that," Old Smoke said. "You would be within your rights to do so. I would be arrested, tried, and most likely convicted. But, sir, I have to ask you . . . how many more people will die in that process? I do not want that, and I would surmise that you do not want that either."

"Yes . . . that's most likely true," James said with a bit of curious surprise at Old Smoke's reasoning.

"Well, I propose we come to an arrangement. I have been here a long time, but it is past time for me to leave. I have thought about it for the past three years, and now it is time for something different."

"And what is that?" came James' weak-voiced reply.

"I leave today to head north," Old Smoke said. "I will make my way to the free states, most likely New York. You will give me a written document that I am a freedman on my way to meet distant relatives there."

James suddenly was curious. He had not considered the slave would make demands of him, let alone ones that seemed to be part of a larger plan. "What happens after that?" he asked. "Are you going to work your voodoo there as well, killing more innocent men who brush against you on the sidewalk?"

Old Smoke looked down with a slight smile on his face. "No, sir, I will not. I have had enough of this life of servitude. I have stewed in my pain and mistakes here for too long. I aim to start a business and make my way just like any other man. I read that a man can earn a good living providing transport in the city. That is what I will do. Now, can we come to an arrangement, sir?"

James sat still for a moment, then reached for his drink. His hands shook as he took a long draught, small drops falling onto his pressed shirt and coat. James then sank back in his chair, thinking of his father and what he might do.

"You know, Smoke, my daddy would have found a way to discipline you, some way to overcome your dark magic. Maybe he tried. I do not know. But . . . " Several minutes passed in silence. The two men stared at each other, neither showing any sign of their next move. "But," James continued, "I am not my father. I accept your proposal. We will draw up the papers, and you can be on your God-forsaken way before sundown."

Old Smoke nodded. "That would be the best thing that could happen to me, to be forsaken as you say. It would have saved me and a whole lot of others a lot of pain and misery. But that is not my path. I've had enough of serving others. I think I will serve myself for a while. See where that takes me. I will be in the quarters. First, I will stop in the fields to say goodbye to the friends I have here. If you will tell the overseers to allow us a few moments, I would appreciate it."

"Agreed, Old Smoke."

"One more thing. Old Smoke is not my name. I never have liked it. Call me . . . Tyson. Tyson Green. Please use that name when you sign the papers to show I am, once more, a free man. I will return in a few hours for them. Then you will never see me again."

CHAPTER 18: ON THE ROAD AGAIN

Gabby eased out onto the road in a car older than she was but faster than she expected. The RX-7 was surprisingly quick and agile. It handled the twists and turns of the Maryland back roads with ease and precision. They were leaving the mountain retreat behind to begin their search for Daniel, Razhael, and the wraiths. *I can see why people like these things,* Gabby thought. She always had seen sports cars as something old men drove while trying to regain their youth, but she was starting to see the appeal the more she drove the thirty-year-old Mazda. *You learn something new every day.*

The tracks leading away from the campsite where Daniel was abducted went north out of the forest then vanished once they came to the main road. Gabby and Cain were relying on Cain's private network of satellites, police informants, and other things Gabby didn't want to contemplate to give them direction. In her heart, though, she was sure the trail went west. "We don't have any good leads, so let's try intuition," Gabby said. "It's not a vision, but maybe it's related. Maybe there are different levels of seeing, and this is one."

"Without further information, one direction is as good as the next," Cain said, gripping the passenger seat a little more tightly than he had planned. Gabby was an excellent driver, but he was not used to being in the passenger seat. It made him uneasy. "Anything else we can use to guide our search? Anything else you have seen or felt that could aid us?"

Gabby frowned a bit. "No, that's it. Just a strong sense that things are happening in the west and we should head there. It feels like it should be in the southwest too. That's because when I think about it, the intuition always feels warm, if that makes sense. Definitely west of here . . . and probably warm. That's the best I have for now."

"It has not steered us wrong so far, your gift," Cain said.

"That's a funny way to put it. 'Gift.' Doesn't feel much like one. Kind of the opposite, really. Is that . . . how it is for you?" Gabby asked with genuine concern.

"It can be," Cain replied. "But when you have lived close to 13,000 years, time can begin to feel meaningless. Watching people I know and love grow up, grow old, then depart this plane of existence is . . . more difficult than I can explain. For most of my time on Earth, I have walled myself away from getting close to people. But I always return to it, and it is always painful. There are great moments to be sure, but everyone I know eventually dies. And I, as my eternal punishment for a moment of anger and a regretful action, stay the same."

Gabby thought for a moment. "I do have something I want to ask you, with your permission. About your family."

Cain prepared himself for the same questions he'd been asked time and time again from those who knew his secret. *Where is the Garden of Eden? How do I find it? What did Adam and Eve look like? Did you see the serpent in the garden?* Occasionally, there was an amusing one. In 1521, Cain was asked by his girlfriend of forty-two years, on her deathbed, "When did you start wearing clothes? And where did you get them?" Clara always had been one of his favorite people, and she made him laugh as she left this life. What he would give to see Clara and hold her close once more.

"Yoo-hoo, Earth to old man," Gabby said. "Are we still talking? You kind of zoned out. I hope I didn't offend you."

Cain raised his head. "No, Gabby, you did not. I was lost in a memory. A good one. Now, you want to ask about my family? What can I tell you?"

"What was your brother like? Tell me about him. How did he act? Did you two look alike?"

Cain was not prepared for this. No one had ever asked about Abel or Seth. They would ask how he killed Abel. That was a question he had heard many times and one he steadfastly refused to answer. But he never had been asked what Abel was like as a person and brother. He never really got to know Seth, but he and Abel were extremely close for many years. A small tear gathered in his left eye, and he held back the urge to sniff. He drew a deep breath and answered.

"He was . . . great. A wonderful brother and a good companion. We had such fun growing up, playing together. I can tell you the very first game of hide-and-seek ever was in the Garden between Abel and me. He . . . he found me after just a few minutes, but he was kind enough to pretend not to see me in the upper branches where I was hiding. We were no more than eight or ten. He let me think I had fooled him for an entire afternoon. He made a big deal about it to our parents as the sun went down, saying that I was such a good 'hider' that he could not find me at all. He went on about searching all over, never seeing me. I felt immense pride that my brother liked something I did . . .

"Gabby," Cain said suddenly. "Do not believe everything you read. Just . . . please keep that in mind as you live your life. And also, once we save the world and go back to what you were doing, when you remember me." Tears now were freely running down Cain's cheek. A few moments of silence followed. Gabby glanced over at the immortal, cursed man as he had an openly emotional moment. She had only known him a few days and was pretty sure Cain was a lot of things, but emotional was not something she expected. She reached over and patted his leg gently.

Cain sniffed loudly, drawing up a deep breath, then spoke, a tinge of happiness creeping back into his voice. "Oh, Abel was such a show-off. He was big and brawny and didn't have to work at it. He was happy all of the time. He was so confident in himself and what he was doing, even when it was just the four of us. Now that I think about it, he was what you youngsters would call an alpha male. The very first one." Cain was crying happy tears and fighting back a wide smile and a runny nose.

"Who are you calling a youngster?" Gabby said. "I'm twenty-eight."

"Which makes you about eleven thousand, nine hundred and seventy-two years younger than me," Cain said, still wiping tears from his eyes. "Definitely a youngster. Please watch the road."

***

Gabby and Cain crossed through a strip of northern West Virginia and most of Ohio without saying much else. Cain had flipped through the radio dial, but he never found anything that suited him. Gabby asked to leave it on a modern rock station from Columbus as they drove just north of the city, but Cain wasn't having it. "A cacophony through and through," he said. "I cannot stand it. Please, choose something else." They eventually settled on the public radio stations they could find at the low end of the dial. Gabby and Cain discovered they both enjoyed National Public Radio, especially the news reports. They were a little disheartened to hear there was no news about a kidnapping in Maryland the day before, but they agreed it would have been a miracle on top of a miracle for them to get that lucky. Cain stayed glued to his phone and laptop as they drove, checking for any clue or sightings that would lead them to Daniel. He would call and receive calls from people who worked for him, but Gabby was having a hard time determining if their information was helpful.

She heard Cain saying, "Yes . . . yes . . . that fits his description." Then, to Gabby, "Daniel is about six foot, one inch, yes? With dark brown hair? Any distinguishing marks?" She would nod or shake her head, and Cain would relay the information as they drove through the heart of the Midwest.

***

An hour after sunset, Gabby said she'd like to stop for the evening. She was getting sleepy and not thinking as clearly as she would like. Her concern for Daniel, plus weariness from driving most of the day, was taking a toll. Cain agreed, making a phone call to arrange a place to stay for the evening.

"You mean you don't have a hidden lair in Illinois?" Gabby asked teasingly. "Maybe you can call Bill Gates and see if he does."

"I am not calling that upstart," Cain said. "We don't see eye to eye on the future of artificial intelligence, and I am certainly not asking him for a favor. Besides, I already have a place for us to stay. All the arrangements have been made. Take the next exit in about three miles."

Cain directed Gabby to a location she did not expect: a busy strip mall with a Marriott at its north end. It looked good to Gabby, like a place she would pick. But why did Cain choose it? He seemed used to luxury and could afford any place he wanted. "Why here?" Gabby asked.

"Gabrielle, for someone with prophetic visions, you certainly cannot see the obvious at times," Cain said in a slightly joking tone. "Our adversaries know who we are, where we live, and very likely how we think. We cannot presume that they are a pack of wild dogs acting out of instinct. The fallen, Razhael especially, are not only smart—they are supernaturally smart. They have senses we can only dream about. In a straightforward confrontation they will win every time."

Gabby parked near the hotel entrance. She and Cain got out of the car, and they went to grab their respective bags out of the back hatch. "Maybe don't tell me things like that," Gabby said, opening the glass hatch and grabbing the bag that had been packed for her in Maryland. "I'm AWOL from my job and driving across the country with the world's oldest man, looking for my kidnapped boyfriend, who was taken by angels from Hell. You have to give me a little hope, Cain."

"We are still alive and fighting," Cain said. "We also know we can hurt them. And they do not seem to be ahead of us in any appreciable way. It seems they are just getting started, so perhaps we do have an advantage." Gabby slung her bag over her shoulder and looked toward the hotel entrance. Cain grabbed his leather bag from inside the car, then reached up and shut the hatch. "We have adjoining rooms. Please behave yourself." He winked at her as they made their way inside.

***

After a long, hot, and much-needed shower, Gabby unlocked her side of the adjoining doors and knocked. She heard a small thud, then footsteps. Cain opened the door wearing a silk bathrobe and slippers. "What, no pipe?" Gabby teased. "Slumming it out here with the commoners?"

"Gabby, we are traveling light, and trying to remain undetected," Cain said. "A little less obviousness will help us greatly."

Gabby smirked and turned around, flopping on one of the queen-sized beds in her room. "You can come in, but please keep that robe tied up tight."

"Yes, Gabrielle," Cain said with a smile. "Would you like to talk strategy for tomorrow?"

"Sounds good. Where do we start? I still feel like we need to head more to the west."

Cain pondered this for a moment. "Another vision or more intuition?"

"Mostly intuition. No visions while I was driving, thankfully. Or in the shower. I can't imagine which would be worse. But, still west seems like the right way. Nothing more specific."

Cain nodded. "Again, lacking any other information, we stick with that plan. I believe we have the element of surprise on our side. I am sure they are looking for us. They never will think we are looking for *them*. They think we are on the run. That would fit Razhael's ego. If you're a fallen angel and you're back on Earth after a few millennia, where would you stay? Not a remote warehouse or anything obvious like that."

Gabby and Cain remained silent as they thought about where to turn next. Gabby half expected a vision to point the way and maybe even give an address. She was growing frustrated, and she was tired from the past several days. She was increasingly worried about Daniel and how he was faring. Closing her eyes, she tried to prompt a vision. After a few minutes of silence and no vision in sight, Gabby blurted out, "You'd go to a church. You would make yourself appear as good as you can—maybe even show a little wing to convince the pastor you're legit and in need of their services. They probably get bonus points for misleading good people."

"Is this from a vision?" Cain asked.

"No, just taking things to a logical conclusion. And trying to think like a wanted person. Where would be the best place to hide? A criminal might hide close to a police station where no one is expecting him. As long as he's careful, he'd blend in because it's the last place the cops would be looking."

"Good thinking, Gabby," Cain said, impressed with her idea. "I like it. Are you positive you did not have a vision? This is very sound reasoning all the way around. Now, which church? There probably are several thousand in the state of Illinois alone."

Gabby thought for a moment. "I'd go for the biggest, holiest place I could find. It would be positively crawling with righteousness. I bet Rachel would feel right at home. Or back at home for a visit, at least."

Cain hesitated for a moment. "What did you say? What did you call Razhael?"

"I called him Rachel, like the character from *Friends*," Gabby said. "Trying a little cognitive restructuring. If I think of him as funny or see him as a little less intimidating, I'll be better prepared to fight. Because I have to say, he scares the shit out of me right now. I'm working on it. Feel free to join in."

Cain laughed. "You are an absolute wonder, Gabrielle. It would be a shame to have you burnt to a cinder and the planet along with it."

"That's the job, right? To stop the . . . you know, burning. Like you said. We rescue Daniel, then stop Rachel and the rest of his . . . friends . . . " Gabby could not finish the sentence for laughing and Cain soon joined in. She thought for a minute, then said, "You know what, Cain? For the guy who invented murder, you're all right. Let's call it a night, and we can get an early start in the morning."

"Thank you, Gabby, for a productive and very unexpected evening," Cain said. "I think we will locate Daniel very soon." He walked back through the adjoining doors to his room.

"Yeah. Me too. Good night, Cain," Gabby said, closing and locking her side of the door before turning in for the evening.

***

"I stayed up working on our problem," Cain said over a morning cup of coffee in the hotel lobby. "Well, several of my people did as well. We have some good ideas to work through."

Gabby nodded then took a sip. "Umm, okay. Let's hear them."

"I asked my security team to look for aberrations in crime rates, either a marked increase or a substantial decrease," Cain said. "If these people—and again I use that term very loosely—are about, it stands to reason they either will cause a ruckus somewhere, or work very hard not to. It is in their nature. Razhael may be in charge, but those wraiths are going to stand out."

Gabby was not impressed. "Okay, that's all stuff we already knew, more or less. Educated guesses that we need to follow up on. Did anything match or happen that would lead us in the right direction?"

"A bit," Cain said. "One of our analysts suggested that our quarry still needs to eat. Razhael may not have to, but those wraiths more than likely do. So what would easily led, semi-intelligent man-hounds from Hell eat?"

"You got me there," Gabby said. "I have no idea. But I'm guessing you do."

"I do indeed, young Gabrielle," Cain said, happy to be sharing his new knowledge. "I have a little bit of experience with these fellows, but just a little. They do not come to this plane of existence often, and for good reason. The wraiths stand out like sore thumbs. They are good for muscle and seem to follow orders well enough, but they also are unruly and easily distracted. Remember our encounter at the monument? They were on a trail. You, most likely. But they were not really what you would call incognito."

"Yes, I was there," Gabby said. "When is the big reveal? I feel like you're building to a big reveal."

Cain smiled nearly from ear to ear. "I am, indeed. We make fine amateur detectives, do we not?" Gabby just looked at him and folded her arms. Cain drew a breath. "Anyway, back to the wraiths. They seem almost feral, correct? Like wild animals in many ways. And what do wild animals eat?"

"Whatever they can find," Gabby said. "But probably smaller animals. With teeth like theirs, I'm guessing they are meat eaters."

"I do not know why you even need me and my network of highly trained and highly paid intelligence operatives," Cain said with a smirk. "I could just hire you and save a few million dollars. But, yes. You are exactly right, Gabrielle. They most likely feed on raw meat, and lots of it."

"And?" Gabby asked, trying to mask her exasperation. "Why are you dragging this out? We have someone to rescue, you know."

"Right, right," Cain said, taking another bite of his lettuce and tomato salad breakfast. "Here is what we found. There are four locations within a day's drive or so from Maryland, which is the last known location of the wraiths, Razhael, and Daniel. We know they left in a few large vehicles and probably continued in them.

"So, a fallen angel, six or so wraiths, and Daniel as a prisoner are driving somewhere. Not exactly an inconspicuous lot, especially if you know what you are watching for. Extrapolating traffic camera footage from all throughout the Midwest for the past day, together with upticks in raw meat orders or the discovery of more mutilated animal carcasses than expected, plus the location of a large-scale religious institution, and our trail narrows itself down to . . . Notre Dame. It all fits. A large religious presence, plus a college—anybody can disappear in those places—and a rash of deer carcasses found just outside the campus. Plus, an Italian restaurant several blocks away has been making larger than normal orders of steak. As much as five times as normal."

Gabby was stunned for a moment. Somehow, against nearly all odds, they had a good lead in less than a day. Maybe her visions did guide her to suggest a church setting. How else could she explain it? It just came to her when she was trying to think things through the night before. Maybe the visions were controllable after all. Or at least directable? "So when do we leave?" Gabby said. "Poor Daniel has to be worried and scared out of his mind."

Cain smiled. "The car has a full tank of gas. We can be on campus in three hours if you drive sensibly. I already took the liberty of having one of my assistants pack our things and put them in the car. Let us finish break—"

Gabby already was up and walking toward the door.

CHAPTER 19: COLLEGE BOUND

Gabby was driving faster than normal. Now that they had a solid lead on finding Daniel, she was becoming anxious. *What have they been doing to him? Is he still alive? What if we're wrong, and he's somewhere else and in pain?*

"Cain, this all sounds good and I do think it's a good plan. But it almost seems too easy," Gabby said, worry creeping back into her voice. "What if they want to be found? What if they are waiting for us?"

"Then we fight. We are going in armed, and we will have backup nearby. In fact, they are already on site and scouring the area."

Gabby frowned. "That will just tip them off that we know they are there. They can't be that clueless. They could hurt Daniel. Call it off. Please."

"Yes, yes, of course," Cain said. "I will do as you ask. We do not want any harm to come to young Daniel or to tip our hand." He began typing on his mobile phone, and after nearly three minutes, he looked up and said, "All done. Everyone is quietly retreating to several blocks away from campus. They will be ready to go in with us as well."

"Thank you. I do appreciate everything you are doing," Gabby said. "We'd probably be dead or captured—well, all of us captured, not just Daniel—if not for you. It took some time to believe, but all this craziness has been consistent. Everything you have said has been true, as unbelievable as it is. You should know, though, that I will feel a thousand times better when Daniel is back home safely."

"As will we all, Gabrielle," Cain said with the utmost sincerity. "We should take a little time—a day or so perhaps—to recuperate. It is imperative that we stop whatever Razhael is up to, but we cannot do that if we are physically and emotionally drained."

"That makes sense, which is saying something considering the past few days," Gabby said. "Let's talk a little bit more about what we're getting ready to do. Can we really take these people on? Should I even call them people? What works against them? How do we get them to give back Daniel?"

"They are preternaturally strong and resistant to damage, so we have to overcome that first," Cain said. "That's just the wraiths. Razhael himself is a whole different matter. We can't beat him if we go at him head-on. He's much, much stronger, faster, and smarter than a human."

"What about holy water?"

"That is for vampires, Gabrielle. He probably could bathe in it and not care."

Gabby frowned a bit as she passed a semi-truck that was going slightly over the speed limit. "So, what works?"

"Well, ramming a tank into them slows them down. We know that," Cain said. "So Razhael is susceptible to the laws of physics, more or less. Electricity to the midsection did the trick, but it required getting close to him, and that is not the best idea in the world. Plus, it was enough of a jolt to down a rhino, and it only slowed him down. It is good if we need it, and we all will be well-armed with enough electrical weaponry to light up a city block. But it most likely will not be a primary means of doing what we need to do."

"So, what do we do?" Gabby said. "Sword fight?"

"No, Razhael is an experienced swordsman. There are many passages in the book that detail angels with swords. We cannot hit them where they are strongest."

"Well, that's encouraging. Can we throw rock and stones, or have they all played dodgeball for ten thousand years too? Wait a minute," Gabby said. "You said Razhael is an experienced swordsman. What about the helpers? The wraiths? Are they? And are they as strong and formidable as their boss?"

"Are they capable with a sword too?" Cain said. "That I do not know. I have never seen that or heard of it being the case. It is possible, though. As for the strength part, they seem to be stronger than the average human, but not excessively so. They are very strong but not super strong, if that answers your question."

"Yes, I get that. But you don't know for sure, right?" A plan was forming in Gabby's mind and she wanted to talk it through.

"Challenging them to a duel is not a good idea, Gabby. What if we are wrong, and they grab the blade and take it from you? Then what? It is too risky."

"No, no, I get that. I'm thinking of something else," Gabby said, having a waking vision. "What about oxygen? Do they need to breathe?"

Cain thought for a moment. "I . . . do not believe so. Once, on the Grecian coast, I saw a pair of them stay underwater for nearly a full morning. I was watching from a safe distance, and they did not know I was there. That was a long time ago. Now that you bring up the subject, though, I wonder if they evolve? Do they grow and change over generations like humans?"

"You compared them to hounds when we were talking in the apartment," Gabby said. "And everything else you are saying sounds like they are more animal than anything else. Is that a fair assessment?"

"They are tougher and stronger than humans, but that is all I know. They are definitely not smart. You have seen evidence of that yourself. But never forget that they are extremely vicious. I believe they are what the modern world would call quote-unquote 'demons,' but maybe there is more to them than meets the eye. Like a Transformer from Hell."

"Did you just make an eighties joke, Mister I'm-so-old-no-one-can-relate? Maybe you're the one evolving."

"Amusing, Gabrielle. One day we can debate that on a beach somewhere. We can spend days on it if you like. But to get to that day, we must focus on the task at hand."

"How about this?" Gabby asked. "What if we take my clothing from the bag in the back and leave some at various points around campus? Wouldn't the wraiths sense something and come looking?"

"Maybe," Cain said. "It is difficult to know whether they are keyed in on you, and if you leave any detectable traces on your clothing. It is a good idea, but it leaves too much to chance."

"I'm all ears if you have a better plan," Gabby said, more than a little smug, "that doesn't increase the risk of Daniel being hurt."

"Of course, Gabrielle. I hope, before all of this is through, that you come to see that I am trying to do the right thing for everyone involved. But until that day . . . My plan is simple. We use our people already on the ground to find where on campus Daniel is being held. They already are working on this while staying far away. They are using satellite imagery and a small cadre of drones to search for heat signatures that match up to Daniel, Razhael, and the rest. What they do not know—but I do—is angels have a very different heat signature. Very different in that they do not have one. Which, given where some of them were banished to, remains not an insignificant blessing. Honestly, I do not understand why that particular bit of biology was allowed to remain. Working in mysterious ways, I suppose.

"Regardless, we are looking for a group that includes our friend Daniel, plus six to ten malcontents loping about, plus one body that is present but does not appear to register any sort of heat when every other body in the world does. Not exactly stealthy, is it?"

"No, it's not," Gabby said, impressed and heartened with this development. "Why don't they think of things like that? I mean, I'm thrilled at the news, but if you were trying to bring about the end of the world, wouldn't you think to hide yourself a bit better?"

"You would think," Cain said. "Despite all their power and general scariness, they are hopelessly stuck in a pattern of revenge and destruction because that is all they know. In a way, I feel sorry for them. But then I remember the hundreds of thousands who die every century because of the influence of these 'people.' These once-proud angels who decided they knew better, then paid the price for it. Well, Gabrielle, I tell you now—they are not going to work out their daddy issues by destroying our planet. They are not, they will not. And I would be happy to die if it meant sending every last one of them back through the gates of Hell never to return.

"If I could."

CHAPTER 20: BEING HELPFUL

Gabby was silent. In the few days she had known him, Cain had not struck her as a particularly deep person. She thought perhaps his extraordinary life had made him a bit reckless, as if everything was a game—one where he didn't have to worry about winning or losing because he had nothing to fear, and he could always move on to the next game with no consequences.

She glanced over at him. There were no tears this time—just a steady gaze outward, to the road ahead. "Cain, that's . . . that's a lot. You make me want to cry. But still, what are we going to do about getting Daniel back?"

"Oh, that," Cain said, shaking himself out of his reverie. "Once we find them and map out all the entrances to wherever they are holed up, we split up. You and several of my best people will wait near the closest entrance to where we believe Daniel is being held. You will be waiting for my signal."

Gabby glanced over once again. "Your signal? And where will you be? Are you going to fight them all by yourself?"

"Yes, Gabby, that is exactly what I am going to do," Cain said matter-of-factly. "They cannot hurt me or impede my progress. They can try, and that is the plan. I can chest-bump with the best of them. One of them, and hopefully more, will try to stop me. They will not. While I am the distraction *du jour,* I will lead them away from Daniel. Before Razhael and his goons figure out that I am a decoy and not the cavalry, your team goes in, gets our man, and beats a hasty retreat. If it is just my people, Daniel may hesitate to leave. Sending you into the field is a little risky, but you have done extraordinarily well so far. Plus if I am lucky, I get to fry a few wraiths and maybe get another shot at Razhael."

"Cain, that's brilliant," Gabby said. "Have you done something like this before? Does it hurt when it happens?"

"Yes, I have. Many times. It is sort of a last-ditch effort, but it will work. And yes, it hurts. It hurts to watch my enemies be driven before me and fried to a burnt crisp while I remain youthful and good-looking. Please let me know when we get close to the school."

Cain leaned against the car door and went back to dozing.

***

Gabby was focused, with two hands on the wheel, thinking about Daniel. Three hours is a long time to travel in a car and be alone with your thoughts. Add in the anxiety of knowing a loved one is in danger and it seems as if time and space are actively working against you getting where you want to be. The RX-7's speedometer was edging close to eighty.

Getting to Notre Dame meant they would have a chance at rescuing Daniel. He'd been gone for more than a day at this point. Gabby half-remembered a documentary stating if kidnapping victims weren't located within forty-eight hours, the chance of finding them at all diminishes greatly. At least that's the time limit she thought she remembered. Things were getting fuzzy in her mind as her worry grew. *He's going to be all right. He has to be,* she repeated in her head over and over. *It's my fault he was dragged into this.*

Gabby really did think Cain's plan was brilliant, but her nerves were frazzled. She listened to everything Cain had shared during the car ride, hoping she would pick up something that, interpreted through a modern sensibility, would help their cause. She also was discovering she liked driving fast. You learn something new every day. Even if it's one of the last days. She started putting together a list of pluses and minuses as she drove. Cain was dozing, muttering in a language Gabby didn't recognize. *My life has changed just about as much as it possibly could over the past three days,* she thought. *Better get back to the plan. Go through it one more time, Gabby.*

In their favor: herself—a semi-clairvoyant with meager defense training but a good sense of humor. Also, the oldest and richest man in the world, who apparently had people working for him in every part of the country, perhaps the world. As a plus, he was indestructible, with what had to be the world's best defense-as-an-offense. They were traveling in a thirty-year-old sports car, hunting for Gabby's boyfriend, who had been abducted by a fallen angel and demonic wraiths.

"The situation," she said out loud as they crossed into Indiana, "would be a great indie film if Daniel's life—and all life on the planet—was not at stake."

This plan had better work. Two more hours to go . . .

***

At the first road sign that read "South Bend 50 miles," Gabby started to become more anxious. She was doubting the plan again, although she could not think of a better one. There really wasn't a guidebook to rescuing your boyfriend from fallen angels from Hell. Maybe she could write one when all this was over, she mused.

"Cain, Cain . . . Cain!" she said in an increasingly loud voice. "We're almost there. Come on, time to get to work."

Cain turned over from dozing while facing away from Gabby. "Okay, I am waking up. No need to shout. Are we there?"

"Close enough," Gabby said. "Any updates?"

"Let me check." Cain sat up in the passenger's seat. After a few minutes of reading and typing, he said, "Nothing different that we can see. The satellite imagery puts them in . . . son of a gun. They are in the Center for Religion and Society, of all places. Maybe Razhael does have a sense of humor. For, you know, an angel who lives in Hell.

"Anyway, it seems as if there is a level below the basement. Maybe some space for heating, cooling, electricity and the like. It would definitely would be off-limits to students and just about everyone else. Hanging out in one of the buildings on campus would certainly would give them plenty of cover too. No one is going to bat an eye at Raz or his goons. People probably take them for a professor and maybe some staff."

"Or really out-there students," Gabby interjected. "Those wraiths are not going to blend in. They seem too unpredictable. They did at the monument, anyway."

"Yes, they did," Cain said, nodding his head in agreement as he typed. "But these fellows may be different. Number one, they have Razhael . . . excuse me, Rachel . . . riding herd on them. They are sure to be more in line and focused with him around.

"We can get past them, I am sure. The big prize is, of course, returning Daniel to us safely. If we can get in a shot or two at Rachel, so much the better. Maybe we can learn what they are up to. That would certainly help in planning our moves after this one."

"Hmm," Gabby said. She was on a different train of thought, one that she was choosing not to share yet. She needed time to make sense of it herself first. Plus, she would be relieved and ready to act once she knew Daniel was back safely. Then she could pick back up on the world-saving.

"Okay. And thanks, Cain," Gabby said with genuine concern for the man beside her. "I know you have a lot going on and way more issues to deal with. I appreciate you helping us at the monument, and helping us now. We'd probably be dead if it wasn't for you."

Cain blushed, but just a little. "Thank you, Gabrielle. I feel most alive when I am helpful and have a purpose. Which, after several thousand years, can be a little difficult. We have a purpose and a plan. We rescue Daniel, then get back to figuring out what these goons are up to. As a bonus, let us see what we can discover during our rescue mission. Even beings from Hell have loose lips."

Gabby nodded. Yes, that was the plan. *Fingers crossed that this works. Then I can share with both of these guys what I saw and what I believe is coming.*

***

"Turn in here and look for a Sprinter van. Like you see in film production sometimes," Cain said.

"We really don't hang around the Hollywood crowd, you know," Gabby replied. "It's a big van, though, right?"

"Yes, yes, Gabrielle. They are in use in many places other than Hollywood. Most video projects will have at least one on set. They can store a remarkable amount of equipment when filming on location. Or if you are hunting someone." A moment later, Cain received a text message with directions. "We are almost there. Turn right at the next light, then go down about six or seven blocks. Our team should be parked on the right side of the road a few blocks from campus. We can gather, go over the game plan with everyone, and then move out."

"Cain, do your employees know who you really are? Not just Mr. Green, but . . . you know."

"They do not, and we need to keep it that way," Cain said. "The ones who would not quit instantly would think I am a madman or worse. A few may even believe it, and we definitely do not want that. Please, Gabby, keep it to yourself. When the lightning comes, my staff believe it is because of a prototype electric war suit I am wearing. They have been briefed about it, and the fact the boss likes to get his hands dirty. They are paid well and are professionals—we will not have a problem."

"Sounds good," Gabby said. "Just wondering what happens if the plan goes sideways."

"It is not going to, Gabrielle. Please, trust me. We will have young Daniel back by the early evening. You have my word. Look. There is our van and our team. Let us go say hello and get this party started, as you young people say."

Gabby rolled her eyes, smiled as she got out of the car, and walked toward the Sprinter.

***

Several quasi-military types were inside the van, watching multiple closed circuit video feeds from the Notre Dame campus. The most officious-looking one broke away from the screen when Cain and Gabby knocked and entered through the rear door.

"Mr. Green, it's an honor to be out in the field once again on your behalf," she said. "I'm sorry it's a kidnapping case. Corporate espionage can be terrible. Please give my sympathies to the family."

"Thank you, Commander . . . Pleasants," Cain said mock sheepishly. "I meet so many people sometimes I get confused. My apologies. But mostly, my thanks for helping to find young Daniel. His girlfriend, Gabrielle, is here too. She will be accompanying you on the mission."

"Is that wise, Mr. Green?" the commander said matter-of-factly. "We can't guarantee her safety once we're inside. And she could turn into a liability if things go south."

"I appreciate your concerns, Paula, I truly do," Cain said after a quick peek at his phone to remember his commander's first name. "Gabrielle here is a national park ranger with experience in handling difficult situations like this. She will be fine. If you would please give her an electric rod as well. She is versed in their use." He gave a quick wink to Gabby that was not unnoticed by Commander Pleasants. "Now, when do we leave?"

"We have seven additional people around campus, in addition to our command staff here, waiting for the signal," Commander Pleasants said. "But I do want to ask for the record, are you sure you want to go in alone? Can we at least send two of the team to go in with you? It's very risky, going in solo."

"It will be fine, Paula," Cain said, beginning to grow tired of being questioned. He had fostered open discussion and idea exploration in all of his businesses, and he sometimes regretted it. "I've practiced with the electric vest here," Cain patted his midsection, "and it will work as advertised. It comes with a guarantee." He made another wink toward Gabby.

"I will be the distraction, while your team and Gabby rescue our man. We will be out before lunch time."

"Yes, sir," Commander Pleasants said. "That's the idea. We are ready when you are." Cain nodded back. "Our people are around the building. We haven't picked up any surveillance on the part of our targets, so we should be able to just walk in. If you will walk the few blocks to the entrance, and find the emergency stairwell to the left once you get in, we can spring the electric door on the basement level. We'll be watching you all the way."

"All right," Cain said. "Let us go to work."

***

"Cain, please be careful," Gabby said as they prepared to set out on their rescue mission. Gabby had changed into plain jeans and a button-up shirt to help blend in with the rest of the team and the college students in general. "These guys are scary, and you don't have a tank with you this time."

"I appreciate your concern," Cain said. "But this will go fine. I have done this before but never with so much backup. So, I will change my prediction. This will go more than fine. Daniel will be back with us, and we can continue our mission now that you have more fully embraced your role." He smiled as he laced up his boots and double-checked his retractable bo staff.

"Well, maybe I have," Gabby said. "I will feel much more at ease once Daniel is back. We are kind of a package, you know." She began to grin when she thought about Daniel and how good he had been for her life. He had helped her feel settled and comfortable as they moved into adulthood. They had talked about having children one day when one or both of them had more regular work hours. One of the things Gabby had always appreciated about Daniel was his way with kids. Most kids gravitated toward him naturally. He must exude safety and willingness to listen for kids to pick up on that consistently. *Too bad adults forget how to do that,* she thought. Gabby drew a deep breath, took a moment to appreciate the good thoughts about Daniel and to make a mental note to tell him this when he returned, then stood up. "Let's do this. Daniel needs us."

***

Cain exited first and began his walk toward the Center for Religion and Society. He had a brisk pace and a hoodie pulled over his head in case he ran into any wraiths or anyone working as a spotter along the way. The rest of the team—Gabby, Commander Pleasants, a woman named Katrina, a slightly older man named Matt, and a younger man named Zander—left about five minutes later and took a different path to the building. They all looked too old for college, Gabby thought. And the bulges near their waistlines and the dissembled rifles in their backpacks weren't going to fool anyone for long.

The plan, once it started, would be brief. Gabby had a collapsible electric rod in her sleeve. It had been coded to her fingerprints so only she could wield it. She was thankful for the safety measure and very hopeful she would not need to use it. In her mind, she dubbed the team "The Brat Pack" while envisioning the poster for *The Breakfast Club*. That's how they must look to everyone around them, she thought. Normal enough to a casual observer, but very, very strange if one took the time to look.

She tried to make small talk with Pleasants and the rest of the team, but they seemed reluctant to engage in anything that wasn't focused on the task at hand. Finally, Commander Pleasants spoke. "Ms. Sullivan, it's not that we don't want to talk, but we are about to go into a very dangerous and unpredictable situation—potentially life-threatening. We are mentally preparing ourselves. We can talk when this is over. Please."

"Got it," Gabby said sheepishly. "Sorry. This is my first time."

"Approaching from the south side of the building," Pleasants said into her collar. "The boss is about ready to go into the main door. We are coming up on the maintenance entrance."

Gabby was trying to pay attention to what the commander was saying while watching campus life all around her. She glanced up at one of the nearby buildings and froze. Something at the top looked familiar, and not in a comforting way. It took her a moment or two; then the realization hit her.

"Oh my God. These things are gargoyles!" Gabby said a bit louder than she intended. Then, quieter and to the group: "We keep calling them wraiths, but they are honest-to-goodness, never-thought-I'd-see-the-day gargoyles. Statues of them adorn buildings all over the world. They are taller in real life, but still just as ugly."

The group had paused when Gabby had spoken. They all looked at one another as they absorbed the new revelation. "Sir," Zander said to Pleasants, "our 'plus one' knows the targets are supernatural. Does that change anything in our mission? She's not going to freak out, is she?"

Cain came through on all channels, meaning the entire group could hear him. "That young lady has seen more supernatural occurrences in the past three days than your team has in a lifetime combined. She will be fine. She will do as you ask. If there is a question on how to deal with something out of the ordinary or if Gabby asks you to do something, no matter how unusual it may seem, please follow her lead. She will not let you come to any harm. And she is, quite unwillingly, a bit supernatural herself. She is just coming to grips with it. Be nice, help her, and listen when she talks.

We will all get through this as planned. I promise."

"Yes, sir," replied the commander, a minor bit of annoyance in her voice. "We're approaching our entrance. See you on the inside. Good hunting, sir."

"You too, Commander."

Before they entered the service entrance that would take them to their destination, the group stopped. Matt spoke up. "Gabby, that conversation wasn't really about you. We need to be ready for anything. And the more information we have, the better things will go. Mr. Green is, as you might have noticed, not the most forthcoming boss. That's his right, but it makes our jobs difficult sometimes. We'll do everything we need to do, including protecting you." The rest of the group were gathered around and began to nod in agreement.

Gabby blushed. "I hope I don't need it, but I appreciate it. More than I can say. I didn't ask for any of this, but now I feel like I . . . " She paused, thinking of everything that had happened since the monument. "Well, we—Daniel and I, and now Ca . . . Mr. Green—have to see this through. If I stop and think about it too much, it scares me, to tell you the truth. I'm not going to be very good in a fight, just so you know. I won't run away or anything, and I can defend myself." She was thinking back to self-defense classes during ranger training and the electric rod concealed in her sleeve. "But actively fighting? That's not me. But please, if we can get Daniel back safe and sound, I will owe you all so big and will spend the rest of my life finding ways to say thank you."

Everyone was silent, and a few had lowered their heads. A tear or two graced more than one cheek as Gabby continued. "Those things in there are tough but not invincible. Don't try a crotch shot either. That doesn't work. Brute force, maybe more than you've ever used before, and electric will be just fine. Just . . . don't hold back at the beginning. I don't think they will give us any second chances."

"Thanks, Gabby," Commander Pleasants said. "We know the risks, and we're ready. It's good to know your stake in this too. We're gonna get in there and make some gargoyles bleed." She then radioed back to the van to have the door opened for them remotely. It clicked. Matt, who seemed to be second-in-command, pulled it open as the group quickly entered. "Now, let's find Daniel and the boss before he does all of this by himself, and we have to listen to the constant bragging."

***

Cain walked in the front doors of the center, his hoodie still up. "You have to show your face when coming inside, young ma . . . uh, sir," said the clerk near the entrance. "It's a requirement."

"Very well," Cain said. "We do not want to upset Big Brother, do we?" Cain grinned as he said it, but inside he regretted losing what little cover he had. His opponents surely now would know he was coming for them. Cain hoped they remained focused on him and not the other team making its way inside from the other side of the building. It would give them a much better chance of winnowing the herd of their enemies and getting Daniel back safely.

Cain found the stairwell he needed and began his descent. No word from the command center or the other team since the revelation that Gabby carried a touch of the supernatural with her. *I hope they are not distancing themselves from her,* he thought. That was highly unlikely, though. They were trained professionals, and Gabby was one of the most likable people he had ever met, visions or not. She did not deserve what was in front of her. Neither did Daniel. But people usually rise to the occasion despite the difficulties. This was one of the everyday miracles that made Cain happy to be alive and hopeful about their chances against Razhael and his forces.

At the bottom landing, Cain found the door unlocked. He stepped through and was faced with a long, tan corridor with several doors on either side. There were many places for people to hide down there, Cain thought. This may be a little trickier than he planned.

He made his way down the hallway, listening for any signs of life. The map his team had shown in the van put their targets near the back of the building. This was fortunate because the other team would not have to venture far once they were inside. The downside was that Cain would have to make up that distance and face any obstacles in the way.

Why hadn't Razhael placed his captive in the center of the building or in a more defensible location? *That can't be good,* Cain thought. Something else was going on with this kidnapping but Cain could not deduce what it was. There were precious few clues, and they were extraordinarily lucky to have found Daniel through satellite and drone imagery. Maybe Razhael had gotten sloppy or was extremely behind on modern technology. Either would be a blessing to their team. Coupled with Gabby's abilities and his team's training, Cain believed it almost gave them an even chance of coming out on top. *One battle at a time, old man,* he thought as he moved down the hallway, listening for signs of life. He didn't hear any.

Near the end of the hall, Cain paused to check in with his team. He spoke into a microphone in his collar. "They are in here, correct? I have been to nearly every door and there are no signs. No voices, no heartbeats, no . . .

"Wait one moment. I may have something. Voices, but almost low and whispering at the very end of the hall. Four doors down on the left. Everything else has been storage or maintenance. That has to be them, right?"

Cain listened to the response, then nodded. "Yes. Thank you. I will be careful. And the others are in place close by? They can be here how quickly? . . . Okay, I will. Please stay on the channel in case something goes awry, Zander. We will see you soon."

After finishing the conversation, Cain extended his electric staff, switched it on, and walked to the door Zander had indicated. He drew a breath, grasped the door handle, and prepared for the worst. He hoped Daniel had not been tortured, but Cain thought the odds were against it.

He had rarely been more wrong.

CHAPTER 21: BREAKOUT

Cain stepped into the room, letting his vision adjust to the dim lighting. He was expecting a storage room with a gang of wraiths, and Daniel tied up somewhere out of reach. Instead, the room looked very much like a slightly upscale college efficiency apartment, complete with a small kitchen area, a decent-sized couch, and a mammoth flat-screen TV. Daniel sat on the couch watching the late 1960s Japanese show *Johnny Sokko and His Flying Robot* with a woman who appeared to be in her late twenties to early thirties sitting very close to him, hanging on his every word. She had red hair.

"You see," Daniel said, "this show was so far ahead of its time with the use of miniatures and models. It helped kick-start the manga movement . . ."

The woman was listening intently. If Cain did not know better and the circumstances were very different, he would swear they were on a date. Daniel had been gone less than forty-eight hours—how had he become so comfortable so quickly? He must have been hypnotized, or they were giving him very powerful drugs. Cain hadn't known the boy long, but he seemed very committed to Gabby. Maybe he was feigning interest and being a model prisoner while waiting patiently for an opportunity to escape or awaiting rescue. That must be it, Cain thought. Or this was one of the fastest cases of Stockholm syndrome he'd ever seen.

Cain moved as quietly as he could through the storeroom/makeshift apartment. There was about 100 feet of open space between the door and the living area. *Looks like the set of a television sitcom,* Cain thought. Why go to all the trouble to abduct Daniel, then treat him like this? A happy prisoner can be more compliant. *Maybe that's what they were going for,* Cain thought. But that would be a first for these vicious angels.

As the couple continued their conversation, Cain made his way silently along a wall until he was within about ten feet of Daniel and the redhead. The couple still was entranced with the show. Daniel was talking about the subtle differences in the actors who played the Flying Robot, and the red-headed stranger was hanging on his every word.

This must be a set-up or this lady is getting paid a small fortune, Cain thought. No one cared this much about old television shows. Even ones with giant robots, which Cain had to admit was pretty interesting. Just not as interesting as Daniel and this unknown woman thought they were.

Since no wraiths were present, Cain would incapacitate the woman and allow Daniel to more easily escape his imprisonment. Cain moved slowly and stealthily, thankful for his time in feudal Japan, where he learned the art of moving slowly and undetected, among other things. The 1600s had been a great century, and still was remarkably relevant and helpful in the modern age, he thought.

Cain moved closer and prepared to strike the woman with a shock from his staff when she suddenly turned her head and said casually, "We wondered when you would show up, old man," with a smile that was anything but friendly.

Daniel turned around, saw Cain, and seemed happy to see his newfound friend.

"Here I am, lady," Cain said defiantly. "There is nothing to stop us from leaving. Daniel, let us get out of here. Now."

"Cain, what are you doing here?" Daniel said.

Daniel surely must be drugged, Cain thought. His reaction time was slow and he was acting dopey. Cain was improvising—he had planned to take on the wraiths while the others rescued Daniel. He had not foreseen a scenario where Daniel would be reluctant to leave. He also did not want to tip his hand that a squad of experienced search-and-rescue professionals, plus one anxious girlfriend, were waiting nearby for his signal. *Think, old man, think.*

Should he tase the girl and beat it, and hope Daniel went along, or should he tase them both and carry the boy out of there? Decisions, decisions. Why were things never easy? Cain mused on the fact that his infamous curse might not be the only thing he carried with him today.

"Good to see you, Daniel. Let us get out of here before the goon squad comes in and things get violent."

"Oh, it's too late for that, firstborn," the redhead said, standing to face Cain with the couch and Daniel in between them. "We've been expecting you, and I'd hate for you to leave before we get a chance to know each other." As she spoke, she picked up a large, high-tech-looking device that had been tucked in beside her on the couch. She raised it suddenly and aimed it in Cain's direction.

A green mist shot out, surrounded Cain, and hung in the air. Cain began to feel woozy and expected to see a flash of lightning any time. But it didn't come, and his legs were becoming rubbery as he struggled to stay standing. He had never felt this feeling before.

"Anesthetic gas, in case you're wondering," the redhead said. "We've had some time and brain power working on how to take you off the board, little man. And we've found it. Physical attacks will get us fried. But chemical attacks? They put you to sleep or deprive you of oxygen just like the rest of us. Chemical warfare. Who would have thought going further and thoroughly modern would be the key to taking you down, all without laying a finger on you? Certainly not Razhael and his little helpers. But they will do their jobs well enough. Not only can we injure the masses more easily, but best of all, we can hurt you without engaging your little party trick."

She moved closer to Cain as he fell to his knees, gasping for breath. Drawing back her leg as if to kick Cain as he crawled on the floor, she feigned a kick and stopped short of striking him, then let out a long laugh. Cain was trying to put some space between him and the redhead. He managed to click a button on his watch, sending a signal for help. He hoped Pleasants' team was close by so they could even the odds a bit.

***

Daniel remained on the couch, watching with morbid fascination as his captor walked around the gasping Cain. He shifted so he could see Cain better, and momentarily thought about helping him. But the redhead waved him back. "He's not your friend, Daniel. He never was. He used you to get what he wants."

"Which is what, Lorelei?" Daniel said. "You said he was dangerous and delusional, but this looks like he was telling the truth. Why are you doing this?"

"He's been trying to separate you from Gabrielle since the beginning," the redhead said with a slight sneer, walking toward Cain. "Think about all you told me. He believes she's some divine last-ditch effort at stopping Armageddon. But really, what has she done? Guessed at a few things, and she was at the scene of the stupid attack from Razhael's little helpers. That's it. He's filling her head with lies and delusions of grandeur so he can take her away. From her life. And from you."

"That's not Gabby," Daniel said. "Not at all. We've been together a long time. I've met her parents and everything. We live together, for Heaven's sake. She's as true blue as they come. I don't know a lot, but I do know Gabby."

"You think you know her," Lorelei said. "But the last few days, since the Monument, how much of a comfort to you has she been? Has she been there for you, or has she just dragged you around on a goose chase, and now this fool's errand?"

"Look, Lorelei, I appreciate you helping me out during this and being a pretty good caretaker considering I was kidnapped," Daniel said. "But you're wrong. Why are you hurting this old guy all of a sudden? I thought you were just here to keep an eye on me? Are you telling me you're a part of all of this too?"

"More than you know, sweet Daniel," she said. "We've gotten to know each other a bit, but there's a lot more to know and see and . . . do. If you're willing." She smiled at him with her best come-on look. It touched something deep and buried within Daniel. The feeling of being wanted and desired that he felt had passed him by in his younger years. Lorelei was a statuesque beauty—about five-foot-ten, Daniel estimated, with flowing red hair, blue eyes, and a body that seemed to be very fit. She was the kind of girl who Daniel thought wouldn't have given him the time of day in high school. Or college. Or afterward, for that matter. He had soaked in all of the attention from her moments after his abduction, when he met her in the van back in Maryland. The wraiths had skittered about until Razhael gave them their marching orders. Lorelei slid close to him until their shoulders were touching. "We'll be okay if we just listen and do what they ask. Please. I'm sorry for the rough treatment, but I have to talk with you one-on-one."

One wraith climbed in the driver's seat and another rode in the passenger seat for security while the rest were to walk to an undisclosed location. Daniel had caught most of the conversation, but he had missed the part about where they were headed. Once in the makeshift apartment, he could hear a few wraiths nearby but never saw them. Once or twice, he thought he heard Razhael just outside the doors.

Now, with Cain crawling across the floor after being hit with anesthetic gas, Daniel had a choice. Stay with this beautiful woman who hung on his every word or try to make it back to Gabby and their improbable mission. It wasn't as easy a decision as Daniel thought it might be.

He hesitated for a moment, lost in thoughts he never had experienced. His mind wandered with strange visions of his own that were equal parts unsettling and comforting. He was in charge; he was looked up to. Lorelei was at his side as throngs cheered him on. People listened to what he had to say. He was in front of a large crowd. In his mind, it looked like Red Rocks Amphitheater. He had never visited it, but he had watched several concerts filmed at the iconic location. To Daniel, that was the same as being there. As he moved up the podium, throngs of people cheered and shouted his name. "Dan-yell! Dan-yell! Dan-yell!" Lorelei stood behind him to his left, smiling like a politician's wife. Daniel walked up the podium to begin . . .

Then, he snapped out of his reverie and once more saw his new friend struggling to crawl along the unfinished floor. Lorelei was staying a few steps behind, taunting him. Daniel leapt over the couch and ran toward Cain. He pushed Lorelei out of the way as he took a big breath, scooped up Cain, and made for the back door of the storeroom apartment. Cain was groaning, fighting to regain consciousness as Daniel kicked open the door and began to look for a way out.

Daniel heard activity around the corner and proceeded as slowly as he could while carrying his semi-conscious friend. He walked slowly and quietly, and in his mind—very similar to the speech he had imagined a few moments before—he was doing pretty good. *I'm super quiet,* he thought. *We can avoid the wraiths and get the heck out of here.*

He peeked around the corner and was met at eye level with the tip of a semi-automatic rifle.

CHAPTER 22: LINES IN THE SAND

"Daniel!" Gabby said excitedly from the rear of the would-be college group. She gestured for the commander to lower her rifle.

Paula did so slowly with a slightly dissatisfied look and murmured into her collar microphone, "Everyone stand down for a moment. Our two assets are out and mobile. Stay alert for the others, though."

Gabby bounded forward.

"We've been looking for you. Cain was supposed to tell us when to come in, but "

"It's okay," Daniel said. "I have him. He's much heavier than he looks. He has to be close to two hundred pounds. We ran into a little trouble. Let's get out of here." Two of the team stepped forward to take Cain, who still was groggy and talking semi-coherently. Once Daniel was free, Gabby wrapped her arms around him and hugged him tightly. He hugged her back, but with not quite as much as fervor. "Thanks for coming for me. It was . . . rough."

"I can't imagine, Daniel," Gabby said. "We got you back in two days, but it seems so much longer. How are you? You look . . . well, you look great. Much better than I had feared. Did they hurt you?"

"No, I'm okay. They didn't hurt me. They drove me here and put me in an apartment back there." Daniel gestured behind him. "They fed me and gave me a television. I had a guard but that was . . . it was okay. I have no idea why they took me. Do you?"

"We think—or really it's Cai . . . Mr. Green—Mr. Green thinks they did it to distract us and try to scare us off the mission of stopping Armageddon but it didn't work," Gabby said breathlessly. She was relieved to have Daniel back but also was worried about what could have rendered Cain unconscious. "Anyway, mission accomplished. Let's beat feet and get out of here before some of those goons show up. Also, I think I figured out what they really are. I'll tell you later on."

"They aren't around much," Daniel said. "I think most of them were sent elsewhere. Don't have any idea where, though. They didn't tell me a lot, but I did hear a lot of talk outside the door. I would hear Razhael a good bit, but I never saw him after we arrived. I haven't heard him for about a day or so. It was late last night, maybe around ten, when *Andy Griffith* was coming on . . . " Daniel said.

"You've been watching television?" Gabby asked.

Daniel froze, afraid she was going to give him a lecture about not trying to escape. If that happened, he would end up telling her about the redhead before he was ready. She had already had a vision about her, and he was more than a little nervous to talk about her. Gabby would be mad, and she would probably be really mad if she found out how cozy he and Lorelei had become in a very short time.

"Yes, a little," he said. "I couldn't go anywhere and had a guard. They did give me something to do, which kept me occupied and gave me time to think of how to escape." Daniel regretted this little white lie. Once he was in the apartment with Lorelei, the notion of escape mostly retreated to the back of his mind. He hoped he didn't have to elaborate further. The more he thought about his behavior, the more shame crept into his mind. *I should have tried something,* he thought.

"We're here now, and we have our person. Let's return to base," Commander Pleasants interjected. Daniel was happy for the renewed focus on getting away from his temporary prison (and new friend and apartment, he thought just a little more thankfully). "We'll navigate out of the building, stow our weapons, and make our way back to base."

Gabby stood up straight and gripped her weapon. "Yes, Commander. You're right. We can talk when we're all back safe and sound, and Mr. Green is on the mend. Thank you."

The group turned and began to move through the maze of corridors that brought it to this destination. The plan was to exit the building where everyone had entered, concealing their weapons before they emerged back into the open. With their weapons stowed away, they would be vulnerable, but it was a calculated risk. They would have access to the electrical weapons if needed but not the guns.

They needed to leave the building as quickly as possible while avoiding any engagements with the wraiths or anyone who might be working with them. They would walk the several blocks to the van and get medical attention for Mr. Green.

"We need to get moving," Commander Pleasants said. "The more time we give our adversaries to realize what's going on, the harder this will be. I want to be well out of town in the next twenty minutes. Everyone ready?"

The soldiers plus Gabby and Daniel all nodded and murmured their agreement. Cain groaned and managed a very slight tilt of his head. "All right, here's the exit," Pleasants said. "Time to switch back to college mode." Rifles quickly were disassembled and stowed in backpacks along with handguns. Electrical rods were collapsed and tucked in sleeves, ready to spring out at a moment's notice. They would be the only defense available to everyone on the walk to the Sprinter. "Let's finish this job."

Pleasants opened the door and started the walk out. The door was on the service entrance side of the building, so not many students or bystanders would be around. The group, however, was met immediately by nearly twenty wraiths dressed as college students. They had surrounded the exit, creating a deadly choke point.

Pleasants took a defensive stance, and the rest of the group did the same. Daniel took Cain off the hands of the soldier who had been carrying him, thinking it would be better if the soldier fought while Daniel protected Cain, and he and Gabby could stay in the back.

Gabby, though, already had extended her electrical staff and walked forward to stand just behind the commander. She led with her left leg and, for a novice, looked surprisingly ready to fight. She looked over at Commander Pleasants, who was giving her the side-eye while smiling. "We watch a lot of kung fu movies. You pick stuff up," Gabby said. "At least, I hope I did."

"Good enough for me," the commander said. "Let's knock these guys down a peg or two. You don't come into the boss' house and kidnap his guests. It's not polite."

The gargoyles stirred around as if waiting for a command. After the

Washington Monument encounter, Gabby had suspected they were not very bright. This second run-in confirmed that, and it all lined up with what Cain had mentioned at their initial meeting. These creatures were cannon fodder. Foot soldiers, nearly mindless and extremely susceptible to coercion and a strong-willed leader. If this many gargoyles were around, Razhael or someone like him must be close by.

Pleasants took an exploratory jab at the shoulder of one of the creatures near the front. It howled in pain and swatted at the crackling electric staff, but it did not advance or retaliate.

The small tactical group all were seasoned fighters, but a wave of nervousness was palpable. They had rarely encountered supernatural beings, and they never had seen this many at once. They all gripped their electrical staffs. Commander Pleasants had made it clear in the mission prep that the rifles were to stay stowed away at nearly all costs. They would signal for backup long before a gun was used openly on a college campus—or nearly anywhere else, for that matter. This had been one of the few lines in the sand Mr. Green had laid out for the group and their latest mission. Inside the building and only if necessary, and never out in the open. The electric rods had proven effective against foes far greater than these. It would be more difficult, but it still would be much, much quieter and far less messy.

As the groups eyed each other and waited for someone to make the first move, Daniel came trudging around the tactical group, still carrying the semi-conscious Cain. He nudged his way in front of Commander Pleasants.

"Let me try first," Daniel said as Gabby watched in wide-eyed disbelief. Daniel was many things, but brave in a fight was not one of them. At least, that's what she always had thought. But now, in front of her was Daniel, preparing to walk unarmed and carrying an unconscious immortal through a group of supernatural predators. It was one of the most amazing things she had seen in the past few days, which was saying a lot considering everything she and Daniel had experienced since the incident at the Washington Monument.

Daniel advanced slowly, Cain mumbling in his induced sleep. Gabby, Commander Pleasants, and the rest of the team were ready to strike at the first sign of violence, but the gargoyles remained in place. They did not move out of the way, but they did not impede Daniel's progress either. He made his way through the small crowd, bumping into a few gargoyles on purpose, usually with Cain's limp body. The first few, surprisingly, took the jostling and didn't react. When Daniel went to pass his fifth gargoyle, who was still standing in an attack position, the creature broke ranks and struck out at Daniel. It grazed Cain's shoulder, however. Storm clouds and thunder suddenly began to roil overhead, followed by a swift streak of lightning to the chest of the erstwhile attacker, frying him where he stood. Daniel stepped over the smoking corpse, still cradling the unconscious Cain, and kept walking.

When the gargoyles moved out of the way, they did not fill back in the space. Commander Pleasants saw the opportunity and took it. "Everyone, move single file and very tightly behind the boy. Stay within kissing distance of your teammates, but don't touch anybody, least of all our ugly friends here. Follow Daniel's lead. We may make it out of this unscathed if we all stay calm and keep our heads on straight."

Daniel continued to walk slowly through the strange gathering. He picked his way carefully around the stationary gargoyles, who snarled and gnashed their teeth but did not strike Daniel or his charge. They treated the passing paramilitary group and Gabby with the same deference. It was obvious they did not like it, but some unseen force or instruction kept them from lashing out.

Near the end of the group, as Daniel made his way past the last two gargoyles, one attempted to stop Daniel's passage by edging closer to him, daring him to stop. Daniel kept walking but inadvertently stumbled on this last gargoyle's errant foot. Daniel tripped and ended up losing his grip on Cain's body. Cain tumbled to ground with a loud *thwack,* followed by an equally loud crack of lightning that incinerated the trip-causing gargoyle where it stood.

"Two down, you dopes," Daniel said, brushing himself off and picking up the old man once more. The rest of the group made their way through the stationary gargoyles, who were very obviously annoyed by their two brothers being fried and not being allowed to do anything about it. Gabby counted herself and the group fortunate to be leaving with everyone they arrived with uninjured, and with Daniel safe and sound.

The walk back to the Sprinter was deliberate, fast, and quiet. If Gabby didn't know any better, she would think the group was in mild shock. She didn't entirely understand why everyone was so serious. They had achieved all their objectives. Yes, Cain was down. But if any of them could recover from an injury, it would be him. Gabby wondered when the last time Cain had sustained an injury was. Could he even be injured? Whatever they did to him in there must have been intense. She was eager to get to safety and hear the story.

***

Back at the building exit, the gargoyles were just beginning to stir again. A few of them kicked at the remains of their burnt companions. The husks came apart like well-burnt cinders in a fireplace, drifting off into the morning sun in this hidden corner of campus. The door opened and the gargoyles tensed up, ready to stop or injure the unlucky soul who was going to walk out into their brood.

It was Lorelei. The gargoyles froze and lowered their heads as she walked past slowly, her hand gently caressing the heads of several of the creatures. "I am sorry to see two of your brothers are gone," she said. "They will pay for this affront, and it changes nothing about the plan. In fact, we are going to move things along a bit more quickly now. We'll be leaving within the hour. Go inside and remove and destroy all evidence we were here. And gentlemen, please do it quietly. No more attention today."

The gargoyles started moving about and headed inside. Lorelei watched Daniel, Gabby, and their group walk to the north, heading off campus to what they presumed was safety. She knew better, though. Soon there would be no safe place on Earth for them. Or anyone. As she turned to walk back inside, she whispered aloud, "See you again soon . . . brother."

CHAPTER 23: EXIT . . . STAGE WEST

Back in the Sprinter, everyone slumped down for a post-rescue breather. The adrenaline was wearing off and several of the team were tired and hungry. Cain was coming to enough to make a bit of sense to anyone listening. When he spoke, all of his employees grew silent as they tried to hear what he was saying.

Gabby and Daniel quietly had talked on the way back that Cain's secret was not theirs to tell, but it might be a little problematic explaining two lightning strikes on demand to seasoned fighters with experience in the supernatural. If any of these professional warriors would deduce their boss' true nature, neither was sure what their responses would be. Cain was on a stretcher in the middle of the van. He had an IV drip of saline in his arm. Gabby had wondered if a needlestick would trigger the curse, but there was nothing but clear blue sky above when the team medic deftly inserted a needle in Cain's arm and started the IV. What was it that Cain had told them that first night? That intent was a factor? A needle in the arm trying to help the man was pretty safe.

"Where are we headed?" Gabby shouted up to the driver, an even-keeled man named Gerald who had remained behind during the mission so he could help run logistics. He leaned his head back and glanced back over his right shoulder. "Not supposed to share that info just yet, ma'am," he said matter-of-factly. "Boss' orders, in case anyone was compromised during the mission. Can't spill what you don't know. Until he wakes up and gives the all-clear, I can't share that. But you'll like it."

"How long will it take to reach this mystery destination that you're sure I'll like, Gerald?" Gabby shot back with a bit more sass in her tone than intended. "If you can tell us, that is. And it's not too secret squirrel for everyone."

Gerald grinned. Like most people, he found Gabby likable and easy to talk to. The jury was still out on Daniel, though. He seemed nice enough, but he was fairly quiet and more reserved. They seemed like an odd pair. Daniel was probably not hiding too much behind that nerd exterior, but there was a little something there that was unpredictable, and therefore dangerous. Gerald wrote it off mostly to nerves after he had been kidnapped. He had seen people come back from similar experiences in much worse shape. Daniel, he decided, was lucky and probably still in mild shock.

"West, young lady," Gerald said with a wide grin on his face. "We are headed out west. More than that, I cannot say. Try to get some rest. We'll be driving for a while."

***

Most of the passengers dozed while traveling. Two were reading, saying they could not sleep in the car. Daniel thought that was one of the strangest things he'd ever heard, but he took it at face value. *Everyone is a little different,* he thought. Gabby slept on Daniel's shoulder while he struggled to sleep, his mind racing.

What if I did the wrong thing? Daniel wondered. *What if Lorelei is on the good side, and Cain is on the bad one? How would I know? What would Gabby think?* If only he could ask her without letting on how much he enjoyed the company of the incredibly attractive redhead. Best to stay quiet about it and see what happened, he decided. He already felt as if he had cheated on Gabby, even though it was just two days and Lorelei never did more than sit close to him and rub his leg. *That's not bad,* Daniel kept telling himself. Plus, he was a prisoner. What was he supposed to do? Scream and fight the whole time? He'd tried to be a model prisoner so nothing worse would happen. *And you know what? It worked.*

But the memory of Lorelei stayed with him, much more than he thought it would. He hoped it would fade with time.

***

The van raced through the night with only two stops to refuel and change drivers. Far west of the Mississippi, the sun came over the horizon behind them. Some of the passengers began to stir, including Cain, who had been set upright and strapped to a chair as whatever had incapacitated him wore off. Commander Pleasants had guessed he had been gassed with an anesthetic, which was supported by the team's medic. As a precaution, she had monitored Cain's vital signs throughout the night. She also had taken a swab of saliva from the sleeping man for testing later.

"Where are we, and what has happened?" Cain said.

The commander looked up from her book and said, "We are about halfway through Missouri, sir. How are you feeling? You had a rough day yesterday, but the mission was a success."

Cain smiled at this, and glanced around the van as best he could. "Will someone please get me out of this contraption so I may move like a normal man?"

The commander slid over toward him and loosened the straps holding Cain upright in his seat. "Doctor's orders, sir. We didn't want you sliding all over the place and hurting yourself."

Cain grinned and thanked the commander for her help. He stretched his arms and legs, rotating his wrists and moving his neck from side to side as much as he could.

"How are you feeling, sir? You had quite an adventure, but we were successful. Thanks in large part to aid from our would-be rescuee," Pleasants said, nodding in Daniel's direction. "He carried you out and managed to activate your electric vest in the middle of a dozen of those . . . things. It was spectacular, given that they are not really human. Then once Daniel began walking through them and zapped two of them, they all stopped and let us through without a hitch. I've never seen anything like it, and I really wouldn't want to. Too much adrenaline and excitement for an aging soldier."

"Well, thank you for your service once again, Commander. And thank you to everyone as well. And apparently an extra thank-you to you, Daniel," Cain said, turning to face Daniel fully and look into his eyes. "I did not know you had that in you. I am impressed." Cain was smiling with genuine admiration as Daniel looked down and began to shuffle his feet in place.

"Thanks," Daniel said. He had noticed no one in the group called their boss Cain, and Daniel didn't see any reason to share that knowledge. He wondered if some of them already suspected there was something very different about their employer. "And thank you for coming to get me. I wouldn't have made it out without everyone."

"Any time, Daniel," Cain said. "Those of us on the good side have to stick together, right? And we have a job to do."

This last statement made Daniel a little uneasy. "Uh, sure. A job for the good side. Sticking together and all that. That's what we're doing."

Cain looked at Daniel seriously for a moment as if he might either hug him or shock him with one of the nearby staffs. Then he burst out into a wide grin. "The boy is in shock from his ordeal. We need to properly see to his health, both mentally and physically. They are equally important. Although I would not have minded being kept captive with such an entrancing redhead, if you know what I mean." Cain laughed heartily at this, as did most of the soldiers in the vehicle. Daniel shrunk down in his seat a bit. Gabby stared ahead in disbelief before slowly turning to Daniel.

"Excuse me," she said. "What did you say? A redhead? Like in my vision that you both knew about?"

"Why yes, Gabrielle," Cain said. "I suppose that is correct. In the heat of the moment and my unexpected incapacitation, that fact slipped my mind. Bravo to you for staying up on things when no one else is. That is how we are going to win this war."

"Yes, I guess so," Gabrielle replied with enough sarcasm to fill the van and then some. "It's how someone is going to win something."

Daniel continued to look down, deeply embarrassed. "Sorry, Gabby. I was so happy to get out of there and then actually help toward the end, I hadn't really thought of that. Sorry . . . "

Gabby continued to glare at Daniel for a moment; then she softened her gaze. She nestled in beside him and stroked his hair softly. "That's okay. You went through a lot. I'm sure being kidnapped is terrible. Like Ca . . . Mr. Green said, you need a good doctor. Hopefully, we can find one soon."

"That we will, Gabby," Cain said. "That we will. But probably not until we are west of Texas. We need to put some miles between us and our adversaries. We need to ensure the safety of everyone we can. I am increasingly distressed at the creativity of Razhael and his goons. They have never before shown such creativity or adaptation. This is new, which is terrifying when you consider who we are up against. We need to plan our next moves. Quickly and correctly."

CHAPTER 24: POST-MIDWEST DISTRESS

After driving for more than twenty-four hours with very few stops and occasional changes in drivers, the van and its weary passengers stopped at a mom-and-pop hotel several miles away from the interstate called The Sagebrush Shareaton. The last part of the name was misspelled on purpose, so potential guests would get the joke but different enough to keep any corporate types away. Daniel let out a small "ha" when they pulled into the dirt and gravel parking lot.

"Do not worry," Cain said. "I do not own this one, and they are much less likely to find us off the beaten path. Plus, we have discreet security stationed throughout the area now."

"And that worked so well in Maryland," Gabby said, still nursing a grudge about the fact Daniel kept something vital from her. She was relieved to have him back, but deceit had never been a big part of Daniel's life. "He's too honest for his own good," she heard his mother say on one of his parents' infrequent visits to the East Coast. Why was he different now? What happened to him when he was abducted? Could he have been turned against them—or her—in that short amount of time?

Surely Daniel's faith helped him through. It wasn't for Gabby, but she knew how much it meant to him. For the first time in years, Gabby couldn't read him. She normally could decipher his tics and facial expressions. He smiled when he was really nervous and furrowed his brow too much when he was deep in thought. But his demeanor since being rescued was puzzling. Gabby thought he still might be in shock. Who wouldn't be rattled after going through such an ordeal?

Commander Pleasants distributed keys to everyone. They all had rooms next to each other on the three-story building's top floor. The commander explained it made good defensible sense, plus she said they had extra protection nearby keeping a watch out. Most of the team shared rooms.

As she handed a key to Gabby, Pleasants said, "Two to a room is safer, and gives everyone a good sense of not being alone after a tough experience. You two will be in the middle section of rooms, so you'll be surrounded by us. We'll be resting, but we'll also be ready to move quickly if needed. Everyone will be safe for the night."

Gabby thanked the commander and began to walk up the stairs. "You coming, Daniel?" she said, glancing over her shoulder.

Daniel hesitated for a moment. "Yeah, I'll be there. I'd like to hit the vending machines for a nighttime snack. Room 306, right? I'll be there in a few minutes."

"Okay," Gabby said, thinking this was a little odd. He was not usually an evening snacker. At times Gabby thought Daniel might be a little OCD.

She'd had a discussion about this during a recent lull in visits at the Monument. Gabby was working at the top of the Monument with Louise, a fellow ranger and her supervisor. Their discussion veered into obsessive compulsive disorder and family members. Gabby liked Louise, even though they were almost always at opposite ends of most issues. They both were agreeable about it, though, for which Gabby was thankful. Gabby mentioned her theory about Daniel and asked what Louise thought about it.

Louise said, as she understood it, either someone had OCD or they didn't. A nephew of hers had been exhibiting signs of OCD, and the boy's parents had him evaluated. After a lengthy interview with the boy, then another with the parents separately, the physician gave a diagnosis of OCD. The parents were equal parts shocked and relieved, and they asked what they could do for their son. The doctor said to give him space and to not bring attention to his issue. It was something to live with and understand, not cure. The doctor said he would be fine.

Gabby asked, "If you don't mind, can you tell me what kind of things happen? Does it affect every part of his life or just certain things?"

"He likes to put the pens in the house in order by color, and I think by size too," Louise said. "My sister said they could never find any pens in the house. She and her husband thought they were throwing them away and would buy more. When those disappeared, they asked their kids if anyone had a pen. Their daughter said that she didn't. Their son said he had a small collection in his bookcase in his room. When they went to look, there were about three hundred pens lined up on one of the shelves, as neat and orderly as could be. Her husband got mad at first because he thought Matthew was stealing them—oh, darn it. I said his name. Well, you would have figured it out anyway, Gabby. You know I have just the one sister.

"Anyway, Robert, Mathalia's husband, got mad and grounded him. Matthew didn't understand why and said anyone could come in his room and get a pen when they needed one. He would be happy to get it and put it back in order. He said it made him happy. Robert kind of calmed down a little after that. Mathalia made a doctor's appointment for Matthew, first with his pediatrician, then a psychiatrist who works with kids. He's the one who made the diagnosis."

Gabby was listening and nodding attentively when Louise was speaking. She'd never heard Louise share so much personal information. When she finished, Gabby said, "Wow. Thanks for sharing that, Louise. I'm glad your family was able to get a diagnosis. That probably was a relief."

"Yeah, kind of," Louise said. "Robert still gets a little annoyed at never being able to find a pen, but otherwise it's fine. Matthew doesn't organize pens at school, thankfully."

Gabby felt a small pang of regret at mentioning Daniel possibly having OCD, but she still believed he had a touch of it. OCD *lite,* she thought to herself. He did a lot of things the same way and often, but he wasn't completely fixed on it. He almost always made the bed, for instance, but there were a few days here and there when he didn't. The same with weighing himself, grocery shopping, and complaining about bad drivers. He usually did all these things, but not always. He was just flexible enough to not seem like he had OCD.

Louise said she didn't think there was middle ground for a medical diagnosis, and she still agreed that Daniel might have OCD. She thought it was great Gabby recognized it and wanted to help him. Gabby smiled and thanked Louise as they got back to work.

Gabby still thought Daniel, the love of her life, had OCD lite and that she loved him no matter what. All of this reverie made her more interested to see exactly what Daniel would bring from the vending machines. Maybe this was how he was coping with the abduction.

Daniel was chipper and humming a hymn as he came into the room. He had a smile on his face and seemed energized. "Hi, sweetheart," he said as he jumped a bit and landed on the bed with a mild thud. "Want some snacks?" Daniel had brought several packages from the vending machine: potato chips, candy bars, and a few sodas. Daniel was usually a healthy eater. He occasionally would indulge in a small dessert when he and Gabby were dining out, but it was rare. And he never finished when he ordered one. This trove of junk food, Gabby thought, was very out of character.

"No thanks," Gabby said. "I'm still full from the early dinner we had in the van. I will grab a water, though. Are you, umm, going to eat all that by yourself?"

"No, no. A little bit tonight and some in the morning. I have a sudden craving for sugar, I guess. I know it's not usually my thing, but with all this excitement lately, I feel a little sluggish. I'd like to perk up a bit."

"That would do it. And maybe send your cholesterol and blood pressure off the charts too." Gabby smiled as she said it, and knew she still sounded as if she was getting on him a bit for his eating choices.

"It's okay," Daniel said. "Today is a good day to celebrate, and this is all I could find. So here it is."

"What are we celebrating? Your rescue or the end of your healthy streak? Either would be fine with me. I'm still so happy we got you out of there. It was frightening to think about you being in danger and maybe . . . you know, losing you."

"We're celebrating us being on this adventure together," Daniel said. "I know that sounds weird, but even being kidnapped, interrogated by demons, being rescued by Cain and you, then having to rescue Cain, driving across the country with the A-Team, on the run from the bad guys and . . . "

"Daniel, please stop for a moment. I'm getting a headache from all of this. I don't think it's another vision, though. I think I just need to eat some real food and get some rest. Let's see if we can order something for delivery."

Daniel was unfazed. "Really? Okay. Sorry about your head. Can I get you anything to help? Delivery is fine if that's what you want, but I'm going to start on these things now. I'm starving."

Gabby was beginning to get annoyed. "Forget the food for a minute, Daniel. Were you going to tell me? A very specific part of my vision came true—one that involves you—and you didn't tell me? Were you ever going to tell me?"

"Yes, Gabby. I just got back from being kidnapped by freaking demons and a fallen angel, and I'm having a little trouble adjusting. Things are kind of messed up in my head. Thoughts that . . . I'm having strange thoughts. I'm remembering strange dreams from when I was a kid. I'm sorry for not telling you. Really. To tell you the truth, that thought didn't even hit me until Cain was talking in the van. Then I realized what a dunce I am. And I'm starving and I know this stuff is bad for you, but tonight I don't care. I'm so damned happy to be free and back with you and not being watched by . . . whatever those things are. They're creepy, Gabby. And I was . . . "

"You were what?" Gabby asked. "Trying to escape? Happy to be taken care of? What exactly was going through your mind under that dark brown mop of hair that you can't even tell me?"

"Gabby, no. It's not like that at all." Daniel was fumbling for words. The evening was not going as he hoped. "It wasn't like that. You're making it sound like it was a date or something."

"Is that what you think? That I thought you were on a date? I was terrified for your life and thought we would never see you again. Why would you think that? I know what you went through was stressful and I can't imagine how you must have felt being alone among the enemy."

At the word "enemy," Daniel winced. He hadn't thought of his captors that way. At least not after being in the makeshift apartment and eating some of the best food he had eaten in a long while. Then when Lorelei showed up, he . . .

"Daniel, please say something," Gabby said, her worry about Daniel's mental state growing with each word. "Tell me something. That you and I are good, and that we're going to be okay."

"I was scared, Gabby. Okay?" Daniel said, his voice trembling. "I

142

was scared out of my mind. This thing we're doing, your visions, Cain, getting attacked—I think it's starting to take a toll on me. I can't shake the feeling that we're on the wrong path. That maybe we're on the wrong side of things. I mean, look at who is leading this whole thing. The guy who committed the world's first murder. He is literally a biblical figure, but not one you would want to meet. And why is he even still alive? That's as unnatural as all get-out. Are you sure we're doing the right thing? With the right people?"

"Yes, I'm sure," Gabby replied. "We're on the side of life. Of the Earth continuing to spin with all of humanity still striving to be better. We're with the good guys, Daniel. Look at what's happened so far. We were attacked by a band of demons and fallen angels. We have to be doing the right thing. If nothing else, we know the forces of darkness don't want us to succeed. That's enough for me."

"I don't know, Gabby. Would it be so bad, would it be so wrong, to start over? Look at all the terrible things in the world. Crime. Disease. War. Kids starving and much worse. People do horrible things to each other every day. Every single day. If we asked Cain if he's ever seen an entire day without something bad happening, I bet he'd say he hasn't. And he's been here for all of it. Heck, he started the whole thing by offing his brother. Of all the biblical figures we could meet, he's the one we get?

"I'm telling you, it's not such a bad idea to wipe the slate clean and begin again. Without those mistakes, without people messing it up for everyone. Without pain or misery or suffering."

"Daniel, what are you talking about? That's not what Razhael and his goons are doing. They want the world to burn. Your superhero movies have left a mark on me, I guess. Razhael and those like him are actively working for the complete and utter destruction of everyone and all we know."

Daniel reached out to touch Gabby's arm. His hand was cold, as if it was winter and he couldn't get warm enough. She clasped her hand over his.

There's still a spark there, Daniel thought. *We can make it through this together.* "Maybe, just maybe, we've ruined things for all of humanity, and this is nature's way of cleaning up the mess we've made and starting again. I'm not sure either side is in favor of things continuing as they are. Aren't we just caught in the crossfire?"

"Daniel, please tell me you are joking. You've always been a big believer. What's changed? What happened to you when you were taken?"

Daniel stopped and thought for a moment. "I don't know. I mean, I still believe, and I want to be on the side of the righteous. It's just that now, I'm not sure which side that is."

***

Cain watched Daniel return to his room, his arms full of junk food. He shook his head and wondered if the boy was going to be all right. He had his doubts. Cain didn't know Daniel well, but his brief kidnapping had changed him, perhaps deeper than anyone knew. Cain didn't know if Daniel had been broken by Razhael and his goons, or if he had become entranced with his babysitter, or if it was something else entirely. These were matters for tomorrow, though.

He walked through the parking lot, giving nods to his security team on duty for the evening. The veterans of Cain's company nodded back. The newer members stared in disbelief as their boss walked into the desert stark naked and barefoot except for a strategically wrapped blanket.

Cain made his way far into the desert, where no artificial light was visible. He stopped near a rock that was about fifteen feet high, dropped his blanket, and climbed up. Cain sat down cross-legged at the top, facing east. The sun would rise in nearly eight hours, and he wanted to watch it as he had 100,000 times before.

It never gets old, he thought. The improbability of life on Earth. Evolution. The animal species he had watched grow, evolve, and disappear into extinction. The advancements of humankind. They were slow at first—storing water for later use had been a big one. The rise of villages, then cities, then mega-cities . . . those Cain did not care for. He enjoyed the hustle and bustle when groups of human gathered and decided to live in close proximity to one another. But there was a limit. Mega-cities were the worst. Moscow, Los Angeles, Rio—all were terrible with only a few redeeming qualities.

He wanted to remember. He wanted to dream of his first home in the garden, his loving but imperfect parents and his brothers. Cain's mind drifted throughout the millennia he had walked the Earth, and all he had done and all he had achieved. He also thought of his losses and failures. He had wasted so much time chasing fruitless dreams and spent passions. Cain dwelled on all he had gained and all he had lost over many lifetimes. And most of all, as he had countless times before and hoped to continue, he wanted to dream of what was next.

***

"Daniel, please. Stop for a moment and think about what you're saying. You sound like . . . well, you sound like Lucifer. 'What would be so wrong about this? Wouldn't this be a little bit better? You know you're not getting the whole story—do this instead.'

"I've sat with you in church enough to know that's temptation creeping in. You're trying to justify genocide on a scale that's beyond imagination. Stop for a minute and think how that sounds to someone else—how it sounds to me."

Daniel was listening intently to Gabby. Her intensity for things she believed in was one of his favorite things about her. By the time she finished speaking, he thought she was positively glowing. Maybe it was just in his mind's eye, but she was glowing nonetheless.

"Gabby . . . you're . . . you're right. I am being foolish. Maybe being kidnapped affected me more than I know. I wouldn't really know, would I? But you—my rock, my constant, the love of my life—see it, and you pulled me back. Back from the brink even. I was having some pretty out-there thoughts, wasn't I? Maybe they did brainwash me. I'd be the last to know, right?

"But you would know. Thanks, Gabby. I need to work on getting rid of these thoughts. Let's ditch this junk food and order a pizza. Or two, I'm really hungry now. Maybe getting brainwashed makes you hungry because I'm nearly starving now. What kind of delivery do you think we could get out here?"

***

Gabby awoke, sleep in her eyes and slightly groggy. The sun was streaming through the blinds of the tiny motel room window. Two empty Pizza Pi boxes ("Constantly Good Pizza") sat on the tiny table where Gabby and Daniel had tossed them from their bedside perch. Daniel was nowhere to be seen, but Gabby could hear him. He was a shower singer, and he didn't know Gabby had been able to hear him their whole relationship. Most mornings, Daniel belted out hits from the eighties. This morning it was "Since You've Been Gone."

Gabby flipped through television channels until she found a local weather forecast. The day was supposed to be temperate, with highs in the low seventies—not as warm as she thought it might be. It would be a good day for traveling to wherever Cain and company thought they would be safe. The drive would give her time to think as well. The night had been eventful, even on top of the pizza discussion. But it could wait.

The sound of the shower turning off was followed a few minutes later with a chipper Daniel, hair still a little wet and shaggy, walking out dressed for the day. He was wearing jeans, white sneakers, and a gray sweatshirt. A delivery from the closest department store during the night had provided fresh and nondescript clothing for everyone. Daniel looked about as nondescript as someone could get. He never was one to stand out, so the new clothes were indistinguishable from his regular ones.

Gabby asked him if there was any hot water left. "Yes, ma'am, there is. Plenty of hot water for a hot woman." Daniel gave Gabby a bear hug and a longer-than-usual kiss on the cheek. "It feels good to be free and with you, Gabby. Maybe this life suits us. Traveling the countryside, righting wrongs, and having adventures. They'll probably make a movie about us. Minus all the end-of-the-world mumbo-jumbo, though."

"Someone woke up on the good side of the bed," Gabby said. She was relieved the disagreements from the night before were behind them. "Let me jump in the shower and get ready. I think we're supposed to meet outside about 8:30."

"Sounds good, babe," Daniel said. "I'm going to watch some TV while you're in there. Anything good on?"

"I don't know. Haven't had it on much," Gabby replied from behind the bathroom door, her voice garbled as she brushed her teeth. "So much going

146

on, I kind of forgot the rest of the world."

"No problem. I'll catch up on the news while you're in there." Daniel flipped the TV on and found a local station. He turned the volume up louder than normal and started to carefully unwrap a small, leftover candy bar from the previous evening. Daniel threw away the bar and scrounged through his pockets until he found a small package. He placed it inside the wrapper and did his best to reseal it. When he felt he had the wrapper as good as it was going to get, he shoved it back into his pocket.

"Not much good on the news," he said loudly so Gabby could hear. "World didn't end last night. Maybe tonight. News at eleven. Let me know if you need any help in there."

***

A little past 8:30 a.m., Gabby and Daniel came down to find the rest of their group waiting in the parking lot. "Sorry to keep everyone waiting," Daniel said. "You know how it is. On the run, a couple in a hotel room—everyone needs a little stress relief." He nodded and looked toward the male members of the team. No one laughed or smiled. When Daniel turned around, Gabby was glaring at him.

"Not funny, mister," she said. "Let's get our stuff packed so we can get moving. I don't like staying in one place too long."

"Well, Gabby, we're still short one member of the team," Commander Pleasants said. "He took off last night into the desert, and we haven't seen him since."

"Who's the knucklehead who did that?" Daniel said. "It looks like everyone is here. Well, except for . . . oh. I get it. The boss is missing."

"Does he do this often?" Gabby asked. "It sounds a bit dangerous and eccentric. Which, come to think of it, sounds exactly like him."

After ten anxious minutes, one of the soldiers spotted Cain walking toward them from the desert plain. He was moving at a leisurely pace, still wrapped only in a blanket. As he approached the parking lot, the group walked over to greet him and to see if he was injured.

Cain looked like a different man. The worry of the past several days had left his face, and he was grinning from ear to ear. He shouted ahead a hearty "good morning."

"Boss, it's good to see you," Commander Pleasants said. "We were getting ready to send out a search party. You had us worried."

"Nothing to worry about at all, Paula. A night under the stars was great for thinking, planning, and resting. I feel like a new man, and I am ready for what lies ahead once again."

When Cain reached the group, Gabby walked ahead to give him a hug. She thought his bare skin would be rough after so many years, but it was surprisingly soft and smooth. Cain gripped tight to the blanket around his waist as Gabby hugged him; then she whispered something in his ear. Cain nodded and then was surrounded by the rest of the group coming forward to greet him. Daniel stayed toward the back. He was the only one gathered who didn't hug Cain or shake his hand. He did say "good to see you again" when Cain passed by. Cain smiled at him and turned around to address the group.

"My friends, Gabby is the reason we are here, and she has something to share. Please come close so everyone can hear."

The group gathered together, eager to hear what Gabby had to say. As she drew a breath to speak, Daniel piped up. "Gabby, if you would, please. I'd like to say a little something first." Gabby nodded and added this moment to her growing list of odd things Daniel never did before but now did.

"Well, first, I'm glad everyone is here," Daniel said, starting off slowly and gazing downward more than once. Gabby knew public speaking was not something he enjoyed. She was more than interested in what he was going to say. She thought it would be more thanks for his rescue. Daniel eventually cleared his throat and spoke again. "I'd like to thank everyone again for getting me out of the situation in Indiana. To have to talk to and be around those things, people, whatever they are, was rough. I'd never been so happy to see people with weapons in my life. So, once more, thanks for coming for me.

"In the group the other day was someone very special, my girlfriend Gabby. Everyone knows her, I think. Anyway, what we're about to do, what we have to do in the foreseeable future, is terrifying. At least, it is to me.

Maybe you all fight demons and fallen angels all the time, but it's a pretty big change for me. So what does the future hold?

"Well, I'm a big believer in hope, and that's what I want to share with everyone." Daniel turned to Gabby and brought the candy bar out of his pocket. "Gabby, I wanted to do this last night, but things didn't go the way I wanted, and I decided to see how the morning was. After everyone was here, and Mr. Green came back in from the desert, I knew it was time."

Daniel bent down on one knee in front of Gabby and held up the candy wrapper. "I know we're not where we wanted to be, and we certainly aren't doing the things we thought we would be when this moment happened. But that's okay. Because there's no one else I want to spend my life with than you.

"So you have to save the world. I think that's great and I'll be with you all the way. But I was hoping we could face what is to come as husband and wife.

"Gabrielle Sullivan, will you marry me?"

Daniel unwrapped the candy wrapper to reveal a small diamond ring, set on top of a silver band. Gabby was looking into Daniel's eyes when a small tear formed in one of his eyes. "I've had it with me this whole time. I was hoping to ask you closer to your birthday so I could talk to your parents. Then I thought I'd do it at the retreat in Maryland, but that didn't work out so well. Asking you in the van didn't seem like a good idea either. Things have been happening so fast, and I didn't want to wait any longer."

Gabby looked down at Daniel. She started to feel a wave of panic, then joy and a strong urge to say "yes" and celebrate and get married as soon as they could. She did love him with all of her heart. From the moment she started dating Daniel, she was fairly certain he would be the one. After two years together, she was certain he was. The years after that had been happy and harmonious as they built their lives together, working their way to making it official.

She tried to put the events of the past week out of her mind and focus on the man—this loving, generous man—kneeling before her, asking her the question she had wanted him to ask for a long time. Gabby thought of her mom, who had given up on waiting for Daniel and just hoped the two of them didn't get pregnant before they were ready. She looked at Daniel and gave him her best smile. She opened her lips a fraction. She didn't want to answer. If only this moment could be frozen in time.

Then she whispered, "I love you, Daniel Masterson. You mean the world to me. I never thought I would love someone as much as I love you, but I do, and the thought of that makes me so happy, I know all of this end-of-the-world stuff will come out just fine. If for no other reason than I cannot imagine a world where you and I are not together.

"But my answer is no. At least for right now."

Daniel kept looking up at Gabby in disbelief. He stood up, his gaze still locked on Gabby. "I'm . . . I'm not sure I heard you. Did you say 'no'?"

"That's right, Daniel. My sweet, loving Daniel," Gabby said, trying to harden her heart enough to get through the conversation that was coming. "We have so much to do, so many things in our way, that getting married now seems like, I don't know, an afterthought, a consolation prize. 'Oh, you have to stop the world from ending, Gabby, but first get married and be happy.' I can't do that. Too many people, too many things are counting on us getting this exactly right. I want you to be with me when we do that. I want that so badly that I almost said yes. I almost took a moment for myself to say, forget the world, let's get married and be a happy family.

"But we already have that, Daniel. A happy couple with a huge, maybe impossible, task in front of us. I'd love to get engaged and married the moment we know the world is safe. It would be the best thing I could think of for that moment. For you and me to commit to each other for all time. But this thing, this mission, this whatever it is, is here and now. I know that's not fair, and I can hardly believe the words coming out of my mouth. But I can't do this now."

Daniel had been listening to Gabby's response so intently, listening for signs of hope to counter what he was hearing, that he momentarily forgot the group standing around them. Everyone was watching silently, either out of fear or respect.

"Daniel, I love you. Please say something," Gabby said. "I love you and need you, now more than ever. Please, try to understand where I'm coming from. Your love has helped bring us this far. Please stick with me. I didn't ask for any of this, and I know you didn't either. It's the hand we've been dealt. Let's get through it together."

Gabby was sure everything was going to be all right when Daniel began to nod—that he understood her reluctance and this didn't change anything between them.

"It seems like you have everything figured out, Gabby," Daniel said. He spoke slowly and softly at first. "You have to do this pretty big thing, and that's good. It's all good. I've always been amazed at your mind and the way you solve problems and still manage to make everyone around you smile.

"But this, I cannot do. I love you and I always will. But if you can't say, in the middle of the Earth potentially ending, that you love me forevermore, what does that say? How do you think it makes me feel? To be appreciated and relied upon, but not loved? At least not loved fully? To be second to a cause? Why can't we do both? It's worked up until now. The only thing I'm asking for is to make it official. So when we end up punching demons, we leave the imprint of our wedding rings on their faces.

"You're saying you're so dedicated to something you didn't even want and probably wouldn't be around for if it wasn't for me, that we can't get married before charging into the end times? Is that your answer?"

"Daniel, it's not like that," Gabby said, tears streaming down her face. "Please, I need you and I am so happy to have you back and last night was a great night together. Let's get packed . . . "

"Please stop right there, Gabrielle. You've made your choice, and that's fine. I don't understand it, but I respect it. I am going to need some time. Maybe this was a bad idea." Daniel took a step back and tripped over the foot of a team member who had been standing nearby, dumbfounded and intrigued at the same time.

Daniel took a few more steps back as the crowd around them gave him room. "I can kind of see your point, Gabby. I really can. 'No time for love, Dr. Jones.' I get it. Mostly. I was hoping we could do this together, and I guess we'll just do it . . . " Daniel stopped, still looking at Gabby's feet, tears streaming down his face.

"No, we won't do this. I won't do this. I can't. I'm heading home. Goodbye, Gabby. Good luck saving the world."

Daniel turned and walked toward Cain. "You. You got all this started. I guess we're supposed to be grateful, but I'm not feeling very grateful right now. So, Cain, can I borrow a car to get home? I know you have some around here. It doesn't have to be armor-plated or shoot missiles or anything. A small car is fine. Just one passenger." Daniel looked back at Gabby as he spoke.

A little bit of shock in his voice, Cain said, "Yes, yes, of course, my boy. But my name is Gage. Or Mr. Green if you are asking a favor. And how did a doctor get involved in all this? Where is this doctor now?"

"Whatever," Daniel said. "Playing 'Secret Squirrel' never was fun for me when I was growing up. Just another thing I'm not good at. Right, Gabby?"

Cain motioned for one of the soldiers to come over. He whispered in the man's ear. The soldier reached in his top jacket pocket and handed a set of keys to Daniel. "It's the red Dodge at the end of the lot. Idaho plates. Should have a full tank of gas."

"Thanks, Gregg. Good luck with the mission. Truly. Stay safe and kick their ass a little for me, will you?"

The soldier nodded and said, "Sure thing, Daniel. You take care of yourself too. Drive safe."

Daniel tossed the keys in the air and caught them as he walked toward the Dodge. He stopped and seemed to reflect for a moment, then turned around and walked back to the group.

"Desert's a little cold in the morning." Daniel snatched the blanket from Cain, leaving him entirely naked. "Might need something to warm up." Daniel turned around once again, pulling the blanket around his shoulders while he walked to the car without a look back.

Tears were streaming down Gabby's face. No one in the group moved. Daniel got in the car, pulled out of the lot, and drove away as fast as a lifetime of being a rule follower would allow. He headed toward the rising sun.

Gabby walked back to the motel steps and picked up her bag, leaving the one Daniel had packed. "Come on, we have a job to do. We're losing valuable daylight. Let's get moving."

The group began to break up and gather their packs. One of the soldiers picked up Daniel's and tucked it under his arm. "Just in case," she said, walking over to the Sprinter to help secure everyone's luggage.

Cain still was standing in the parking lot stark naked. "Where is this doctor? How did he or she get involved? Is anyone going to tell me where Dr. Jones is?"

CHAPTER 25: IVORY COAST, 1591

A lush forest ran along the coastline. Roughly 100 feet of sand separated the dense thicket of trees, vines, and flowers from the sea. The beach stretched as far as the eye could see no matter which way one looked. Take twenty or thirty long strides into the forest, and one would be hard-pressed to find signs that a beach and an endless expanse of saltwater thrived a short distance away.

Just outside the tree line, where a thin ribbon of sand and stone jutted out into the ocean, a man was walking. He stopped occasionally to draw in the sand with his foot. A child, no more than ten years old, was holding his hand as they walked along the narrow beach.

"*Agya,* why are we walking near the poison water?" The boy, Cahnya, looked over to his father when he did not answer.

"Son, this water is home to more lives than we can count," the man answered. Cain had not used his true name in eons, and this life was no exception. The people of the forest saw him as a god and had named him Shango, master of thunder and lightning. He enjoyed the notoriety. His friends and family did not know his true past, his curse, or the reason he did not age. He thought being labeled a god was just fine and only a little ironic—life was better than it had been in a very long time.

He had persisted with his wife to name one of their children something reminiscent of his true name, without giving away why he was enamored with the idea. He would come up with suitable permutations of Cain, and Yuguroyo would reject them and laugh at her husband. With his seventh child, though, he succeeded.

When he answered his son, he spoke slowly and carefully to allow his son the opportunity to let this knowledge sink in. "While it is not for us, many sea creatures live in the water. Were we able to ask them, they may say the same thing about the air we breathe and the woods where we live. Tall trees, vines, flowers, and curious little boys probably would be as unpalatable to them as the ocean is to us. Both are good for a visit, but living beings are made for only the environment into which they are born."

Cahnya pondered this for a moment. "*Agya,*" he said once more, out of respect for his father. "I understand that much, I believe. I know that the ocean sustains and protects many, many lives. Many of us are thankful for the food the ocean provides. For fish, crab, and shark. And every so often, the remains of a whale. We ate very well that season."

The boy's father looked down at him, curious to hear what he would say next.

"Well," the boy continued, "many of us ate well. You and several of my brothers and sisters, you do not eat flesh meat."

"Thank you, Cahnya," the father said. "I appreciate that you know the difference, and that you know why we do not. I still am saddened that you, your mother, and the others partake of such things." The father smiled as he said this, so his son would know that, while he did not enjoy such feasting, he was delighted that his children were becoming more and more independent and were making their own choices.

Cahnya nodded. "You did not answer my question. I know all of this and am grateful for the knowledge. But why are we walking alongside the poison water now, *Agya?*"

"I hear your question now, my youngest," the father answered. "Forgive me for not listening to the wisdom in it when first you spoke. We are walking because the beach is here, and it is a beautiful day. It would be a shame if we did not walk a bit and be humbled by nature's beauty. Also, your mother wanted to take your brothers and sisters to the eastern market for things we cannot grow, make, or catch. I believe your sister Onyeko will be married soon, and she wants to find something to wear for her union day. Your mother and I both agreed you would not enjoy the trip, so I stayed behind to help you pass the time. Walking the beach seemed as good an idea as any other. Do you not enjoy it?"

"Yes, I like it. But, why cannot I go to the eastern market? I could trade a few hunks of gold for something from far-off lands."

"You are too young for the chaos of the market and the crowds there, son. You must listen to your mother's wisdom, if you will not listen to me. She will be angry with me when she hears that I told you that, though. I am enjoying this walk. If we keep going, we will be able to see the outskirts of the market soon. Would that raise your spirits?"

"Yes, Father. Thank you. But I would be happier if I could go into the market with you."

"You are trying to create dissension between your mother and me, Cahnya. You must stop that at once. It will not work, anyway. I am terrified of her."

Shango looked down with approval at his youngest son. When he was born, Yuguroyo, his wife, said the boy, against all odds, looked like the man who would raise him, and so she agreed to the name finally. All of his children were born from Yuguroyo and one of the other men in their small village. It was considered an honor to help father a child for the mighty Shango, protector of their village. He had traded his virility for uncommon strength and command of thunder and lightning as well as immortality. Everyone thought even the chance of a child being born with those abilities would be a danger to everyone, so a bargain was struck. Men from the village would be chosen by lottery to lie with Yuguroyo, with her consent and that of her husband. The children born from this union would be raised by Yuguroyo and Shango as their own. In this way, the village was kept safe, and its future assured.

The stories of Shango had spread throughout the forest and beyond. He was starting to be seen as a god walking among men in some parts of the continent, and the small jungle village where he lived had flourished for many years. He went along with the ruse because he enjoyed having a new purpose in life and having a large, thriving family.

He did not know how long he had lived there, but he knew he had been married to four different women during this time. He had buried three already, as well as many of his children. The frequency with which this happened did nothing to ease the sorrow of losing a loved one. In this way, Shango felt his humanity as deeply as any other man.

"*Agya,* what is that ahead?" Cahnya said, pointing to the first glimpses of the market ahead on the shoreline. Shango strained to see what his son was talking about. When he did, he wished he hadn't.

"Come along, son. Now we have to hurry. Those are ships that cross the ocean to faraway lands, come to pillage and take from us. That is never good for our people."

He began to increase his pace, while encouraging his son to keep up. Eventually, Shango broke into a full sprint when the outskirts of the market city were close. He turned back to his son, yelling over his shoulder, "Find your brothers and sisters and stay close to them. Follow me as best you can. I am going to find them."

Shango ran as he never had before. His young son tried to keep up, but he was only ten and not as muscular as his father. Still, Cahnya kept running and tried to heed his father's words.

When Shango reached the edge of the market, there were people everywhere. There were baskets, pottery, brightly colored dresses and necklaces. He searched in vain for his family in the crowd, making his way toward the large vessels that were moored in shallow water nearby. *Please,* he thought. *Please be safe and do not go near the pale men from the boats.*

He thought he saw a glimpse of Yuguroyo ahead of him. He ran as fast as the bustling crowd would allow. He was careful not to jostle anyone too much, for fear of bringing down the lightning on an innocent. He looked behind him and saw that Cahnya was just reaching the outskirts of the market. He was torn—he could press on and search for his wife and children or wait a few moments for his young son to catch up and help him.

Inspiration struck as he deliberated where to search next. He ran to Cahnya and hoisted him up and onto his broad shoulders. "Son, please search for your mother, brothers, and sisters. Guide me so we can ensure they remain safe."

"Yes, Father," Cahnya said, "I am proud to be helping yo . . . I see them! They are to our left, six, no seven stalls ahead. I can see Mother's hair."

"Excellent, my son. Let us make our way through the crowd quickly. Please be as loud and as attention-getting as you can be. I know you can do this. Today, that skill will be just what we need. As loud as you can, Cahnya. Yell for your *mama* like you do when you want her attention.

Now, Cahnya. Do it now!"

Yelling and perched on his father's shoulders, Cahnya drew stares. The crowd began to part to let the pair through. Shango walked steadily in the direction his son led. After a few minutes, they saw Onyeko looking over brightly colored cloth that could be made into a dress. She looked so much like her mother, it sometimes was difficult to tell them apart.

When she saw her younger brother and father, she hugged them both. "Father! And little Cahnya! What are you two doing here? I thought this was a trip for the adults in the family." Onyeko was one of the oldest children, and she enjoyed ribbing her little brother whenever possible. Cahnya didn't flinch at the jab.

"It is. Can you not see how tall I've gotten since you left this morning? Father says I'll be the biggest member of the family one day."

"One day, maybe. But not today, little brother."

Shango was growing more nervous the longer they stood still. "Onyeko, where is your mother and the others? There are boats from across the great ocean docked nearby. That is never good for our people. We need to get away from the market. We need to get everyone out of here."

"Really, Father? What do we have to fear? We have the mighty Shango as our father and protector."

"Yes, yes, my daughter. That is true, but even I have limits. A large contingent of slavers from the lands to the north is a bad sign, and I will avoid a fight if there is another way. And we have one, but we will lose it if we keep standing here talking. Let's find the others and be away. The sooner the better."

The trio made their way through the crowds, Cahnya still yelling from atop his perch. "Mother! Ororo! Adah! Kasim! We are looking for you. Please come to us!" They wandered through most of the makeshift streets in between the stalls, Cahnya and Onyeko taking turns calling out for their family.

Shango was becoming more distressed the longer it took to find everyone. He knew what the men from the boats were there for, and he knew what they were capable of. He would confront them if necessary, but stories of magical lightning strikes would just bring more interest and more slavers. Even the mighty Shango could not fight them all.

The closer their path came to the docks, the more distressed Shango became. He loved Yuguroyo with all his heart, and she was growing noticeably older every year. Shango knew what would come one day, but he hoped that day was far, far off. He hoped he and Yuguroyo would have many more happy seasons together. He would feel much better when his family were all safely back home.

"Onyeko, did they say where they were going? Anything anyone was looking for in particular? We could wander here all day and night."

"Yes, Father. Mother was looking for a special type of thread to make a gift for you. She has been working on it in secret for many months."

"I see," Shango said, trying to guess which direction thread merchants might be, if there even was such a thing. Clothing had always been a bit of a mystery to him. "Let us keep looking."

While wandering, he noticed the ships that had been moored nearby were moving away from the market. He set Cahnya down and ran toward the water. He leapt over merchants and animals as he made his way to the shoreline, his heart racing ever faster. *Nothing has hurt me in this long, damnable life,* he thought. *But if my Yuguroyo has been taken, my heart will break and burst out of my chest and onto the ground.* What of his everlasting curse if he lost the will to live? How would the curse deal with that? Would blood still pump through his ancient veins without a heart? *I would not want it to,* he thought as he ran along the beach to catch a glimpse of the ships and any passengers still above deck.

When he was closer to the boat landing, he could see several familiar figures in the distance. One, two, three . . . there's another, four . . . now where is my beloved? Shango ran so fast that he did not know if his heart would give out from heartbreak or exhaustion. He called out to his children, who began to wave and excitedly yell, "Agya!"

Shango greeted the group with hurried hugs and questions about everyone's well-being. "Where is your mother? Where is my Yuguroyo? Please tell me she's here. Where did she go?"

"Father, she spoke to the men who came off the boats, and they took her."

Shango looked toward the boats and asked his children, "Which boat? Which one is she on?"

"That one, Father, the one still closest to shore."

The boat was about fifty yards into the ocean and starting to unfurl its sails. Shango dove into the water and began to swim after it. He was a powerful swimmer but slow. He kept up his pace, covering half the distance to the ship before it moved. As the wind picked up and billowed the sails, the ship began to move into deeper waters. Shango kept swimming, focused on his goal. He was gaining ground, but the wind was starting to pick up. If the wind got any stronger, the ship would be too far away to reach. He kept swimming, his powerful legs kicking behind him to propel him toward Yuguroyo.

He was about ten yards from the ship and nearly out of breath when he heard a loud splash toward the front of the boat. Shango grabbed onto one of the ship's errant ropes that dangled near the water's surface and began to climb. He was prepared for a fight, but wanted to get to high ground quickly. He knew a bigger fight awaited him on deck.

As he neared the boat's edge, Shango glanced down to see who or what had leapt into the water after him. Just before he clambered over the railing, he saw Yuguroyo, floating behind the vessel and struggling to stay afloat.

That amazing woman freed herself and jumped to safety, Shango thought. *She is incredible and much braver than any man I know.* He braced his feet against the ship's side and pushed himself away from the vessel, hitting the water about thirty yards from Yuguroyo. She was a strong swimmer, but she had never been this far out into the ocean. Shango swam toward her, and she toward him.

"Yuguroyo, I am so happy to see you," Shango shouted out in between waves, his long, white hair covering his eyes. "I thought you might be gone forever."

"Well, old man, I am not," Yuguroyo said, happily paddling alongside her husband. "Those men grabbed me when I was shopping with some of the children. Everyone except Onyeko. She was still looking for cloth and the others were getting irritated. We split up and ended up near the shore. That is when those men took me. I tried to tell them my husband was the lightning god and would come for me, but they did not listen.

"When the boat began to move away from shore, I decided I had enough and liberated myself—those white men do not know how to tie a knot—and jumped off. I thought I saw you swimming toward us, but it was difficult to know for sure. Then, I was in the water and saw you climbing up. I do not think I ever saw such a wonderful sight, husband. Thank you for coming for me."

Shango smiled and tried to kiss his wife's forehead. The waves made this difficult, and he was tossed up higher than he anticipated and landed on top of Yuguroyo, sending her under the waves for a brief moment. He half expected a bolt of lightning to strike, but the skies remained clear. Yuguroyo resurfaced, spitting water at her husband and laughing.

"You great fool, you come out all this way to help, only to try to drown me. The next thing you know, your lightning will be chasing me all the way home. Come, husband, let us swim ashore, gather the children, and return home. There has been enough excitement already."

"Yes, my love," Shango said as they began to swim toward the shore and their waiting children. "Enough indeed. I hope Onyeko found what she wanted. I hope that boy is worthy of her. She is much like her mother and will make a wonderful wife and mother. And for that, I am beyond thankful."

CHAPTER 26: SOCIAL CALLS

Razhael walked down a bucolic lane in the small West Virginia town of Elkins a little before sunrise, humming and singing to himself.

"Glory, glory, hallelujah.
Don't let that ol' Christ child fool ya,
He's not coming back, and you're out of luck
Hell is coming from above and below,
Humanity is tee-totally, absolutely and most assuredly fucked."

"Gods, I love music," Razhael said to Lorelei as they approached a nondescript neighborhood house. The name SULLIVAN was spelled out on the mailbox in gold and black block letters. "Of all the things we could have lost, we didn't lose that. I could just sing all day. But there is work to be done, so . . . "

Lorelei glanced over at the fallen angel, interrupting his rambling. "We're here. Let's get this over with."

Razhael walked up and rapped the gold knocker against the door. "Anyone home? Hello? Traveling salespeople here. Won't you come see what we have? It's a blast." There were sounds of someone getting up and footsteps coming toward the door, then nothing. Lights from the home's second floor indicated at least some of the occupants were inside. Razhael knocked once more.

"Razhael, knock it off. You're terrible at this," Lorelei said. "Let me try. Excuse me, is anyone home? We are a little lost. Please excuse my . . . " Lorelei glanced over at the fallen angel, looked him up and down, then frowned. Razhael shrugged and rolled his eyes—eyes that were old before the Earth had formed. "My uncle," Lorelei said. "He thinks he's funny but, well, there's one in every family."

A few moments of silence. Then definite sounds of activity behind the door. "Who are you? We don't get many visitors." The voice behind the door was male, a little muffled, and a bit ailing by the sound of it.

As Lorelei began to speak, Razhael stepped in front of her. "Enough of this," he said. "I'm done waiting." Razhael unfurled his wings, black as pitch, and thrust them both, with razor-sharp feathers, through the door like it wasn't even there. They heard a gasp on the other side of the door, a groan, then a slightly louder thump, as if something heavy landed on the floor. Razhael retracted his wings from the door, pushing it open as he stepped over a man's body slumped in the foyer. Razhael's wing tips now were red. Tiny bits of flesh were stuck in some of the black feathers.

"Oh, great. Now I have to get them washed entirely before the damned things will be usable again. Thanks, Mr. I'm-Not-Answering-The-Door. If you just would have let us in . . . Well, we would have killed you anyway. Maybe this was faster and, dare I say it, more humane. Can't have the fellows knowing about that. Anyway . . . you are welcome, Mr . . . " Razhael took a moment to glance back at the mailbox " . . . Sullivan. You are welcome for a much swifter death than you deserved. You're going to miss all the fun we have planned for you and the billions of others like you running all over the face of this forsaken planet. Why we are fixated on ruling it, I have no idea. Too much of a fixer-upper if you ask me.

"But still. Orders are orders. If the boss wants to rule this pitiful mudball, that's what we're going to do. Let's see who we got here," Razhael said, stepping over the body.

"That's not her father, Razhael," Lorelei said in a disapproving tone. "I don't know who this is, but it's not one of our targets. You've messed up again. Father is going to be cross. With you, not me."

"Don't threaten me, little girl. I was killing humans eons before you were even a thought in your ancestor's worst dreams."

"Razhael, there's no need to be angry," Lorelei said, crouching down beside the body. "That's what got you kicked out of Heaven in the first place—no patience and no appreciation for your station. Who were you before? 'He Who Watches From Above'? You were the Almighty's stenographer? Maybe a reporter? Town crier? Which was it? I forget."

"I am The One Who Sees Afar, which you damn well know. Your paltry human education wasn't that poor. Your manners are worse and . . . "

Lorelei moved forward, putting her finger in the face of the fallen angel. "I'm not here to make friends, Razhael. And you aren't here to strike poses when you finally do something, which is all you seem to be good for lately. You're too fixated on this girl. You're getting distracted. You should be in Russia by now. It's almost time for the first launch. I don't want to miss it."

"I'll make it," Razhael said, wiping his wings on the back of a nearby recliner. "You have distractions of your own. We'd be there already if you weren't playing house with that man-child."

"Who is worth more than a dozen Razhaels, which it seems you've forgotten," Lorelei said. "He has a part to play in all this. You do too. But he's special."

"If you say so, my . . . what's the inane word you people use? Niece? Let's get out of this depressing place and where we already should be. There's a lot still to do. If we've learned anything it's that just because it's written down, it doesn't mean shit. We have to see it through and then some."

"Finally," Lorelei said, licking her lips. "Something we agree on. Grab your winter coat. Vladivostok is colder than normal this time of year."

CHAPTER 27: REVELATIONS IN THE DESERT

Gabby stared out of the passenger side window, searching for something in the endless Arizona desert. "Where do you think he is?"

Cain was driving the RX-7, trying to enjoy the experience despite the circumstances that put him behind the wheel. His people had brought it to them the day before in a separate transport, along with several other vehicles from Maryland so the group could split up and not appear as conspicuous as they would in the Sprinter. Gabby thought it was unnecessary because their opponents seemed to find them any time they wanted to. "That hurts, Gabrielle," Cain said. "Everyone here is dedicated to our cause and has been preparing for this far longer than you have. Please, if you will not be positive for me—which I understand—be positive for them. It will help. They see you as a leader whether you like it or not."

"I get it," Gabby said. "Sorry. Just taking out some frustration. And I miss Daniel. I hope he's okay and is getting home safely."

"We did not follow him, if that is what you are asking," Cain replied. "Daniel made his choice to leave the battlefield. I hope he finds the peace he needs. Perhaps he was injured more psychologically during his brief capture than we know. He really should have some professional help. We offered, but he turned it down."

"You and I have to talk too," Gabby said, still leaning her head against the car window. "We haven't talked about last night's vision dream thing. Daniel kind of overshadowed it, but it's big. It's the most specific, vivid one yet. I know what they are up to. I thought we all should hear it, but I'm not sure. Thoughts?"

"Gabby, there is nothing to gain with secrecy at this point. We all are fighting this war. We all have a stake in it. Most of us have families, not to mention friends, and also the general notion that we do not want the world to end. Now, having said that, when and where would you like to share what you have seen?"

Gabby sat up in her seat. "No time like the present. How about we do it over lunch?"

"I can have a restaurant cleared out for us," Cain said.

"No, no, that's no good," Gabby said. "Word will spread about something like that. Even if someone heard just the basics, it could tip off Razhael. That's too risky."

"Good thinking, Gabrielle. Your natural leadership tendencies are coming out. What do you suggest?"

Gabby continued to gaze out into the desert, lost in thought. Cain cleared his throat, ready to speak again, when Gabby said, "Now. Let's do it now. Pull off the side of the road. Tell the others to do the same. If they are ahead of us, have them double back. Tell the ones behind us to stop when they see us. This will work just fine."

"Okay, Gabrielle. It is unconventional, but perhaps that is what we need."

"They've found us at every turn, Cain. We have to stop that and get ahead of them, or else it's lights out. I know what they're doing now. And Daniel . . . Daniel can. . . . " Gabby did not break her gaze into the desert Southwest. Her eyes welled with water, but not enough for a tear. "Daniel can save himself. We have work to do, and not much time."

***

When the team had gathered, all of their vehicles several yards away from the highway, Gabby asked them to move away even further so they could talk. They had only been driving for about forty minutes, and most seemed irritated at the change in plans. Gabby read the mood of the group, which was obvious to her and didn't require any supernatural assistance. "Look, everyone, I know you think this is odd, and maybe it is. But there's a good reason for that," Gabby said as she paced around the semicircle the group had formed, their backs to the sun. Gabby squinted a bit and continued. "How many times have the bad guys found us or been a few steps ahead? Two? Three? More than that? Well, it's going to stop. Here. Today. We're going to switch things up and hit them where they least expect it. We have to be unconventional to stay ahead—and away—from them.

"We are almost always going to lose in head-to-head confrontations, no matter how good you all are. These are fallen angels and, well, gargoyles from Hell. The worst of the worst. I know you all know that. We can't let our guard down or get cocky. We managed to save one guy"—Gabby had already decided she wouldn't say Daniel's name, at least for the time being—"but I'm not convinced they didn't let us get away with him. I'm not sure why, so it's just a hunch. I haven't had a vision about it yet, or one I can connect to it. If that changes, I'll let everyone know.

"And that's how we are going to beat them." Gabby's voice was growing louder, bolder, and more focused. "Working together, sharing what we know, and countering what Razhael is doing before they can react. I've seen him up close, which I really don't want to do again. He's a little terrifying, and his breath stinks. Good thing he lights up when we hit him with some juice. That's a huge break and something we always have to be ready for. Plus, there's the very likely chance there will be more like him out there. Why would they only send one to the big dance? We have to think there are more fallen angels and who knows how many gargoyles. We have to plan for that. How? I don't know, but I bet you all can think of some ways. I have the visions, but you all have the know-how and the experience."

Gabby stopped for a moment, looking into the horizon and lost in her thoughts. She had to tell them what she saw. They had to know what they were walking into, what the stakes were. She had to tell them how the world might end. *Take a few deep breaths, Gabby, you can do this. You don't have much of a choice, so get on with the show.* One last deep breath and a glance upward toward the mid-morning sun, and she began again.

"Last night I had my most vivid dream yet. I don't call them visions because that sounds a bit too New Agey or like I'm some televangelist, and I'm none of those things. At least I don't think I am. Anyway, the dream. I've actually had it twice: once back in DC, and the one last night. Last night's had more detail and felt more real. Like it's closer now. Like there's a specific date.

"Which there is."

The group had been listening intently to Gabby as she paced back and forth. They all grumbled, gasped, and moved around a bit at this news. Gabby took another deep breath.

"The end of the world will be December 21, 2032. That's a Tuesday, in case you're wondering. On that day, the northern hemisphere will be its farthest distance from the sun; then it begins to draw closer again in a never-ending elliptical orbit. But not this time. On that day, the top half of the planet will freeze, along with nearly all of its people. The meteor that just went by, Boemer, had given Razhael the idea years ago. Maybe on its last pass. He's been on the Earth much longer than we think, making plans for this. We're just coming in at the very end of what they have been doing in secret for a very long time. Before that, they had been on the path we were expecting—fire, devastation, that sort of thing. Then they got creative.

"They think it's hilarious. We're expecting fire and brimstone, plagues and everything else, and they're going in the complete opposite direction. They are very proud of that fact. They think we're too stupid to figure it out."

Cain had been listening quietly, his head down. "That is truly scary because those putzes are very stuck in their ways. I'm amazed they know how to drive, let alone find their way around. But they have."

"And they continue to learn," Gabby said. "They've come up with a way to make this happen. That's what they are doing now. Everything I've seen and experienced in the past few days is just a distraction to them. They don't like it but they haven't deviated from their plan either. They are laying all of the groundwork now so no one suspects what's really going to happen. It won't be with flooding, as promised. And it won't be in fire, which everyone suspects.

"It will be ice and temperatures so cold virtually no life outside the equator can survive. The Southern Hemisphere will be slightly better since they will be in summer. But a few months later, they will get it too. If there are any of us left in the north, everyone will be trying to get to the south, to where it's warmest. People will tear each other apart trying to survive. Then the vultures swoop in, finish us off, and that's it. Game over."

The group was silent. Most were listening with their heads down, not wanting to meet Gabby's gaze as she told them how and when the Earth would end. "We can't let it get that far," Mr. Green said, still staring down. "How do they do it? How do they get a planet to freeze?"

"Well, it's scary beyond words," Gabby said. "They have a plan and apparently have thought this out. They don't have a meteor, so they will try the next best thing and make some of their own. Most of you seem like you're ex-military or have experience with things like that. What do you know about kinetic bombardment? That term kept surfacing in my dream. I think I can figure it out, but it would be helpful if we had more informed knowledge as well as your thoughts on how it might work."

"Holy cow, Gabby, that's some scary stuff you're seeing," Katrina said. "I know a little bit about kinetic bombardment. The basic premise is simple. You drop something big from space. Aim it with enough precision to hit your target—or get close enough to it—and boom. Your target receives a blast akin to a medium-sized nuclear bomb minus the radioactivity."

Cain spoke up. "I am, *ahem,* familiar with the concept. One of my defense companies has been working on the idea for the last few years. It was first suggested as a concept during the Cold War. Strategic strikes without the nuclear fallout, as Katrina shared. Once the object is released, it is nigh impossible to stop. One just needs to get the projectile above the Kármán line—about sixty-two miles, give or take—then strategically release it over your target, allowing for drift and wind. Reagan was very interested in it, but the technology at the time wasn't precise enough. It is, I am very sorry to say, now extremely viable. It may have even helped stop an insurgency or two in some very politically sensitive places.

"If it were really a thing. Which, officially it is not," Cain added.

"So that's how they plan to do it," Gabby said. "Those sneaky bastards. It makes sense now—my dreams and how this all fits. I kept seeing logs floating down a frozen stream. Hundreds of them, maybe thousands. I was chasing Razhael, who was jumping from log to log. I almost slipped a couple of times. The further we went downstream, the colder it got. I've dreamt about the cold consistently since this all started. It's been staring me in the face all along. They are going to drop enough objects to knock the Earth out of its orbit. Not a lot, but any deviation is going to affect the weather worldwide. It'll take a few years for the new course to do any real damage, but weather patterns will be extremely unpredictable until we get to 2032 and the winter solstice."

Cain spoke first. "Gabby, thank you for sharing your prophetic dreams with us. That is how we are going to win. By working together and sharing what we know and thinking it through. Followed by quick, decisive action to wipe those angel scum from the face of the Earth once and for all." The group remained silent, soaking in the knowledge that the planet suddenly had an expiration date. There was not a coward in the bunch, but many of the team were thinking of family, friends, and things left unsaid and undone. Suddenly, a few years didn't seem like enough time.

"Gabby. Mr. Green," Commander Pleasants said, "how can we, this small group of people, stop Armageddon? A fallen angel or two, sure. But the end times? The war to end all wars? Can it even be stopped? What about the prophecies? What about the Book of Revelation?"

"What about it?" Gabby said, her voice suddenly rising with conviction. "It foretells a lot, but it's not exact. Heck, I'm in there and none of us knew it. Not one. Not even Green here knew it, and he's been . . . never mind. He didn't know either. That means we have a chance. Just because it's written doesn't mean it's going to happen. My dreams are proof of that. What if we are meant to save the world precisely because of that small, inconsequential technicality? I don't know about you, but I have no intention of lying down and letting those things ruin our beautiful world. We do that to ourselves enough. We don't need their help." Gabby now was speaking more loudly, and standing a bit taller than when she began.

"Our world is flawed, yes. But it's ours. Not theirs. They made their choices and have a home. I say we put our heads together, however many it takes, and come up with a plan to stop them once and for all. For good. Send them back to Hell with their tails between their legs. Or wings. Or whatever those rotten bastards have. Let's send them packing, then let's work on cleaning up our big, blue, beautiful, and flawed world. It's ours. The neighborhood bullies can go to Hell. How's that for a mission statement? Who's with me?"

Everyone in the group raised their hands and stepped forward. Cain said it was one of the most inspirational speeches he'd ever heard. He then made it a point to speak to every member of the team, thanking them for their service. After a few minutes of well wishes and thanks, one of the team asked what their mission was. It was Gabby who spoke up. "We have one mission. Make sure whatever Razhael and company are going to drop from space never makes it there in the first place. Let's get to it."

***

Cain slid into the passenger's seat after Gabby waved him away from the driver's seat. "My turn, old man," she said, laughing. After a few miles, Gabby turned to Cain, who was almost asleep. "Cain, wake up."

He roused himself and sat upright. "What is it, Gabby? Did something happen? Another dream?"

"No, nothing like that. Just thinking things through. We know what they are doing now, and I'm confident we can stop it. Except . . . "

"There is always a catch," Cain said, nodding. "What is it?"

Gabby stayed focused on the road. "There's one part of all this that we haven't talked about. I'm amazed no one has mentioned it. I left it out on purpose, but it's going to be a big factor. We have to be ready for it. Razhael isn't the only leadership they have. There's got to be at least one more. One they all defer to."

"Oh no, Gabrielle," Cain said. "There's no evidence the Adversary is on the Earth yet. We know it is supposed to come. But given the time frame, he most likely will make his debut closer to the date you mentioned. To rule over the remains. To take up his father's mantle and complete the destruction of Earth."

"I hear you, Cain, and you've been right on nearly all points up until now. But I'm telling you, the anti-Christ is here, and he—or she—is up and running. Maybe they're behind the scenes, but the presence is palpable."

"You have seen this?" Cain asked. "It has been in one of your visions?"

"Yes, although I didn't see it at first. I was so focused on Daniel that I missed what was right in front of me the whole time. I think the redhead is the Anti-Christ; she's the one behind all of this."

Cain pondered this for a moment. "I had not thought of that, but you may be right. She certainly fits the bill, now that you mention it. The forces of Hell seem more clever all the time. A female Adversary. That certainly puts a new spin on things. Still, if we can stop Razhael from getting into space with whatever he is going to drop, we will stop them right in their tracks, yes?" When he finished speaking, Cain's telephone began to ring.

"Yes, that should do it," Gabby said. "We will figure it out. I'm sure of it. Are you going to answer that?"

Cain was listening so intently to Gabby's reply that he barely had noticed the phone ringing. "Oh yes, thank you. Maybe this is some positive news. This is Mr. Green. What do you have for us? I see . . . okay . . . How long ago? That does seem to line up. You have taken care of the arrangements? Thank you. Yes, we will discuss it. Please let me know when you know more. Thank you again."

Cain turned to Gabby. "They have struck again. Gabby, they went to your parents' house. They rang the bell and . . . I am sorry."

CHAPTER 28: AULD LANGE SIGNS

"What happened? Who went where? Are you talking about Razhael? He went after my parents?" Gabby was trying to remain calm while driving. She pulled off the road so she could talk without having to watch where she was going. She shut off the engine and turned to Cain. "Tell me everything you know. Give me the details."

"Gabby, that is not going . . . "

"Dammit, Cain. Tell me. Now."

"The police report says two unidentified people—a man and a woman—were walking through Elkins and went to your parents' house. They knocked, but no one answered."

"Okay, what else? You're leaving something out."

"The man apparently thrust two swords through the door when he heard someone coming to the door. Your father was hurt. He has been flown to a trauma center in Pittsburgh."

"Okay, okay, thank you," Gabby said. "That's terrible, but that wasn't my dad. Mom and Dad are in Florida for a few weeks. I had called them after we left your apartment and suggested they be snowbirds and take off for a while. And, uh. I'm pretty sure you are paying for it."

"How did that happen, may I ask? And if the man who was stabbed is not your father, who is it?"

"That's probably Mr. Blibeck from a few houses down. Mom and Dad ask him to check on things when they are away, but he hangs out over there when Mrs. Blibeck is mad at him. Which is almost always. You don't know how he's doing?"

"Just that he was flown to Pittsburgh with two stab wounds," Cain said. "My guess would be those were made by Razhael's wings. They can be deadly in any number of ways, if I remember correctly. You cannot underestimate a fallen angel. They are desperate, have no honor, and are very, very tired of living in Hell. But how did your parents make their way to Florida?"

"Well, after the attack in DC, I talked to Merrison on the phone, just to check in on her and to see how she was doing after the fire. She was the one who suggested I discreetly send any family I had close by away for a bit. Mom and Dad have a pretty good savings account, but they are in their early sixties and aren't retired. So, Merrison helped them out and told them they won an all-expense-paid trip to Clearwater. They've been there for about three or four days now. We'll have to call them and let them know what happened, if they don't know already. Mom will have a cow."

"I see," Cain said. "That was very good thinking on Merrison's part. I will have to thank her when things settle down. Also, I think you need to go home for a day or two."

"Why, I like Mr. Blibeck and all, but . . . oh, I get it," Gabby said. It dawned on her that Razhael thought he had wounded Gabby's father and was trying to lure her back home where he could find her. "I go back, but we know it's a trap. Then we trap the trapper, right?"

"Something like that, yes," Cain said. "We will have to make arrangements soon. They are going to be lurking around town until they know you are coming. This does lend credence to your theory about the redhead too. Razhael never would take orders or be seen as an equal to a human. He was one of the proudest angels before the Fall. Maybe only second to the Morningstar. I would think he is none too happy to be second fiddle to the boss' daughter now."

"Poor Rachel," Gabby said, smirking. "No wonder he's cranky."

"And that is why we must be doubly careful, Gabrielle. He is very powerful, and it is becoming more apparent that he has a well-thought-out plan. I doubt we will be able to hold him at bay with electrical rods the next time we meet."

"Why is that? I thought you said that would 'do the trick.' Isn't that how you put it?"

"Yes, and it should work. However, Razhael and his followers seem to be adapting at an alarming rate. It has been puzzling me for days. We now may know why—the influence and intelligence of the Adversary. If that is correct and Lorelei is their chosen one, we should rethink our strategy. We cannot send our people into harm's way unprepared. Or worse, ill-prepared. They would be slaughtered."

"What do you mean, rethink it?" Gabby said. "I thought you said this would work? You've been so calm and collected about this, you've made it seem as if it will be a walk in the park. Why are you nervous now? Because of the girl? The one who was couch surfing with Daniel? Surely she would have better things to do than that. I mean, Daniel is a catch and all that, but still . . . "

"Now that you have said it out loud, I see what you mean," Cain said, his brow furrowed. "I am not saying Daniel is not a fine man. But would the Adversary, the offspring of Lucifer, really lounge on a couch with him for two days? Or be the one to spray me with anesthetic, negating my natural defenses? That does not sound much like a leader to me. More like . . . a loose cannon, as the kids say these days."

"Cain, 'the kids' haven't said 'loose cannon' since the 1960s. But I get your meaning. It is puzzling. What if we're wrong, and that's not who she is? Or what she is?"

"Then we breathe a sigh of relief and use everything at our disposal to neutralize her. Take her off the board. If she is not who we think she might be. If she is . . . "

"How could we tell? Any signs to watch for?"

"Oh, the Bible is full of them. You have been catching most of them lately. I am not sure how we might determine if she is the Adversary, though."

"What about the number? Would she have that on her?"

"Highly unlikely. That makes for good drama. But if you were sending your child to set the end of the world in motion, would you tell everyone that by branding the child in a manner that most of the population is going to recognize as being straight from the pits of Hell?"

"Umm, good point," Gabby said. "So that's most likely a no on discovering the Adversary is here by finding a number in her hairline."

"I thought Daniel was the movie connoisseur, but in truth you both are," Cain said with a slight guffaw. "Regardless, the number was a coded reference to the Emperor Nero, one of the first scourges of the early church. The believers wanted a way to share information about him and his unbelievably horrific actions, and that is how that came about."

"Well, that does make some sense," Gabby said, still pondering. "But what if that also is a red herring, like I was. Or am. You know what I mean? Maybe these secret, coded messages are beginning to pop up everywhere. Maybe I was just the first."

"Or the first that we know of," Cain said.

Gabby turned to Cain, her face showing exasperation and irritation equally. "Can you please not be negative all the time? It's wearing a little thin. We could use some positive vibes. I'm doing my best, but if you keep being Captain Bring Down, I'm going to tie that long mop of hair of yours around your mouth so you will stop saying cryptic and depressing things."

Cain was stunned and, for the first time in a few lifetimes, speechless. After a minute or so, he spoke up as Gabby continued to look at him disapprovingly.

"I am sorry, Gabrielle. I let my mind wander, and then I have to get it out and . . . I am sorry. Truly. I will strive to do better. Very old habits die hard, I am afraid. As much as I try to stay current with the world around me, I often find that I am still very stuck in my ways."

"Try to unstick it then, old man," Gabby said. "We aren't going to accomplish much if you're always a downer. Now, if what you said is true and Razhael is prepared and waiting for us, what do we do? How can we overcome those odds?"

Cain looked to Gabby, who switched the engine back on and pulled back onto the highway. "We need to keep moving," she said. "Now, what is your plan? Because unless it's better than mine, we go with mine."

"You thought up something that quickly? You are a marvel, young lady."

"If you grew up where I did, you learn how to take care of yourself and the people around you. I'll have to make a few calls, but we should be able to handle Mister Mean Old Angel just fine, electrical weapons or not. You don't come into my hometown and stab my friends without some good old-fashioned payback.

"Help me out a little, though. Would Razhael be as strong as, say, a full-grown elk, or stronger? A bull elephant maybe?"

"I cannot be sure, Gabrielle, but I would say stronger and more durable than an elk and as tough as an elephant but not as strong. But, as you know, in a much more compact frame."

"Okay, got it. I think this will work then. We'll have to plan it out carefully, and we will need a good cover story. We may have to fib just a little about what's going on. But only a little. I'm not sure the people in my hometown are ready for Apocalyptic war, but they are pretty good in a fight. Speaking of which, where were you during the American Revolution and the Civil War?"

"Gabby, I was a slave in the American South for many, many years," Cain said, sadness creeping into his voice. "I was there, but I was . . . not as I am now. I had given up."

"Put a pin in that story. I'm sure it's difficult to share, and I want to hear it—and I mean I really want to hear it. But not now. Let's make a promise to swap stories when we win this fight. Not the one back home, but overall. When we stop Armageddon together. Deal?"

"Yes, that sounds like something we all can look forward to when we win."

"Okay, great," Gabby said. "What I was going to ask was if you knew why West Virginia was separated from Virginia, and why Lincoln was in favor of it?"

"I know no more about it than what is taught in schools and is part of history. The plains of Virginia had slaves, but the mountainous sections did not."

"Good enough," Gabby said. "That's true, but there's more. Lincoln and Washington before him prized the mountain people for their grit and their cantankerous, fighting nature. Over the generations, they had adapted to the terrain and knew how to fight in it. And most of them loved to do it. So this whole state full of wily mountain people who are usually good in a fight are pretty big assets when push comes to shove. When you can, look up Woody Williams and World War II and you'll see what I mean. So, to make a long story short: Razhael and that red-headed bitch are in for a world of hurt. I don't care how strong they are. I need to make some calls to get things moving."

CHAPTER 29: FRIENDS IN THE MOUNTAINS

Cain had arranged a flight from a small airport in southern Nevada to Cleveland. The drive to Elkins would take more than four hours and give them time for last-minute planning and any questions. Gabby said Elkins was small enough that most of the people she knew would notice out-of-towners. No one had reported seeing the perpetrators of the knife attack at the Sullivan house, though.

"They could be waiting anywhere," Cain said. "I cannot imagine they would stay in a hotel or even an Airbnb, but they have to be close by. I would not be surprised if Razhael knows how we found them the last time and is compensating for his lack of a heat signature."

Gabby thought for a minute. "What if they split up? What if one of them is in Pittsburgh near the hospital, and the other is watching the house? They could have reinforcements too. Or, we could be totally off the mark. Any advance word?"

"No, nothing. Our eyes in Pittsburgh have seen a few gargoyles nearby, but nothing more than that. They may have learned to be low-key. That is not unexpected. If they were traveling with a lot of gargoyles, that would be a little more difficult. So, perhaps we will just have the two to deal with here."

"What are the odds of that?" Gabby asked. "I can't imagine they would be very good."

"You are most likely correct," Cain said. "In our favor, however, is the fact that this is happening in a small town. It would be much more difficult to hide there than in, for example, Pittsburgh. So not visiting your parents' friend makes sense. You would have to think Razhael and the redhead would know they hit the wrong person by now."

"One would think so. It's been on the local news. They released Mr. Blibeck's name this morning. His wife set up a donation account at one of the local banks too."

"I will be happy to cover all of his costs," Cain interjected. "He would not have been wounded if not for us."

"Thanks," Gabby said. "I'm sure they will appreciate an anonymous benefactor. However you make the donation, make sure they get it to Mr. Blibeck and not his wife or that new account. She will spend it before he's even out of the hospital. Mom and Dad say the two of them must really love each other, because he never met a penny he couldn't pinch and she's the exact opposite. Maybe that's why it works."

"Why what works?" Cain said. "Did I miss part of the story?"

"The Blibecks' marriage. They are opposites in a lot of ways, and you know what they say about opposites. Sometimes they attract. They sure have made it work over the years."

Cain thought about this for a moment. He recalled hearing the expression but had very rarely seen it in action. *After all this time I still have much to learn,* he thought.

"I haven't had any dreams about what we're doing now," Gabby said, getting back to the task at hand. "I'm not sure it would work, either. Up until now, it's been all biblical prophecies through a much different lens, like an early warning system, but only I can see it. Or a secret code that I have the key to. Sometimes my dreams don't make a lot of sense at the time. Like the elevated train and the snow. Eventually it made sense, but usually it's after the fact. I don't like thinking that way, but I'm not sure what else to do. It's not very helpful if I can't make heads or tails of what's going on. I had the big snow dream twice. I think that was to really hammer the point home. The second time around, I saw way more specifics. How they planned to do it, and when."

"Interesting, Gabrielle. I wonder if it is possible to direct your dreams. To think about the types of things you want to see and lead this ability to see things that you believe will be helpful. No, wait. That sounds too easy now that I said it aloud. Forget that idea."

"Actually, Cain, I really like that. I used to do that when I was a kid. I would have nightmares and wake up so scared. I kept having dreams about being chased by a monster that only I knew about. When I tried to scream for help, my voice was gone. That went on for about six months. Mom and Dad took me to a counselor, Mr. David. I forget his first name, but he was great. He suggested I try to direct my dreams before falling asleep. I didn't think it would work, and I was scared to try it. The dreams kept coming, so I finally gave it a try. It took a few nights, but it really did work. The bad dreams lessened. When they did come back, I was able to take control of the narrative. I still do it, to tell you the truth."

"That is impressive, Gabrielle. Maybe you can dream of certain things that way. There does not seem to be much rhyme or reason to when you have them, does there?"

"No, they seem really random. There's no pattern I can figure out. I try to remember as much detail as I can, but it does make me wonder."

"About what?" Cain said, glancing over to look at Gabby.

"I had this crazy notion, but I'm trying to forget it."

"Gabby, how many times have we said the more information we share, the better off we are?"

"Yeah, you're right. But the idea is really out there, and it kind of makes me sound like a jerk."

"Then I must hear it as soon as possible, young lady."

"Okay, but please don't look at me with that disapproving look of yours when you do. I was thinking that if I know—really know—that something is going to happen, does that mean it won't? Like the date. Since I know it and have shared it, does that automatically reset the clock? Sort of like this: 'No man will know,' but then *I* do, so technically the passage still is accurate. But does me knowing it change anything? Like someone up above or down below is saying, 'Darn it, Gabby has figured us out again. Back to the drawing board.'"

"You are not being serious, are you?" Cain said with the disapproving look Gabby had hoped to avoid. "You are—what do you say—winding me up? Telling me a tall tale? Pulling my leg?"

"I'm not, I promise," Gabby said. "I really would like to know. I mean, I have so little control in my life now. I'm looking for something to pin my hopes on, something that says I'm in the driver's seat with this role. That someday my task will be done, and I can go back to being regular Gabby."

"Then we must see this through and defeat the evil that is growing around the world. Then and only then can we return to our normal lives."

"Yeah, yeah. Exciting pep talk, coach," Gabby said, although she could not help smiling as she said it. "Win the game, then we can go home. If I have a home to return to."

"What do you mean?" Cain asked. "Will you not return to the house in Virginia?"

"Yes, eventually. It depends on where Daniel is. If he's moved out, then yes. If he's there . . . I don't know. Maybe. Then there's the slight matter of my job. I haven't talked to anyone since the attack. I presume they think I'm on leave. If there's anything the federal government loves, it's rules and paperwork. Both of which I have broken and am woefully behind on. If I haven't already been fired in absentia."

Cain began to speak, but Gabby cut him off. "And I don't want you to 'make some calls.' I'm in this mess, and I can get out of it. Plus, if you did that everyone would know, and I would never live down the fact that some rich guy called and had my job restored. The world doesn't work that way. Or at least it's not supposed to."

"But, Gabrielle, what you . . . "

"Cain, I said no. I do appreciate the offer. Really I do. But no. This I have to do on my own. You can pay to help repair the monument, though. That would be worlds better and help a lot more people. I don't know about Daniel's job. He may want you to help him there."

"You know, we have not discussed Daniel since he left," Cain said. "What is Daniel's occupation? I do not believe we ever talked about it."

"He's a computer programmer for a private security firm in Bethesda. He's insanely good with computers."

"Hmm, I did not know that," Cain said. "That does help to answer some questions about the boy. His mannerisms and social skills at the least. And maybe more."

"I know he's a nerd," Gabby said. "But he's my nerd. Or was." She thought for a moment, staring ahead at the road. There were no tears and no sadness in her face or her voice. Just determination. "Let's talk about something else. Like how we are going to beat these jerks in my hometown."

***

The flight to Cleveland was uneventful. There was a nondescript older Mercedes waiting for them near the hangar where the plane stopped. A little less than four hours later, Gabby and Cain saw a sign that read "Welcome to Elkins." In town, there was another sign: "Welcome to Historic Downtown Elkins."

"The people really seem to love their history," Cain said.

"You have to go with your strengths," Gabby said. "Tourism is big here. Lots of hikers and weekend trips in the Monongahela National Forest. It takes up most of the eastern part of the state. It's absolutely beautiful if you've never visited."

"I am sure I have, but maybe before it was enshrined by the US government," Cain said. "When it was full of natives and wild beasts. The America I know differs from yours. I visited this continent several times before I was enslaved. There used to be a land bridge, and there were a few times I was able to hitch a ride with some Vikings. That was fun. Vikings are very non-judgmental, it turns out. We got along great. When there was a big fight, they would strap me to the front of their lead war wagon—with my permission of course—and charge into battle. They loved to see the lightning hitting everywhere and their enemies scattering. So did I. Those were the days . . . "

"Are you telling me a 'when I was young and fun' story, old man?"

"Yes. Yes, I am," Cain said proudly. "We have shared so much hurt and pain these past several days. Something positive like a fond memory can lift the spirits like nothing else."

"Cain, you are probably the only person on the planet . . . scratch that, you *are* the only person on the planet who would think sharing a first-person account of Viking warfare—and apparently very barbaric Viking warfare—counts as a fond memory."

"*Suum cuique,* Gabrielle. 'To each their own.'"

After a few turns, Gabby and Cain found themselves on the street on which Gabby grew up. "A few more blocks, and we'll be there," she said, searching ahead for signs of activity nearby.

"Is that your house?" Cain said, returning to the task before them. "The one with all of the very worn vehicles in front and . . . is that . . . wire? Why do they all have wires strung around their vehicles? And why do all those burly men and women seem to be brandishing firearms?"

"Those," Gabby said, "are my friends. And they are about to be your friends too. Think of them as modern-day Vikings, minus the ships. Try to keep up."

***

Gabby greeted every person who had gathered at her parents' house one by one. She hugged everyone, and made small talk about how they had changed since high school or about their children. Some spoke about their own parents and how they were upset about what happened to Mr. Blibeck. One of the men showed Gabby where they already had replaced the damaged front door with a new, metal one.

"No knife or anything is going to get through that," Gracie Joseph, one of Gabby's best friends growing up, said. They had known each other since kindergarten and had been friends ever since. During their teens, each of their parents gently asked them if there was something more to their relationship. Both Gabrielle and Gracie said no, explaining that they were just friends and that's the way it was and please stop asking. Gracie had been the first person Gabby called when she needed help with walking into Razhael's trap.

She had been surprisingly accepting when Gabby said the stabbing was the work of something supernatural. Gracie and Gabby had talked many times in their youth about how there had to be something more out there than anyone knew, and they would watch for it and share anything they discovered. She was proud that Gabby called her first, and that they were right.

Gracie, however, was most proud of what was waiting inside the Sullivans' living room. She could not contain her grin when Gabby and Cain walked in and saw a man with black wings, hands tied to the ceiling fan, his clothing in tatters, and the rest of him tied tightly to a makeshift wooden structure that supported his weight. The wings were tied down as well, along with the angel's feet. Small electrical wires were wound all around his body and his mouth. A large portable battery sat several feet away. Gabby could see the leads going from the battery to the fallen angel. It was not Razhael.

Cain began to laugh uncontrollably. He excused himself and walked back outside with the others. "Your friend likes what we did," Gracie said. "I think I like him already."

"Yeah, he has that effect on people," Gabby said. "How in the world did you maniacs end up with this thing trussed up like a Thanksgiving turkey in my parents' living room?"

"We found him and a girl, maybe twenty-five to thirty years old, a little bit outside of town to the north," Gracie said. "They were lurking in the woods when someone spotted them and passed the word around. When I got your call, I went out that evening to see the two for myself. Sure enough, they were in about the same spot, just waiting.

"I went home, called everyone else we knew and might believe me, and we got to work. It took most of the night, but we wired up all our trucks to electrify at the flip of a switch. Wish we'd thought of that before you said something about it on the phone. It would have made a few instances in the past few years more enjoyable. But that's another story."

"What about the girl you saw?"

"No sign of her when we came back."

"Gracie Jo, what have you all done?" Gabby said. "I asked for help, not to take matters into your own hands. You all could have been killed or worse. Much, much worse."

"I know, but it sounded like you really needed help. And that's not really like you, so . . . "

"Are you going to tell us how this happened? Mr. Green and I have been working on this since . . . "

"Since what happened at the Washington Monument, Gabby?" Gracie said, with a little jealousy creeping into her voice. "You were all over the news for days. Your parents said you called and had someone pretend to give them a trip. Your dad said they weren't going to turn a trip down and that they'd never heard you or Daniel sound like that. They packed up and went along with it. We've been watching for more news, but it's been quiet. Then you called . . . "

"Gracie, thank you, really. I owe you big, but you all have put yourselves in more danger than you know. I'm sure you can guess what the implications are." Gabby gestured toward the bound angel.

"Yes, I kind of figured. But there's something else too. Something that really helped me make up my mind."

"Oh, yeah? What's that?"

"Him," Gracie said, pointing to the gargoyle who came out of the kitchen, eating a sandwich and carrying a large fountain drink with a rubber straw. He was gaunt and looked as if too little skin was stretched over too much skeleton. His hair was a haphazard mess of gray. Only his eyes seemed alert.

The trussed-up angel began to squirm and try to speak at the sight of the gargoyle. His struggles led to an automatic switch being tripped, sending several thousand watts of electricity coursing through him. The angel twitched, tried to talk again, then settled down. No one knew if he was angry, upset, scared, or had a warning for them not to trust gargoyles. Gracie and her friends all had decided they would rather take their chances with the friendly gargoyle than the demonic angel. Gabby drew out her collapsible electric rod, ready to fight. The men around her backed away. Only the gargoyle remained in the same spot. He looked up from his food and frowned. "Not again," he intoned.

"Gabby, Gabby, Gabby," one of the other women said, stepping forward and in between the two. "Tuna here is A-OK. He's with us, more or less. Since he helped us capture Mister Bad there, he's been with us. Hanging around, learning to eat real food, watching some TV. Did you know they have to find all their own food in Hell? I mean, the place doesn't have a farm, a dairy, or even a kitchen. That really does sound like, well, Hell."

The gargoyle still hadn't moved. "She hurt me?" he said in slow, halting, but understandable English.

Gracie walked up to the gargoyle to reassure him. "No, Tuna, she's not going to hurt you. She's not used to seeing your people being friendly."

"Friend. Tu Na," the gargoyle replied.

Gabby was confused and impressed. "How did you all get him to talk? You know he's a gargoyle, right?"

Gracie put her hand up on the gargoyle's shoulder. "Without him, most of us would be dead. He helped us capture that thing in the living room. He says he wants to help. We believe him. He just wants to eat. A lot. And he knows more than you think. It takes him a while to put the words together, but he can do it. He also knows you. Or knows of you. That was one of the first things he told us when we got back here. Right, Tuna?" Gracie motioned toward Gabby, pointed at her head, then made the near-universal gesture with her hand for talking. Tuna followed Gracie's every move. When he saw her hand gesture, he perked up.

"Yes. Ga Beer Ah is her. She stop bad friend. My bad friend more."

"Take it easy, Tuna," Gracie said. "You did a brave thing. You left your people and helped us. You defected to the other side. To the good guys. You can stay with us. We'll help you. Tell Gabby what you told us."

"Yes. I tell," Tuna said, slightly faster than before. He glanced around the room. All of the men and women nodded affirmatively, as if to tell the gargoyle it was okay to speak and they supported him. "Bad drop from sky high up. Drop big. Lots. Three. Three drops." Tuna stopped for a moment, with a look of concentration. "Flor day first. Cal ee for na then." At that he stopped, took a breath, and closed his eyes. "V la vla . . . ostock then. Three. Last. Must stop. Must stop. Tu na make friend. No want to die back to Hell. No die back to Hell. Please."

***

Cain walked back into the house with several of the men and women. They were laughing and back-slapping as if they had known each other forever.

"Gabby, you are absolutely right. These fine ladies and gentlemen would have made excellent Vikings . . . Good grief, what is *he* doing here?" Cain said just as he caught sight of Gabby and the others talking with a gargoyle, still holding his snack from the kitchen.

"Cain, it's fine. Calm down." Then, "I mean, Mr. Green. Gage," she said, trying to recover from her slip of the tongue. "He's a good guy. He helped Gracie and everyone capture Big Bird in there. His name is Tuna."

"This is the truth?" Cain said, turning around to ask his newfound friends. They all nodded and said yes. A few even gave positive nods toward Tuna, and more than a few thumbs-up.

"Hmmm. I have never known a wraith to be smart enough to be a double agent," Cain said as he walked toward Tuna. "Let me look you in the eyes, gargoyle." The group bristled when Cain spoke, but they remained behind him and watched for signs of trouble. Cain walked up to Tuna and looked up at him. The gargoyle met his gaze and did not blink. Several tense moments passed in near silence. Then Cain said, "Welcome aboard, my boy. I must hear how this very unusual turn of events came to pass."

"We just finished with that," Gracie said. "He told us their plan, more or less."

Gabby followed this up quickly before Cain had a chance to speak. "He told us exactly what they are doing. It matches my dreams. We need to check things out, but what he said sounds like the real thing. And for what it's worth, it feels right too."

"Hmm," Cain said. "That counts for a lot. But I am still suspicious. I have a lifetime of seeing these fellows do very bad things. It will take some time to get used to. But, everyone here seems to have accepted him, and that is more than enough for this old man. Welcome aboard, uh . . . what is your name again?" Cain put his hand out for a handshake, and Tuna stared at the outstretched hand.

"Tuna is me," the gargoyle said, clasping Cain's hand in both of his. "You are Cain? The first and never die?"

"Whoa, whoa, there, big fella. Let us not get ahead of ourselves. I did not know gargoyles had such an imagination," Cain said, mock laughing as he glanced around the room.

Once again, Gracie spoke up. "It's okay, we figured it out. We're not stupid. When you have an angel trussed up in the living room, believing Cain is still around isn't that big of a stretch." She extended her hand in friendship. "Plus, Gabby says nothing but good things about you. That's enough for me. It's a good feeling to know you're on the right side of things and can pitch in to help, though." Then whispering into Cain's ear, "You gotta show me that lightning trick sometime. Promise?" Cain nodded his assent.

Once again, the group nodded and murmured their agreements. Cain returned the handshake. With everyone's attention turned elsewhere, the captive angel managed to loosen his head restraint. He caught nearly everyone by surprise when he said, his voice booming, "Betrayer. Traitor. False friend. I curse you. I curse all of y . . . " His voice was cut short as one of the women turned up the amperage on the battery and the angel began to convulse.

Cain walked over to the fallen angel as he writhed in pain. "Hmmm, I do not know you. Are you new? Or have you been kept in Hell until you showed some maturity?

"Ladies and gentlemen." Cain stepped back and looked around at the men gathered in the room. Every gun was pointed at the angel. Gabby had come up behind Cain to look the fallen angel in the face. Tuna had retreated back to the kitchen. "Can we talk with this fellow for a bit? Can you keep him restrained but allow him to speak? Will that work? We must make sure he cannot get away, first and foremost. He would kill us all in a heartbeat were he free. But we may learn something if we talk to him."

"We can give it a try," Gracie said. "He can talk if he wants to. If he starts to act up, we can still give him the juice."

"Perfect," Cain said. "Let us see how chatty he can be. If he answers our questions truthfully, we can set him free."

He turned to the angel. "Which one are you? I do not recognize you, so you must not have visited this plane of existence much."

The angel eyed his captors. If looks could kill, no one in the room would be left standing. "I am Hadrael. I was the angel of the waters. Now, I burn with nothing but the desire to wipe every last human from the face of the Earth. Nice to meet you, firstborn."

"Well, you are pleasant enough for someone with your history," Cain said. "Let us see if we can do some business together; then we will let you go. It is as simple as that. Help us, then we set you free. Do we have a deal, Hadrael, former angel of the waters?"

The crowd grew nervous. It had taken all of them and several electrified vehicles to subdue the fallen angel, and that was with Tuna setting him up. Now that he was talking and looking at all of them, many started to doubt the wisdom of what they were doing.

"I don't make deals, let alone with traitorous filth like you," Hadrael said. "I cannot wait to see you burn in . . . what are you doing?" As Hadrael was making his threats, Cain stepped back and took one of the shotguns from the assembled group. He pressed the barrel behind the angel's right shoulder at the base of one of his wings, and squeezed the trigger. Tiny bits of flesh hit the Sullivans' television and went into the dining area. Most of his right wing was hanging by a few remaining bits of muscle and sinew.

"You will pay for that, firstbo . . . " Hadrael's threat was drowned out by another shotgun blast, this time to the left wing. Most of it fell to the floor and, alarmingly, began to smoke. Hadrael wept. Black tears were running down his face as Cain asked for a fresh weapon.

"Not in a talkative mood, my friend? What was that you were saying? Here, speak into the microphone so we can all hear." Cain took the new shotgun and placed it under the angel's jaw. "Gabby, I will be happy to pay for any repairs to the house." He looked back at Gabby with a mischievous grin. "And of course any cleaning that's required. Still feeling defiant, Dumbass-el or whatever your stupid name is?

"Brave men and women, this creature would not hesitate to eviscerate you or your families. He can do it, and he probably would enjoy it beyond measure. But he is not going to because we are going to set him free. We will show him more mercy than he ever would show us. And that is why we are going to win. We will remove as many of their players as we can from the battlefield, and we will try to do it without killing anyone. If you are put in a situation where it is you or them, that is different. Do what needs to be done to survive and win. No one will weep for dead fallen angels or gargoyles.

"Umm, except for you, Tuna." Cain saw their new gargoyle ally peeking around the corner. He seemed delighted to be singled out and called out by his new name.

"But it is imperative that we stop Armageddon the right way. If not, what is left to save? We would be no better than him." Cain gestured toward Hadrael, who had slumped back against his makeshift prison, his wings in bloody pieces below. "We can get him down from there. He's not a threat to anyone now. Without his wings, he can't travel and his body will be busy repairing itself for a while. His strength will be depleted for weeks, if not more. That's more than enough time to stop what he and the others are planning. A secure jail cell should do the trick. If we survive what is to come, we can release him after we win. Do any of you fine folks know where we can find one?

"We need to get him secured so he cannot cause any havoc, and we need to get all of your friends to safety. With the Maryland compound compromised . . . "

"Please stop for a moment, Mr. Cain," Gracie said. "Gabby is our friend and so are you and Tuna now. If you need help with more dirty angels and who knows what else, we want to help."

Cain looked at the woman, then turned toward Gabby. "I am so happy to meet your friends. They have done a great thing, but they also have put everyone they know in great jeopardy. However, I do have a good feeling about this. Like the tide is turning in our favor."

Gabby glanced down at Cain. "YOU have a good feeling about something? That has to be a first. But yes, I agree. They are in this now, more than I wanted, but . . . "

"Like I said, in for a penny, in for a pound, Gab," Gracie said. "You're our friend. We'll do whatever you need."

"I hope it doesn't come to that," Gabby said. "One battle down, the war to go."

CHAPTER 30: TROUBLE COMES IN THREES

"Three sites, so three teams. Everyone good with that?" Gabby was deep into planning mode with Cain, most of the original team from Maryland, some of her friends from Elkins, and Tuna. There were fourteen in all. Fourteen people to stop Armageddon before it started. The Maryland retreat had been hastily fortified with more fencing and dozens of additional sentries patrolling the grounds. When they arrived, Gabby felt as if they were entering a military installation rather than a peaceful, relaxing hideaway. Site director Eric Ballencourt was not on the grounds. He was home with his family, recuperating from a week earlier. Gabby thought it had been much longer. It had been just ten days ago, according to the assistant site director. She also shared that the Ballencourts were all doing well. They had an African vacation—something they always wanted to do—planned once everyone was feeling up to it.

Cain already had called dibs on Russia. Vladivostok was the most likely location for finding Razhael and gleaning any further information about his plan. He'd been spotted in Eastern Europe the day before. Plus, Tuna mentioned Russia considerably more than the other two sites. It stood to reason that's where most of the preparations and planning was taking place.

Commander Pleasants and four of the team—Jonn McNeil, Reece Cleaver, Gregg Coffman, and Zander Snyder—would go to Florida.

That left California to Gabby. She wanted to go alone, despite nearly everyone agreeing it was a bad idea. She was too valuable. What if she discovered new information to share and had no way to relay it? In the end, the California team ended up being the largest. In addition to Gabby, there was second-in-command Matthew Peak, Milla Tran, Katrina Lee, Roland McIntyre, Lewis and Candy Reed from Elkins, and Tuna.

Gracie had stayed behind to help keep watch over Hadrael and share anything he let slip. Gabby hugged the Reeds and thanked them for making the trip. "It will be good to be with people I've known most of my life," she said. Everyone had been making light conversation within their groups, but all conversation stopped when Gabby spoke.

"No offense," she said. "You know, it's kind of a lot to process. The last week has been the craziest one of my life. You've all been more than great and let me do . . . whatever it is I bring to all this. An early warning system, maybe? The town kook? Regardless, we all want the same thing: to stop Razhael and his side from setting the Earth on the path to Armageddon. After we do that, we can swap stories and give me more funny looks like you're doing now. I want to get through this with all of you so we can laugh about this moment for years to come."

The groups went back to conversing. Lewis and Candy walked over to wish the Florida team good luck. "And happy hunting," Lewis said, trying to hide the quiver in his voice. Candy smacked him on the shoulder.

"Wait a minute," Commander Pleasants said. "The boss can't go to Russia alone either. He needs some backup." Cain began to speak, but Pleasants cut him off. "Sir, they gassed you in Indiana. You have to know they will do that again, or worse. You cannot be a one-man show this time."

"Paula, I will be fine." Cain had arranged the groups for maximum safety for all involved and so he would have minimal responsibility for the safety of those around him. He believed he would be able to cut loose if it was just him versus Razhael and whoever he had with him.

"Sir, it makes sense operationally if you have a support team close to you," Paula said. "I know you can handle whatever gets thrown at you. But please, if nothing but for the sake of the rest of us—take some people with you. You can use it as an opportunity to work on your social skills."

"All right, Commander, your point is well taken," Cain said. "Who do you have in mind?"

Pleasants already had decided who would be going. "Gregg, Roland— you're up. You'll be accompanying the boss to the steppes of Russia. Like we've discussed before, please try to keep him from winning this thing all by himself before we even have a chance to do something." Both men nodded and moved over to stand beside Cain, who nodded courteously to both. "It will be nice to have some company on the trip. Thank you for coming along. I am not used to working with others like this, but I am sure I will learn quickly. Now, tell me a bit more about yourselves . . . "

As everyone made small talk about the upcoming mission, Gabby got up to get a breath of fresh air on the nearest veranda. Zander walked through the door and joined her. "Going to be a lot of activity really soon, huh?" he said as he came up beside Gabby, standing just a little too close for her comfort.

"Yes, and we have to stay focused . . . Hey, do you mind? Give me some breathing room, Zander!"

"Just want to talk and see what you're thinking, Gabby. I mean, we're all putting our lives on the line here, mostly because of your visions. I'd like to know what kind of person really gets this gift and what you plan to do with it."

"Well, Mr. Snyder, I think you already know the answer to that question. You're trying to test me—goad me into doing something that shows weakness. Or you want me to say something that shows I'm out of my mind. Is that about right, *Mr. Comms?* And why is it that you are almost never in the field? I'm all for equality, but how did a young man like yourself, who probably did a few tours in the military right out of high school, then decided to cash in and become a soldier for hire, end up running the communications grid for a private enterprise like Mr. Green's? Couldn't find a young lass back home who would fall over your every word? Your tales of derring-do not thrilling enough? Your soldier of fortune stories? Hmm?"

Zander looked Gabby straight in the eyes. She met his gaze and stepped forward a half step: The soldier was a good five inches taller than Gabby. Zander breathed deeply and slowly raised his hand. Gabby made a fist, preparing for what might come next.

Zander's hands rose and he made the universal sign for surrender, both hands palms forward in front of his chest. "Just seeing what you're made of, boss lady. I'll do what I'm paid to do. Just want to see what you're getting out of all this. See you for final planning in the morning, Gabrielle." The soldier then made a quick turn-around and headed back inside.

"See you then, Zander. Try to find your manners in your quarters. You're going to need them."

***

The library was the largest gathering area in the retreat. Cain and the staff had worked most of the night preparing maps and instructions. Dozens of electric rods were laid out on a far table, along with flak jackets and more traditional weapons. One large map of the world had three large X's on it. Vladivostok, Russia. Mojave, California. Cape Canaveral, Florida.

As the last members of the group sat down, Cain stood up. "Everyone will be headed out later today. I hope no one became too comfortable last night. We all have our assignments. If our intelligence is correct and we do this right, we will stop three space transports, each carrying payloads of metal rods that are designed for only one thing: a highly coordinated pummeling of the Earth from space. Many of you may have heard about this idea in your military careers. It has several names: Project Thor; Divine Hammer; Rods from God. It's all the same thing—drop a big enough object from space to Earth, and it will create an explosion akin to a medium-sized nuclear device. Drop several things in short succession in enough locations and . . . "

"It will be enough to knock our planet the tiniest fraction out of orbit," Gabby said, standing up as she spoke. "It will wreak havoc with our weather. There will be massive rain storms, lightning, the tides will change. Almost overnight, the face of the Earth will be permanently affected. Then it gets worse. The sun will be blotted out by dust for years. And eventually in a few years, on the Winter Solstice, the northern hemisphere will freeze. A few months later, the same thing will happen in the south."

"I have a question, Gabby, if you don't mind," Katrina said while holding her hand up. "How will a bunch of dust make the Earth freeze? It's bad, of course, but it can't do that much in the long term."

"Very good point, Katrina. You're absolutely right. It's bad, but it's just a side effect of the real damage." Everyone in the room has been talking among themselves quietly during the question and for Gabby's answer. Everyone stopped at "real damage." "The problem," Gabby continued with everyone's attention, "is the barrage from above will be enough to move the

Earth's orbit. It will be just a fraction and probably unnoticeable, but it will be more than enough. Enough to move us from the sun just a bit, and then in a few years we all freeze to death.

"Most of my dreams have had an element of the cold, and that's been increasing. At first it was a background element, but lately everything has been enveloped in white—snow, rain, sleet, people freezing to death in the streets. Just last night, one of the dreams was full of snow. One of my favorite things used to be concerts. Well, it was a favorite thing for Daniel and me. Anyway, last night was a dream about everyone freezing at an outdoor concert we went to years ago in Colorado. It was terrifying. Whatever is going to happen is going to happen soon. And with that, I'm going to turn it over to our host."

Cain rose and walked toward the head of the large table. "Gabby, thank you so much. Your bravery is an example to us all. Perhaps most of all to me. We now have verified the three sites. Cape Canaveral has a rocket sitting on a launchpad. In California, we have seen a commercial rocket practicing with a heavy payload. We believe these are the weak points in their plan. If these launches can be stopped, their plans are done. We believe all three payloads are needed for what they are planning. One or two will be extremely bad, of course, but we believe they need all three payloads to make their plan work.

"Which brings us to the third site. There is no official launchpad in Vladivostok, but that does not mean one is not there. We have verified reports of Razhael in the city, and that's been corroborated by our new friend here." Cain gestured toward Tuna, who stood just a bit taller at his recognition. "At first we did not know why, but satellite imagery and people on the ground and near Rachel—that still makes me laugh, so let us try to use it as often as possible." Cain was trying to stifle a laugh but he was the only one. Tuna, however, still had a big grin on his face and was nodding in agreement. "Allow me to regain my composure . . . Thank you, everyone. I do believe a sense of humor can help us all get through this most weighty of tasks. It is almost more than the human mind can take. A little levity could not hurt.

"But, back to our intelligence reports. We do have someone in the city

196

who has noted significant activity at an old Soviet military site north of the city. The launch site is not an official one, but it is there nonetheless. It appears the site has been receiving updates recently. The jobs are simple enough: prevent all three rockets from launching. Either by hook or by crook, we can stop them. We must stop them. The world and . . . other interested parties are counting on us, whether they know it or not." Cain pointed upward slightly as he spoke. "Let's get to planning."

"Commander Pleasants, you are Group One. You have Florida. Stop that launch, then go say hello to the mouse for me. I do love that place. Your team flies out this evening on one of our planes direct from Pittsburgh to Cocoa Beach."

"Thanks, Mr. Green," Commander Pleasants said. "We can get it done." The members of Group One looked around, nodding silently to their partners.

"Group Two, and Mr. Peak," Cain said, gesturing toward the second-in-command. "Matthew, you have done an outstanding job and are fast on your way to a full command of your own. All of you should know he has my full faith and trust during this mission. You have all won an all-expense paid trip to sunny California and the fine folks at Vandenberg Air Base.

"Which leaves Gregg, Roland, and myself to bundle up and head to Mother Russia. While I should be able to handle things myself, your points are well taken. This is no time for grandstanding. And I will be very glad for not only the help, but for the company."

"I'm glad you are not trying to sneak away and go solo," Gabby said. "There's too much riding on this."

"You are correct, Gabby," Cain said. "So before we leave, I have one more bit of information to share. Gabby knows this, and as do Candy and Lewis by happenstance. It is far past time to share this with the people I am asking to risk their lives.

"If any of you had been in Elkins to see the thorough shaming of Hadrael by Gabby's friends, you would have heard him refer to me as 'firstborn.' To their credit, Gabby's friends accepted this knowledge without much question, but nearly all of you here have worked for me a while, and we all have a relationship to one degree or another. And you deserve to know. Not only so our opponents cannot use it against you, but also so you may see, I hope, the utmost faith I place in every one of you.

"The truth is, I am many thousands of years old. I really have no idea how many. I have not aged since the day I slew my brother. My name is not Gage Green, or any of the other pseudonyms I have used throughout the eons. I am, to my eternal shame, Cain."

The room was silent as everyone stared. Zander was the first to speak. "Who would name their child that? And you said that thing back in West Virginia called you 'firstborn.' I can see wanting to use a different name if my parents named me . . . " All the faces in the room were looking at Zander. They were somber, but not angry. Zander grew quiet.

Commander Pleasants spoke next. "You are right, Zander. Who would name a child that? I can think of only two people. And it's not like we couldn't tell there was something special about you, boss. Chatter throughout the organization does get around. But no one would win the office pool on this one."

All eyes suddenly were on Cain. He'd revealed his true nature only a handful of times in his very long life, with varying results. Some cursed him where he stood; some hugged and loved him anyway. Most took a few moments to accept the impossible that was standing in front of them. This group—a supernatural visionary, experienced military veterans who signed up for a lucrative job as part of a private army, two civilians who had helped capture a fallen angel, and a reformed gargoyle—gathered around Cain and laid their hands on his shoulders or arm. Then, a cascade of compliments and thanks began.

"Thank you, boss."

"I don't care about your past, but I'd sure love to hear about it one day."

"Well, this explains a whole lot. I love my job, by the way. I'm with you no matter what."

"Geez, how old are you then?"

"So when you took over for your dad, you really just replaced yourself? That's awesome."

"When this is over, can you take us to the garden? Also, I love my job too."

"I bet you've seen a lot, huh, boss?"

"You've helped protect the world this whole time? That's amazing. You should write a book. Maybe several."

As the comments and well wishes subsided, Cain began to weep openly and thank everyone standing around him. Never had so many learned his secret at once, and never had he heard such positivity and thankfulness.

Katrina stood up. "Mr. Green, I have a question . . ."

Cain, a smile on his face from ear to ear, interrupted her. "Dear Katrina, I have heard just about every question that can be asked over the years. What can I answer for you? I will do it if I can. By the way, in case this is your question—my parents did not have belly buttons."

Laughter filled the air, only this time it was more raucous than a week ago as several people doubled over with tears in their eyes from laughing. "Never mind. You beat me to it," Katrina said as she sat down and tried to regain her composure.

Once everyone settled down, Cain spoke once more. "I cannot thank you all enough. My life has been extraordinary, and I will be happy to share as many tales as I am able when we are through. And thank you for that most unexpected affirmation. Yes, I am *that* Cain. I really have no idea how old I am. When I have given my true age to those who know my secret, it has been a guess. But I am really old, and I am really rich. And anyone who lays a hand on me in anger gets hit by lightning. So, as many of you have surmised, the lightning jacket does not really exist. My curse was the inspiration for the electrical rods that have been so useful against our enemies.

"And we do have enemies, and we are going to stop them. Two of our groups have someone with supernatural abilities or senses. This is very much on purpose. It should give those groups a slight edge. The California team has two: Gabby and Tuna. The Cape Canaveral team has no supernatural help, so they get the most experienced people. As for me, Razhael and every denizen of Hell know who I am. Which, by the way, is why I wanted to go alone. They know to attack me is death. I can do this by myself."

"But you don't have to, boss," Commander Pleasants said. "What's the point of this organization, of this mission, if we can't rely on each other? Even you. Please, for our sakes if nothing else, don't go back on your word to take Coffman and McIntyre. Plus, those guys never bathe and they can smell pretty damn bad after a while." The commander was smiling as she said this, and nodded toward the two men on Team Three, who returned the gesture.

"Very well, Commander. Your point is taken. The teams stay as is. Now, we all have flights to catch and fallen angels to trounce. Everyone, please grab your gear so we can stop with the speeches and get to work."

CHAPTER 31: SPAIN 601

"Good morning, *imperecedero,*" Isla said, sitting on the edge of a window of a large home in the sprawling Roman city of Hispalis.

Ordoño Falcond rolled over in a bed of straw, stretching his well-muscled arms to help wake up. He had several bits of straw from the bed entangled in his long white hair, and he began to pick them out before getting up. The day before had been taxing but a good one for Ordoño and his family. He not only had solidified his role as a city elder, but he had ensured his family would remain one of the most prominent in Hispalis for generations to come.

Ordoño had bought a large block of land in the city's center so his family could expand their market with a much better location before diversifying into a wider variety of items. He planned to begin importing food that city dwellers never had tried so his stand would become a destination. Hispalis had grown into a major trade location in Andalusia under the rule of Rome. Spaniards, Romans, and Moors made up the majority of the city's population. Living in this crossroads city meant lots of different tastes and customs were pouring in all the time, and this included the palates of many who longed for the food of their homelands. Plus, there was the city's established citizenry. Ordoño thought he and his family soon would be running a very successful—and profitable—market.

"Come, Isla," he said. "Let us walk down to the new space once again. We can enjoy this sunny day and talk of our plans once more."

"Of course, husband, my *imperecedero.* I will get dressed so we are presentable as a family on the rise, thanks to you."

"And you too, my Isla," Ordoño said.

***

Ordoño and Isla, along with Isla's sister Maya and her children Santiago and Gabriella, walked south along the wide, dusty streets for many blocks.

The outskirts of the market area had vendors of less expensive and less valuable items. The heart of the market area ran alongside the Guadalquivir. The Falcond's new market area ran for 300 feet along the riverbank. There was not a better location in all of the city. Ordoño had bought out four other merchants to give him the space he needed. In a few days, they would move from their current location a few blocks away to this new, very well-traveled area. Ordoño was paying some local ruffians to keep people away from the space. They greeted him as he approached.

"*Señor* Falcond, good morning, sir," one of the leaders of the group, a tall, heavily scarred man named Toribio, said. "All is well with your land here. We are protecting it from all sorts of trouble. It has not been easy. Some of our men were injured last night. I am afraid our price will go up."

"That is not what we agreed to, Toribio," Ordoño said. "The price was for full protection until we are moved and open. I am disappointed you are trying to renegotiate now."

"You did not factor Roman patrols into your price," Toribio retorted. "Those centurions came poking around, looking for handouts and protection money themselves. We are good, but those centurions have a lot more armor and weapons than we do."

"I am a Roman citizen, Toribio. I will inquire about these centurions and their illicit activities. If they injured someone, they will pay restitution. However, the price remains."

Toribio looked down at the man before him. Toribio thought he had one of the strangest combinations of features he had ever seen: extremely dark skin, with snow-white hair down to near his waist. He edged closer toward the man, still staring into his piercing blue eyes.

Without breaking his gaze, Ordoño hit the professional criminal with a very quick, undefended punch to the groin. Toribio fell to the ground, doubled over in pain. The remainder of Toribio's men fled. Ordoño and Isla backed several feet back away. The injured man managed to choke out the words, "You are going to pay for that, mongrel."

"That is doubtful, young man," Ordoño said. "As I said before, I am a Roman citizen, and you are not. That is strongly in my favor. Then there is the matter of you being a criminal. One I hired for a job—that you did not do very well—but a criminal nonetheless. And third, any attempt to harm me will not work out, I assure you. If you have a bit of sense rattling around in your head, you will take what I pay you and depart. Do not come around my market again. Do you understand?"

Toribio stood up very slowly, still wincing in pain, and limped away. He turned to look back at the small crowd that had assembled around his erstwhile employer. Ordoño was being congratulated for standing up to the city's criminal element with some people cheering and some giving him pats on the back. Ordoño saw Toribio looking his way, waved to him, then went back to talking to members of the crowd. When the crowd had dispersed, Isla turned to her husband and said, "You should not have humiliated him. This is not going turn to out well, Ordoño. You hired a criminal to do an honest job. What did you expect?"

"I wanted to give him and those around him a chance at a decent living. I had hoped they could complete this, then continue doing small jobs for us. Jobs that are honorable. As a way to rise above his station, as I once did."

"Ordoño, you are tender-hearted but foolish," Isla said. "Those men have had hard lives, much harder than you or I." Isla knew there was something different about her husband, something rare and dangerous, but she did not know the truth. "He is not going to forgive you. I promise you this will not turn out well."

"I hope you are wrong, my Isla," Ordoño said. "For all our sakes, I hope you are wrong."

***

On the walk home, Ordoño and Isla, along with Maya, Santiago, and Gabriella, stopped for a cask of honey to share after the evening's meal. After exchanging pleasantries with the shop owner, the group turned to leave and were suddenly face-to-face with Toribio and a group of his men. Toribio drew a blade from inside his clothing and moved toward Santiago and Gabriella. Ordoño moved quickly past his wife and sister-in-law to reach the children, who had been standing behind the adults and now were the closest to the criminal gang.

Toribio lunged toward Santiago, cutting him on the arm. The blade was not made well, and didn't do much damage. Ordoño threw himself in front of Gabriella as Santiago fell to the ground and his mother rushed to his side. Toribio scoffed at the display. "What will you do, little man who does not pay? Try to hit me when I am not looking again? There is no chance of that and no chance of you stopping me now." Toribio lunged toward Maya as she tried to stop the flow of blood from her son's arm. This time, Ordoño was successful in preventing any further harm to his family as the blade slid into his chest and pierced his heart.

Everyone surrounding the two men—Isla, Maya, Gabriella, and Santiago—and Toribio's gang suddenly grew silent. To assault a Roman citizen like this meant death. As if directed by an unseen choreographer calling for more drama on an already dire scene, thunder began to roll and lightning could be seen in the distance. A large storm had materialized out of nowhere and, according to multiple witnesses, was moving directly toward the city. And not just the city, but the spot where Ordoño had just been stabbed.

Ordoño was lying on the ground gasping for breath. Remarkably little blood was leaking out. "Please, Isla, Maya . . . get the children and move back. Far back. Please. This will be . . . it has not happened for a long time . . . and this wound . . . it will not be safe."

"What do you mean, husband? The open wound in your chest is not safe? I do not understand."

"Isla, please, now, there is not much time. Move away now. Several blocks at least. You must do this. Now."

Maya and her children already were heeding Ordoño's warning and were hurrying down the street as the storm moved closer. Isla stood up, her gaze still on her mortally wounded husband. "I am going, my love. I do not understand it, but I am going."

"Thank you. I love you, Isla. Now, make haste."

Toribio had watched this scene from a few steps away. His knife was still in his hand, and still bloody. His fate, he thought, was sealed by this crime. He hoped that his family would forgive him and visit him while in prison.

With his family safely away, Ordoño turned to look at Toribio and his men. "You fool," he said, with a surprising amount of anger considering he had just been stabbed in the heart and should be dead or well on his way to it. "You have brought ruin on yourself and your men, all over a few *lira.*" Ordoño looked at the sky; the storm was upon them. "I have not seen this in more than three hundred years. Goodbye, Toribio."

"What do you mean, three hundred yea . . . " Toribio began, when the heavens suddenly opened up and eight bolts of lightning struck him, leaving just the barest suggestion that, a moment before, a human had stood there. A few blackened wisps drifted through the spring breeze, much of it getting caught in the hair and clothing of Toribio's men. Several of the men fell to their knees in prayer. Most fled.

Ordoño leaned back and groaned. His wound was healing, but it had never been a fast process. The pain was the same as if a mortal man had sustained the wound. Isla ran to her husband and saw that his knife wound was markedly better in just a few minutes. She stepped back from Ordoño, who was beginning to sit up. "Isla, my love," he said, his voice a shade raspier than before. "I never wanted you to see that, or see me like this. I am . . . "

"A hero, my *imperecedero.* You are a hero. You are Hercules reborn, come to save the city you founded. You command the storm. You are, you are a . . . god. A god among us and my husband. I never knew, Ordoño, I never knew. Please forgive me."

"Isla, no. That is not who I am. Not what I am," Ordoño said. "I am cursed. All this I would trade in an instant for one more day with you, my lovely and faithful wife and partner. I must leave now. And quickly. Please listen to me. All of my holdings—the house, the market, my stash of Roman coins hidden in the casks on the roof—are now all yours. Work the market with your sister. You will have lots of help, and you always had a better mind for business than me. See to it that it grows and your wealth along with it. And Isla, please . . . remarry when the time is right. That is my wish for you before I leave this beautiful city."

"Why, Ordoño, why must you leave? You won. You brought justice to the criminals and have revealed yourself as the reincarnation of Hercules here in his city. Your city."

"Then I leave my city in the very best of hands, Isla. Yours. My actions may not seem to make sense to you now, but people will come looking for me here. People I need to avoid, for at least a few years more. When asked, tell them nothing. They will menace you, but they will not harm you. I have seen to that."

"Yes, if that is your wish, husband," Isla said, her eyes beginning to well with tears. "Will we ever see each other again?"

"No, my love," Ordoño said, now standing, his chest not showing any sign that a mortal wound had been dealt there just a few minutes prior. "I may see your descendants one day. Please, if you can, retain the name we have shared. It would be a welcome thing to hear the name Falcond spoken with honor and pride throughout Hispalis, and Andalusia, all of Spain and all of the world, for generations to come.

"One last thing, my love," Ordoño said. "The market is wonderful, and it is vital to our family now. But it will not last the centuries ahead. Grow it as best you can. Put most of our money, our savings, into land and buildings. The need for both is eternal and will bring great wealth and prestige to the Falcond name. This I promise and leave to you and your most capable and lovely hands."

The couple shared one last embrace. Then Ordoño turned away, tears streaming down his face and his tunic still smoldering, and began to walk to the nearest city gate. He did not look back.

Note: The city of Hispalis had a name change sometime after the year 712. Since then, it has been known as Seville.

CHAPTER 32: WHO ARE YOU?

Daniel was beginning to regret his decision to leave Gabby in Texas. When he took off, he planned to drive back to Virginia and use the time on the road to sort through his thoughts. He would return to work and wait for Gabby to get back from saving the world. But that plan didn't last past the exit from the motel. Daniel decided to seek answers for himself by heading west.

He never told Gabby, but he also felt a calling to travel in that direction. Behind the wheel for the better part of the day, he made it to southern Colorado in the early evening. He had made multiple stops along the way at nearly every roadside attraction he saw. His only purchases were a Navajo dreamcatcher and a bottle of Nehi. The dreamcatcher now dangled from the car's rearview mirror.

Daniel didn't know exactly why he was traveling west or why he bought the dream catcher, but he knew both decisions felt right. It was as if a new part of him was just waking up. He tried to ascribe the feeling to having met Cain and getting caught up in his self-appointed task of stopping Armageddon before it started. He briefly thought perhaps Gabby's gift of prophetic visions had rubbed off on him a bit and this was a side effect.

But deep down, he knew better. He felt it with the awakening that began during his captivity—during his time with Lorelei. Something primal lived inside him, and he was discovering it the more he drove and thought about it. It was a feeling Daniel had trouble describing and even more trouble reconciling with his beliefs. He prayed as he drove, but he could not maintain his concentration enough to pray as he believed he should. He gave up on it, promising himself he would try again when he stopped for the day.

The feeling didn't leave his mind, and it had grown into a small buzzing by late afternoon. Daniel thought of his long courtship of Gabby. How he had wished for more, but she didn't . . . at least not yet. He thought of his career. He was good at being a computer programmer, but not great. Already, the kids coming out of college were more advanced than he was, and he suspected, at age twenty-eight, they looked at him as an old man.

His relationship with his parents was good but unremarkable. They visited every so often from South Dakota and called every few weeks, but it was nothing any of them thought of as close. The relationship was perfunctory and loving, but nothing special. His parents, Linda and Clive, still worked and had busy lives of their own. Daniel thought they were almost relieved he didn't live close. He loved them and they loved him, but in a distant, almost required sort of way.

Then his thoughts drifted back to Gabby. He knew he loved her with all his heart. Daniel never had been a passionate man, but Gabby was the perfect woman for him. She checked all of his internal boxes: tall but not rail-thin; long auburn hair that he found insanely attractive. Even the long, flowing, deep red hair of Lorelei didn't compare.

Then Daniel wondered why he was comparing his girlfriend to some chick who kidnapped him. Where did that come from?

Gabby was smart and clever in a way very few women Daniel knew were. She loved a good joke and showed more than a little interest in his genre movies. She often would ask him about the characters in science fiction movies and why they did what they did. The best he could think of usually was "That's what the story calls for." She smiled and would say thanks, but Daniel knew she was holding back out of respect because the movies were something he really enjoyed. It was a good relationship, and Daniel could not exactly say why he left her at the Texas motel.

His thoughts then drifted back to Lorelei. He always had been faithful to Gabby to a fault, but his kidnapping and time with Lorelei had awakened something. Something he didn't know he had in him. The voice in his head post-kidnapping was insistent: you are special in a way that Gabby never can be. You are destined for great things. Take the hands of your brothers and sisters and make a stand. Daniel didn't have any siblings, so he took the last part with a grain of salt. Maybe the voice meant fraternity brothers—which Daniel also did not have. He had avoided the raucous socializing of the Greek system in college as best he could. He had friends in a few fraternities, and they urged him to try it out, but Daniel always demurred. He had to study, he wasn't feeling well, he had a big project due. His friends eventually stopped asking. He lost track of most of his college friends after graduation. Whatever his new internal voice was trying to tell him, it was lost on Daniel. Or he needed someone to interpret his thoughts. Maybe he would see a psychologist when he got home.

But home was a long way off, and Daniel needed answers quickly. Before he had to be home to greet Gabby as if nothing had been amiss. He had planned to tell her he merely was frustrated with Cain's mission and was in a bit of shock from being kidnapped. His unexpected jaunt out west to find Lorelei and join his . . .

Wait, Daniel thought. *I never thought about finding Lorelei.* He had been recounting how things would go with Gabby when she returned. He was on a short trip to the West Coast to see some sights and put his mind at ease, but that didn't count. He would leave that part out of his tale. Where did Lorelei fit in this? He tried to disregard the thought, but he kept coming back to it. Daniel knew about Stockholm syndrome, but some part of his rational mind knew what he was experiencing was not that. It was something much more—much deeper. When he had been beside Lorelei on the couch, he would quickly forget how he arrived there and that he had been kidnapped. Daniel had soaked in her presence. Her hair, her eyes, the smell of her, and much more . . . it was almost all he thought about when she would leave the room for short periods. He anticipated her return like a high school boy watches for his first crush: giddy anticipation that often cannot be put into words, with wild fascination and the thoughts of what she was concealing under her clothes.

Daniel was having trouble keeping his eyes on the road. It was 7:30 in the evening, and he'd been driving for nearly twelve hours minus his short stops. He would look for a place to stay for the night, thanks to the credit card and its generous spending limit Cain had supplied the night before. He should make it to the northern California coast by late afternoon the next day. He kept an eye out for a place that would offer some degree of safety but was off the beaten path to avoid making him or the car a target for Razhael and company.

After driving another forty minutes and no hotel in sight, Daniel was beginning to wonder if there were any in the Colorado high desert. He started thinking he could just sleep in the car, but he almost immediately discounted that because of the anticipated temperature drop. The land he was passing through would get extremely hot during the day and come close to freezing at night. Sleeping in his car would not work. There had to be something close by.

After another twenty minutes of driving, Daniel saw a small road sign for a motel. It wasn't part of the usual big blue highways signs directing passersby to the nearest Econo Lodge or Holiday Inn. It was a small white billboard with black lettering that read, "Two Horns Motel, Two Miles Ahead. No Credit Cards."

Great, Daniel thought. *I have absolutely no cash on me, but I do have a card that could probably buy anything I wanted.* He decided to risk it and hoped the sign was out of date. How did a place like that even function these days? From the looks of his surroundings, not very well. But with limited options, Daniel thought, how bad could it be?

The motel was about a quarter mile from the exit. He passed a small mom-and-pop gas station that was closed for the evening, then came up on the motel. The only other vehicle in the lot was an older Mercedes, and it was at the far end of the lot. Daniel parked and went inside. The desk clerk looked up from his magazine as Daniel approached the counter. He said, "You saw the 'cash only' sign, right? It's a big hassle these days, but it's how the owner likes to run things. Don't even have a machine to process cards, if you can believe that."

"A card is all I have on me," Daniel said. "Isn't there something we could do? Call my bank or the card company, maybe do a cash advance? I'm beat from driving, and don't think I can make it any further."

"Nope," the clerk said. "Cash only. The owners are real funny that way. I'm sorry. There's a Holiday Inn about seventeen miles from here, though. They take cards."

"Thanks, but I can barely keep my eyes open. Would it be okay if I sleep in my car in the parking lot for a while?"

"That's fine," the clerk said. "You wouldn't be the first person to do that here. Not sure why they won't take cards, but it's the rules. I get paid in cash too. I guess it's some kind of tax dodge and no one's caught on yet. You can park under one of the overhead lights. It gets down in the twenties at night. You gotta blanket or something to help keep warm?"

"I have a blanket, but that's it. I'll check the trunk, though. I borrowed the car from a friend." Daniel had a slight twinge of guilt referring to Cain as a friend. He liked him well enough when they first met, and he was super happy when Cain and Gabby and their private army showed up to rescue him from sitting on a couch with a gorgeous redhead who hung on his every word. After that, he felt like Gabby and Cain were growing closer and he was the odd man out. Even with Armageddon looming, he still was on the sidelines.

Daniel walked slowly to the car. He already was parked under one of the few lights in the parking lot. He opened the Dodge's trunk and rummaged for a blanket or two. He found two thin blankets—one black and one gray. They both smelled relatively clean but a little musty. Daniel thought they would work fine. He would continue his trek in the morning and be sure to drink plenty of coffee to help counter what he thought would be a long, difficult night with little sleep. He eyed the Mercedes as he climbed into the driver's seat of the Dodge and began to recline the seat. Who else was traveling through this desolate stretch at night? *I bet my reasons are a whole lot more interesting than theirs,* Daniel thought as he covered himself with the two trunk blankets and attempted to sleep.

***

It was 11:49 p.m. when Daniel awoke and needed to pee. *Too many Nehi's on the trip,* he thought. He stumbled out of the Dodge and walked about sixty feet past the hotel where no light shone so he could go without anyone seeing. After finishing, he wrapped the blankets around his shoulders and made his way back to the car.

There was someone leaning against it.

"You've got to be kidding me," Daniel murmured to himself. *If they steal anything I'm going to lose it.* He patted his pockets to reassure himself that at least the credit card was still with him. If this went badly, he had that as a backup.

Daniel was able to determine that the figure leaning up against the Dodge was female. That's a small relief, he thought. Maybe it wouldn't be a fight. Maybe she was just a lot lizard looking to score. Although he wondered why she would work such a desolate stretch of road. As he moved closer, the streetlight overhead shone brighter on the red hair of the would-be street walker/car jacker. *I know that hair,* Daniel thought, *but that can't be her.* When Daniel was fully under the streetlight, Lorelei waved to him. Daniel checked and rechecked that he had zipped his fly and tried to run his hands discreetly through his hair while walking toward the car. Lorelei was leaning against his car like she didn't have a care in the world. Neither of them noticed that the dreamcatcher dangling from the Dodge's rearview mirror was starting to smoke.

When Daniel was within talking distance, Lorelei straightened up and said loudly, "Daniel! It's so good to see you again. Fancy meeting you here. And we meet outside this time. You can't beat good old Mother Nature and the fresh night air. You are looking well. I presume you are traveling on one of Mr. Green's credit cards? He seems to be very generous with his friends. I would like to show you how generous we can be to our friends too. Daniel, it's time you learned just how special you really are."

CHAPTER 33: WHO YOU ARE

Before the three teams left the Maryland sanctuary, they agreed on several things. First, they would stay in constant contact with one another. All three missions were planned to take place within a two-hour period to minimize any advanced warnings or extra defenses at the other sites. The plan was simple: blow up or disable the space-bound rockets at all costs.

All teams would be armed with electrical staffs and conventional weapons. Everyone except for Cain and the Reeds also would be carrying enough plastique to blow a hole in the side of a small mountain. Cain said he didn't need it, and the Reeds said they never had done anything like that before, and the rods and guns would be just fine for them. No one thought any differently about them for their decision.

"Probably a good call, you two," Zander said. "This is no time to be learning on the job. You'll do fine." Both Lewis and Candy nodded to the communications officer, then joined newly promoted Commander Peak and Gabby for a short group talk. The Cape Canaveral team, led by Commander Pleasants, would reach their destination and tackle their mission first, mostly because of proximity, the team's familiarity with the launch site, and, last but not least, the time differences between the sites. An early morning strike in Florida would put the Russian team at about noon the next day, with the California team beginning in the middle of the night. Tactically, everyone agreed this made sense.

The Florida team, however, would have to wait until the other two teams were in place. This presented some risk, Cain said, but Commander Pleasants spoke up and assured everyone they would be fine. "All four of us are seasoned veterans. We know how to sit tight until it's time to get to work. Don't worry about us, boss."

"And that is why you are the commander, Mrs. Pleasants," Cain said with genuine admiration. "Which brings us to our newly promoted second-in-command, Matthew Peak. Matthew, you are in charge of the California mission. However, if Gabby asks you to do something, I highly encourage you to listen and do as she asks. You were chosen for this command for your adaptability. Please don't forget to use it now that you are in charge.

"Which, lastly, brings us to the Russia team. Truly, this team is overflowing with testosterone. And experience. Let us not forget that." Cain said this last part with a wide grin on his face as his two teammates went from unreadable expressions common to military veterans to smiles and proud glances around the room. "I am honored to have you along. Thank you for joining me. And now, the time for speeches is over. Our ground transport arrives in an hour. Let us get packed and ready."

***

"What do you mean 'special'? Like Gabby special or something else?" Daniel was excited to see Lorelei but confused about the conversation. What he had in mind when seeing her again was something very different than this. In his happiness to see Lorelei, he hadn't even considered how they both ended up at this far-off-the-beaten-path motel at the same time. The motel setting, though, did give him hope.

"Definitely something else, Danny boy," Lorelei said, her head lowered slightly so she was looking up at Daniel. It was one of the most suggestive things Daniel ever had seen. He knew he was showing a response but he didn't care.

"Are you going to tell me, or are we going to stand out here all night making googly eyes at each other?" Daniel asked, hoping Lorelei wasn't feigning a sense of humor back in Indiana.

"Neither. We're going to go inside and get to know each other better; then you can ditch the Dadmobile and ride with me," she said, nodding toward the Mercedes. "We're all headed west, but I think you already know that."

"Uh, okay . . . inside. Ditch the car. Got it. Lead the way, Lorelei," Daniel said with an equal dose of anticipation and dread in his voice. He was going to cross the line he and Gabby had agreed would be a deal-breaker. There was zero chance she wouldn't find out, either from her dream visions where she could see everything or from Daniel's inability to hide his actions.

Lorelei looked back and, as if reading his thoughts, said, "There's no shame in sharing a moment with someone, especially someone you're attracted to, like us. Not one bit, Daniel. You'll see."

"Okay" was the best Daniel could manage to say as they reached the third floor and found the room. Lorelei opened it with a key on a plastic diamond-shaped key ring, room number 301. Daniel walked inside and Lorelei locked the door. She turned toward Daniel and looked him directly in the eyes as she began to slide her top down to her waist and turned the room light off in a single motion, leaving just moonlight streaming through the shabby blue curtains. She walked slowly toward Daniel and guided him down onto the plain double bed. His legs quivered and he surrendered, finally, to the hidden desires that had been inside him all along.

***

All three groups were flying in private jets out of Charleston, West Virginia, in the middle of the night. The Pittsburgh airport would be under observation, Cain said, along with other major airports in the region. They were lucky to land in Cleveland the day before and didn't want to push their luck. Razhael would know about the capture of Hadrael by now and perhaps knew about it as soon as it happened via some unknown angelic—or demonic—sensory mechanism. The drive was a little more than two hours from the Maryland retreat, which, despite the late hour, gave everyone a chance to make small talk along the way. The caravan was chosen carefully so it looked like state government vehicles—West Virginia vanity plates with lots of zeros and only a few numbers on four older model SUVs with dark, tinted windows. The teams mostly were grouped together. The Reeds sat next to Tuna. He nodded enthusiastically to what they were saying, which consisted mainly of helpful tips for the gargoyle to blend in.

Matthew sat next to Gabby and asked her what it was like to have the visions. "They are very dreamlike, like I know it's a dream and I want to see where they take me," Gabby replied. "I've tried to direct them, to see more, but so far that's not working. I'm still getting the three sites, still with lots of snow mixed in. At times I see Daniel in the snow walking toward me, but he never gets there. Just endless trudging. I can't figure that one out yet, which is unusual. I guess the powers-that-be will let me know when I need to know something."

"That must be frustrating," Matthew said. "I can't imagine having what you have on my shoulders. If you need someone to listen, I'd be honored to help."

"Thank you, Matt," Gabby said. "I may take you up on that, but I'm good for now. I'm looking forward to getting back to regular life." Matthew nodded in agreement and moved to talk to another member of the team.

Gabby sat silently, lost in her thoughts for a few minutes. She had been trying to convince herself that there was nothing wrong, that she had adjusted to Daniel leaving. She still was mad at him for prioritizing his needs over everything else. She rarely had seen him so self-centered. They would have a lot to discuss the next time they saw each other. If they saw each other again. Gabby was loath to admit it, but she felt his absence acutely. She wondered where he was, what he was doing, and if he had told anyone about the events of the last several days. She pecked on Matt's shoulder lightly when there was a pause in his conversation with Katrina. "You know, Matt, maybe I can take you up on your offer. You too, Katrina, if you want."

They both leaned up to listen more closely. The rest of the team still were talking, but their conversations became noticeably quieter when Gabby spoke. "You know, I dream of regular life at home too. Something is always off like dreams are, but I'm home, I'm happy, and I know that we finished our jobs. What we're doing now. I thought it was just me having a regular dream, sort of to compensate for the visions. But maybe they've been visions all along too. I really dislike that term, but maybe I should embrace it—not fight it so much and call them what they are. Not dreams, but visions.

"I'm kind of backpedaling here, but maybe I need to. It has been a gift. Not necessarily one I wanted, but that's okay. If it helps us survive, it's worth it. So yes, Matt, Milla, Katrina, everyone—I'd love to share my visions with you. I've heard that there are people with visions and also interpreters of those visions and they are rarely one person. I've done okay with it so far, but maybe we stand a better chance if we all have a little more insight into what's going on or what's going to happen."

Everyone in Team Two liked and admired Gabby from their first encounters with her. At this moment, though, they began to look up to her and see her as a leader. Matt, sensing the positive but interested to hear more vibe from everyone, said, "Gabby, will you share with us the visions you've had? We have some travel time. And, like you said, maybe one of us will pick up on something new."

Tuna spoke up just as Matt finished, in slow, halting sentences where he was careful to enunciate as best as he could. "Stories yes. Tell so we know what to do. Please, Gabbee. We do what you say. Also do what Mat Tew say too. Promise. No want to go back Hell. Stay here with friends. Can Dee, Lew us, say I stay."

The group was silent when Tuna finished speaking. Most of them were astounded at how much better he was after just a short time. Candy had been quietly helping him, and he had been an unexpectedly avid learner. Lewis patted Tuna's shoulder as if he was a proud father.

Unbeknownst to everyone and especially Lewis, Tuna never had experienced physical contact that wasn't meant to hurt, chastise, or worse. Tuna's first reaction was to throw his bony elbow into Lewis' jaw.

Everyone in the SUV suddenly went quiet as Lewis bent over and began to spit blood. After several throat-clearing efforts, he sat up and looked at Tuna, who was now cowering against the seat in front of him. "Tuna, it's fine. Don't worry. I am not mad. I wasn't thinking. My fault. When we get back, you might have a career as a professional wrestler. And I may need to see a dentist. Now, I think Gabby was going to share some magic stuff with us before I so carelessly interrupted."

***

Daniel rolled over as Lorelei lifted herself off him and sat up on the edge of the bed. He stumbled to the bathroom to splash water on his face and to catch his breath. He didn't think being breathless in front of the gorgeous woman with whom he had just shared the most intimate of acts set the right tone for whatever was going to happen next. He walked out of the bathroom expecting to see Lorelei lounging on the bed and waiting for him. Instead, she was fully dressed, brushing her hair and putting her belongings carefully into a travel bag. She turned her head to see Daniel, just in a towel, with a puzzled look on his face. "Darling, we have things to do. More than the things we just did. There can be more of that later, but it's time you heard the truth. Get dressed and grab the worn-out book in the nightstand."

***

"They are like movies in my mind," Gabby said. "My first vision was at a bar, of all places, a few Sundays ago. I thought maybe I was dehydrated or hadn't eaten in a while. The overhead music and my vision started to blend together. Daniel said I had seemed a little zoned out. Anyway, I saw that meteor that passed by a week or so ago and then pools of blood on the moon. All the talking heads on TV and online were explaining it as a scientific wonder, but I just saw a moon filling up with blood. Things got more specific after that first one."

***

After hurriedly getting dressed, Daniel opened the bedside table and found a Gideon's Bible. Lorelei sat beside him, and asked him to read a verse from Revelations, Chapter 13. "It's short. Go ahead. You will recognize the part. Read it and tell me what it says."

Daniel flipped to near the end of the book, and found the section Lorelei referenced. "'Here is wisdom. Let him who has understanding calculate the number of the beast, for the number is that of a man; and his number is six hundred and sixty six.'

"Okay," he said. "What does Nero have to do with me? Am I his great-great-great-grandson or something like that?"

"No, Daniel," Lorelei said, looking deep into his eyes. "This may come as a shock to you, as it was for most of us. Just as your girlfriend's part in Armageddon was masked, so was ours. But we are on the right side of things, despite what that thing says." She glanced down disdainfully at the book in Daniel's hand. "We are for change, for survival of the fittest, for sorting out the weak so that the strong may thrive. We are for exploring this planet and the hundreds of thousands of others in the universe. We are for free will and for doing as we please." With the last part, Lorelei placed her hand on Daniel's thigh and leaned toward him until he could feel her breath on his neck.

"Who are these 'we'?" Daniel asked, not yet making the connection Lorelei wanted him to make. "Are you saying you're working for Razhael?"

"No, my dear Daniel. I'm saying Razhael works for me. Me and my 665 brothers and sisters. We have covered the globe for generations. We are of different ages and nationalities. Some may pass on, but there is always another to rise up and take their place. The one thing we have in common is our parents. Or more precisely, our parent. The human sows who bore us don't know the grand plan. They fulfill their tasks and usually are none the wiser. When our father visits this plane of existence to build his family, he has to disguise himself from the prying eyes of his rival." Lorelei sneered as she said this and pointed up. "But that will not be the case for much longer.

"Just like that bitch and her visions, we also have a secret. A secret that you've known all your life but couldn't accept. Daniel, why do you think the lessons you heard every forsaken Sunday morning didn't stay with you? How could they slip away from your mind as easily as water passing through your hand? Because they were not meant for you. You and I were made for greater things than restraint and fake piety. We are made to rule. You, me, and our 664 siblings. There is no Adversary. There are Adversaries. You, me, and our brothers and sisters will do as we please with this world. We are the numbers of the Beast, brother, and we will tear this world to shreds long before it freezes."

CHAPTER 34: COMPARATIVE DECEPTION

"What the heck do you mean we're Adversaries?" Daniel asked, trying to grasp what Lorelei had shared. "Are we going to fight or something? Like that kind of Adversary? Or do you mean . . . ?" Daniel began to pace around the tiny room, running one hand through his hair while the other kept his towel from falling and leaving him stark naked. Lorelei sat back and smiled as Daniel worked through the knowledge she had shared.

"Oh, shit. That IS what you mean. The Devil is our dad? That really sucks. But you know, it does clarify a few things for me. Like, I love going to church but never really feel anything. And sometimes I write extra code at work just to see what it will do. And sometimes I don't make the bed even when Gabby asks nicely, and if he's our dad, and you and I just . . . what about that? You're not supposed to sleep with your . . . your half-sister!"

Lorelei sat up on the dingy bed. "Things are very different for you, me, and the others. We can sleep with whoever we like. Some of us even try to do the right things, but ultimately it never works. The immortal side in us is very strong."

"What about wings? Am I going to grow wings? Black ones like Rachel or maybe giant bat ones? Tell me I'm not going to grow wings. Do you have wings hidden somewhere? Wait a minute, maybe it would be cool to have wings. Like Hawkman." Daniel still was pacing the room, his towel occasionally slipping down; he would have to stop to fix it before resuming his pacing. Lorelei was beginning to laugh at his response.

"We don't have wings, Daniel. But we do have other attributes that will help bring about a new age on the Earth. A more just and balanced age. We will rule the remains of Earth and help our father claim his rightful place as its new god. The cycle of punishment, death, and rebirth will be broken, then we remake Earth in our image. When that is complete, we travel—to other planets, other systems, other galaxies. It is our destiny to rule."

"You have spaceships?" Daniel asked, stopping momentarily. "We can do that?"

"It's an expression, Daniel," Lorelei said, starting to tire of Daniel's mania. "But yes, we believe space exploration should proceed at all costs. The better to spread our message."

"And you know people are out there? That's something you can confirm?" Daniel stopped to sit on the bed and begin getting dressed. "You're not pulling my leg? Or any other part of me? Which was great, by the way."

"Daniel, I think you are missing the point of us meeting, fucking, and learning our true parentage. We are to be the new masters of this world. Together, we will bring the world's governments to their knees before the Big Freeze. After that, the stage will be set for our father's glorious return to Earth."

"You mean he's not underground? Hell is not below us? Jesus Christ, I've been lied to my whole life. I can't believe this shit!"

Lorelei took a deep breath, stood up, and straightened her skirt. "There is so much happening, Daniel. It can be a lot to absorb all at once. Especially now. Everything I have told you is true. You are one of us. One of the 666 who are destined to rule this world. This is our time. We can use your computer skills to our great advantage. You simply have to embrace who you are . . . who you have always been."

"And we get to do it again, right?" Daniel said, thinking through the several impossibilities he had accepted as fact recently. "Like, a lot maybe?" Lorelei nodded, but was starting to have misgivings about it. "And no wings unless they are super-cool and retractable."

Lorelei stood up and cupped her hands around Daniel's face, looking at him with a gleam in her eyes. "The world can be yours, Daniel. All of your dreams," she ran her hands up Daniel's leg, "can become reality. We can literally do anything. We can do that together. If you come with me, I can show you."

Daniel stopped and felt Lorelei's caress and the stirring of feelings he never knew he had—feelings of empowerment, of domination, of feral brutality that once would have been unthinkable to him. In this moment, he accepted his unique place in the world and fell further under the spell of his parentage. "I . . . I would like that. I can see it now. Please, Lorelei. Take me there and help me understand who I am, and what I can do to help. I've never been a big joiner of causes, but this is different. This is family, and it seems like destiny. I can feel it calling out to me. To be better, to be bolder . . . to be stronger.

"Please, Lorelei, let's go visit our family. I have a lot to learn."

***

" . . . then the wraiths showed up where I work, at the Washington Monument. We didn't know what the heck was happening. It happened really fast, but things seemed to be in super slow motion at the time. I thought we all were going to die. The door burst open, and there was Cain. I thought he was another terrorist at first, and we were doomed. Then he started flipping around and ducking and grabbing. It was impressive. He had the wraiths—I still think of the ones from the first encounter that way, and sorry for this next part, Tuna—banged up and on the run and the crowd down the stairwell before I knew it. I was astounded and knew I was way out of my depth. I just didn't know how much until later."

"And what happened with the boss again?" Katrina asked.

"We got the visitors all to the ground safely. Then the stairwell bursts open, and there is Cain walking out like he didn't have a care in the world. Then a limo leaves the White House and the Secretary of State comes over and, well, starts thanking Cain and kissing his ass. It was the darndest thing I had ever seen. Up until that point. Everything since then has been, you know, even stranger."

"And you didn't know who he was, or who he said he was?" Candy asked.

"Not a clue," Gabby said. "I thought he was some whack job or was in on the whole thing for whatever reason I do not know. He made some crack about six-thousand-year-old salad, and I took off not long after."

Everyone in the vehicle laughed at Gabby's recollection. Cain even managed a guffaw. He was pleased the teams were coalescing so quickly.

Teamwork and a sense of trust in one another would be key to completing their missions. Cain thought it was one of the biggest advantages they had. All the other side had was hate and hundreds of thousands of years being stuck somewhere they did not want to be. These modern humans, Cain mused, may be just the thing they needed to win. Their adaptability, their sense of community, and their willingness to follow when needed were remarkable.

While Cain was lost in his thoughts, Gabby continued her story. "That evening, though, was the big vision. Maybe the biggest one I've ever had. I've had longer ones with more detail, but this one was a show-stopper . . . "

Cain continued to let his thoughts drift. He had seen so much and lived a hundred thousand lifetimes that the thought of life on Earth ending seemed impossible. He had found out the hard way that the human mind can only retain so many memories. He knew he had forgotten far more than he remembered, and he was thankful that he had written down his memories every few years to help remind himself of what he had lived through. He also knew he wasn't ready to leave this life, but he also wasn't exactly sure where he would end up when he did.

How can we win? Cain asked himself again. They had a good plan but there was still something missing. Something elusive that he couldn't quite pin down and, to his shame, didn't share with the people who were risking their lives beside him. *Of course, I am not really risking my life but they are, he thought. Old man, you have to keep it together and find out what is missing. And fast.*

Cain rustled in his jacket pocket and pulled out his mobile phone. Ingenious devices. Nearly the whole knowledge base of the planet was accessible to everyone from their pockets. Simply wondrous. He typed a message, looked at it once more, then hit send. That should get the ball rolling.

***

Daniel's phone had not buzzed or pinged since leaving the motel in Texas. Not Gabby, his parents, or his few friends from work. He had almost forgotten it was in his pocket when he and Lorelei left the motel in her

Mercedes. The muffled but unmistakable ping came from his left jacket pocket. Lorelei glanced over and asked, "Are you going to answer that?"

"What? Oh, the message. Yeah, I guess. Can't imagine who is texting me at this hour." He took a look but didn't recognize the number. It did have a 202 area code, so it could be work. Computer glitches happen at all hours, and they have to be fixed pretty fast. Daniel hadn't given much thought to his job since being kidnapped. He wondered if he was still employed. He wanted to find out. The message was brief.

"Know you are out west. Doughnut blame you. Beautiful scenery. Hope UR doing well. How is the company?"

Who was texting him at this hour and would know where he was? The message didn't sound like Gabby. It wasn't her style. Besides, he knew she wouldn't contact him for a long time. He would have to be the one to make the first move there. Which left really only one person.

"Everything okay, Daniel?" Lorelei asked.

"Yeah, just some work outage. We get these all the time. I'm not super sure if I'm still employed or not. If I'm getting this, maybe I am. Let's see."

Daniel: "I'm fine, Cane. Car in Colorado but you already know that right? U tracked it? Sprying on me?"

A few minutes went by, then a response. "Stand urn issue on car fleet. Did not mean to but here wee are. Gabby misses you but will not say it. With the redhead?"

Dammit, Daniel thought as he clicked his phone off hurriedly and shoved it back in his pocket. How the hell did he know that? Did Gabby see it? Maybe the car had audio and video surveillance as well. Lorelei glanced over at Daniel and began to rub his leg with her right hand. "Work giving you trouble, Daniel? Not for much longer. You will not need to work anymore when we're through."

"Uh, thanks. That would be great. What exactly are we going to be doing, though?" His phone buzzed once again.

"I told you, Daniel, we're going to see the rest of the family and see where that takes us. Believe me, everything is going to be all right. You'll see. Work still texting you?"

"I guess. They can wait. It's the middle of the night there. Must be a problem with the servers again. They always go out at the worst times. Maybe I should just quit." Daniel folded his arms and leaned his head against the door. He thought if he could get some sleep it would help, and he could forget Cain's texts. Daniel thought he should have blocked the number. *I'll do that in the morning.*

About fifteen minutes later, the phone buzzed again. This time it was twice, which meant two messages. Daniel had just begun to doze. What the heck was going on? He took his phone out of his pocket.

The same 202 number had written twice more.

2:32 a.m.: "Do not worry. Secret is safe with me. You now I have plenty of my own."

3:14 a.m.: "Headed to Megiddo in the am. Sure you want to miss the fun?"

3:16 a.m.: "Texting tix for you Justin case."

The last message had a link to a boarding pass good for any airport to fly one Daniel Sullivan to Pittsburgh, where a private plane would be waiting to help him complete the journey. Daniel grew red-faced and pressed the button to lower his window. He threw the phone out and watched it shatter into a thousand pieces in the passenger side rearview mirror.

"I take it you quit?" Lorelei said, looking over at Daniel with a smile.

"Yes," Daniel replied, trying his best to sound convincing. "That place was driving me nuts. Wasn't going to advance there anyway."

"Good." Lorelei was suspicious of the texts and asked if the texts were from Gabby.

"Yes, you got me. It was Gabby. Sorry for not coming clean the first time. Still embarrassed a bit, I guess. She wanted me to come back and help them, but I said no. They even sent me a plane ticket. They are headed to Israel and the plains of Megiddo. Guess they think things are coming to a head pretty soon. Are they?"

Lorelei turned her attention back to the road. "Oh, yes. They are indeed. Thank you for telling me. That had to be difficult."

Daniel sat still for a moment, staring ahead at the gathering clouds in the distance. "No, it wasn't difficult at all. I know who I am now. Gabby and the others, they treated me like a prop. Like a sideman. I've had enough of that. I'm all yours, Lorelei. Can't wait to meet the rest of the family."

CHAPTER 35: NEXT STOP, MEGIDDO

Cain was thankful he chose to text Daniel rather than call. He would have been much less likely to believe him if he had heard several voices, including Gabby's. Cain didn't like not telling the others what he had done, but he believed it was necessary. He couldn't risk Gabby losing her focus. He could share the details when their tasks were complete. If he had calculated correctly and thought things out to their logical conclusion, he had sown some doubt and arrogance in the minds of their opponents, and bought his army of fourteen an extra day. He hoped that time would make a difference.

To complete the elaborate ruse, Cain left the open-ended ticket in Daniel's name in case anyone followed up on it or intercepted his texts. He also arranged for fourteen of his other private soldiers—nine women and five men—to leave the Pittsburgh airport for an all-expenses-paid trip to the Holy Land. They were briefed on their mission and were ready for any unpleasantness they might encounter up to and when the deception was discovered. Cain was determined to finish this job with as many people—particularly those in his employ—as alive and well as possible. The other side, he hoped, would not be as fortunate.

***

Their caravan arrived in Charleston a little before 8 a.m. In addition to hopefully sending Daniel and, through him, a lot of the bad guys on a wild goose chase in the Middle East, Cain also had arranged for complete wardrobes and essentials for everyone for the next several days. At the gate check-in, everyone found their bags and began to say their goodbyes and give well wishes to one another. The Florida team would arrive first and find somewhere inconspicuous to wait for the other two teams to get in place. The Russia team would be the last one to arrive at its destination. Gabby walked toward Cain for a final prep talk. "I have a good feeling about all of this," she said. "Like, it's going to work, and we'll meet back in Maryland soon to celebrate."

"Was this a vision?" Cain asked. "Dream, I mean. Was it a dream?"

"It's okay. I'm starting to make my peace with the 'v' word. It's the least crazy of the crazy things I've seen or heard lately. And to answer your question, no. It wasn't a vision or a dream. Just a really good feeling that this is going to work. That we're on the side of angels, and we'll do it."

The rest of the team were saying their goodbyes all around Cain and Gabby. Zander walked past the two and gave a slight smile. Gabby couldn't shake the feeling he was going to be trouble on the Florida mission.

"Have you ever met an angel, Gabby?" Cain said. "I have. They are pompous windbags who mostly look down on humanity. They are very full of themselves. Come on, let's get to our flights."

***

When a rest stop sign advertised bathrooms just two miles away, Lorelei said she needed to take a break. "Just need to powder my nose, Daniel darling. How about you? Need to go?"

"No, thanks. I'll just wait here."

Once inside the ladies' room, Lorelei withdrew her mobile phone from her skirt pocket and made a call. "I need a few of you to find something for me. Send at least one who is good with electronics. Yes. That's good. Yes. A little past mile marker 141. That's right. Let me know when you find it."

***

The three teams walked out onto the tarmac and headed toward their respective flights. The two domestic planes were first. They appeared to be standard private jets, similar to those used in the corporate world and for medical emergency flights. The last plane, though, was different. Sleek and angular, it resembled the photos of a stealth fighter. But this plane was much, much larger. Cain directed Gregg and Roland toward its stairway.

Gabby, Commander Pleasants, and Lewis both walked up beside Cain to get a better look at the aircraft. Lewis whistled and asked what kind of stealth plane it was. Cain smiled and thought he would take a few minutes to show off.

"This, my friends and fellow warriors, is indeed a stealth aircraft. It also is much more than that. This is one of the few aircraft on the planet certified for low-earth orbit."

"You're kidding," Lewis said as he walked toward the plane to get a closer look. "I thought all space plane prototypes were government property."

"They are," Cain said. "But as Gabby learned a few days ago, defense contracting can be an extremely interesting business. Very difficult to make money in the field, but you do get to create some interesting things. And if a fully operational working prototype remains with the contractor and the keys are left in it, who are we to turn down the ride?"

"Can we switch teams?" Lewis said, only partially joking. "California will be nice and all, but it would be awesome to fly in this beautiful machine. It's like a work of art."

"Thank you, Lewis." Cain was rarely humbled, but to hear praise from someone capable enough to have helped capture a fallen angel with no training or guidance made him blush. "Tell you what, Lewis. When this is over I will take you and Candy and as many friends from Elkins who want to go for a ride. Anywhere you want to go as well. It is the least I could do."

"That's a deal, sir," Lewis said, extending his hand in friendship. "I look forward to it. You'll be there too, right?"

"Yes. Yes, I will," Cain replied. "It would be an honor and a whole lot of fun for all of us. I look forward to it as well."

As the groups made their way to their flights, Gabby remained behind for a last one-on-one with Cain. He asked her, "Still have that good feeling?"

"Yes," Gabby replied. "This is going to work. Do you want to talk about your texting fest back in the car now? It couldn't have been about our supplies. Everything here would have taken much longer. Anything you want to share?"

Cain looked at her, a little dumbfounded and in amazement. He believed no one caught on to what he was doing, but Gabby saw and knew it was something big. He decided to come clean. "Yes, I bought us some extra time. Sent a message through a channel I know Razhael is watching to throw him off the trail."

"And what channel is that? It was Daniel, wasn't it? You texted Daniel."

"Yes, Gabrielle. It was Daniel. He did not go home, which I think you already know."

"Did he go to the redhead? The one from Indiana?"

"I am so sorry," Cain said. "I did not want to tell you this way."

"It's okay. I thought that might be it. That dummy always has had a thing for redheads," Gabby said with a slight smile and a tear welling in her right eye. "They set him up good, didn't they?"

"Yes, they did. I do not believe he is actively helping them, though I am not positive. I got the impression he is along for the ride, so to speak. He doesn't know about this plan, so I gave him a false one. It should buy us some time."

Gabby wiped away a tear and sniffed a little. "That's great. What did you tell him?"

"That we are all headed to the fields of Megiddo for the final battle. I sent look-alikes on a flight out of Pittsburgh this morning."

Gabby stood up a little straighter and gave a slight chuckle. "Oh, that's good. You've had a lot of time to work on this, haven't you?" She was slowly returning to her old self.

"All the time in the world, my dear."

"Okay. First, thank you for telling me. Second, we need to tell the others. Let's do that when everyone is airborne. Have the commanders do it. Tell it all, though, including the part about Daniel. They need to know what he's done. Now we can go. Thanks for telling me, Cain. I know you wanted to protect me, but I don't need it. I promise. I'm as focused as I can be. See you back at the retreat, okay?"

***

Ferdinand, one of the 666 and the brother Lorelei had spoken with on the phone, drove slowly along the Colorado interstate in the morning sunlight. It was glaring and made it much harder to see. At mile marker 141, Ferdinand pulled over and got out. Two gargoyles got out of the back seats. "Okay, let's start walking. You know what to look for. No stopping until we find every piece. Let's go."

After twenty minutes of searching and grabbing pieces off the pavement, they had found the majority of the shattered phone. They returned to the car, and Ferdinand motioned for one of the gargoyles to drive. He was going to ride in the passenger seat and work on extracting information from the remnants. "Let's head back. I can get this thing working while we are on the way. Time to see if our new brother is on the level or trying to play us for fools."

CHAPTER 36: LEAVING

The first two Lear jets left the Charleston airport in the early morning within minutes of each other, one headed west and the other south. The exotic aircraft taxied to the beginning of the longest runway. The pilot had requested the all-clear, but there was no response from the tower other than "Sit tight, please."

Cain walked up to the cockpit and asked what the delay was. The pilot, a genial ex-fighter pilot named Charles Johnson, said there was an issue in the tower. "Have they told you what the issue is, Captain?"

"No, sir. Just that we are to sit tight for a few minutes before we are cleared for take-off."

"May I speak to them?" Cain asked. It would be a bad harbinger if Razhael was already onto them. At least the first two flights were in the air. "Captain, please radio the other two flights. Do it securely. Let them know we are held up and we may have trouble sooner than expected."

Captain Johnson handed Cain the radio, while he made the secure call on another device. "Hello, control tower, this is . . . uh . . . one of the passengers. Can you tell us what the hold-up is? My wife is very nervous to fly in this thing, and I keep telling her it is safe."

"We hear you, Starbird One. No hold-up really. We just wanted to get photographs of your aircraft and try to get some video of your take-off. Just for posterity. Again, there is no issue. Just a little bit of envy here in control."

Cain felt a wave of relief. "Thank you, control, sir. If you would do me a favor and wait about seven days to post anything, please. We are, uh, carrying a few more people than the FAA allows and I would hate to get Captain Johnson here in trouble. I had to talk him into it. Now he is, uh, he is not happy with me. It is totally my fault. Can you do that for me, sir?" Cain shrugged his shoulders as he handed the mic back to the captain.

A minute went by, then two. The radio crackled a moment, and then a new voice came through the plane's loudspeaker. "This is tower. Roger that, Starbird One. We have some great photos and hope to get some good video too. Come back and visit us any time."

"That is affirmative, tower. We would love to visit. Will call ahead when we are in the neighborhood again." Cain, Captain Johnson, and the rest of the team breathed a collective sigh of relief. They all knew what the stakes were. Every detail, every move they made was a potential catastrophe. The call clearing the massive aircraft for take-off came through about two minutes later. Cain made his way back to his seat near Gregg and Roland. "Buckle up, gentlemen. This baby packs a punch on take-off."

***

Two and a half hours later, the Florida team landed at Space Coast Regional Airport and left quickly via a small van that had been left for them. Several crates were stacked in the back. Commander Pleasants peeked inside and seemed satisfied with the contents.

Cape Canaveral was about an hour away via car. Pleasants shared with her team that they would be staying on the lower cape in the hotels normally frequented by departing boat passengers.

"It will be crowded, which will help us blend in," Pleasants said. "We'll drive there and get checked in. As cover, we are booked for a cruise that leaves in two days. We, however, will miss that boat. We should have plenty of time to achieve our mission and get out safely. The others will be in place by midday tomorrow, our time. This evening we can do some light reconnaissance, then relax. A typical adult family of siblings, out for a family reunion. The real party starts tomorrow.

"First, though, I want to scope out the launch site. I've made a career out of being prepared. It helps and never hurts. We are not going into this mission—out of all the ones we've had—half ready. We will do a complete and discreet review of the area, then report back."

Reece, who was driving, and Jonn nodded in agreement. Zander still had his headphones in. Commander Pleasants reached back from the passenger seat and smacked his knee. Zander sat up quickly and said, "I heard, Commander. Check out the site tonight, the mission is tomorrow. Probably in the afternoon or early evening but still TBA. I got it. I promise."

"What are you listening to, Snyder?" Commander Pleasants said. She had not worked with Zander before. She knew he had a good service record and had bounced around in Cain's private army until landing in communications about six months ago.

"Just some music that reminds me of home, nothing special. Want to take a listen, Commander?"

"Probably not, Snyder. Your reminiscing does not come before the mission. I just briefed everyone on the plans for this evening."

"And I heard them, Commander. I'm a comms guy, remember? Keeping up on multiple things is my jam." The young soldier sat up and, without removing his headphones, said, "Traveling as a family. Staying at a rube hotel nearby. Blend in. Recon this evening. Action tomorrow. Did I miss any of it?"

"No, you didn't. Thank you for your attention to detail, Zander. You could be a great soldier if you had a better attitude. Maybe that should be your 'jam' for a while."

"Yes, Commander," Zander said before sinking back into his seat.

***

The team arrived at their hotel and unpacked quietly. They all were sharing a suite that would sleep everyone and still allow enough privacy for four adults. Everyone was checking their equipment, ensuring electrical rods were charged fully and earpieces were connecting properly. After a few minutes of adjustments, Zander gave the thumbs-up that they all would be able to stay in touch with each other.

Commander Pleasants was the first to be ready to leave. She was dressed in khaki shorts, a faded T-shirt, and sunglasses. "Let's get out there, spread out and keep the 'family on a cruise' cover going. See what we can learn about what's going on at the launch site. See if the payload has been loaded yet, how many guards are between the site and us. I don't want this to be a one-way mission for any of us. Let's figure out a way in and a way out that brings everybody home."

Everyone left the hotel at different times and through different exits in case they were being watched. Commander Pleasants, McNeil, Cleaver, and Snyder each headed in different directions. They would meet back at the hotel in ninety minutes.

There were several launch sites at Cape Canaveral. Satellite images showed a heavy and private payload being prepped for Launch Complex 46. They all were assigned different reconnaissance tasks centered on getting to the pad, disabling the rocket, and destroying the payload.

Getting close to the launchpad was going to be difficult, but Commander Pleasants was ready. She had requested scuba gear from their local contact. It was ready and in the van when they arrived. The team would leave in the very early morning, get in their gear, and swim as close as possible to the launchpad. Getting through the perimeter fencing would be easy by comparison. Making it to the rocket undetected, however, was nearly impossible. They would have to choose the best time to make a run at the rocket, destroy it, and get out before any security could reach them. If they were caught, they would be labeled terrorists and not see the light of the day for many years—if they were not shot on sight. The connections and money of Mr. Green would not be able to help them.

If they were caught. If they failed, the consequences would be worse. Commander Pleasants planned to avoid both. "All right, team, let's get out there and figure out how we're going to blow that thing to Kingdom Come."

***

Once outside, everyone went in different directions. Pleasants and Reece Cleaver headed toward the southwestern side of the main entry point. Zander was going to act like the typical lost tourist so he could get a look at the main gate. Jonn McNeil headed east, hoping to spot a weak spot in the security from Jetty Park Pier. The plan was to swim to a spot nearest the launchpad, get over the fence, and disable the rocket with explosives.

McNeil reached his destination first. The pier offered a great view of the entrance and southern end of NASA's campus. Jonn took several close-up photos of the coastline and, in the distance, Launch Complex 46. His mission completed, he put away his camera and strolled about as every other tourist was doing. He was one of dozens of people looking and taking photos of the most well-known American spaceport. As he turned to leave, he bumped into a man standing right behind him who was at least 6'7" and half that wide with muscles. He wore Air Force dress blues. "Excuse me, sir," he said, with no trace of an accent. "Busy night on the pier."

"Yes, it is," Jonn said. "Excuse me. I need to meet my brother and sisters in a bit. Have a nice evening." Jonn maneuvered past the man, only to feel a too-strong grip on his left shoulder from which he couldn't break free.

"You forgot something," the man said. "You forgot this is our time and the end of yours. Come with me."

***

"My name is Gaderel. There is no way you are leaving here alive. Depending on your choices, it can be quick and painless, or slow and terrifying. Your choice. Call your friends. Tell them to meet you at the bleachers just past the main gate in fifteen minutes. If you lie or try to send a coded message, I will know. So don't."

Jonn kept his composure despite the circumstances and a slight tremble in his legs. He radioed to the rest of the team. "Found something very helpful. Meet at the first observation station in fifteen."

"Good job, Jonn," Gaderel said. "A human who listens. How unusual. Let's sit together and enjoy the view for, oh, let's say fifteen minutes."

***

Commander Pleasants and Reece were the first to arrive. They saw Jonn at the top of the bleachers, and a tall man sitting a few feet away and down on the bottom bench. They approached Jonn cautiously, who, when he turned around to greet them, was stone-faced and pale. He managed to say, "I'm sorry" before the man was up and behind them faster than humanly possible.

Zander arrived five minutes later and was quickly subdued. He had offered no resistance and remained silent when Gaderel stood up and walked toward him. He did, however, let go of his bladder and pass out when the hulking figure stood behind him and said, "Welcome."

Gaderel shook his head as he picked up the limp body of the communications expert. "What are they making humans out of these days? Nothing sturdy. Let's go. I want to help you, you know. You came to see what we are doing, and you will get the opportunity much sooner than you planned. It's glorious beyond measure."

***

Commander Pleasants was the first to wake up. The four of them were tied tightly with a combination of rope and zip ties. Wherever they were, it was dark with lots of sounds nearby. She felt the ropes around her everywhere. Despite the darkness, she could tell she had been stripped naked, and so had the other three. She squirmed to get out but to little avail. She called out, "Jonn, Reece, Zander. Wake up! We need to get out of here. Come on, you three. Let's move it. It can't end like this. We still have work to do. The others are counting on us."

"That's admirable," said a deep voice just beyond the wall. "Loyal to the end. I have no doubt about where you all will end up. Which is in about T minus ten minutes. Engine tests are so exciting, especially at night. The people line up all around to watch even the most minor things when it comes to these rockets. I don't see the fascination with them, but as long as they do their job, I'm sold. Now I need to get clear before things heat up around here. I've had enough of that. It's time you humans experience the blast furnace doom of several thousand degrees searing your flesh without mercy. Tell the good guys upstairs we said hello."

Gaderel laughed at his joke and walked away from the wooden container he had single-handedly placed out of view of the control tower, underneath the main engine of the rocket on Launchpad 46. He was dressed in green coveralls, sunglasses, and a helmet. He looked like every other payload specialist as they walked briskly to catch the tram and watch the test from a safe distance behind the control tower.

The upcoming launch was for a private company with an undisclosed payload. The engine test was for the NASA leadership, who were privy to the materials being launched for the first privately funded and manned space station. Two-hundred twenty-two solid metal pylons, four feet in diameter and more than seventy feet tall. Each pylon weighed more than 1,000 pounds and would be the framework of the new station.

At T minus two minutes, everyone was in place. Civilians sat on the observation bleachers, excitedly watching the launchpad, ready to take photos of the event. Families with small children had made the trek just to watch the rocket take off the next day. Gaderel smiled and looked at his watch. As a former angel of discernment, he appreciated a good schedule and punctuality. *Almost time, you plucky band of adventurers.* In the team's hotel room, gargoyles were combing every inch of the place as well as the abandoned van for clues as to what the doomed team had planned. Commander Pleasants always insisted on strict mission security, and had left behind nothing but suitcases of vacation clothes and a van with diving equipment.

Inside the box, the four members of Cain's would-be saviors were struggling to free themselves. The ropes and bindings were tight and expertly done. No one spoke as three of the four tried to break free while also praying and mentally saying their goodbyes to loved ones. Only Zander remained silent, his gaze unfocused as he looked to the side of the container.

Then, over a loudspeaker broadcasting from a safe distance but still within earshot of the rocket. "T-minus ten . . . nine . . . eight . . . seven . . . six . . . five . . . four . . . three . . . two . . . one. We have ignition."

After forty seconds, the loudspeaker activated once more. "All systems functional and ready for launch. Commencing engine shutdown."

***

The crews would have to wait two hours for the launchpad to cool down enough for human contact. Gaderel was so pleased with himself that he had missed the tiny transponder Commander Pleasants had hidden in a hollow tooth. With less than one minute remaining, she bit down on the transponder and felt a slight electrical surge on her tongue, letting her know the signal had been sent successfully. The boss would get the message and know something had gone wrong. She knew all of their families would be taken care of for the rest of their natural lives. Their mission had failed but she hoped with her final act she would sound the alarm that the enemy was on to them.

***

Two hours and twenty minutes later, the crews approached the rocket to do a visual inspection and, if everything checked out, give the all-clear for launch. Gaderel walked under the massive engines and searched for any sign of the box or the four people who had been trapped in it. The temperatures had burned at nearly 5,800 degrees Fahrenheit, more than twice the temperature to melt steel and more than enough to get rid of four bodies and a wooden crate without a trace.

Without a trace to human senses but not angelic ones. Gaderel found the spot where the box had been secured. There was nothing but scorch marks and burnt concrete. He looked down at the launchpad and saw what no human would detect if they ever thought to look. The remains of three humans who were roasted alive. *Three?* Gaderel thought. There were four of them. Did one escape somehow? He had neither seen nor heard any evidence of that during their final moments, but there was the ten-minute trip back to the control tower. He had tied the bonds himself. No one could have escaped. They must have been so thoroughly disintegrated even he could not find a trace of them.

CHAPTER 37: FAMILY REUNION

"I need a new phone, Lorelei." Daniel was getting antsy in the car without his primary contact with the world he knew. He regretted throwing his phone out the window as soon as it left his hand. "Can we stop somewhere so I can get a new one? My data is all backed up, so it will be just like my old phone but newer."

"Yes, Daniel," Lorelei said, sounding more like a caretaker than a sister or a lover. "How about if I call ahead and have one of the wraiths pick up a new one? You can get it set up at the compound. What would you like?"

"The latest iPhone. I can't remember what version that is. The people at the store will know. Be sure to get one with plenty of storage, though. That's important."

"Okay, Daniel. I'll do that for you since it will make you happy. I hope you are as happy when you meet the rest of our family. Everyone is looking forward to meeting you."

Daniel looked over at Lorelei and gave a weak smile. "And I'm, um, eager to meet them too," he said, somewhat unconvincingly. "You know, I spent most of my life in church. This new information, this feeling, it's . . . different. It may take me a while to get used to it."

"That's normal, Daniel," Lorelei said. "Many of our brothers and sisters experienced the same thing when they learned of their true heritage."

This piqued Daniel's curiosity. "What about you? When did you learn it?"

Lorelei smiled. She thought this was a good sign. "I've known since I was a small child. My mother was . . . progressive. She believed in very early child development and expected her children to behave as adults while we still were young. I didn't have much of a childhood, really."

"You said children. Are your siblings, you know, the same as you and me?"

"No, they're not. Mother gave birth to me when she was in her teens. She didn't know the truth about our father at the time. That changed shortly after I was born. She said he visited us just the one time, but it was enough. Mother raised me to know exactly who I was and what my destiny could be. She later married my stepfather, who also knew. They both helped me grow and learn. My stepbrother and stepsisters didn't know, but they knew something was different about me. One of them actually became a pastor, believe it or not. We . . . really don't speak these days. I think I scare him. How about you, Daniel? What's your story? The real one?"

"Not much to tell. Grew up in South Dakota, went to school in the east, met Gabby. Stayed in the area, got a job, bought a house together. You know, the American Dream, minus the kids. I'm sure that would have happened sooner or later."

Lorelei looked over at Daniel. "And no twinges of angst? A desire to break things? Control people? Anything like that?"

"No, not really. My parents are great. Pretty good upbringing overall. They helped out with college as much as they could. I had a small scholarship and financed the rest. I guess there are times when I think I might have a temper, but I usually simmer down after a bit. Gabby doesn't like it when I get mad. She says I get unreasonable really fast.

"So, about my mom. She . . . does she know? That would be kind of a hard thing to miss."

Lorelei almost laughed at this. "Oh, Daniel. Most women do not know at all. Mother was one of the lucky ones. She accepted it and saw the future for me. Most women are probably like your mother. They had a one-night fling, or else Father masqueraded as someone they knew if they aren't the one-night stand type. Pretty sneaky really. But what else would you expect?"

As Daniel looked over at Lorelei, a large hawk or eagle flew overhead and partially blotted out the sun. Strange shadows danced inside the car for a moment, and Daniel thought he saw Lorelei's eyes glowing red. He had been trying to not think of his mom being unfaithful to his dad, especially this way. He quickly decided she had been tricked into it, and neither she nor his dad were none the wiser.

"So back to my question that you so deftly avoided," Lorelei said. "Any desire to rule or command armies, things like that? These are common traits in our family."

"Umm, no, not really." Daniel searched deep for an answer. "I mean, the usual schoolboy angst and hijinks but nothing major. I do sometimes write code that I know won't work and the other programmers can't fix. That way, I look like I'm really doing well at my job."

"You are a rebel, Daniel," Lorelei said with the slyest grin Daniel had ever seen. "The family is going to love you. We will be there in a few minutes. I hope you are as excited as I am."

"I am," Daniel said. "This is an adventure. And for once, I'm not in the back seat."

***

Cain felt a buzz from his phone, his watch, and the very small transponder he had implanted in his upper left leg a few years ago. They all had the same purpose—to let him know one of his high-level employees was about to die. Only six people had the corresponding dental implant; five of them were not active at the time. The signal coming through now could only mean one thing: Paula and the rest of Team One had failed to stop the Florida launch and were most likely dead. It also meant Razhael and his followers undoubtedly knew they were coming for them, and would be prepared at the other sites. He wondered if Gabby already knew.

He walked up to the cockpit and asked Captain Johnson if the California flight had arrived yet. "I'll check for you now, sir," the captain said. "Let's see . . . it looks like, yes, they landed about ninety minutes ago. Would you like us to contact them for you?"

"No thank you, Captain. If they are on the ground, I can call them directly." Cain walked back to his seat and past the others until he was far in the rear of the passenger area. He took out his phone and selected Gabby's number. She answered on the second ring.

"Hi, Cain. We arrived about an hour ago. It sure is hot here. I presume you're not calling to check the temperature, though. What's going on? Did something happen?"

So she didn't see it, Cain thought. Thank the fates for that, at least. The girl was burdened enough. He didn't enjoy adding to it. His eyes welled with tears when he shared the news that the Florida team was gone. He didn't know any specifics yet, but it was almost a certainty that everyone was dead and they didn't stop the upcoming launch. He also shared that Razhael and those who were working to bring about Armageddon would know shortly, if they did not already. Their jobs had just become exponentially more difficult. When he finished, Gabby was silent.

"Gabrielle, are you there?" Cain said, hoping to hear the resiliency he had quickly come to admire in her.

"Yes, I'm here," Gabby said. "Just . . . I just need a moment. I didn't know any of them very well. But they changed my life. Paula, Reece, and I had a few good chats back in Maryland. Jonn I didn't know as well. And Zander was—he was a pain in the ass, but he still tried to help." Gabby was weeping and didn't speak for a few minutes. Then, "They helped me, helped Daniel, all because we asked them to. I know it was their job, but still. To die trying to stop Armageddon. Cain, there has to be a special place in Heaven for people like that. Please tell me there is."

"Gabby, I . . . I do not know that. I would like to think so. It would be the right thing, the just thing."

"Then . . . " Gabby said, choking back her tears. "Then that's where they are. Because I cannot imagine fighting for a cause where heroes like those four are not honored in death."

"I am sure you are right," Cain said. "May we meet them again someday in a far better place."

"We will," Gabby said, determination returning to her voice. "But first we are going to wipe those demons from the face of the Earth. That's still the job. I'm still having these damned visions, so we're not done yet. We stop for a moment to honor our fallen friends. Then we finish this. Let's talk revised strategy, Cain. You have some time?"

"All the time in the world, Gabrielle. All the time in the world."

"Good, because I've been thinking. We need to change our plan. And yes, I did have a vision about it, before you ask. Here's what I saw, and what we need to do . . . "

CHAPTER 38: WEST COAST MANEUVERING

"Captain, please land the plane in England. Radio ahead to Heathrow. We have a hangar there where we can refuel and make other preparations. When we are airborne again, I will be asking you to do some fancy flying. Are you ready?"

Cain was thinking through the specifics of Gabby's plan. It was a good one strategically. It also took into account the fact that the Florida mission had failed. Cain wondered if Gabby was telling the truth about not seeing what happened to the team there. He walked back to speak with his two teammates. "Roland, Gregg, we have updated our plan for Vladivostok. We will be landing shortly to refuel and resupply. The mission has become much more perilous. However, Gabby shared her vision about it, so I believe we ultimately will succeed. It does require going into the upper atmosphere and the fringes of space. This plane and her pilot are more than capable of that, and have in fact been on similar journeys many times. But that's where the similarities end. I have one more call to make; then we can talk through the plan."

***

Daniel's new phone was exactly like his old one, the one he had thrown out the car window, and was surprised that the gargoyles had brought the model he requested. He began the restoration process so everything from his old phone would soon be on the new one. The compound that Lorelei called her "home away from home" was a massive estate situated in the Colorado Rockies about an hour northwest of Denver. It was crawling with gargoyles and others who Daniel surmised must also be some of his other brothers and sisters. He recognized news anchors, actors, and politicians. He also thought he saw an extremely well-known basketball star practicing on the outdoor court. They all paused briefly to watch as he and Lorelei walked from the main house toward a breathtaking view of the mountains to the west.

"Everyone is here, Daniel. All of our beautiful siblings," Lorelei said. "We are among the late arrivers. Everyone will be here today. Tomorrow, we will gather just a bit west of here on the estate and launch our plan so we all can take our rightful places as rulers of this world."

"And how is that going to happen?" Daniel asked. "What are we going to do, overthrow some governments and install our own people?"

"Nothing as crude as that, Daniel. That is an option if needed, but we prefer the modern approach. Charismatic leadership in times of great trouble, ready to take the reins from the current slate of world leaders, will reveal the current slate of quote-unquote leaders for the inept fools they are. It's not political power or religious power, but the power of leadership— soft power, oddly enough—which can take many forms. The power of a reporter appearing on your screen every day. Someone you know or look up to. Some of our brethren are leaders of industry, and a few are, as I'm sure you saw, world-famous athletes. Most of us are like you and I—regular people who happen to be extraordinary."

"So people are going to listen to us because they do that already? That's pretty sneaky."

"Yes, Daniel, that is precisely what we are going to do. We are poised to provide examples of strong, courageous leadership from several different vantage points. Including your world of technology. We hope you will take part in our efforts."

"I have no idea how I could help with what you just said. But sure, I'll do what I can, Lorelei."

"Good. We gather to launch everything tomorrow morning. The grounds extend into the mountains. There is a point at which the mountains give us a natural amphitheater. It's the perfect place for us to begin our plan. That's why all of us are here. I'd like to ask you to help with some of the technical parts, if you would."

"Okay. Maybe I can help after all. Thanks, Lorelei. I think . . . I think I'm really going to like it here. And thanks for the new phone."

"Any time, my faithful Daniel. Any time."

***

In California, there was nothing to do yet but sit tight and wait for the right moment. Gabby thought it was a bit anticlimactic to be sitting so long inside a massive hangar when there was work they could be doing. But she knew this was the best thing for the time being, mostly because she saw it in her latest vision. Sometimes the best results come from a few key decisions at the right time. This was one of those times. Plus, Cain and his team were busy getting ready for their part, which was going to be incredibly dangerous. In her musings, it took her a moment to realize her phone was ringing again. And not just any ring—it was the one she used for Daniel. At first she hesitated to answer. She looked down at the screen. On the third ring, she answered.

"Hello, Daniel," she said, trying to use as unemotional a tone as she could muster. She was not going to reveal anything to him if she could help it—her feelings, their current whereabouts, or the plan—over the phone to the love of her life, who abandoned her when she needed him most. "I hope you are doing well."

"Gabby, it's so good to hear your voice," Daniel said.

She almost believed him.

"You too, Daniel. Are you safe? Did you make it home?"

"No, not quite. I stayed out west, going to see some . . . some family while I'm out this way."

Gabby was surprised. "You went to your parents' house?"

"No, not there. I'm in Colorado. A little west of Denver. I had a call from some old friends and met them here. It's a hotel retreat. Going to work on some, um, some programming for them. Do a little freelance before I head home."

Gabby waited a moment before speaking. She knew Daniel's tone of voice backward and forward. He was lying. She wanted to see how far he would take it. "Daniel, that's great. Fresh air can do wonders. Good luck with the programming. I know that's something you really enjoy."

"Thanks, Gabby. I really appreciate it. I figured you would be upset with my dumb ass. Heck, I think I'm upset with myself a little. I've never been good with my emotions. Which you know."

He's really laying it on thick here, Gabby thought. And when did he start referring to himself that way? It didn't sound like him at all.

"To tell you the truth, I got so mad the other day, I threw my phone out the window, if you can believe that. Just got a new one. I had to ask my, uh, one of my friends to pick one up for me. It's just like the one I had. Exactly the same, in fact. It's great."

"That's . . . great, Daniel. A new phone just like your old one. Doesn't really sound like you, though. You usually get the latest and greatest."

"Yeah, you know me. I like to stay with what I know."

Gabby thought that was the complete opposite of him. Had Daniel been drinking? It was completely out of character for the man who usually couldn't wait for the latest devices. Why would he . . . *Oh,* Gabby thought. *He's trying to tell me something is wrong. Something specific.*

"Yeah, that's you to a 'T,' Danny," Gabby said, using the informal version of his name, which he hated. She hoped this was enough to say, "I get it. You can't talk freely."

"I've taken a small job here to help with a convention too. I may not be home when you make it back. This place is great. You should see it one day. Everyone is here. Everyone." Daniel emphasized this last part to imply something, but Gabby didn't know what he meant. Who was "everyone?" Something had happened to him in the few days they'd been apart. Something fundamental and also something that scared him. Gabby couldn't piece it together, though.

"All right, Gabby, I gotta run. Things to do here and get used to my new phone. I need to make sure all the settings are the way I'm used to. Privacy first. You know me." This part Gabby agreed with wholeheartedly. Why did he keep talking about the phone? Were they listening in somehow? What was he trying to say?

"Okay, Daniel. Thanks for calling. It's good to hear from you. See you . . . when I see you, I guess. I do love you, you know."

"Yep. Sounds good, Gabrielle. Good luck. Talk to you soon."

Gabby then heard the line cut off. He didn't give her time to be mad at him for not returning the "I love you."

Either he'd gone completely over the deep end for the redhead, or he was mixed up in something that he couldn't get out of. Gabby wondered which was worse. She would follow up with Daniel when all of this was over. She wanted to stay focused on the task before them before she could let something else distract her.

***

Despite the upcoming mission, Gabby kept trying to make sense of her strange conversation with Daniel. Some of it she expected and some of it didn't sound like him at all. *Colorado, of all places!* He didn't have any connections there that she knew of. And she never had heard of any college friends before now. Daniel was as insular as could be in school. Or . . . oh my, he *was* trying to tell her something, Gabby realized.

Several years ago, Daniel had created an app just for her. It was a tracking app so when Daniel was running late, Gabby would know where he was. It was not reciprocal. Its sole function was to tell Gabby where Daniel was. Earlier in their relationship he would lose track of time and forget when he and Gabby had a date. She had almost quit trying with him until a heart-to-heart talk where he showed her he was not chasing other girls or doing something else he shouldn't. He truly lost track of time when deep into his work.

He had created the Find My Dumb Ass app as a way of saying, "please don't give up on me." Daniel submitted it to the app store several times, but it was always rejected because of the name and its limited usefulness as it only worked for two specific people. He eventually got it in the store by changing the app's name to Find My Dumb A and leaving it as a beta version. That way he could claim to still be refining it for mass use when, in truth, it functioned just as he intended. Gabby thought it was it was a heartfelt gesture from the socially awkward man she had fallen in love with.

She opened her phone and found the app, tucked away in a seldom used folder titled Miscellaneous. The app opened, then started to narrow down where Daniel was. When it gave his location as Devil's Ridge, Colorado, on the map, Gabby stared at it. *That name can't be a coincidence,* she thought. *What has he gotten himself into?*

In the hangar, one of Cain's other aircraft began to taxi toward the entrance doors. It looked like a smaller version of the plane Cain boarded back in West Virginia. Commander Peak looked out the window with envy. "Oh, wow. Someone is taking the Blackbird out for a spin. I wonder who is flying her today?"

***

On the ground in England, at the rear of Starbird One was what looked to be a flight simulator console. In the pilot's seat sat Cain, wearing a virtual reality headset and making adjustments to whatever he was up to. He laughed a bit as he activated the radio headset, saying, "This is SR-71 Blackbird Three, taxiing into take-off position."

***

In California, the Blackbird rolled outside, then moved out of view of the hangar doors. "Did anyone see a pilot get in that thing?" Commander Peak said. "I didn't, but I could have missed it. Only a few of our pilots are certified for it, and I don't believe any of them are in California at the moment."

Gabby came up behind Matthew, with the others right behind her peering out the tiny windows of their plane. "They aren't," Gabby said. "But she has a pilot nevertheless."

Commander Peak turned around to look at Gabby. "You mean it's being flown remotely? I didn't know it could do that. How do you know?" Gabby looked at the commander and raised both eyebrows slightly and shrugged her shoulders. "You saw this? You saw the Blackbird flying on its own in a vision? How? When? You don't mean it's being flown by," Commander Peak pointed upward, "you know, someone up there?"

Gabby shook her head. "Oh no, the pilot is definitely earthbound. Can someone please turn on the TV? Any national news channel should work." Milla found the on button for the nearest one and pushed it, flipping through the channels until she landed on CNN.

The Blackbird's engines grew louder and louder. Then suddenly, the plane accelerated down the runway and took off into the morning sky. Once it was airborne, the plane turned and headed inland away from the coastline. Now on a straight course, the aircraft accelerated until it generated a sonic boom and very quickly moved out of sight.

"Wonder where it's headed?" Candy Reed said. "I've never heard a sonic boom before. Does that happen a lot around here?"

"No, it does not, Mrs. Reed," Commander Peak said. "And I have a feeling when it arrives at its destination, there will be some people who wished it hadn't."

CHAPTER 39: SEVENTY-TWO MINUTES

Traveling at its top speed of 2,200 miles an hour, the SR-71 Blackbird can cross the continental United States in a little more than an hour. Cain was not one to sit still for that long, but since he was remote piloting the fastest plane ever made, he thought it was a decent trade-off. His virtual reality headset was trying to keep up with rendering the passing cloudscapes and ground below, but at times it just showed amorphous blobs. Cain wanted to look around a bit before the aircraft arrived at its destination, but he thought any distraction at this point wouldn't be a good idea.

Traveling from northern California to the Florida peninsula meant a slightly longer trip than Cain preferred. He hoped he could best the cross-continental record set in 1976, not counting the fact that he was traveling diagonally and not just straight across the country. *That has to count for something,* he thought. His heads-up display showed he had another seventeen minutes until the plane would arrive at its destination. Cain set the automatic pilot and made a quick call.

"You are sure it is clear? No bystanders? The ocean? Just the fallen? How many? Perfect. I do appreciate a good plan, especially when you can see it before it happens. Do you think I will get a chapter named after me for this? The Book of Cain? Maybe Cain the Redeemed? Cain the Conqueror? How about more than one? First Cain and Second Cain has a nice ring to it. That seemed to be popular at one time. No? Okay. Well, I better get back to it. The autopilot sometimes gets a little wonky past the speed of sound. We will have to work on that. Talk to you soon, Gabby. And good luck out there. I know you will do great."

Cain listened for a moment, then said, "Yes, I know you know what will happen. Just give an old man the chance to be nice during the Apocalypse, please? Is that too much to ask? Thank you. Talk to you soon." Cain resumed control of the SR-71 making its way toward Florida. *Eight minutes to go,* he thought. Time to prepare for landing.

***

Gaderel was proud of himself for disposing of the meddling humans so thoroughly. The plan was going exactly as expected—what else could one expect from a former angel of discernment? The launch still was on schedule for later in the day. The other two spacecraft were due to launch over the next eighteen hours, and then the world would be reshaped by Gaderel and his fellow fallen angels, aided by the Adversaries. Gaderel didn't think they needed the help, but they were the boss' children and everyone expected it.

After the Earth was sufficiently pummeled from above, the rest of the fallen would arrive. Together with the 666, they would rule the Earth until it finally froze and the experiment that was humanity snuffed out for good. Gaderel was pleased with his work and the fact that the rocket under his command would be the first to launch and deliver its payload. The puny, insipid humans in Europe and northern Africa would never know what hit them. He and three of his fellow fallen, together with one unwitting human, would board the rocket in the early morning for their journey. It would be the last flight for the human pilot.

He joined Molingel and Asphaserel on the main walkway to begin their long trek down the stairs. They all would be happy when they could openly use their wings again. Up until now, they had been cautious and stuck to their plan, which, to give credit where it's due, came mostly from the redhead and a few other of her kin. Razhael never had been this sophisticated. He was more of a doer than a thinker. Together with the demi-humans, they finally were fulfilling their destinies. It was not quite in the manner most of the fallen envisioned, but that fact made them like the plan even more. They believed they were being innovative.

As the three made their way down, they all heard something in the distance. Too slight for human senses, but it was there. A quiet, steady hum that was growing louder. *Did one of the dimwitted humans leave a phone up here?* Gaderel wondered. There were no outside devices allowed above ground level. If so, Gaderel was going to kick it off the plank and watch it smash on the reinforced launchpad below. He hated the things.

The humming grew louder the further down the stairs the trio went. None of them, however, could pinpoint where it was coming from or what might be causing it. It was growing louder every second and now seemed to be coming from everywhere. Asphaserel said if it was a human tinkering around the rocket, he was going to kill him on the spot. The other two did not argue the point.

When they reached the bottom of the stairs, the extremely keen hearing of the three fallen angels was nearly shattered by a sonic boom. With eyes more powerful and much faster than a human, they all watched as a sleek jet flying faster than the speed of sound broke through the Florida clouds and flew directly into the rocket.

The sound of the collision alone was deafening. Large bits of burning rocket and aircraft went flying into the nearby ocean with the kamikaze aircraft. Everything around them—the rocket, the stairs, most of the launchpad, and their carefully crafted payload of 222 large metal rods—was on fire, falling, or both.

The three fallen angels were mostly incinerated. The rest of them were either broken or on fire. They made their way to the ocean and jumped in among the wreckage to quench their burning flesh. After they all surfaced, a voice came over a phone wrapped in a plastic bubble and drifting nearby in the plane's wreckage.

"Hello, boys." Cain's voice came through much better than planned, thanks to Gabby's suggestion of the plastic bubble. "That is one down. Enjoy the warmth of the fire. Probably reminds you of home. Which is where you will be headed once again very shortly. I presume their view on failure has not changed in several millennia? No answer. That is fine. We all know how it will go for you.

"By the way, look up."

The rest of the launch tower and rocket, still burning and weighing several hundred tons, fell into the ocean where the three had been floating and listening to Cain boast. The crash and subsequent explosions were violent and deafening, but there was no one left to bear witness to it.

***

Several thousand miles away, Cain laughed and let out a loud and uncharacteristic full-throated, celebratory, "Woo hoo!" He removed the VR goggles and pushed back from the console. "That's for Paula, Reece, Jonn, and Zander. One down, two to go."

As he walked up toward the front of the plane, he shared the news with his two teammates. All three entered the cockpit to share the news with Captain Johnson and to await Gabby's next signal.

CHAPTER 40: CALIFORNIA LAUNCHPAD

Gabby knew her team needed to get moving. It was almost time. She walked over to Commander Peak, who was going over a map of the Vandenberg site. "Commander, we're up. How far to the launch site?"

"Not far. About twelve miles and about three military checkpoints. So it should be a walk in the park. And please, call me Matt." He still was getting used to his title and asked everyone to use his first name. He told them formal titles could be used at the celebration after they finished the mission. Until then, he was in command and should be addressed as Matt and nothing more.

"You sure this is going to work?" he asked. "We will have an awful lot riding on you four for the majority of the mission. If it succeeds, we still need to get out of there in one piece. Destroying private property on this scale is going to make us wanted for a long, long time by a whole lot of people."

"If things work, Matt, we shouldn't have to destroy much," Gabby said. "But being prepared for it is a good idea. Things could change. Things I haven't seen yet."

"Has that ever happened?"

"Sometimes there are subtle changes. It depends on the intensity of the vision too. Everything I've seen has come to pass, or it seems like it will in one way or another. I know that's a lot to put your faith in, let alone risk everyone's lives, but . . . "

Matt spoke up quickly and cut her off. "But nothing. You've seen it. It happens. Good enough for me. Just please don't tell us too much. Won't that ruin it? Maybe make things change course?"

"I don't think it works that way," Gabby said, enjoying the conversation a little more than she thought she would. "The visions take that into account. Like, if I see you eating a peanut butter and jelly sandwich tomorrow and tell you, you're still going to eat it."

"So what if we do nothing? What happens then? Does someone else do it, or does it mean you saw something that might happen but didn't?"

"Honestly, Matt, I don't know. This has all been in the past two weeks, and it didn't come with a manual. Sometimes I see things that allude to a big snow or things freezing—it's the idea of what is to come. Other times, it's as if I am there and see things that are going to happen as if I'm standing there watching. That's what just happened with Florida."

"Hmm, interesting," Matt said. "Do you know if you will still have the visions when this is over? When we win?"

"I don't know," Gabby said. "I haven't seen anything past the next few days. And sometimes I don't know what I am seeing. At times it seems I'm in the American South a few hundred years ago, or some place under Roman rule. I don't know why. It seems random. I try to remember those, but right now I'm focused on how we can win this war before it really starts.

"Speaking of that, it's close to time to leave."

***

Matt and Gabby's plan was simple. Gabby, Lewis, Candy, and Tuna would drive through the main gate with forged credentials—posing as visiting academics from West Virginia University. Matt had arranged for their identification cards to be created before flying out the day prior. The cards were waiting for them when they pulled the plane into the hangar.

Matt, Milla, and Katrina would be carrying the explosives and would get to the launch site with high-power electric drones, which were electric, like so many other weapons of war to come from Cain's companies, and could carry a person short distances. They also were equipped with electronic baffling so they and their passengers would not show up on any surveillance cameras. At worst, it would seem as if everything on camera was out of focus. The baffling devices, another invention from Cain's companies, spread out for several feet all around to aid in masking the devices and passengers. The downside was they would be visible to anyone who saw them in person. Matt said it was an acceptable risk because not many people would be walking around a rocket launchpad. They would wait just outside the northeast side of the campus until the others were near the launchpad, and provide as much distraction as possible. Gabby also shared that they would have help once they were inside, but she didn't elaborate.

On the way to Vandenberg Air Base, Gabby sat next to Tuna. He was going to be crucial to the success of their mission by providing a distraction. Tuna seemed very excited to take part in the mission. "Tuna be he ro. Like you," he said to Gabby as she went over the plan with him one more time. She had seen it in her last vision, but the implausibility of it made her nervous. Satellite reconnaissance of the launchpad had shown it was crawling with gargoyles, the most anyone had seen in one place. They were dressed as technicians, but their task seemed mainly to be security.

A few hours earlier, Tuna had listened as closely as he could when Gabby told him he had appeared in one of her recent visions. She told him that because of his decision to defect to their side, he had changed in a fundamental way, and the other gargoyles, having nearly animal-like senses, would sense that and listen to him. Gabby said it was the same principle as the fallen angels commanding them. They acted as if they were in charge, and gargoyles—save one, Gabby noted to Tuna's delight—listened to them as such. It was this part of the plan that made everyone nervous. Gabby assured them it would work.

***

Gabby, Lewis, Candy, and Tuna made it through the first checkpoint without a hitch. Their next step was to get as close to the launchpad as possible before being detected. They parked near the control tower for launchpad four and got out. No one came to greet them or stop them. "Is this a good sign or a bad one? I can't decide," Lewis said as he checked his concealed electrical rod for the seventh time.

"Let's go with good," Gabby said. "Come on, we have to go through the control tower entrance to make it onto the launchpad."

The team walked unimpeded into the lobby. The countdown clock inside showed the rocket was scheduled to launch in one hour, thirty-seven minutes. Gabby relayed the message to Matt. He immediately responded,

"Okay, we now have a deadline. Let's get out there and shut it down." The foursome made their way out to the rear doors and onto the tarmac. The launchpad was at least a quarter mile away. There were no vehicles nearby, and Gabby said they would have to make a run for it.

But first, she needed to make a call. She pulled out her phone and dialed. Cain answered on the first ring. "Time to take off," Gabby said. "Get airborne and head toward Vladivostok. Make sure everyone is ready for zero-G flight. And good luck."

Gabby put her phone in her back pocket, then turned to face the Reeds and Tuna. "Okay everyone, we're going to run as fast as we can toward the launch site. Everyone ready? All right, on the count of three we make a break for it. One . . . two . . . three!"

Gabby and the Reeds started to run as fast as they could, but Tuna remained still. Gabby looked around for him, and stopped when she realized he was at least 100 feet behind them, and hadn't moved an inch. She yelled for the Reeds to stop, then went back for Tuna. "Come on, Tuna. We have to run!"

The gargoyle looked at her. "Tuna thought that. Then Gabby say break it. Tuna not have thing to break so Tuna stay. Tuna do bad?"

"You're fine, Tuna. We have to run to the launchpad. Will you please run with me?"

"Yes, Gabby. Tuna run." With that, the gargoyle took off running toward the launchpad. He was considerably faster than a human. Gabby now had to run to catch up to Tuna and the Reeds. She saw Tuna pass the Reeds, who had restarted their sprints when they saw Gabby and Tuna headed their way. *At the rate he's moving, Tuna will be there in two minutes,* Gabby thought. *Time to pick up the pace.*

She could see a group of people at the base of the launchpad. In the distance, she saw that Tuna had stopped in front of the crowd, and the Reeds were getting close. Gabby began to breathe deeply and focus on running as fast as she could. *Almost there,* she thought. And still no response or alarms from the tower.

Gabby arrived next to the Reeds, who were standing behind Tuna. In front of them were more than fifty gargoyles, all dressed as flight technicians. It was the most surreal thing Gabby had ever seen, which was saying a lot given her life lately.

She moved up directly behind and slightly to the right of Tuna. He was gazing at the crowd of his fellow gargoyles, who were restlessly waiting for . . . something. They looked as if they were ready to overrun the quartet, but they mostly were silent and did not advance. Gabby gently said in Tuna's ear, "What are they doing?"

"Tuna not know. They stop when Tuna say stop. Like Gabby said."

Gabby was relieved. She had seen this in a vision, but it felt much different standing in front of dozens of creatures from Hell that would love to tear them apart. The only thing holding them back was the presence of one of their own who only recently had decided to switch sides.

"Tuna, they are listening to you. Do you remember what we talked about? What to tell them?"

"Yes. Tuna knows."

"Then you're up, Tuna. Tell them," Gabby said close to his ear.

He didn't say anything. Gabby waited. Still nothing. The gargoyles were getting restless. All it would take was a command from one of the fallen, and they would be on them in an instant.

"Tuna? Are you going to talk to them?"

"Yes. But Tuna not up. Tuna right here. Why Ga-bee say Tuna up? Is Tuna bad?"

"No, no, no, Tuna. You are doing great," Gabby said. "It's a figure of speech. That's my fault. Please tell the gargoyles what we practiced."

Tuna nodded, then turned his attention to his fellow gargoyles. They quieted down when it was apparent Tuna was going to speak.

"You all. Stop. No more. No more bad. They use us. Not like us. No be nice. Ever." Tuna took a deep breath. "Be good. Help. Not hurt. Feel good help. Good here." He pounded lightly where his heart was. "Hoo-mans friend. Good to Tuna. Now Tuna family. Tuna say so. Be good.

"Change. All change. Now.

"Please."

Gabby, Candy, and Lewis all held their breath. Their survival and the mission depended on the gargoyles listening to Tuna, who had defected to their side and now was trying to convince his fellow gargoyles from Hell to do the same thing.

No gargoyles moved.

Then, toward the front of the group, one gargoyle stepped to the side. He was followed by the one behind him. A gargoyle to the left stepped over one step, leaving a small gap in their ranks. Slowly and one by one, the crowd parted, leaving a walking path in between them all for Gabby, Tuna, and the Reeds. Tuna stepped forward and began to walk in between his fellow gargoyles. Then he stopped and turned around and motioned to Gabby. "You first. Please.

"Gabby.

"Our Gebirah."

Gabby walked in between the throngs of gargoyles who, until a few moments ago, wanted to kill them all. All of the gargoyles kept their heads and eyes down. Some reached out to touch Gabby as she passed by. She tried very hard not to recoil from their cold, bony touches. The Reeds walked through right behind her, not wanting to allow any space between them and Gabby. Tuna followed behind, nodding to his fellow gargoyles as he went. When all four had made it to the other side, the gargoyles closed ranks and followed behind the four.

"Gabby, what just happened?" Candy asked. "Are those . . . things like Tuna, are they on our side now? Just like that?"

"Yes, Candy, I believe they are. He did it.

"Let's meet up with the others and get things going. Hopefully, we won't have to use the explosives. I'm not wild about the thought of living the rest of my life as a fugitive from the US Government if we can help it."

***

At the top of the gangway stairs, Matt, Milla, and Katrina had just landed and sent the drones back to their home location beyond the perimeter fence. If needed, they could call them, plus four others for extraction. Katrina said she heard someone coming up the stairs. The three soldiers-for-hire drew their electrical staffs, just in case.

After a tense three minutes of waiting, Milla said she saw the Reeds about two floors below, and it looked like Gabby and Tuna were in front of them. She leaned out a little farther to take a look, and saw the large group of wraiths waiting below. "That's not good," she said. "We're going to need the drones again."

"Hi, guys, miss us?" Gabby said, a little winded as she reached the top of the landing. "You haven't already opened the . . . okay, I see it's still intact. Never mind."

"Gabby," Milla said, "what's with the waiting party down there? How did you all make it through that? We've called for the extra drones to be ready."

"Thank you, but that won't be necessary, Milla. Those folks down there have followed Tuna's lead and joined the winning side. I'll explain more later, but we all owe Tuna big time. He came through and then some."

Tuna, who had stuck close right behind Gabby during the trip up the stairs and had been standing right behind her the whole time she was talking, poked his head around Gabby's shoulder and said "Hello, Matt. Hello, Mill-a. Hello, Ka-trin-a. We have new friends. Friends down below wait ting."

"Wow, Tuna, that's amazing," Matt said. "You are one impressive . . . man." He stumbled to find the right word for the moment. When Tuna heard the word "man," he stood a little taller and looked to be thrusting his spiny chest out as much as possible.

"Thank you . . . Matt," Tuna said, taking time to enunciate what he wanted to say. "It was . . . good. Very good. Thank. You. Tuna stop talking now. Time for miss on."

Gabby stepped up and hugged the trio as the Reeds joined everyone else on the gangway. "Let's see about opening that capsule and getting those astronaut wannabes out of there."

The six humans began to bang on the sealed hatch of the capsule. They could see the four astronauts, already strapped in their seats awaiting launch.

When they realized Gabby and the others were trying to open the door, they frantically began to flip switches to begin the launch early. The massive engines rumbled, sending the gargoyles down below running for cover.

"Come on, we didn't get this far to fail now," Matt said. He was powering up his staff in an effort to short-circuit the door. The others began to do the same thing. Tuna was using his considerable strength to try to pry the door off its hinges, but he was unable to make any progress. The engines were now sending out large plumes of fire, and the entire structure shook. Gabby yelled as loud as she could, "Everyone stand back! It's going to be all right. We have incoming."

She looked to the east and pointed toward what appeared to be a large bird headed right for them. As the figure got closer, it was apparent the figure was much larger than any bird and was coming straight for them. Gabby motioned for everyone to clear away from the capsule doors. Coming in very, very fast, with a flaming sword in his hand, was Zander. He had large white wings spreading out from his back, and was completely naked except for a belt. He slowed his approach a little when he was within several hundred feet of the capsule door. He led with the flaming sword and slammed into the capsule door, his sword easily cleaving through the metal and penetrating deep into the capsule's interior.

He removed the sword, which then seemed to move on its own to a scabbard at his side. Zander looked at the stunned faces of his teammates; then he sunk his fingers into the metal door and ripped it off its hinges.

Inside, the crew members closest to the door were attempting to unbuckle their harnesses when Zander removed the sword and thrust it through the midsections of the three men. The sword stopped just short of cutting the fourth astronaut, who was staring in disbelief at his crew mates. All three had been run through but still were moving and writhing in their seats. As the three wailed in agony, black wings began to sprout through their spacesuits, taking up what little extra room there was in the tiny capsule and beating against the capsule's lone human occupant. Zander ripped each of the fallen angels from their seats and threw them onto the gangway.

Gabby and Lewis climbed into the capsule to help the seemingly hapless astronaut escape his restraints. He stumbled out of the capsule to see his three crew mates writhing on the metal floor, black wings beating all around them, while another man with white wings pointed a sword in their direction.

"You," Zander said, gesturing to the man. "Did you know who you were about to fly with? Are you in league with these traitors? Answer with the truth. I will know if you are lying."

The astronaut struggled for a moment to remove his helmet. Zander carefully placed the tip of his sword where the helmet was joined to the man's spacesuit and gave the sword a short, swift flick that sent the helmet flying off the platform, crashing into the metal structure surrounding the rocket.

"Are you kidding me?" the astronaut responded. "I've known these men for more than a year. We trained together for this mission. We talked, we shared family stories. They never said anything about being . . . that." He gestured toward the motionless bodies, even as some of their wings still flailed about.

"Very well, human. You can go. But remember this, I'll be watching you."

The astronaut retorted, "Oh yeah? What makes you different from them? You're the one who just killed three men . . . or whatever they are, after flying in here like a bat out of hell."

Zander listened to the man, considering what to say next. "Those angels once were like brothers to me, and it pained me beyond measure to slay them. As to our differences, we made different choices many years ago, my friend. Just like you or any human can do every day. You can choose to be good and choose to make a difference. Or you can choose to be selfish, arrogant, and believe your very existence entitles you to more. It is the same for us. We are not so different—angels, whether above or fallen below, and humans. Our choices make us who we are. Our bodies and heritage only provide the raw materials to do what we choose with the time we have. These three, and others like them, thought they were better. They were not. I mourn their loss twice—once when they fell, and now when I was forced to end their existence."

Matt stepped forward to place himself between Zander and the astronaut. "Zander, wow, that's . . . that's something. Have you always been an angel, just waiting around and watching us?"

"Yes, friend Matthew. Please call me by my true name: Xanusel. I have been on Earth for many years, placed into anonymous service with the firstborn to observe and guide him—and his followers—away from any foolishness."

Gabby stepped up to speak to both men. "Well, Cain seems to be doing your job for you. Why did you hide for so long? And what was with the arrogant jerk act all the time?"

Xanusel broke into a wide grin. "The firstborn's actions have been, happily, a surprise to us all. Perhaps not *all* of us, but most of us. You never know. And I was attempting to act as a venal human to further my disguise, lest I be mistaken as a spy among allies."

"You mean you're not a jerk when you're all angeled up?" Gabby said. "You were a bit of an asshole, to tell you the truth. Pompous and acting like you're superior to everyone else. I guess a disguise can only hide so much."

"It was enough to hide my true self and complete my mission, Gabrielle. It worked for many years. It even fooled your new senses, I am happy to say."

"Zander . . . excuse me, Xanusel, I knew who you were a day before I met you. Nice try. *I see all. I know all.*" Gabby said this last part with a smirk and a really poor attempt at sounding like a carnival fortune teller.

"You did? My apologies, Gabrielle, but I don't think that is possible."

"We'll just have to agree to disagree then. It really doesn't make any difference now. This launch is stopped, and Cain is on his way to stop the last one. We have some new allies waiting for us below. Let's go down and make what I'm sure are going to be some awkward introductions."

Everyone began to walk toward the stairs. The Reeds and Tuna were helping the human astronaut—who said his name was Bran Foster and kept repeating he didn't know his crew mates were from Hell—make his way down and prepare him for meeting fifty-odd gargoyles once they finished their descent.

Xanusel waited until everyone else was headed down the stairs, and placed a hand on Gabby's shoulder. "Gabrielle, we do need to talk."

"What about? Cain and his team are on their way to intercept the third rocket. They will prevail. I've seen it. What else is there? Do I have some unpaid parking tickets somewhere? Am I in trouble because I sometimes nod off during church services with Daniel? What is it? And please make it fast. We have a lot to do still."

"Gabrielle, it's about Daniel. There's something you need to know . . ."

CHAPTER 41: AIR VLADIVOSTOK

"You have got to be kidding me," Gabby said. "There's no way Daniel is the Adversary. Or one of them. I would have seen that. I sure as hell would have known it. Wouldn't I? How did I miss this? He loves to attend church. He goes all the time."

"Perhaps that and your influence had helped to hold his ancestry at bay," Xanusel said. "But with that gone, he has joined his brethren. I saw it with my own eyes. They are only waiting for the chaos of the bombardments so they can come forward to throw the world further into darkness."

"Wow, that really doesn't sound like Daniel. Like, not at all. Does he have a choice in this? Can he choose to be a conscientious objector? That would be more like him. He told me he was at a conference in Colorado. He even told me where it was, which, come to think of it, was odd."

"He did? Then there may be hope. For him and for us. We cannot sense them, but we can observe them. They appear as normal humans to us. We know they are here but not who they are or where they all are. We know the woman from Daniel's kidnapping, Lorelei, is one of the leaders. She's been very blatant about it. That's how we've learned most of our information. As always, the seeds to their own defeat are sown from within. But if they are all gathering in one place to prepare for their world debut, we have a chance at stopping them now. How can we find them?"

"Do you have a smartphone?" Gabby said. "Daniel built this really funny app a few years ago . . . "

***

Starbird One was flying sixty-two miles above the Earth, just below the Kármán Line, which separates the planet's atmosphere from the cold, unforgiving environment of space. They were within 100 miles of Vladivostok when Captain Johnson announced they would remain in a holding pattern for the time being.

"What are we waiting for, boss?" Roland asked. "Shouldn't we be there by now?"

"We are there," Cain said. "Or as close as we can get at the moment. We are the proverbial cat waiting for the mouse to make an appearance." He was putting on a custom-made spacesuit for someone his size. A helmet sat on one of the seats beside him. "Although I do recommend suiting up, just in case." Cain gestured to a storage locker near the front of the plane. The two men opened the locker and removed their suits.

Just then, the overhead speaker came to life with a crackle followed by the voice of Captain Johnson. "Everyone, we do have confirmation of a launch near Vladivostok. The rocket took off about eight minutes ago. We should see her in a few minutes. I have them on our radar. Watch for the engine flare. That's the easiest way to trace them visually once they are airborne."

Cain, Gregg, and Roland all began looking out windows on both sides, watching for signs of the rocket. Captain Johnson said their quarry was about sixty miles east and several miles below their current position. The Starbird's stealth technology would keep them masked from the rocket's crew and their ground crew. Once they were in visual range, though, the element of surprise would be gone.

Roland pointed out his window excitedly. "I see it! It's . . . it has two boosters which just separated, and something else. I can't make it out from here."

Cain walked over to the window beside Roland with a pair of binoculars. It took him a few minutes to focus and then track through the sky to see their target. When he stepped back to hand the binoculars to Gregg, he said, "It appears we have our work cut out for us. Take a look."

Gregg focused in on the rocket that was just about level with their altitude. He saw one larger booster engine, which was just starting to fall away, and separating from it was a jet-black space shuttle.

***

"He's showing us exactly where he is. Where they are," Xanusel said. "Perhaps Daniel has not changed sides entirely. Perhaps there is good in him still."

"People don't change that fast," Gabby said. "And especially Daniel. He may have had his head turned, but he's still a good man. I could hear it in his voice. He was torn over something. This must be what it is. No wonder he was so evasive on the phone. How do you tell your girlfriend something like that? Can you imagine? Living your whole life believing one thing, then finding out you literally were born to do the opposite."

"No I cannot, Gabby. Should we go to him, if this is his hour of need?"

Gabby looked at the angel. "You can take me to him?"

"Yes, Gabrielle. The location Daniel sent to you is not far, especially when we would be flying in a straight line. Take my hands and do not let go."

Xanusel's wings lifted him off the gangway; then he pulled Gabby up close to him, wrapping his arms around her and using one of his legs as a support for Gabby's legs. His arms were as firm and steady as steel, and he even managed a smile when they took off. "Hold on," he said. "We will be there in a matter of minutes."

Down below, Matt, Milla, and Katrina had successfully helped Bran down the stairs, still in his bulky astronaut suit. Tuna and the other gargoyles all were pointing into the sky, as if tracing the path the angel and Gabby had just left on.

"I hope she knows what she's doing," Matt said.

Tuna turned toward Matt. "She does. Gabby knows."

***

Lorelei and Daniel walked past the house and toward the natural amphitheater nearby. Many of their siblings were doing the same, while others continued to mill about and talk with one another near the pool. "When do we start?" Daniel asked. "And what do I do? Do I listen in the crowd or help backstage? Where will you be?"

Lorelei smiled at Daniel's eagerness to help. "Go wherever it suits you. If we need you, we will call. Things will be getting started soon. Everyone will be here by noon. I do have a small role to play, though. Will you be all right by yourself? Perhaps you can use the time to meet more of our family.

Most of them know about you already. The mate of the seer. You have some cache already, dear Daniel."

"Thanks. I think I'll walk around and get to know some of the others. See you in a bit."

***

Captain Johnson had watched the final booster jettison off the shuttle as it crossed into low-earth orbit and activated its own engines. He followed the shuttle, remaining at least ten miles back and still radar-invisible, past the Kármán line and into the thermosphere.

"What are they doing, Captain?" Cain asked through the ship's intercom. "Anything you can tell?"

"Not so far, sir. It looks like they may be getting ready to roll over as if to deliver a payload. But there doesn't appear to be any other structures nearby to receive it."

"That is because they intend to drop their payload, Captain," Cain said. "That is what we are here to stop. Tell me, Chuck, how close can we get without them knowing?"

"With the ship's stealth technology, plus the fact that we both are black spacecraft and absorbing heat and they are just floating, I'd say within thirty meters."

"Excellent, Captain. And you can maintain that distance for a while?"

"Yes, sir. Should not be a problem. If I may ask, what are you going to do?"

"I am going for a neighborly chat to point out the error of their ways. Moving on, anyone have any ideas what it would take to pry open those bay doors? Captain? Gregg? Roland?"

Roland said the shuttle bay doors mostly likely had mechanisms inside to open them, but in zero G they might be easy to pry open. "They aren't built to keep people out. The designers probably never envisioned a scenario where keeping someone outside in the vacuum of space was desirable."

"You all are missing the obvious," Gregg said. "They want to open the bay doors, right? Why not go over and wait until they do, then destroy the payload or send it out somewhere?"

"Gregg, that is brilliant," Cain said. "I knew you were a more than capable soldier, but you have a good tactical mind. That's exactly what we need to do."

"What's with the we, boss? I was talking about you out there, not me. Not us. That's way outside of my knowledge base."

"You and Roland will be tethered to the Starbird and under the watchful eye of Captain Johnson. I will go out without a tether to work the payload loose and deal with any threats. My suit has a small booster attached in case I need to change direction. What can I say? I spent a lot of time reading James Bond novels. Gentlemen, this can work. This is what we signed up for. Please suit up. We need to take a walk and say hello."

***

The natural amphitheater sat in the base of the Rockies with a formation of rocks that resembled steps. Daniel could see Lorelei near the staging area, talking to two women and a man. They all looked in Daniel's direction and waved; then they went on with their conversation. A few gargoyles were putting the finishing touches on several loudspeakers and the lone microphone stand sitting at the largest outcropping.

The set-up was minimal but impressive. Daniel thought with the microphone in place and someone speaking from the rock, it looked a little like a scene from *The Lion King*. He wondered if they would want him to speak.

***

Twenty minutes later, a hatch in the belly of the Starbird opened up. Cain, Roland, and Gregg were floating near the exit in full spacewalk gear. The two men, as promised, had very long tethers attached to the midsections of their suits. The other end was attached firmly inside the ship. All three held onto grips near the hatch's opening.

Captain Johnson moved slowly toward the dark shuttle as it hung in zero gravity like a bird of prey, the Earth slowly turning beneath it. The captain had turned off all of the Starbird's external lights to further conceal its presence from the other ship. The usual procedure with such a maneuver was close communication between the two ships to ensure both were traveling in the same direction at the same speed. Captain Johnson was doing it without the benefit of additional guidance. When they were roughly sixty meters away, the Starbird began to slow. Cain thought for a moment that they might collide or give away their position, but the Starbird slowed its movement until its belly was matched with that of the shuttle and at least one ship length behind. It was now or never.

A light turned green above the hatch, and Cain pushed away and headed toward the shuttle. Roland and Gregg followed, albeit more cautiously and mindful of their tethers. Cain landed feet first on the top of the rear part of the ship. He used handrails to pull himself closer to the bay doors. The other two arrived a minute later.

Cain looked toward the Earth and saw they were above Russia and parts of China. The sun would catch up to them within the next hour. They would need to move fast when the bay doors opened. They waited, all three floating in space and ready to either fight or send the metal poles into the sun. Three minutes, then five. At ten minutes of waiting, Cain became impatient.

This is taking too long, Cain thought. *We are going to lose the element of surprise.* It was time to act before it was too late. He removed a brick-sized block of plastique he had strapped to his side and motioned to the others that he was going to try to open the doors himself. They didn't want to risk radio communications that might be picked up inside the shuttle.

Roland waved frantically at Cain, crossing his hands back and forth several times. Cain replaced the plastique in its case and pointed to his head. Roland moved his head up and down, and pointed to a crowbar he had strapped to the outside of his suit. Cain nodded in agreement.

At the top of the shuttle, Roland motioned for Cain to stay behind him. When Cain was in position, Roland used the crowbar to pry open the bay doors enough for Cain to slip inside and loosen the cargo. Cain undid the main straps on the mammoth metal rods, letting them float inside the cargo area while he made his way toward the bay door controls. The metal rods were strapped together in bundles of twenty-five.

Roland still could see inside from where he had pried the doors open.

He gave Cain the thumbs-up signal, then disappeared from view. Cain flipped the switch to open the bay doors. They would have to move quickly to get rid of more than 200 rods before someone from inside the shuttle suited up and came outside.

With Cain feeding the stacks up to them, Gregg pushed the stacks to Roland, who began to send them in the general direction of the sun. During each push, Gregg held onto Roland's tether to keep him from flying backward. It was awkward and slow going, but they were making progress. In a little more than five minutes, they had sent seven bundles to melt in the fiery nuclear blast furnace of the sun. Cain was getting the eighth and final bundle ready to pass up when the cargo bay access door opened. Razhael stepped out in a modified spacesuit that allowed his wings to be free. Cain finished lifting and passing the bundle to Gregg, then activated his in-helmet microphone. "You two get out of here. Right away. I will handle this."

Captain Johnson started to move the Starbird away from the shuttle, pulling Gregg and Roland along with him. Roland gave the final bundle a good shove, then a supremely defiant look to Razhael. As the Starbird began to move away and pull the two to safety, Razhael leapt out of the cargo area, using his wings to maneuver toward the two men. He flew straight at them, then turned at the last minute to slice both of their lifelines with his wings. Roland and Gregg already were in motion from the Starbird, and both went careening further into space.

Cain activated his helmet communicator. "Captain Johnson, go after those two and get them on board. Then get out of here. Your job is done. I can handle the rest."

"Yes, sir. I can get them," Captain Johnson replied. "They may be bruised, but they will come home. They are as good as got. Let me know if I can do anything else."

"No thank you, Captain," Cain said, never taking his eyes off Razhael. He had landed about twenty feet from Cain, who still was inside the shuttle's cargo bay. "You three have done more than enough. You all have. I can finish this. Get those two on board and head home. Wait for me there."

Razhael eyed Cain warily. "For all your efforts, firstborn, you will lose.

This is a temporary setback and nothing more. The world will freeze and we will be there to pick up the pieces. Humans will serve us as they were meant to. The Adversaries can do what they want with them. If it keeps them busy, so much the better. I can't stand having to work with half-breeds."

Cain was listening to the fallen angel as he checked his helmet's HUD display for the Starbird. Gregg and Roland were on board, and the ship was heading back in the atmosphere and toward home. *Okay,* Cain thought, *time to end this.* "Razhael, you know what? You talk too much." From the lower back of his suit, Cain pulled the sawed-off shotgun he had brought from Elkins.

Razhael looked at the gun, then at Cain. He began to laugh. "Oh, this is wonderful. You are so desperate to stop us you've brought a gun. Into space. You do know how they work, don't you, little man? Aren't you an arms manufacturer? You and your humans are pathetic. It would almost be a pity to kill you. Almost."

Razhael started to slowly move toward Cain. Cain's bottom lip began to quiver as he looked deep into Razhael's eyes with a look of surrender. He raised the shotgun and pulled the trigger. A soundless blast blew apart Razhael's chest, sending him floating back into the wall of the cargo bay. Thick black blood oozed from his suit and instantly froze. Razhael had a look of bewilderment on his face as Cain launched himself toward him, grabbing onto his shoulders. Razhael said weakly and in a daze, "How . . . ?"

"You missed the twentieth century. I have lived here my whole life." Cain placed the shotgun on the base of Razhael's left wing and pulled the trigger. Both men were sent spinning out of the cargo bay and into space. Cain still hung onto the injured Razhael. "They have worked without oxygen for a long time."

He moved the shotgun to the base of the remaining wing. "You live with your regret and bad decisions in Hell trying to scheme to destroy our beautiful planet and do not know shit." Cain pulled the trigger and watched the wing tear free from Razhael, black blood freezing as it spurted out of his suit.

Razhael's voice came through Cain's headset. It was a wail of agony, followed by a language Cain did not recognize. He lined up another shot, this time on the visor of Razhael's helmet. "I know this will not kill you. In fact, I am counting on it." He pulled the trigger once more. The unknown language stopped but the body still was moving, still trying to recover. Cain moved away from the floating angel, looked out into the stars, and chose the blackest section of the void he could see. He activated his thrusters, ramming himself into the fallen angel and sending the newly defenseless fallen angel into the cold depths of uncharted space. "Enjoy eternity," Cain said, hoping there was enough of Razhael's hearing left to get the message.

Cain watched as the incapacitated Razhael tumbled helplessly through the void until he was out of sight. Cain then drifted for a few moments, enjoying the view of Earth from above. He thought it looked so peaceful and so colorful that if these were his last moments, he was glad to see his home one final time. He could see the edge of the United States as he drifted slowly back into the Earth's gravitational field.

Cain reached up to his helmet and found a button on the side and pressed it. His Russian was a little rusty but he thought he could manage. "Russian shuttle, please come in. This is Cain, the man who just sent your boss flying toward Jupiter. And in case you might be wondering, he is not flying on his own on account of me severing his wings. Since no one else is coming out, I presume the rest of you are human. If you were knowingly working with Razhael, I will find out and deal with you later. I suggest you close the bay doors and head home. Your mission is over."

Cain then turned away from the shuttle and used his remaining boosters to propel him toward Earth. "Siri, call Gabrielle. I need to say goodbye."

CHAPTER 42: FALLING IN LOVE ALL OVER AGAIN

"Young lady, answer the phone." Cain had entered the upper atmosphere and was beginning to pick up speed. He could see the Pacific Ocean below and hoped he could make the most of his time before falling to his death from outer space. He didn't age, healed from minor wounds, and had never been stricken with a life-threatening illness, but Cain did not see a way he would survive being a human meteor.

On the third ring, Gabby answered. "Hello, Cain. Are you all back already?" She sounded positive. Perhaps she hadn't seen what happened.

"In a manner of speaking," Cain said. "We stopped them, and the team is flying back to land in California."

"It sounds like there's a 'but' coming. What is it?"

"Well, Gabrielle, I have developed a small problem."

"I thought all your problems were small," Gabby said jokingly. She was thankful that the two missions had stopped the launches and was trying to put on a brave face for seeing Daniel. Xanusel had landed a few miles away so as not to attract the attention of the Adversaries. Gabby called Daniel and told him she had rented a car and would be there soon.

"Very funny," Cain said. "This is a new one, however. One that . . . that I may not survive. I am speaking to you through my helmet. I am falling through the upper atmosphere at a somewhat alarming rate. I do not expect to survive the landing."

In an instant, all of the color drained from Gabby's face. "What do you mean you don't expect to survive? I thought you couldn't die?"

"So far I have not, but I also never went skydiving from space without a parachute. So after countless millennia of not putting you-know-who to the test, it looks like today we all will learn something new."

"Cain, I'm on my way to meet Daniel. What about Xanusel? Can he catch you?"

"Who is that? Another angel? They are crawling out of the woodwork these days. No thank you."

"Don't be stubborn, Cain. This is your life we're talking about."

"Yes, I am fully aware of that. Has it ever occurred to you that I might want this? That I am tired of endless life? That, after helping to save the world from the Apocalypse, I would want to take my chances at the Pearly Gates? See if I have made up for my brother?"

"No, I hadn't thought of that," Gabby said, desperately trying to think of a way to help. "Wait a minute! I didn't get to tell you, Cain. We aren't done. There's one teeny-tiny part of the Apocalypse we overlooked."

There was silence from the other end. Gabby started to speak, but Cain beat her to it. "The Antichrist? Is that it? He's already here? He's not foretold to be here until the . . . son of a bitch. They out-Gabby'ed us, did they? We have a hidden ace, and they had one too. How could we have missed that?"

"We all did, Cain. Even when it was right under our noses. There's not just one, there are 666 of them. It wasn't just the number of rods they were going to drop. I think we got caught up in that and missed the rest. But they are all here, ready to overrun the world through subtlety and persuasion, believe it or not. And the worst part is . . . the worst part is . . . Daniel is one of them."

"You have got to be kidding me! Your Daniel? The guy who follows you around like a lost puppy? The guy we rescued from . . . She is his sister, is that it? He got his head turned and that is why he jumped ship?"

"There are a few more details there, but yes, that's pretty accurate. Except he told us where they are. Where they all are. Every one of them. Xanusel and I are going there now to try to stop them."

When there was no response, Gabby spoke into the phone again. "Cain? Cain? Are you there? Please don't be gone. Please answer. Say . . . say something. Please."

A moment. Then two. Tears started to well in Gabby's eyes.

Then, "Sorry. Had to put you on hold. I called Daniel. I needed to clear up a few things. I also told him to get the hell out of there as fast as he can. You and bird boy need to pick him up and get going too. Meet in California at the hangar. Text Daniel, he's expecting it. Two calls in a row will look suspicious. He will come to you. Don't waste time trying to find him."

"What? You called him? Why? What's going on? Why is he leaving?"

"Because I just told him there is a missile strike heading toward him and his new family, and I hoped he really had not changed sides. He said he had not. I then asked him how you two found him. He gave me the coordinates. Clever boy, even if he did have his head turned. Lust will do that to you, believe me. I hope you can forgive him. But first, and I cannot emphasize this enough, you three need to get out of there."

"Lust? What were you all talking about?"

"Gabby, this is not the time. Let me summarize. Daniel gave me the exact coordinates where you and all of the Adversaries are now. In northern Colorado. I am currently exiting the thermosphere somewhere above the California coast and moving fast. We accomplished our mission. And now we can remove the Adversaries we did not know about before now. It is almost like it was planned, is it not? With this final move we will completely stop the Apocalypse in one fell swoop. I have always wanted to say that. We can still stop them. Or I can. I told Daniel to meet you at the western side of the property. But you have to leave, and you have to leave now. Ask birdman to get you and the boy and hightail it out of there."

"Cain, what are you talking . . . "

"Gabby, I know what he's doing," Xanusel said. "He's right. We have to leave. We can pick up Daniel if we hurry. Whatever he's doing, he needs to walk away quickly and get out of there. Text him, please. We can pick him up on our way out. Tell him to watch for us and be ready for extraction. Tell him to walk away right now and head west, steady and quick but not enough to tip them off. We can get him and be out of there quickly. We have enough time, but not much to spare. It should be enough.

"And, Cain. I know you are still listening. You always have been a marvelous bastard. You may have caused us no end of trouble at the beginning, but you've more than made up for it. This is the icing on the cake. You have our respect."

"Thanks, bird brain. That is much appreciated. Also: my parents were married. You would think you all would remember details. Gabby, you have been beyond wonderful. Now, get Daniel and get the hell out of there."

Cain ended the call before she could respond.

Xanusel picked Gabby up, and flew east toward the retreat to find Daniel. In the distance, they both could see several hundred people listening and cheering someone speaking passionately from atop a large rock.

***

" . . . And we will rule the world for the next several years in precisely this way," Lorelei was telling the throngs of her brothers and sisters. "It will be unexpected. When the Great Freeze comes along later today, we will be poised to take control and rule all of humanity when Father joins us. We will remake the world in his image this time. Anyone who opposes us will be put to death without mercy. With a few examples, the sheep will follow. It will be a glorious ti . . . " The crowd of Adversaries still were cheering as Lorelei stopped speaking when she saw something out of the corner of her eye. It was too big to be an eagle, and it was flying extremely low.

She pointed to the sky and said, "Look, my sisters and brothers! It is one of the angels from on high, come to show us the error of our ways. They wouldn't dare invade us now. Let's say hello." The crowd started to surge toward the approaching Xanusel, Gabby still in his grasp. Xanusel swooped down lower as Daniel stood alone, his arms outstretched. Xanusel moved Gabby to his left arm, and extended his right to pick up Daniel without stopping. He had not done something like this in a few thousand years. "No time for niceties," Xanusel said. "We need to vacate the area. We have incoming."

Daniel grabbed onto the angel's arm, then felt himself rising up over the fast approaching crowd that began to throw whatever they were holding at the trio. Daniel managed to grab a basketball that narrowly missed smacking him in the head.

"You're not getting this back," Daniel yelled down at his surprised half-brother. "I'm going to sell it and give the money to a church, you big phony."

Gabby looked over at Daniel, who was looking down below at what he was leaving behind. "Hi, Gabby. I appreciate the rescue. Again. I'm, uh, sorry about leaving earlier. I didn't know about all this," he gestured downward to the crowd as they began to disappear the further and higher Xanusel flew, "then. I do now. And it's . . . it's not me. But I don't know what is anymore."

Daniel then glanced up at the angel carrying them high above the Rocky Mountains. "And thanks to you too, big guy. You're not going to get in trouble for helping one of . . . whatever I am. For helping me, are you?"

"Friend Daniel, rescuing wayward humans—even those with unfortunate parentage—is our specialty."

Daniel looked over at Gabby, who was smiling ear to ear. Then he looked up to Xanusel and asked, "Did you just make a Phantom Menace reference?"

"A truly underrated masterpiece," Xanusel said. "I never understood why it wasn't received better. And that Jar Jar—comedy gold."

"Um, yeah," Daniel said. "We're going to have to talk about that when we land. Also, has anyone told you that you look just like that jerky comms guy?"

***

Now in complete free fall within Earth's gravity, Cain used his helmet's HUD to plot his course. He would ride the wind past California and find his target.

He had been using his body as a windbreaker to maneuver where his helmet computer was sending him. He ignored the flashing red warnings and concentrated on getting to the location at the exact right moment.

As he passed the 8,000-feet mark, Cain figured he might as well enjoy the rest of the trip. He tucked his head down, pulled his legs behind him and stretched his arms out in front of him as he turned his free fall into a dive. *Black Superman is on his way, you nitwits.* The wind rushing past him felt glorious. *I should have spent more time skydiving,* he thought. *Well, I did get to do just about everything else under the sun.*

In the distance, he saw a winged man carrying two people westward into the early afternoon sun. They were safely away. Against all odds, they had stopped Armageddon and hopefully found each other again. *And this,* he thought, *is a fine way to die.* The wind rushing past him was exhilarating. Saving the planet he loved and the people he loved even more. *It's been a good life,* he thought.

But I need to make sure none of them leave. And I'm no hero.

Cain changed position when the Rocky Mountains were in sight. He curled his body up into a ball, and wrapped his arms around his knees. He could see the gathering below him. He imagined his arrival would be visible through the mountain fog but not completely. What a surprise this would be, he thought. His best one yet. This would be a fine death. After a lifetime of poor choices and wasted time.

When he broke through the clouds, he saw the assembled crowd. Lorelei was on stage shouting to the cheering throngs. A few looked away and up just in time to see the world's oldest man, in a tattered spaceflight suit, cracked helmet, a shotgun still tied to his back, heading straight for them at more than 800 miles an hour.

Then one last sound. A voice that was heard over the crowd, the speaker, and echoed throughout the mountains.

"Cannonball, motherf . . . "

CHAPTER 43: THE ISLE OF PATMOS, YEAR 94

The white hair appeared first. It rose to the top of the murky Mediterranean near the island's easternmost edge. Even in the moonlight, it was visible from a distance. John thought it looked like a very old octopus, and he wondered why Cain bothered to sneak around. He looked like no one else. If those around didn't know about his curse already, they would find out soon. It was bad enough that he faked his own death thousands of years prior.

Cain walked up the shore, setting down the large reed he used to breathe while making his way to the prison. He picked up several large stones nearby and hastily created a place to stand where he could see through the bars. John was sitting in the far corner, trying to look like he was seeing something. In truth, he was waiting for the visit.

"Ho, John," Cain said through crude, rusty bars. "I have come as you asked. I was having a wonderful time far to the east. The people are so much more advanced and refined than this desert garbage. Did you know they invented several systematic ways of combat? Just came up with it! And it works. Not that I need it, of course, but it is wonderful exercise."

"Hello, Cain," John said. "Killed anyone lately?"

"They told me you were a sour one. No wonder you are in prison. No finesse. But that is a hallmark of your people, is it not? You are right and you know it and the hell with everyone else."

"Be quiet, murderer. It is bad enough that I have to deal with you. I will not listen to your jibes about me, our cause, or even your fiendish ways of moving about that you learned from foreign devils."

"John, it is that very attitude that landed you here in the first place. Visions and seers everyone knows and tolerates. But a loudmouthed one who tells everyone he is right and the rest are going to die . . . not a very good look, I am afraid. Why send for me? I came to see your alleged gifts for myself. And I am pretty sure I knew your great-great-great-great-grandmother. Cute lady. She had the brightest eyes and was a handful in the hay. I miss her."

"You are a damnable demon who walks among men, firstborn. I would rather eat my own tongue than talk to you."

"Go ahead. I would like to see that."

John narrowed his eyes and cleared his throat when he spoke next. "But unlike you, I serve a higher power and a greater cause. I am only speaking to you because I saw you, and it falls to me to ensure you do not go astray."

Cain suddenly became quiet and attentive. "What did you see? I do not perish, do I? I still have so much life to live and enjoy."

"No, you foul little man. For reasons that I cannot fathom despite daily communion with the most high, you are . . . important to the cause. You still have a role to play."

"And your ancestors ate dung and enjoyed it. What could I possibly do? You do know who I am? Killed my brother, cursed for all eternity? I am not an ideal soldier on a good day, let alone someone who would help you desert freaks."

John stared at the man who was taunting him through the bars of his prison. He looked at him with distaste at first; then he calmed down enough to show something like pity.

"The killing of your brother was an accident," John said. "You were both attempting to burn your offerings, and yours would not light. Abel walked over to help you while you were fretting. He was crouched over the fire he had successfully started for you to ensure it would stay lit. You still were upset and, in your distress, stood up and inadvertently knocked him headfirst into the flames. You lied about what happened to hide your shame because you could not bear the thought of having killed your brother and best friend. And so you were cursed for all eternity as a murderer."

Cain had been listening in disbelief. He had never told anyone that story, not even his parents.

"John . . . how do you know this? Dark magic? I had heard your lot had strange abilities, but this. This is, this is a truth that has never been spoken. No one would believe you if you said it."

282

"Yes, Cain," John said in an almost conciliatory tone. "I believe it because I have seen it. Would you accept the truth if I told you the color of your brother's eyes? Or the contents of his offering? Or yours?"

"No, no," Cain said. "That is enough. I came here as a jest. But this is not what I expected. Why do you torment me now, John? What purpose does it serve to use your tricks to show me my failures? I have had a good deal more since then."

"For the same reason everyone is tormented. So you may learn something and do good despite yourself."

"Me? Do good? Is that possible? Perhaps your visions have driven you completely mad as everyone says."

"Far from it, Cain. I see far into the past and even further into the future. I will share what I know that you need to know now. Pay attention. Many years from now, there will be a girl. She will be descended from one of your loves. When you meet her, she will be the closest thing you have to a blood relative, even though none of your accursed blood will flow in her veins. Still, you will not tell her. She will receive a terrible gift that will save us all. And you will help her. In doing so, you may be redeemed."

Cain found no words to match this proclamation. Redeemed? He had put off that thought long ago. Instead, he asked, "Who is this mystery woman? When will I see her? How will I know?"

"Because I'm going to show you. Be quiet and listen for once, you impatient and impertinent man. You have wasted all of your life. It's far past time you give something back to this world you love so much. Sit down on the stones and listen . . ."

CHAPTER 44: THIS WAY TO THE EGRESS

Xanusel, carrying Gabby and Daniel, began to descend when they were close to the California launch site and the remaining team. "There they are, Xanusel. We made it." Gabby saw Matt, Milla, Katrina, and Tuna walking far below, outside the hangar. Captain Johnson was walking around the Starbird, noting the damage on a tablet. They all looked up when they saw the large shadow on the tarmac.

Gabby, Xanusel, and Daniel were greeted immediately and almost knocked down by a very excited Tuna, who picked up Gabby as soon as her feet were on the ground. "Gab bee. You are back. Safe. So glad.

"Who this?" Tuna asked, pointing at Daniel. "Bad guy?"

"What in the . . . ?" Daniel said, looking in bewilderment at Tuna. "You know what he is, right?"

Gabby hugged Tuna; then she turned around toward Daniel. "Yes, we know *who* he is. He's with us. Daniel, I'd like you to meet our friend and teammate, Tuna. Tuna, this is Daniel, my . . . boyfriend."

The gargoyle looked at Daniel, then back to Gabby. He repeated this once more, finally saying, "You and he? He not good. Born bad. No good. Mean to Tuna. Like others."

"No, no, Tuna," Gabby said. "He's my boyfriend. He's not going to be mean to you. He didn't know about that until recently. And like you, he chose to do good instead. I promise." The gargoyle eyed Daniel suspiciously, then turned and walked back into the hangar.

"It's a long story," Gabby said. "We probably both have them."

Daniel just nodded. He wasn't sure how much of his long story he was ready to share. As everyone else came up to greet them, Xanusel folded his wings to blend in more easily. Matt walked up to him and asked, "You've been this the whole time?"

"Yes, friend Matthew. My task was to watch Cain and also to protect the seer."

"What about the others? Paula, Jonn, and Reece? What happened to them?"

"We were caught by one of the fallen within hours of our arrival. He shackled us, then placed us under the rocket."

"And you couldn't save them?"

Xanusel looked at Matt, as if he was staring into his soul. Matt stared back, looking for some hint of humanity and compassion. It was Xanusel who broke first. "It was . . . not my task to do so. I grieve for the three who sacrificed themselves to avert Armageddon."

Matt, still looking at the angel, replied, "That's the best you can do? 'It wasn't my task?' You allowed three of the bravest people I know to die when you could have saved them?"

"Yes. For the greater good."

"You couldn't have just said, 'Hey, everyone, we really don't need to do this. We can crash a jet into it, and that will work just fine.'"

"Matthew, if I had . . . "

"You know what, Zander? I don't want to hear it." Matt turned around and walked away.

Xanusel watched him walk into the hangar and strike up a conversation with Gregg and Roland. "Gabrielle, do you understand? Why I couldn't save them and save you too?"

"No, I don't," Gabby said. "Look, Xanusel. I appreciate your help with the rocket, I really do. Then taking me to get Daniel and all that. But this is a tough one to swallow. You're going to have to give us some time.

"For what it's worth, I understand tough decisions. I know your perception of reality and time is very different than ours. That's probably not going to change."

Xanusel looked stone-faced at Gabby for a moment. Then, with a slight smile, "You are wise beyond measure, Gabrielle. My task is almost complete. Then I shall ascend once more and leave this material world behind. I will miss it. And I will miss you."

"Thanks, Xanusel. I'll talk to Matt. I'm sure he will forgive you one day."

"But I don't require forgiveness from . . . "

"No. But you should seek it anyway. Trust me on this one. It's big with us humans."

Xanusel nodded, then unfolded his wings and launched himself into the sky.

Gabby watched as he rose higher and higher until he was out of sight. She then walked toward the remaining group, who were all giving Daniel a wide berth. Gabby motioned for him to join her. He walked over slowly, his gaze remaining down at the ground.

"Gabby, we are so happy to see you!"

"You did it!"

"It seemed touch and go for a moment, but we pulled through. How about your group?"

Gabby spent several minutes hugging and thanking everyone. When she had talked to everyone, she motioned for quiet.

"Everyone, it's so good to see all of you. You each had an almost impossible task, and you did it. I'm not sure if the rest of the world is ready to learn that we just foiled the Apocalypse, but we know. The people trying to end everything sure know it. They were trounced as thoroughly as possible. We lost several good people—Paula, Jonn, and Reece. They gave it everything they had and then some. We will remember them forever, and I hope they are honored now in the world beyond. We also lost Cain. He went out exactly like he wanted. Doing the right thing on his own terms. I only knew him for a week or so. Some of you knew him better and for much longer. He was, at least he seemed to me to be . . . complicated. What an extraordinary life, and we saw just the barest glimpse into it before he left us.

"I should tell you this too. When we were getting ready to leave, Xanusel said some really nice things to him. Things that seemed to unburden Cain's mind in his final moments. I know we all are upset with Xanusel, but he did achieve a lot of good. Let's not forget that any time soon, okay?"

Just then, Gregg came running out from the hangar. "It's on the news now. You have to see this." The assembled survivors stopped talking and all made their way inside to the hangar's lounge. Live video from a bevy of helicopters that were flying around a massive crater in the Colorado

Rockies was playing on nearly every station. Gregg turned up the volume so everyone could hear.

" . . . are unconfirmed, but the meteor appears to have struck a retreat that was hosting a number of international celebrities. Towering figures from the world of politics, media, sports, and business all were in attendance. And, we are sorry to report, apparently there were no survivors. It will be many weeks, if ever, before we know the number of people who lost their lives in this unprecedented tragedy. It follows another tremendous loss yesterday when an apparent spy plane lost its way and crashed into a rocket at Cape Canaveral . . . "

Gregg began flipping through every channel he could for additional facts. Each one showed nearly the same thing. As he made his way through the dial, Gabby saw something and asked him to go back. "Did you all see that? It mentioned lightning. That hasn't shown up on any of the other reports. Go back."

Gregg flipped back and found the local news channel that was reporting several lightning strikes right after the meteor hit. No footage had been produced so far, but several witnesses in different locations all said the same thing. Multiple bolts of lightning were seen hitting the site after the meteor crash.

"What does that even mean?" Milla asked. "Unless . . . Do you think it means he's alive?"

"Maybe," Gabby said. "Or maybe it was after the fact, or maybe it was *because* he died. We probably won't know. But if he did survive, I'm sure he will make himself known sooner or later."

***

"So where will you go now, Daniel?" Gabby asked once everyone had left. A courier had brought packages for everyone except Daniel, individually addressed by someone with extremely flowery handwriting. Cain had left every member of the team a sizable fortune as a final thank you. The packages for the three who died would be sent to their closest relatives. They also all received an invitation to sit on the Board of Directors of a newly established nonprofit called New Eden. It was ridiculously well funded and had a very simple mission statement: Create a better world now. The first board meeting was in two weeks at the Maryland retreat.

As the last of the group left the hangar, Daniel turned to Gabby. "I don't know. I want to do the right thing, but I don't know what that is anymore. I didn't want to help Lorelei and Razhael, but I never really felt a part of all this either, you know."

"But you chose, Daniel. You chose the side of life. Of things continuing as we know them, and hopefully with a little help, improving. If these last few days have shown us anything, it's that we do not have to follow anyone's path but our own."

"I believe that's true. But I'm not certain. And given who I really am, I need to be certain. Like, extremely certain. I don't want to think everything is fine and then, in a few years, feel the ol' genetics kick in. I mean, if I'm the only one left, what does that make me? Am I now the Adversary? Am I destined to do something later that the today me wouldn't want to do? And if so, how do I stop that from happening?"

"Daniel, I think you just answered your own question. What you've been through in the past several weeks is more than most people do in their entire lives. And that's not even counting your surprise parentage. Please, after all this, give yourself a break. You did good. Let's head home and start rebuilding. Our lives and our relationship."

"Gabby, I want that more than anything in the world. Believe me. You have been the very best thing in my life, probably ever. And despite every atom in my body screaming to go with you, I can't. Maybe one day, but not right now. I need to find a nice, quiet seminary and enroll. My mind—it's at war with itself. It may not seem that way to you, but that's because I have it under control for now. We both know it's going to come back, and I want to be ready when that day comes. Ready to do the right thing, no matter what. Just like you."

Gabby looked at Daniel, perhaps clearly for the very first time. She was proud of him. It would be so easy to slip back into everyday life, to ignore the small, insistent voice at the back of his mind. But he—and she—knew better. "Seminary, huh?" she said. "I hope you can make your sermons more exciting than the ones you made me sit through."

"I'll do my best, Gabby. I'll see you soon, though. There are lots of seminary schools around DC. You never know what will happen. He turned away before he started to cry and walked out of the hangar without another word.

***

Three months later, Gabby felt settled enough to accept Matt's date request. She had returned to the house in northern Virginia, but it still did not feel like home without Daniel. She had wanted to write down everything she could remember about her experiences so the details would be there long after she was gone. Three months and still no word from Daniel.

The Park Service had been very accommodating about her leave of absence request. The Washington Monument was closed due to repairs anyway. An anonymous donation that would cover the cost of repairs and much more had arrived shortly after the attack. Matt had called semi-regularly for the past few weeks, and he finally got up the nerve to ask her out again. This time, after several "I'm not ready's," she said yes.

***

He was charming, clean-cut, and very different from Daniel. *Not really my type,* she thought, *with his lengthy military background. But he's nice enough, and knows who I am. Let's see what happens.* Matt had chosen a locally owned prime rib restaurant in Vienna for their night out. The weather was beginning to turn chilly, so Gabby chose a gray pullover with a long gray skirt. She figured she wouldn't have to bring a jacket if she got cold, then end up carrying it most of the time. They made small talk about his new job as a security consultant, and she updated him on her writing. Midway through dinner, Matt excused himself.

Sitting alone and out in the world once more, Gabby's mind started to wander. She was enjoying herself, and Matt was good company. He was a definite possibility for the long term. When she was ready. Her mind continued to drift until she saw a very old man in an even older prison, on an island. He was talking with someone just outside the crude metal bars, but she could not see who. She couldn't make out what was being said, but she had the distinct feeling it was about her. Then, it was just the old man, but he was younger somehow. He was walking alone in a large, modern city. She closed her eyes, trying to bring herself out of the vision. She had not had one since they stopped Armageddon. Matt came back to the table just as she was bringing herself out of her reverie.

"What? I missed that part, Gabby," Matt said. "You said something about seeing a profit? Did you invest what you-know-who left you? That's smart."

Gabby smiled as he sat back down. "No, it wasn't that. It was . . . Do you ever think about what we went through? What we did?"

Matt put down his fork, leaned toward Gabby, and in a hushed voice said, "All the time. Do you? It still amazes me that we did all that and no one knows. It all got written off as accidents, forces of nature or, you know, acts of a higher power."

"Sometimes I wonder if it all was real. That's why I started writing it down. So it doesn't slip through our fingers and become a half-forgotten memory."

Gabby had a sudden vision, as if a flash bulb went off in her cerebral cortex. She saw the Colorado crater, but not as it was now. The area was still cordoned off, and all sorts of science types were running around the place. Then, it was quiet as the scientists and excavators left for the day. The moon, silvery and bright, hung in a western summer sky.

A sound was coming from the northeastern rim of the crater. A distant thumping, perhaps from an animal that had fallen in. Then the sound became closer and more defined. It sounded like . . . like a man. She now could hear grunts, then grumbling that was unmistakably human. Gabby stood up suddenly at the table, her napkin still clinging to her dress. "We have to go. Can you pay the bill, please? Please hurry, or we're going to miss it."

"What are we going to miss? Are you feeling all right?"

"Yes, yes, I'm fine. Or I will be. Come on, or we're going to miss it."

The pair made their way out of the restaurant and into the fall air. Gabby looked up and down the street, searching for . . . something. "We just missed it," she said.

"Missed what?" Matt asked as he pulled his jacket on and stumbled outside. A long, sleek limousine—the kind that were commonplace on the streets of the nation's capital—moved past a stoplight and turned a corner, vanishing from view.

"Nothing. I thought I heard an old friend. I'm sure we'll catch up soon. Come on. Let's go out and do something fun. It's about time."

ABOUT THE AUTHOR

Tom is a public relations practitioner by profession. He has worked at King's Daughters Medical Center in Ashland, Kentucky, since the mid-1990s. He is a graduate of and a big fan of Marshall University in Huntington, W.Va. While at Marshall, he earned a B.A. in Journalism/Public Relations (1992), and a M.A. in Journalism (1999). He also earned accreditation from the Public Relations Society of America in 2001.

He has two children, Chloe and Alex. Together, Tom, Chloe and Alex adopted two dogs, Rusty and Daisy, at the beginning of the pandemic. The kids are not impressed that their father wrote a novel; the dog are impressed when he walks in the front door.

Gebirah is his first novel.

ACKNOWLEDGEMENTS & THANKS

George Dearing, Chloe Dearing, Alex Dearing, Chris Dearing, Georgianna Dearing, Merritt Henderson, Mary Lou Sullivan, Sue Snyder, Christa Carter, Debbie Groves, Chris Dickerson, King's Daughters Medical Center, Ebook Launch

Made in the USA
Monee, IL
25 February 2022